Also By Leo Gher

FICTION

NOVELS

Moynihan's Journey

SHORT STORIES

The Bishop of Saint George • A Troubled Spirit

The Legend of Conquering Valley • The Roadhouse

POETRY

Lake Chautauqua Collection

CHILDREN'S TELEVISION

Wonderstar

The Sergeant Pepperoni Club

NON-FICTION

Civic Discourse and Digital Age Communications in the Middle East

The Art & Science of Media Management

A Novel of International Intrigue

LEO GHER

///BookBaby

Book Publishing for Independent Authors

7905 N Crescent Blvd

Pennsauken, NJ 08110

A special thanks goes to my colleague, proofreader, and friend, Roland Person. Without his valuable eye, knowledge, and dedication, this book would not have been completed.

PUBLISHER'S NOTE:

This is a work of fiction. Names, characters, places, and incidents are either the product of the author's imagination or are used fictitiously, and any resemblance to actual persons, living or dead, events, or locals is entirely coincidental.

ISBN (Print) 978-1-54395-998-7
ISBN (Ebook) 978-1-54395-999-4

FOR MY FRIEND AND TEACHER

JOHN GARDNER

"Write to make a difference," he said. "… honest fiction, the kind of novel that readers will find they enjoy reading more than once."

LIST OF CHARACTERS

HOUSE KEDAR
One of the 21 ruling familes of Azerbaijan

Azreal Kedar [aka, Conor Moynihan] Head, House Kedar	Son of Tom Moynihan & Zarifa Kedar
Mira Nadirov	Azreal's aunt & surrogate mother
Tali Nadirov (Mira's daughter)	Azreal's cousin & lover
Seyfulla Nadirov	Mira's husband & father of Tali
Rufet Qurb (trusted aide to Azreal Kedar)	1st deputy of Zumre Corporation
Georghe Markirov	Mira's father
Rayna	Mira's bodyguard

HOUSE KOS (THE DARK TRIAD)
One of the 21 ruling familes of Azerbaijan

Viktor Kos, Oil Minister	Head of House Kos
Vanya Kos, Next in line as head of House Kos	Son of Viktor Kos & Aydan (1st wife)
Vladimir Kos, 2nd son	Son of Viktor Kos & Dina (2nd wife)
Misha	Butler in House Kos

IN CHICAGO:
The family of Tom Moynihan

Jake Moynihan, half-brother of Azreal Kedar	Son of Tom Moynihan & Katie Kowalski
Katie Kowalski-Moynihan	mother of Jake
Lindy Bedrosian	Jake's girlfriend
Mike Bedrosian	uncle of Lindy
Denis de Barras (Jake's cousin)	son of Sean & Julia de Barras
Julia de Barras	Katie Kowalski's twin sister, Jake's aunt
Sam Mansour	photojournalist & university professor
Iza Beggs-Mansour (Sam's wife)	(journalist & university professor)

MINOR CHARACTERS:

Rolan Guliyev	President of Azerbaijan
Alexandr Kazimov	Foreign Secretary of Azerbaijan
Seymur Rezuli	CIA operative in Azerbaijan
Tad Tadesian, (Vartan Alliance)	Armenia-American
Mo Chinske, (American military retired)	CIA Chief – Central Asia
Tom Moynihan / Zarifa [Zara] Kedar	dead father & mother of Conor
Ali Tabak	Hunting guide in Turkey
Chira Beggs	mother of Iza Beggs-Mansour

TABLE OF CONTENTS

AZREAL

JAKE

MOYNIHAN'S DREAM

Fire & Wind

Azreal

W hat demons possessed young Zara Kedar to choose it has always been a mystery. It is a curious and contentious name. It means angel of death. Some said it was prophecy, that she was anticipating the tragedies that would befall her son; others said Zara wanted revenge for the loss of the love of her life. The truth is, she foresaw death looming, her death, and it filled her mind with dread and despair.

But in those last days, it wasn't all anguish. When Zara looked into her baby's blue eyes, she remembered her beloved Tom Moynihan. Accordingly, she gave her son a second name – Conor – in honor of his Irish heritage. That name, however, was a clan secret. Only close family members ever called him Conor because, in most Muslim places in Central Asia, a Christian name was shunned by the public. In Azerbaijan – the land of fire and wind – he was known as Azreal, the vulnerable orphan without the guiding hands of mother or father, the boy-doyen of House Kedar.

1

The Dark Triad

Now and then a grey ember would fall through the fireplace grate and burst into bright flames. The poorly lit study would brighten momentarily, and the hand-painted tiles on the hearth and a few of the Russian icons hanging on the walls could be seen again, if only fleetingly. There was a man in the room, a silhouette resting quietly at his writing desk. He appeared to be sleeping – his head was thrown back against the headrest, eyes closed and elbows folded over a considerable belly – but of course, he was not. Viktor Kos was simply being still with his thoughts, measuring probabilities and outcomes, carefully ordering lists of friends and foes. The kingpin of one of the governing clans of Azerbaijan would soon have his hands full. Allies would arrive within the hour, and action would be required. Knowing that events soon would come to a head, Viktor thought of the old Shia proverb, Fate and fortune at the gate.

The residence was mostly silent, but Kos could hear shuffling feet in the next room as his servants set up for the meeting. He had ordered shekerbura – an irresistible sweet pastry, filled with ground almonds, hazelnuts, and mixed with honey – to be served before the summit. "A way to break the tension of the moment," he told his butler. As Kos took several shallow breaths, pleased with his inspiration, he heard a door creak open. Without opening his eyes, he asked, "Vanya, arrived finally, have you?"

"Vlad, Papa," his younger son replied. "Vanya will be here shortly."

"Never on time, that one," the old man groused. "When he becomes Bey of this House, he will not have the luxury of being late." Viktor Kos took coldhearted satisfaction in psychologically battering his sons, Vanya in particular, as he thought it necessary training for the future head of an elite family.

Suddenly, from the room next door there came the sound of dishes crashing to the floor. Irritated, Viktor sat up. He pushed himself from the table and then shuffled off to the door at the far end of the room. When Kos unexpectedly appeared, the servants picked up their pace, especially the one who had dropped the tray.

The room was dark. The butler had dimmed the lights, so Viktor was unable to distinguish among the servants darting fretfully from table setting to table setting. There was an elaborate chandelier centered over the circular conference table, but it was never turned on. Viktor Kos suffered from corneal abrasions, and light sensitivity often caused him migraines. The only lights allowed in the room were small table lamps above each place setting. Noticing the head of the House looming, Misha expected a reprimand. "We'll have this cleaned up in a moment, sir." Then the butler asked, "Do you have any preference for guest seating?"

Kos was taken aback by the question. "What do I care where they sit?" he sneered. "Does it matter?"

"It always matters, sir," Misha replied. "You said there would be eight. It would be useful if I knew who the others were."

Why was his butler prying? Kos wondered. *What has he overheard?* Viktor glared at the man warily, his concern for household security on full alert. Viktor rechecked a mental list of the recently-hired butler: last job – Russian oligarch; home country – Georgian passport, no apparent local affiliations. The man seemed good enough at his job, but Viktor growled, "Gossip mongering, Misha? I did not expect that from you."

"Not at all, sir. But my previous employer always tried to prevent imbroglios among powerful men, if you get my drift."

A light dawned, and Viktor recognized that Misha was right. "Ah, very good. Bagirov and Vidadi don't get along, so put Vlad between them," he smiled wickedly, then, "He can prevent any fisticuffs that might occur." He thought of his son in the other room. Vlad was tall and slim. He gave the appearance of being fragile, but was, in fact, healthy, supple, and had a formidable demeanor. Vlad was also highly skilled in martial arts and was instinctively prone to settling arguments with violence. Most assumed he was not the brightest bird from his father's nest, but Vlad had proved them wrong time after time.

"Yes, sir. Anything else, sir?"

"Seat Vanya opposite me. It doesn't matter where the others sit." Misha made the mental notes.

"Yes, sir, it shall be done."

Eventually, Kos meandered back to his study. He looked at Vlad, reassured by his decision to separate Bagirov and Vidadi. Vlad was an odd-looking duck. He had fierce, dark, almond-shaped eyes, his hair was incongruously slicked over to one side, and he had, from the age of 13, sported a mustache. It was bushy now, fell over his upper lip generously, and was the color of an aged claret. Vanya called it a Russian cliché, but Vlad liked the image.

Self-assured, Viktor began an old harangue with his second son: "You cannot understand our adversaries unless you go back to the time of Peter the Great. Imperial Russia conquered our lands, and the Tsar ruled the Caspian Sea from Derbent to Baku. Not by charm did that one rule, and so must we."

Vlad raised an eyebrow. "You said rule, Papa. Is that what you have in mind?" Unruffled by his father's insinuation, he immediately thought of his own enemies, and how he would exact a toll on them if, in the end, the Kos clan were in power.

Vlad was sitting on the sofa next to the window that overlooked the courtyard. Viktor marched over, poked him on the arm, and said, "A benevolent dictatorship is vastly superior to any western government. Peter was cruel but just."

History tells a different tale. Vlad knew from his studies that the Tsar had built St. Petersburg on the backs of thousands of serfs and impoverished artisans, who had been forced to travel to the city on their own, without food or supplies. If they managed to survive the trip, constructing Peter Alexeyevich's Venetian fantasy on a disease-ridden, unstable, swampy site, often in the winter, had nothing to do with justice. It was merely cruel, but Vlad said nothing.

At that moment, the door opened. "Again, the Saint Peter lecture?" Vanya boomed out his presence. "Viktor, have you not given any regard to my advice about moving beyond worn-out Russian ways?"

Kos twisted around to see his elder son crossing the threshold. As usual, Vanya was dressed in a black blazer and burgundy turtleneck, which covered most of the Rosacea stain on his neck. But it wasn't the scar that everyone noticed when Vanya entered a room. It was his smell – the reek of cheap aftershave that too often made people gag. "Close the door," said Kos. "We have much to talk about before the others arrive."

"Something more, then?"

"It's not about the Russians, but about President Guliyev, the Kedars, and the Nadirovs."

"I thought we had them boxed in," Vlad insisted. Of late, the ruling powers of Azerbaijan were at odds – House against House – the Kedars and Nadirovs leading one group, and the Kos driving the other.

"Too much thinking, Vlad, will spoil your appetite."

"I'll pretend I didn't hear that, brother."

"The Kedar Bey will pay for his recklessness. His juvenile miscalculations at Council are many." Next, Viktor grabbed the arm of each son and escorted both to the window box overlooking the courtyard. Neither servants nor visitors could overhear his words from that vantage point. "All things come to an end."

The oil minister was referring to the one resource that determined Azeri fortunes: petroleum. House Kos had controlled the oil concession of Azerbaijan for three generations. The rules were simple: 50% of all profits went to the government; 25% went to the President, and the other Houses split what remained, more or less. Of course, Viktor Kos had been skimming off the top for the past quarter-century. Vanya knew this and had long understood what his father would say next. With vain bombast, he spoke up: "And when will the oil reserves come to an end, Viktor?"

Viktor wasn't used to blatant rudeness, not even from his son, but replied just the same, "The last of the wells will be dry in two years, probably less." There had been endless debating among economists: would the wells dry up first, or would oil prices drop so precipitously that pumping was no longer sustainable? The Kos didn't care about academics. They just kept stuffing their pockets, like squirrels storing nuts for the winter. After all, a family must survive.

"And the other countries?"

"The Iranian fields will last a little longer, but that will make little difference to us."

Vlad was alarmed, remembering the fate of Syria when its resources had failed. "Disaster!" he shouted, and then added, "Everyone will blame us!"

"Again, the boy wonder speaks."

Ignoring his elder son's backbiting, Viktor Kos persisted, "Of course they will. It is the nature of vultures. And so, the need for our meeting today."

"Why do we need the other Houses?" Vlad countered. "They're dead weight, as I see it."

"We use them as tools, Vlad, tools."

The butler interrupted just then with a muted knock. "The guests are arriving, Honored Bey."

"Yes, yes, Misha. See them in."

Vanya said, "Offer them a whiskey and shekerbura treats. We'll be there in a few minutes."

Viktor whispered to his sons, "I have a plan. It impacts the President and all the Houses of the Shirvan, especially the Kedars and Nadirovs."

"I could arrange an accident or two," Vlad oozed with malevolent intent, "and we'd be rid of them."

Viktor Kos looked at his son and smiled acidly. "Plan B, Vlad, Plan B."

2

Rufet Qurb

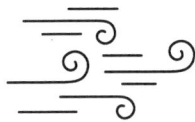

The E9 Sportster had reached 100 miles per hour. The driver glanced down at the speedometer, touched the dashboard button of the rearview camera, and caught a glimpse of the thick desert clouds rising behind him. Not fast enough, He thought. Extreme anxiety – that's what everyone involved in the chase was feeling, especially for those in the vehicles that were trying to block the fugitive's escape. He was headed directly toward them and seemed doggedly resolute as he raced closer. He crushed the accelerator to the floor, and the powerful engine of the Audi Sportster responded instantly: 115... 130... 160 mph. When the driver looked back again, the clouds that had been tracking him out of Cairo had begun to disappear. At this speed, the fugitive imagined he would reach the Mediterranean seacoast in another 20 minutes, but that was no consolation. He would still have to find his friends and then escape the police that would be appearing on streets everywhere.

"Müserif," said David, "Müserif." It meant "the honored one" in the Azeri language, and David was trying to get the attention of the middle-aged man who had been gazing through the car window, lost in memories. The real dust stirred up by the heavy traffic that led to the city had triggered Rufet's oft-recalled nightmare. "Mr. Qurb, the office or the residence?" The chauffeur had reached Neftcilar Boulevard and would need to decide: turn right for downtown Baku or continue north along the Caspian coast to the home of the Kedar Bey.

Snapping out of his daydream, the ruggedly handsome Rufet Qurb responded, "Yes, David, what is it?"

"The office or the residence?"

"The residence," Qurb replied. "I have urgent business with the Kedar Bey."

David was more than chauffeur to the First Deputy; he was Qurb's majordomo and confessor as well. Rufet had never married, and for decades the Zümrə Company had been his only mistress, and Azreal Kedar, his only boss. "The dream of Egypt again?"

"Yes," Rufet hid nothing from David, "I once owned an Audi Sportster, a beautiful car. It was ruby red and one-of-a-kind in that awful desert city."

"What happened to it, sir?"

"I don't know, exactly. The police confiscated it, I suppose." Then Rufet reflected, "In my dream, I always get away, but in reality, I didn't. The secret police gave me these." David looked into the rearview mirror. Qurb was pointing to the cigarette scars on his forehead.

"What happened next?"

"My old friend, Mo, saved me."

"Our Mo Chinske? The CIA guy?"

"The very same." David had reached the turnoff. It was just a few miles along the E119 highway from the Old City to the medieval-walled marketplace and the Palace of the Shirvanshahs. It was forever windy there, especially in the winter when the wind comes from the north, blowing gale-force across the peninsula. The Azeris call that one *Khazri*. It can kill if a person's not careful. In the summertime, the wind comes from Iran in the south. This one, the locals call *Gilavar*, and it cools Baku. But it too can be hazardous, often leaving the skin parched and dry, the lips cracked and sore.

How anyone could call Baku beautiful was a mystery to Rufet. He was a country boy from the small village of Gobustan. In his youth, he had made a living escorting foreigners to the mud volcanoes, the fire temples, and the famous Iron Age petroglyphs on the rising plains west of the Caspian. Nostalgia filled Rufet's mind. He thought of Zara and Mira when they were little girls – five, maybe six. Little beauties. He remembered that they called it their Rock Garden. But most of all, Rufet was partial to guiding international hunters into the mountains and through the backcountry for the big game. He and his brothers made good money when the CIA or MI6 came calling. Those stints, however, were only temporary, so when the Kedar clan came to power, he went to work for old Elman as his chauffeur. Maybe that's why he confided in David so much. After a decade of service, Rufet had climbed to second-in-command under Elshan, Azreal's uncle. When Elshan was executed seven years earlier, the boy Azreal became clan leader, the Bey of House Kedar.

People were astonished by Azreal's rise to power. He was the youngest person ever to lead a prominent Azeri House. It was a good thing that the boy had two steadying hands to guide him: those of Rufet and Mira Nadirov. Although Azreal had been groomed for the position all his life, the 26-year-old still had much to learn, expressly when he dealt with the intrigues at the Council of Elders.

Baku has always been a city of hills and a hodgepodge of architectural styles. In every section of the capital can be found buildings in the styles of the Belle Époque of Paris, Vienna Baroque, soulless Soviet Constructivism, ancient as well as modern interpretations of Islamic design, and of course, the double-walled luxury of the Shirvanshahs. In recent years, a myriad of preposterous skyscrapers had mushroomed along Baku Bay, and most of the 21 elite Houses had built sprawling compounds among the modern showplaces and the out-of-date mansions of nineteenth century oil barons.

Of late, many things had changed. There was an aura of rising fear throughout the city. Old ghouls were reawakening: mob mentality, scape-goating, cultural victimization, and the tyrant's howl about the grand future that will avenge historic Azeri degradations. Mira Nadirov had sensed the shifting mindsets throughout the past year, and Rufet understood them all too well. They both had warned the Kedar Bey of the dangers. They had counseled President Guliyev as well. But he seemed unmoved by their concerns.

When they pulled up to the residence, David hopped out of the car, and then rushed to the other side to open the door for his boss. "This may take some time, David. I've received word from our spy inside the Kos household."

One of the Kedar staff emerged from the residence and took Qurb's briefcase. "Have you sent word to the Kedar Bey?" Rufet asked. The man replied with a nod.

David said, "Sounds like trouble."

"Trouble it is."

"House Kos?"

"And others… cronies of the Dark Triad." Afterward, Rufet added, "Find Mira Nadirov and ask her to join us as soon as possible."

3

Conor and Tali

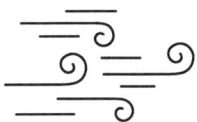

Conor never felt like an orphan. He belonged to House Kedar, one of the prominent families that ruled Azerbaijan. But his parents were gone, so like all orphans, he chased through life searching after their shadows. He had no fond recollections of his mother, or what it was like to be a young child. He blamed his family for that. They never talked about Zara, and that was a mystery. Until he was six, Conor lived with his Uncle Elshan at the Zebeqi compound, north of Baku. Elshan had just become the Kedar Bey, and young Azreal felt the shield of Elshan's position, but not his love. Their relationship was all about inheritance, property, and responsibility. There were no fatherly urges in that man: no warm arms wrapping him up in a bath towel, no tender kissing to ward off quaking lips, and no jumping into bed with a guardian against the shadows of the night. Many years later, when Conor had learned the terrible fate of his mother and had the power to act, he ordered all the buildings of

Elshan's compound demolished. Then he turned the property over to the villagers, who wanted to build a madrassa there. He left everything behind, except Elshan's cruiser, a beautiful Fairlane Targa 62-footer.

When Azreal was a youngster, his uncle Elshan had frequently promised to take him on sea outings, but he never did. It was Rufet who took him on the adventures. With giggly delight, he remembered the speedboat churning up waves past sturgeon fishermen, shooting the water cannon at oilrig ferries, racing against other Caspian powerboaters, and camping on remote islands. Conor grew fond of Rufet. He was the nearest thing to a father that Conor had in those early years.

These days, the craft was moored next to the boathouse at the Kedar residence on Baku Bay. Because it was showing its age, he'd had it refitted and painted. After that, he renamed it. He called it the *Zarifa* – his mother's full name – and did the stenciling himself. Now he could see the Zarifa every day from his bedroom window, which was about 75-80 yards from the shore. Besides the boat dock and the personal residence, there were other buildings on the property known as the Zümrə Estates. From the marina to the front gate, the compound stretched a quarter mile north and about 900 feet east. The three low-lying buildings and a parking lot near the front entrance housed the Zümrə business operations. A walking garden of pink and red Azaleas surrounded the residence, ridiculing testaments to the harsh deserts and barren plains just beyond Baku's seaside location on the Caspian.

Elshan Kedar had been an evil man. He was convicted of many crimes, the greatest of which was the murder – he called it an honor killing – of his own sister, Zarifa. When Elshan was sent to jail, Conor moved in with his close relatives, the Nadirovs. Aunt Mira raised him as if he were her own, but she was more a taskmaster than a nurturer. There was no self-serving brooding in her household, just chores. Because he would one day be the Kedar Bey, which would require discipline and courage, Mira Nadirov took on the duties of rejissor, a regent of sorts.

For the most part, Conor had lived alone on the Zümrə Estates. It was more a business center than a family home. For the past year, however, his cousin Tali had been staying with him. She had finished a degree from Baku State University 15 months earlier and was now working as a political liaison for the company. But Tali was more than a houseguest, she was Conor's best friend. Though a year younger, Tali often took on the role of consoler, and sometimes even as a shrink. Her mother would often advise her, "Tali, you've got to be there for Conor. He often feels lost. He looks to Rufet, but Rufet is not family."

Mira had raised them together as brother and sister. She knew they loved each other, but when Tali moved in with Conor, it worried the ever-prudent, ever-vigilant Mira. She was appalled and told her daughter so. "Tali," she warned, "the offended Mullahs will get you. They will come for your head."

"I don't care," Tali would say, the rebuke falling on deaf ears. "This is a new world, Mother. Conor and I are of a different generation." Conor would never add anything to their discussions. He would just look at Tali – his fiery, gorgeous cousin – with rapturous eyes.

The first time Conor noticed something different about Tali was when she was twelve. Until that tender moment at the Gobustan swimming pool, Tali had always been Little Sis. She enjoyed swimming, which was an oddity because Azeris are not known as a nation of swimmers. But in Soviet times, the Russians had built an indoor pool as part of a high-rise housing complex and recreational facility for expat oil-workers and their families. That's where Tali could be found in the early morning hours three times a week. She would rise before all others, hop on her bicycle, and pedal down to Dom#3. Grandmother Ana would scold, "It's dangerous for a little girl to be out on her own so early. *Ecnebi* are everywhere, Tali." She meant foreigners, of course.

Tali loved her grandmother, but every time ignored her cautions. Ana sensed much of Zara in Tali: tempestuous yet courageous, a brilliant mind, too busy to be pestered by authority, the dominant in all relationships, even with her elders. Still, everyone was concerned about her safety as well as the family's reputation. So, grandfather Georghe decided that he would send Conor as her guardian at least once each week. It was his way of letting the *Ecnebi* know that Azeri clans were watching, protecting their youngest daughter.

The tender moment came on a cold spring day. The 13-year-old Conor – a creature now caught between boyhood and manhood – remembered it vividly. He and grandfather had fought about duties. He wanted to sleep in "just this once," but Georghe would not have it, and had splashed a glass of water on the boy's head. "Tali has already left," he growled, "You must get up, Conor. You cannot allow Little Sis to be at the mercy of those Russian hooligans." Reluctantly, the sleepy-head did as he was told.

Still bleary-eyed, Conor threw his pajamas at his closet door, then dressed hurriedly – no underwear or socks – and jumped into jeans and loafers. Next, he grabbed the light pullover he had worn the night before. It was a mistake. Even though it was spring, the wind was still blowing from the north, which always made the mornings chilly. Outside, he looked for Tali, but she was nowhere in sight. Conor liked Tali, but they fought thoughtlessly as siblings often do, and he did not want another confrontation.

When Conor arrived at Dom#3, it was empty, and that was unusual. Most days a gaggle of Russian babushkas could be found escorting children to and from the pool, but not today. Puzzled, he rushed through the dressing room to the natatorium; again, no one. Then he spotted a lone swimmer under the water, turning at the far wall, pushing off, and then dolphin-kicking for some 20 feet until the swimmer broke the surface for air. It was a woman – dazzling, riveting – and she wore a ruby-red, skin-tight two-piece bathing suit.

Maybe he was still drowsy from the early hour, or perhaps it was the shock of the cold north wind that made Conor question what he saw in the pool – a creature, broad-shouldered like Tali, but full-figured with the muscular arms of an Olympic athlete. She was wearing a swimming cap and goggles. Little Sis used neither; at least he could not remember it if she did. Out of the blue, Conor realized he had not paid much attention to Tali in recent days. Slightly panicked he thought, *Check the hallways.* Nothing. *Had she finished… already on her way home? Check the bike rack.* But her bike was still there, chained and locked.

When he returned poolside, the water nymph was just making another turn at the near end of the pool. *A mermaid,* he quipped mentally. She pushed off the wall and then dipped under the surface for another long dolphin-kick. Instinctively, Conor held his breath. Next, the creature shot upward through the surface gulping for air. Conor was flabbergasted. It was Little Sis, and it was not Little Sis. Then she waved.

"Tali," he shouted. She waved again. Relieved to find her, Conor sat down on one of the lounge chairs next to the pool. Tali continued for two more laps, and when she finished, she set out across the pool for the ladder where Conor was sitting. When he realized she was coming his way Conor stood up. He had always helped her out of the pool, but what emerged poolside was not his Little Sis. She pulled off her goggles first, and when she removed her bathing cap her long, auburn hair fell across her erect, beautifully formed breasts. Eyes glued, Conor was surprised and pleased, *when did Tali get breasts?* He grabbed a beach towel and then pulled her from the pool. Next, he began patting her dry. As he did so, he brushed her nipples, which were hard and conspicuous in the cold morning air. She looked at him purposefully and said, "Conor, what are you doing?"

"I didn't know," he began. Confused and frustrated, the thirteen-year-old felt brutish and geeky at the same time. Eventually, he would learn how to control his testosterone-charged delight, but not today. So, he tried a sheepish smile.

Tali didn't mind. For a long time, she had, as young girls do, wondered about such a moment, and then she kissed him. "It's okay, Conor,"

she said, taking command of the situation, "nothing we can't handle." He
was relieved, but their relationship, which had always been resilient, had
changed forever.

There were no others on the Zarifa that afternoon as Conor and Tali
enjoyed the serene waters of the Caspian. Conor sat at the helm, but he was
not piloting the boat, just watching Tali. She was lying on the sun deck. It
was late September, and probably the last time she would be sunbathing
for the year. The couple used the Zarifa when they wanted to be alone,
away from the tumult of Azeri power struggles. Today they were drifting a
few miles offshore when a few clouds began rolling in from the north. He
thought, *maybe it was time to return home.*

Conor twisted around in search of Baku, but he could see nothing
but haze and sea. He checked the homing beacon; it indicated west by
southwest. Okay. Before he could decide about home, he noticed a flashing
light on the communications console. It was annoying, and when Conor
was annoyed, he would fidget endlessly with the ring on his index finger. It
was his signet ring, and the engraving on it was the ancient seal of House
Kedar. It was 24-karat, but the value of the ring was not in its gold. It was
the seal that mattered, that commanded respect, and permitted him to
order a hundred men into action anytime, anywhere. Many were jealous of
its power. Some thought it magical – able to ward off jinn, uncover hidden
poisons, ensure the favor of grand estates – but to Conor, it was more a
burden than a boon.

As the clouds continued to darken, Conor stood up so he could see
more of the shoreline. On the horizon where he thought Baku should be,
he noticed a swirl of blackness. Odd. It was regularly forming and reform-
ing in the wind. *A storm cloud? A waterspout?* It moved erratically, like
birds trying to avoid a predator. Conor recognized it as a sign of the season

coming to an end, but there was also menace in this murmuration of grackles. He would have to consider its meaning more thoroughly.

Then he thought of Tali. She didn't need protecting, but still, Conor felt an entrenched responsibility for her wellbeing. Returning to the now, he realized that she was wearing only a sundress, and he knew she would soon feel the weather changing. He hurried down to the galley to get a bathrobe and some hot tea. A few minutes later he came on deck. "You read my mind," she said.

"Looks like weather coming in from the north."

"Where has our warm autumn gone?"

"Khazri is coming. We should be heading back soon." But Conor had something else in mind as he sat next to her. They had so little time to themselves when they were on display in Baku. Conor said, "I've been so lonely at times."

"Me too," Tali replied, but then, "hasn't Rufet been there for you?"

"That's different. But yes, he is very loyal. Still, Qurb has his own demons to fight."

"What about your demons?" she asked. "What haunts your dreams, Conor?"

"You, of course," he said smiling broadly.

"Be serious."

"I often dream about my father and his dying moments. I think I could have saved him, but I was off in the wilderness of Zebeqistan confronting Elshan."

"You have to forgive yourself, Conor. It was not your fault."

Wanting to change the subject, he asked, "What about you, Tali, what makes you happy?"

"I'm glad to have a place I now call home. Gobustan had so many bad memories." Then she added, "Do you ever go back there? I mean, to visit their graves?"

"Sometimes," he replied. "The first time was six months after you left for college."

"When Mother decided you needed help running the Zümrə companies?"

Conor laughed, "Yes, she said, 'You can't fight off the Kos by yourself.' I was glad to have Mira's company and her advice."

"Did you go to the cottage, then?"

"We both did. Grandpa Georghe kept everything in good shape. The two trees we planted next to the garden have grown, probably 40 feet tall by now."

"Wow." Tali took his arm, "I remember the day when we buried Tom Moynihan next to your mother. You had no one."

"I had you," he said. "I have always had you."

"There was another."

He thought for a moment. "You mean Jake?"

"Do you ever talk to your brother?" Tali asked. "How old is he?"

"Two years the younger... 23, I believe. Jake lives in Chicago, but no, we never talk." Suddenly, the ship-to-shore com-light began blinking again.

"Probably Mother telling us to come home." Tali had had enough of sea and sun. She got up and went to the cabin to change into her street clothes. Conor headed for the helm to check the message.

It wasn't from Mira but from one of the household staff on shore. It read: "Rufet Qurb has arrived at Estates – reports pressing developments – Dark Triad on the move."

4

Ghost Dancers

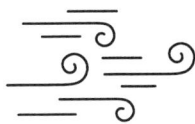

The week that followed saw crises emerge on several fronts. President Guliyev had gotten word of the opposition forces gathering to compel a vote of no confidence. Authoritarian that he was, Guliyev didn't take the threat lightly. Additionally, oil prices plunged, causing panic among world economists. Azeri social media picked up the story and followed with numerous editorials, creating alarm among local bankers and commercial interests. Last but not least, Armenian troops attacked the village of Agdam, killing dozens of villagers along the western frontier. The old conflict was rearing its ugly head and raising fear throughout the region.

Shrewd populist that he was, Guliyev prepared his alt-reality messages to reassure his fellow countrymen that he had anticipated the situation and that Azerbaijan was prepared. For years, Guliyev had been purging independent media outlets, and those that remained free owed their viability to the President and his cronies. The word went out, and all media were required to play the President's communiqué for three days: 1) there was no government crisis necessitating special elections, 2) Azeri cash reserves were plentiful because the President had ordered a sell-off of ten million barrels of oil months ago, and 3) the national militia had been called up 60 days earlier, had completed their training, and they were being deployed to the front immediately. Everything was under control, so much so that Guliyev would be going on vacation as scheduled – for a weeklong hunting trip with family and friends.

Of course, not one thing within the missives was true, except the vacation. It was an old political trick. The opposition screamed that he was a liar, but Guliyev held all the cards in the game. On Wednesday, Conor had received his invitation to join the President. It was a last-minute affair and caused much confusion for everyone involved.

Even the resourceful Mira Nadirov was not her usual self that Friday when she dropped off Conor and Rufet at the airport. In fact, he was irritated and flummoxed. The men were headed for the meeting in, of all places, Kars, Turkey. "You need to get some rest, Mira," Conor said. "Two days of R&R at the cottage will get you back on track."

Relaxation was not what Mira wanted. Obsessive about control, Mira really didn't like days off, and Conor's insisting that she spend the weekend in Gobustan put her in a bad mood. In a rush to pick up Rufet, she'd forgotten her makeup bag. A mild panic attack ensued; the thought of facing the mirror for the next two days without cosmetics was depressing. To top it off, she couldn't find her laptop. *I've left it at the office*, she guessed.

In recent days, Mira had become preoccupied with the drama between her family and the Dark Triad. The constitutional crisis didn't help. She realized that everything hinged on what Conor would say when he met with Guliyev. Once commitments were made, nothing could be unmade. Not being there to advise the young Kedar Bey was driving her to distraction.

But Conor and Rufet were gone, and she was on her way to the cottage for some R&R. As soon as her driver reached the outskirts of the city, Mira found a way to put aside her anxieties and spend some time gazing at the countryside. By the time she was halfway home, she was cheery and daydreaming about her cousin and playmate, Zara Kedar, and simpler times long ago.

Zara shouted out to her mother, "Ana, we are going to see the ghost dancers."

With that, we bolted out the door. It was our holiday ritual. As soon as we arrived at the Kedar summer cottage, Zara and I would head into the hills to what generations of our people called the Rock Garden. I shouted, "We'll bring you some wildflowers, Aunty."

The long slope above the village was called Gobustan Hill. It was a landscape of rock and stone, but scattered within the harshness of the uplift there were many delicate plants and shrubs: ephemeral grasses, tender bushes, wormwood, honeysuckle, dwarf cherries, and wild pomegranates. After each ghost adventure, we'd pick whatever plants looked best and bring them home. Mother warned us, "They're only for decorating, not eating!"

We didn't get far that first day. Outside, on the porch, my mother blocked our getaway, holding two sunhats. She said, "Not without your bonnets, Miss Zara, Miss Mira." The temperature in the hills was always ten degrees cooler than the village, but the sun would blister your skin if you weren't careful. Naturally, we whined about the hats. We were six, but there was no arguing with the two-fisted titan blocking our way. Once we got past the koi pond, and beyond the wooden fence, we cast the bonnets to the ground. We'd grab them up on our return, and then pretend we were obedient little angels home from an adventure. We were no angels, and our hot, pink, sunburned faces didn't fool anybody.

The ghosts were nothing more than prehistoric art on a limestone rockface – petroglyphs – and they were everywhere in our garden. Mother said they told the story of an ancient Azerbaijani civilization: primitive men hunting, warriors with lances at the ready, camel caravans, women gathering flowers, marriage ceremonies, oarsmen crossing a vast sea, constellations, stars, and animals of every sort, including porpoises and even whales. Years later, the Azeri government created the Gobustan State Reserve, and, after a time, it became a World Heritage Site. But for us, it was just the Rock Garden.

We cheerily bounced through the hills and around the switchbacks until we found our special place – a massive pillar with a series of three cuttings that Zara fancifully called the ghost dancers. The figures depicted on the rockface were dancing, undeniably, but Zara was the only person who could see that they were dead. I always asked her, "How do you know they're dead, Zara?

My pretty cousin would shout out, "Their eyes are closed! Of course, they are dead!"

My comeback each time was, "When I sleep my eyes are closed, and I'm not dead."

"It's the way they're closed, Mira."

She could see things I could not. Zara was weird in many ways. She imagined fireflies as specters flying in the night sky, and called them baby ghosts. Zara drew their faces in a little book she kept in her room and gave them names too. Once, she stole a sharp kitchen knife, sprinted past the koi pond, and then carved a baby ghost on the Oriental Planetree in the yard.

It had weirdly contorted, blank eyes, so I asked, "Who's that?"

"Me."

"You're a ghost dancer?"

"You know that I am," Zara insisted, "I can close my eyes and be with them anytime I want."

I screamed back, "You cannot!" That's how it would go – two six-year-olds arguing about life and death in the summer sanctuary of our family cottage.

Once at the outcropping, we would play Queen of the Zebeqis. Zara was always the queen, of course, and I was her handmaiden. What we loved most, however, was the music we created in our garden.

There was a broad, flat rock at the base of the petroglyphs that we called our jingling stone. It was a natural gemstone that made tambourine-like sounds when struck at different thicknesses along its length. Ana told us it was Gaval Dash (whatever that was) and said it was found nowhere else on earth. It sounded perfect for our game, and we played our music for an hour before returning home.

That day, just as we were retrieving our sunhats in the yard, Zara said, "You know, Mira, I foresee things, feel things others do not." She said it with such certainty I did not doubt that it was true. Now, 20 years after my sweet cousin's death, I tremble angrily at that memory, and those words haunt me still.

Gobustan, a bucolic village on the Caspian coast about 60 kilometers south of Baku, had always been the ancestral home of the Kedars and the Nadirovs. Most of the Kedar family had long ago moved to Baku, but many Nadirovs had stayed behind, including Mira's parents, Georghe and Ana. They were tied to country ways and their friends of seven decades. They still lived in their family home at the center of the town, but, after Zara's death, had also taken possession of the Kedar cottage. Conor wanted nothing to do with the place, but Mira found it a peaceful, breathing space from the din of Azeri politics and quarrelsome élites of Baku. Georghe had rebuilt the cottage, refurbished the grounds, and had added new security fencing on the perimeters.

As was her habit, Mira hoped to avoid her parents during the weekend, so she instructed Rayna to drive straight to the cottage. When they reached the security gate, the feelings of dread had been lifted. Time alone was a luxury. Tali was safe and secure in Baku, Conor was off to Turkey, and Mira didn't have to make any decisions for the next few days. It was wine time.

After dinner, and remembering her daydreaming whimsy, Mira decided to visit the Rock Garden. "I'm going for a walk," she called out.

Rayna, who was in the kitchen cleaning up, shouted back, "Not without me." Rayna was more than a secretary, more than a cook. The 27-year-old was Mira's Ranger-trained bodyguard.

"I'm just going into the hills, Rayna. I'll be back in 30 minutes."

"What's up there?"

"Just youthful memories… maybe a wild boar or two, a few snakes, and lizards. Nothing I can't handle." As she thought about it, she wasn't so confident about the braggadocio, but she needed some private time.

Rayna bounded into the living room with a small walky-talky, and said, "Take this. Our phone service is not working as it should. This thing has a locator. I can find you if anything should happen."

"You're such a worrier, Rayna."

"It will be dark in less than an hour."

"I'll just need space and quiet. Besides, I have someone to guide me home."

That response did not reassure the ever-cautious Rayna, "Who's that?"

"A ghost dancer."

"I don't believe in ghosts," replied Rayna. "But I'll turn on the light just the same." Then she slipped a flashlight into Mira's coat pocket.

As Mira stepped onto the porch, she remembered the old skirmishes with her mother about sunhats. But it wasn't summer, of course, and the air was chilly, so she wrapped a knitted scarf around her collar and fastened her parka. The sun was dropping on the horizon, and as she looked upward toward the Rock Garden, the fading light painted the rim in blood reds and burnt oranges. Mira sensed childlike adventure once again.

The sweet whiff of honeysuckle – most potent when the shadows of light are long – filled the air. It didn't take any time at all for Mira to find the jingling stone, and she grew excited because she knew the ghost dancers were near. *Would it be the same,* she wondered? Though she had imagined it many times, Mira had not walked this path in years.

Unexpectedly, she heard a door slam in the far distance and twisted around to see if she could catch the cause. As Mira looked in the direction of the cottage a flash of light – blue light pierced the night sky. She was startled at first, but then she recalled what Rayna had said. It was nothing: the porch fixture coming on, an electrical discharge of some sorts. As she climbed upward, it was hard to find the right path, and there was a reek of rotting food in the air. Mira thought, *the wild boars have turned over a garbage can along the trail.* That was a bit disconcerting, so she took out her flashlight and pointed it along the near path. Then she sniffed deeply, searching for a hint of pigs – nothing at the moment.

When Mira located the ghost dancers just beyond the next switch-back, the sky was bright enough to recognize the rockface – the 2000-year-old images were still dancing around the campfire. Mira laid one hand gently on the first dancing ghost and then swept across the others playfully. It was a carefree remembrance of Zara, and it filled her with happiness.

There was one last thing she wanted to do. Mira stepped down to the base of the rock and found the jingling stone. A moment later, strange sounds echoed throughout the hills. It was the beguiling beat of tambourines in perfect Muğam rhythm. Her recollection complete, Mira decided to head back down.

Just before Mira had finished her descent, she stopped to admire the playground of her youth, and, for just a fleeting moment, to think about the cousin she so loved. She turned off the flashlight so she could admire the stars and the cobalt sky. After a full turn, Mira's gaze settled on the cottage, and that's when she noticed a strange glow on the third floor. It wasn't the porch light that Rayna had promised, but a bluish radiance... flickering high above, splendid and alluring. It seemed to be growing and shrinking and moving – a changeling without boundaries. Mira's heart jumped at the phantasm. And then it was gone. Her mind peaked with unanticipated possibilities. She raced to the cottage. The slamming door startled Rayna, "Oh, good. You're back."

Mira asked, "Rayna, have you been upstairs?"

"No, I've been reading here in the kitchen."

Curious to no end, Mira headed for the staircase, "When I was coming home, just outside the fence, I saw a light on the third floor." That troubled the always alert Rayna because she had armed the security system shortly after their arrival. *Had someone entered the house before their arrival?*

"Mira, I'm going with you." She retrieved her gun. "Let me go first."

Mira didn't argue. After searching all the rooms upstairs, Rayna was satisfied. "Maybe it was the motion light outside, maybe a bird flying by triggered the beam, or maybe it was lightning in the distance." The last room they had investigated was Zara's old bedroom. Once Rayna had finished her search, she said, "Looks okay," and then she headed downstairs to check the first floor.

Mira decided to stay behind. "I'll be down in a few minutes, Rayna." As she looked around, the clutter of memories was everywhere. Then she heard the rustling of leaves outside. Intuitively, she turned off the bedroom light, walked to the window, and peered out across the grounds.

That's when she saw the blue presence again. At first, it was nothing more than a faint shimmering, but almost immediately it morphed into a figure, gossamer and gray. *A woman,* the thought zipped through her head. The figure was standing next to the koi pond. It appeared to be sweeping up debris, and there was another figure nearby, a child. Mira held her breath recognizing the ancient heartbreak about to unfold again. Her mind reeled. She knew she was tired and stressed out. *This can't be happening!*

Next, the phantom turned to the entry gate. It was slightly ajar, and ever so slowly, it began swinging inward. Something or someone was pressing on the door from the outside. As it opened more fully, two brutish figures startled her, and the phantom tripped while backing away. Mira sensed menace and terrible helplessness. There was a struggle, and then a moment later, the woman was on the ground in a fetal position, bleeding out, dying. Another shade swooped down from the house and snatched up the child. An instant passed, and then abruptly, all disappeared.

Again, the leaves rustled, so Mira looked upward at the top-most branches hoping to see the ghost. But there was nothing there. But that's when she heard a voice ever so softly saying, "Protect the child. Protect the child."

She was startled. Had she lost her mind? *Or is it all just my imagination?* Mira struggled mightily between the probable and the incredible: doors slamming, voices from the trees, spectral figures wandering the yard, *protect the child*? One minute she was dismissing the fantasies, and in the next, she was rationalizing about this waking dream.

That night, Mira thought about the events long and hard but said nothing to Rayna. Secretly, she declared to herself, *Real or not, I've got to warn Conor.*

5

The Ibex Head

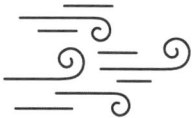

Six hundred miles due west of Baku stands the city of Kars, Turkey. Remote and secluded, it lies on a Central Asia plateau known as the Armenian Highlands. It is an ideal meeting place for those who value secrecy and pursue destiny.

As superintendent of the Kars airport, Mrs. Hazinedar was used to seeing foreigners come and go when the ski resorts were open, December through March. But it was never this busy in October; the snowfalls were at least six weeks away. Both Mrs. Hazinedar and her air traffic controller would cope with the traffic influx, but they were more than curious about these strangers, who were mostly security personnel. Today, the airport had five charter flights scheduled in the morning, four from Ankara and the other from Tbilisi, and of course, there was the daily Turkish Air flight from Istanbul.

Seated at the tower console, Aisha was currently dealing with a Cessna business jet coming in for a landing, "Zümrə XLS-4, standby. Break-Break." At an altitude of 1,750 meters, Kars-Harakani regularly experienced morning fog, but by 10:00 the tarmac was usually clear. There was a pause in communication with the pilot as Aisha checked the radar for any unexpected runway trouble. Though it was late morning, condensed stratus clouds had formed over the region, and a low, white haze still lingered over the airport, "Zümrə XLS-4, cleared to land, Runway 2 south." Aisha gave a thumbs-up to her boss.

"That's the last of the charters for today," said Hazinedar, "now just the afternoon TA at 16:00."

"And tomorrow?"

"That's when it's supposed to get really busy, big shots arriving all day. These early flights are security details, mostly from Ankara."

"The president here?"

"Not Turkey's, but I think Guliyev of Azerbaijan for sure." It was only conjecture, but three jets offloading security forces was ample clue. Then there was the armored black limo. It had the Azerbaijani flag flying on the hood ornament and the Presidential seal on the driver-side door – dead giveaways. The fourth jet from the west was Turkish military, probably the escort for a high-level minister.

"And this one coming in?"

"I don't know for sure." The super glanced out the tower window to see if she could catch a glimpse of the plane. The muddled troposphere was getting worse. "Private jet – the Bey of one of the Azeri Houses, I suppose." Hazinedar thought about which one of the elderly gentlemen it might be, secretly hoping to meet him and have a tour of his luxury aircraft.

Just then one of the ground crew began reporting "a situation" on the tarmac. "Samir says there are two men on the runway. It looks like security, but he isn't sure. He thinks they might be coming toward the tower."

"Turkish or Azeri?"

There was a brief moment as the controller listened, then, "He couldn't say. One is strange looking, a tall thin man with a bushy red mustache."

The Cessna Citation XLS-4 landing was top-of-the-line. The furnishings were all custom made by Bradington Young: the seating was nickel leather, the side tables Persian walnut, the carpeting hair-on-hide cream. Mrs. Hazinedar would have enjoyed a tour, but the Zümrə company jet would not be on-ground long enough for her to wrangle an invitation.

On board were four crew members and two passengers: Conor Kedar and Rufet Qurb. Because they wanted to avoid Armenian radar along the way, the circuitous route from Baku to Kars took more than four hours. They stopped in Tbilisi, Georgia, to refuel and file an alternative flight plan; other than that, it was a quiet yet entertaining ride. Once they achieved cruising altitude, Rufet uncased the rifle he had inherited from his grandfather. It was an antique Weatherby bolt-action model that had been used on family hunts for generations. Rufet had brought it along just in case there was an actual hunt. For the next 90 minutes, Rufet regaled young Conor with one Caucasus Mountain adventure after another. "A noble quest," that was the stated purpose of the Presidential invitation Conor had received one week ago, "a once-in-a-lifetime opportunity to hunt the wild Bezoar Ibex, the ancestor of all domestic goats." House Kedar could not refuse such a summons under any circumstances. After a couple of hours, Rufet ran out of hunting stories, and both men fell asleep.

The men awoke when the pilot announced the approaching airport. Rufet picked up the rifle again and thought he might demonstrate how the old bolt-action worked. But when he looked across the aisle, he could see that Conor was preoccupied. Troubles he imagined, *House Kos, concerns about Tali, and, of course, this meeting with the President.* Qurb knew that Conor was inexperienced with such things. *A young man still searching,* Rufet mused.

Conor was staring out the window fretfully. There was no evidence of a city below, let alone an airport. Everything was blanketed over by the haze. Occasionally, through a break in the clouds, a country road, a pasture, or a rocky outcropping appeared, but only briefly. Conor had never been to Kars, never considered coming here, the easternmost province of Turkey. *If I'm going to Turkey, I'm going to Istanbul.* He was a city boy, and Kars was too bucolic, too out-of-the-way. Such emptiness made him feel detached, exposed, and anxious. Earlier in the week, when he searched the web about the region, Conor found one bright spot: the Sarikamis Ski Resort. It was only 50 km away. Both he and Tali loved skiing, but with no snow likely skiing was not an option. At that moment, he wished he had asked her to come along, but she hated the countryside more than he did. She wouldn't even consider it, so he hadn't asked.

This meeting with Guliyev was a mystery. What made matters worse were that the Azerbaijan security forces had blocked all routes to and from Kars, so Conor anticipated a deserted town and a boring trip. Evidently, President Guliyev wanted to keep the meeting top secret. Then he turned Rufet and asked, "Do you know where we're staying?"

"At the Kars Castle in town," The First Deputy responded. "A historic location, on a hilltop overlooking the river."

"Why there? It's old, right, a relic of a bygone era? Why does Guliyev so relish monstrosities of the past?"

"Presidential security made the call. Its walls are built of basalt masonry, five layers thick, and there are only three access points to the castle: the main gate, a side road that opens on a great fissure, and the rear gate, next to the watchtower that allows for a clear view of the surrounding topography. It's a safe and secure post."

"Sounds like a prison," replied Conor.

"Guliyev's job is a prison."

Conor thought about his most trusted confidante's remark, and as the moments passed, he began to see Rufet in another light. *How old is Rufet?* he wondered. He gazed at Qurb's ruddy face and the old scar that ran from his left ear down to his collarbone. Rufet often complained that it was itchy and sometimes painful.

When Conor was a little boy, Rufet had told him that the Prince of Arabia had slashed him across the face with his scimitar. It was a good story, and Rufet told it well, so the youngster believed every word of it. The scar was pinkish and prominent in those days; today, it was a long brown flab of wrinkled tissue. Conor thought he saw something different in Rufet's demeanor lately, and wondered, *Not the Arabian Prince, but maybe a long-ago knife fight; or perhaps it is unfathomable melancholy... attempted suicide?* Conor knew that Qurb had been tortured in Egypt. He was determined to find out the real origin of the scar, but not today. Hard air turbulence jarred him back to the present. "I want to see the ski lodge at Sarikamis," Conor said.

"The ski lodge?"

"'Sarikamis Ski Resort, the best powder snow in central Asia, set in a scenic pine forest.' That's what the Instagram page said."

"The locals call it Katherina's Mansion, after the Russian princess. But it's been completely revitalized, very modern."

"Whatever it's called, I want to see it," Conor said. "Maybe I'll bring Tali here for a holiday. I want to stay there instead of that dreary old castle. Can you get us a room?"

Rufet said, "That's where we are supposed to hook up with the hunt-ing outfitters on the last day. Clearly, there's no skiing now, so it shouldn't be a problem."

"Perfect," said Conor. "You can shoot that beautiful old Weatherby you brought along, maybe even bag one of those rams you're always talking about."

"They are ibex, city boy, not sheep."

The city boy would never understand. The Bezoar Ibex was the most resplendent of all mountain goat species and had always been Turkey's most famous attraction for international hunters. Of course, there were other prize game – wild boar, the Anatolian red stag, and the Urfa gazelle – but the grand head of the Bezoar was the trophy that most big-gamers desired.

"Okay, a goat then." Later, Conor questioned the sport of killing what he thought was a domesticated animal. "How troublesome can it be to kill a goat?"

"It is mountain hunting. It requires patience and cunning – the spot-and-stalk method – and it takes several days. The Ibex habitat is steep hills and deep gorges." Rufet continued on, "You can't just shoot the beast, you have to retrieve it as well, city boy."

The conversation was interrupted by more rough air. One of the flight attendants announced, "We are on final descent into Kars-Harakani. We should be on the ground within ten minutes. Please buckle up. It's going to be a shaky ride." Conor looked out the window, hoping to see the tarmac. But there was nothing but uncharted land below, and he felt he was falling dangerously fast into it.

The Kars Castle – more a citadel than a palace – was used mainly for tour-ist activities these days. The inner core was a four-story structure. On the ground floor, it housed an archaeological gallery, a restaurant, and a small mosque. The gallery featured local woodcarvings, an excellent collection of coins, and distinctive kilims sold to tourists as prayer rugs. The restaurant was legendary for its first-rate Kasar yellow cheese and delightful honey. On the second floor were military lodgings and an ammunition depot, while two executive suites occupied the third. Above all that was the watchtower, which had an assembly hall that had been converted into a meeting room. That's where President Guliyev conducted his classified business, and that's where Conor was summoned the next day.

Fuad was the president's long-time personal assistant and had always traveled with him on political as well as private missions. This was both. He had been with Guliyev for a decade and knew most of the prominent members of the elite Houses. Today, he was escorting the youngest of that group to a personal meeting with the President. When they reached the top floor, the door was locked. Fuad entered the code, "The president has a private lift." The door swung open. "He will be with you briefly. Have a seat on the divan." Conor nodded and then watched the old man walk away. *How many secrets does that man know?* After four years, the Kedar Bey still didn't remember Fuad's family name.

Guliyev's meeting room was a strange mix of Turkish décor and taxidermy. Of course, there was the ubiquitous picture of the President of Turkey hanging directly opposite the entry. An Ottoman-era desk sat in front of Guliyev's private lift, and two sofas and a coffee table were positioned perpendicular to the only window. Hanging above that window was the main feature of the room – the trophy head of the famed Bezoar Ibex. It was remarkable. Conor finally understood why Rufet was so captivated by the beast and its massive, curled horns.

"It's the largest trophy ever taken in the highlands," said Rolan Guliyev, silently emerging from the lift.

"Mr. President, I didn't hear you," said Conor. Guliyev walked toward Kedar, holding out his hand.

"I'm told Minister Kaplan shot it three years ago. He's from the region." Osman Kaplan was Turkey's Defense Minister and had been the focus of the allies' summit for the past week.

"Rufet intends to hunt the Ibex after this meeting. He wants to show me how it's done. I, however, have no stomach for goats, dead or alive."

"I knew Rufet in former times," said Guliyev. "He was once a famous mountain guide, you know." Guliyev escorted the Kedar Bey to the window under the Ibex head.

"I told Rufet he could do the hunt by himself, and that I would be going home."

"Is that all you want, Azreal… to go home?"

It was not a casual comment. Guliyev was always asking and probing at the same time.

"One day, I wish to marry and have kids."

"Tali Nadirov, I am told." He eyeballed the young man unsympathetically. "That can never happen, Azreal."

"I'm not sure I understand?"

"The Kedar Bey can never marry such a relative," Rolan replied, "the Grand Ayatollah will not allow it."

"With all deference, sir, I will marry the one I choose."

Guliyev ignored Kedar's youthful arrogance, "Nothing more, then?"

"I must restore the honor of my House. The Kos have been stealing from us for a decade," he said, then added, "and my father's reputation, of course."

"Your father sealed his fate when he attacked the Zebeqi Nation. You should be grateful that none vandalize his burial site."

"I will never allow that," Conor reacted stubbornly.

The president then took Kedar's arm and escorted him to the window, "Beautiful view, wouldn't you say?" Pressing matters of state were at hand.

"Indeed," Conor replied, and then, as he gazed across the panorama, he noticed a few buildings and a tower directly to the east. "What is that city in the distance?"

"No city. Just a border crossing," said Guliyev, and then, "That's Armenia, the trophy we seek."

"So, your meeting with Kaplan is about Turkish support for a military campaign?"

Guliyev walked to the Ottoman desk and removed the linen covering. It was a relief map of Azerbaijan, Armenia, and eastern Turkey. "We are planning to employ Hannibal's master tactic, the Double Envelopment. But there will be a twist." Conor was taken aback by the details of the display. After generations of pontificating, the Azeris finally had a president who was willing to act on Azerbaijan's ancient grudge.

"Twist?" Conor now understood the purpose of Fuad's locked door.

Guliyev opened the right-hand drawer and took out several chess pieces. "We will begin with a feigned retreat at the Black Garden, here." He was pointing to the map. "General Aslan will mount a direct attack on the entrenched Armenians at Agdam." He placed a white knight piece in position. "The attack will fail, of course, and Aslan will fall back, luring the Armenian army into fortified Azerbaijani territory."

"The feigned retreat."

"Exactly. Next, Aslan will split his forces into right and left flanks. The Armenians will see that as a tactical mistake."

Kedar thought he understood, "And commit to a full-frontal attack, hoping to destroy the whole of the Azeri Army quickly."

"You've studied military tactics, Azreal?"

"No, sir. It just makes good sense."

"The idea is to hold the Armenian attack in stasis. That's when the signal will be given, and our Turk allies will begin an advance from this very spot to that border crossing." He walked Kedar to the eastern window, "You can see where the attack will unfold. Yerevan is less than 100 km to the southeast."

Conor said, "The Turks' enmity toward the Armenians has always been formidable."

"Not truly Christians, you know."

"The Armenians?"

"Broke from the Roman church in the third century. They hated the western Christians, and created a religious monstrosity of their own."

Conor replied, "I never knew that."

"Once the Turkish Army is within 50 km of Yerevan, General Samir will launch the Air Force on a bombing raid of Yerevan."

Conor looked at the president and smiled. "A brilliant plan, my Guliyev Bey."

"To defeat the Armenian rabble should be simple. It will take a month, maybe two at the most." Guliyev's eyes drifted back to the window, then he pointed, "Our prize awaits, Azreal."

Conor peered out the same window, saw nothing more than the barren uplands, and then said, "I have a question."

"Permit me to guess: How do you fit into this plan?" Guliyev gestured for the Kedar Bey to take a seat on the divan, punched the speaker on his intercom, and ordered tea. "Azreal, you and Ambassador Kazimov will be our voices at the UN Asia Conference in London, the first week of November. This is why I cannot allow you to return home. You and Kazimov will be the new faces of Azerbaijan – youthful and modern, both graduates of western universities – it will be your job to prepare the way for reconciliation. After, of course, we have subdued the Armenian forces and taken back the Black Garden, the highlands, and the Nakhichevan corridor."

At that moment, Fuad entered with a tea service and placed it on the table between the two men. When the servant had departed, Guliyev continued: "So you'll need to be in London no later than October 31st to meet with Ambassador Kazimov. You will lay out a plan for Azerbaijan to be the first to sue for peace."

"Azerbaijan will be made whole again."

The president declared, "Yes, the desire of all nations."

Not nearly so naive as Rufet and Mira reckoned, the young Kedar Bey did not wait for the next shoe to drop. "But there's more you expect from me?"

"Of course," Guliyev replied. "We will need vast financial resources 'to keep the peace.' Your contacts with the London bankers should do the trick."

Conor was a graduate of the London School of Economics and regularly returned to England on business. Because Viktor Kos had slashed the Kedar share of the oil monies over the years, House Kedar was forced to develop other revenue resources. International banking was its principal means.

Next, Guliyev surprised Conor with an offer. "About the honor of your House," he said. "I've been considering you as my next vice president – you or Viktor Kos. If you complete this task, you will not only have great power and wealth, but your family's name will also be restored."

Conor wasn't used to playing mind games with the President, but he recognized that he had to stay one step ahead in this fast-moving situation. "So, the rumors are true?" he hesitated, "That the oil monies are running out?"

"You know, then?"

"Over the years, Mira Nadirov has followed the diminishing oil returns closely, searching for the underlying cause."

Rolan Guliyev moaned, "Basically, it's already gone. Viktor Kos is just playing with the money. Don't worry about the Dark Triad. I will take care of that clan."

Conor wasn't sure what Guliyev meant by the last remark, but he followed up with an assumption about the upcoming war. "As a result, if the UN wants to keep the peace in central Asia, it will have to pay up."

"Exactly."

"The 21 families have taken up sides," said Conor. "The no-confidence vote you faced recently was the result."

"That's why I need you and your allies with me in the fight."

Conor began making mental notes about the people he would have to contact. Then his mind turned to a pleasant thought, *ten days before I have to be in London; Tali and I could spend a little time together.*

Later that day, Conor met with Rufet. "You're free to hunt your Ibex," he said, "but be sure to meet me in London on the 31st of October."

"Where are you going?"

"On holiday."

Then Conor sent a text to Tali: "Meet me in Istanbul tomorrow."

6

Away from Baku, Away from Home

The man who relishes the hunt is a most righteous man. Alive in the moment, he senses a kinship with ancient spirits and feels a purity of purpose. No matter the circumstances that have befallen him in recent times, the frustrations, the obstructions, the betrayals, they are ignored on the mountainside. Such a man enjoys the hardness of pursuit: the aching muscles, the stiff hands and numb feet, the frozen air. In the evening, when he returns to camp, he wonders not about the capriciousness of civilization, but about the cunningness of his prey, and finding the ruse that will bag him. Sleep comes swiftly to the hunter. The genuine joy of being in the wilderness is the surety that tomorrow will bring symmetry to one's life and maybe even a trophy.

When Conor told Rufet that he wasn't needed until the end of the month, the First Deputy was surprised and delighted. He had a business meeting with Mira the following week, but it would not interfere with his plans. He had plenty of time – three days, maybe four if necessary – to seek his Ibex trophy. Rufet was satisfied and relaxed; he would hunt again. *Fifty-inch horns; nothing less will do.*

Qurb often dreamed of his hunting trips on Mount Sheki. He wanted to hunt alone as he did in his youth, and that thought brought a smile to his face. He enjoyed the solitude of the quest. In Baku, there was no time for solitude, just galling mendacity.

But this hunt would require planning. Launching a hasty trek into the mountains was unsettling to the 60-year-old. Rufet knew that his physical capabilities were not what they once were, so he decided to hire a guide. A local outfitter could arrange for provisions and horses, recommend a hunting range, and then escort him to a base camp and spike out his tent. *I'll take my satellite phone in case of trouble, or I need help to retrieve the carcass.*

So, the next morning, Rufet went to the concierge desk to ask about a guide. "I have one good man still available," the clerk said. "A young fellow named Ali. He lives close by. I can call him if you like."

"My time here is short, so I would like to go as soon as possible. Please make the call."

The concierge nodded, thumbed through his iPhone, and then sent a text to a man named Ali Tabak. "He should respond shortly."

"I'll wait."

To occupy his time, Rufet began rummaging through the hunting brochures on display next to the registration counter. He thumbed through several until he found one about the Ibex. He then walked to a nearby couch, sat down, and began reading: "The rutting period is best for bagging your trophy Bezoar Ibex. Typically, the rut begins in late October and lasts through December. In parts of Eastern Anatolia and the Lesser Caucasus mountain range, elevations on the Kars plateau can exceed 1,900 meters.

Summers are brief and generally warm, while winters are especially cold. The average January low is −16 °C. However, temperatures can sometimes plummet to −35 °C. Kars has a wealth of wildlife…."

Tired of the puffery, Rufet drifted off to sleep.

An hour later, Ali entered the lobby of Katherina's Mansion. He was in his mid-twenties, short and stocky, sported a military buzz-cut, and was somewhat pigeon-chested. As he approached the concierge, his smile was as broad as his shoulders. "I'm looking for Rufet Qurb."

"The man on the couch."

"The fellow with the mustache?" Tabak assumed the clerk was referring to the younger man, who was sitting on another couch in the lobby.

"No. The man sleeping," he interrupted to point out Rufet, "there."

"Thanks." He walked over to Qurb. "Mr. Rufet?" He tapped him on the shoulder, "I'm Ali, the guide you requested."

It took a moment for Rufet to regain alertness, "Oh, sorry, it's been a long day. Thanks for coming."

"You'll be hunting for Ibex?"

"Yes, but I have only a few days," replied Rufet.

"If we can get you to base camp tomorrow, I'm sure I will be able to find you a nice set of horns."

"I want to hunt alone," said Qurb, "but I need you to set me up with a base camp and show me the good Ibex territory."

"I don't recommend going alone. It's very demanding out there. The terrain is rugged and steep. Elevations can be more than a kilometer high; a test of physical and mental fitness even for a man my age."

"I've hunted in the Caucasus many times," Rufet said. "If you will provide the horses, sleeping bag, and supplies for a camp, I can do the rest."

Even though he sensed that Qurb knew what he was doing, Ali was reluctant. But he agreed. The outfitter would return in the morning with everything needed for a three-day hunt.

Ali asked, "Do you have a rifle?"

"A Weatherby, bolt-action, with a Swarovski scope."

"And ammunition? The shooting distance will average 200 to 300 meters."

"180-grain Nosler AccuBond bullets."

"You'll be shooting up and down steep angles," Ali said. "I'll bring a rangefinder, so you can calculate the compensation angle." They shook hands, and then the guide left to round up the equipment and provisions. Rufet waved goodbye, then headed upstairs to finish his nap. After they were gone, the man on the other couch – the man with the red mustache, who had been listening to their conversation – closed his book, tossed it to the bellman at the door, and followed Ali outside.

The next day, after three hours of horse-backing onto the Kars plateau, Ali found an ideal location for Rufet's base camp. On a rising slope just below the high range, he came across some level ground that was slightly higher than the surrounding terrain. If it rained, water would drain away without creating a problem. That's where Ali spiked out the tent. Knowing it would be cold at night, he dug a circular pit in case Qurb wanted to start a fire. Then the guide offloaded a supply of ready-to-eat goods. When he finished, there were still several hours before sunset, enough time to get back home. Rufet thanked his new friend, shook his hand, and then asked Ali to return mid-morning in three days.

Still keyed up from the backcountry ride, Rufet decided to explore a hilltop nearby. His best guess told him it was about a one hour's hike.

Once he reached the crest, he sat down, retrieved his binoculars, and began searching the mountainside hills. He was looking for mid-elevation switchbacks, north-facing outcrops, and grassy locales. Twenty minutes later, he found a well-worn Ibex trail angling up toward the north range, and there he spied four bucks. Rufet felt adrenalin surging through his chest, a sensation he had not experienced in many years.

He remembered the last time clearly. That was over a bet with his cousin. They were near the mud volcanoes and had spotted a menacing clutter of wolf spiders, which was unusual because they are usually solitary hunters. Hormones surging, the young Rufet bragged, "I can catch one, and pull off its head before it bites."

His cousin warned, "Wolf spiders are poisonous, and you can die if you're not quick enough." Rufet was not deterred, but he lost the bet. He was decidedly not quick enough. The poison put him in the hospital for a week.

This Ibex hunt would be different – he would not have to be agile or quick to avoid angry spiders. Through his binoculars, Rufet noticed one of the bucks had an intriguingly large head. Brashness returning, Rufet had already claimed the prize. *I'll take that one tomorrow.* Satisfied, he packed up his gear and headed back to base camp.

That October evening on the Eastern Anatolian Plateau, there was a sudden drop in temperature. As Rufet neared his campsite, the sunset was finishing, and a few stars were just now appearing in the cloudless sapphire sky. He hurried to get inside his tent, but he left the flap unzipped so he could admire the rapidly changing nighttime display. He was alone with his thoughts when he noticed a meteor zipping high above in the brilliance. Then there was another and then another. One glowing trail seemed to linger unusually long and extended across the expanse of the heavens. Shortly after that, he noticed a blinking red light and realized it was not a meteor at all, just the contrail of a passing jet airliner. It was racing towards the western horizon… away from Baku, away from home.

After the sky-trekkers had disappeared, Rufet felt hungry. He hadn't eaten since morning, so he began devouring chunks of beef jerky, a power bar, and lots of water. Then he zipped up the tent and climbed into his sleeping bag. It was a grand feeling. He was free from Azerbaijan's warring madness, so he closed his eyes and fell asleep.

The next morning, Rufet slept in. It wasn't his habit, but age has a way of making demands. "Damn!" he cursed out loud. "I've missed the dawn graze." It would be more than an hour before he could return to the spot where he had seen the four bucks. Mad at himself, Rufet grabbed up his gear and charged out of camp.

Once he reached his spot, he began searching the range. Two hours went by without a sighting. After lunch, he moved further up the slope. There, he checked a hidden box canyon and finally caught a glimpse of two bucks, one with half curl horns and the other full curl. They moved behind a large rock outcropping and nipped out of sight. The horns were not exceptional. Disappointed, he set the binoculars down, opened his backpack, and rifled through it for water.

Out of the blue, an intense spark of light from above surprised him. He raised one hand to cover his eyes, and immediately thought of the Ibex bucks. He realized that was not likely. *Another hunter – sunlight reflecting off the lens of his scope – damn!* He explored the surrounding ridge, but there were no subsequent flashes of light. *Am I being followed? Maybe it was Ali signaling.* That made no sense. Ali wasn't scheduled to return for two days. No, just a glint of sunlight, bouncing off a flat rock. It was now 3:30, and time to get back to his search for a trophy. There were only a few hours of daylight left before he had to return to base camp.

At 4 o'clock, Qurb spotted a small herd of nannies in the distance. Following them dutifully were yesterday's bucks. There was a fifth with them today, and he was a Goliath. Rufet identified their well-worn trail angling up to the pasture where the herd had gathered and were now grazing. He headed that way, eager to avoid any kind of noise. At the top of the ridge, slippery shale forced him to turn off the path and onto a sharp cliff edge. The climb was steep, but the rocks there were dry and stable at the moment. Rufet was able to hide from the Ibex coming down the slope toward him. *This is it*, he thought and settled into a shooting position. He was lying next to a deep-cut cliff with a 10 to 15-meter crevasse just below. The wind was picking up, and he worried that he couldn't hold his position or the Weatherby steady enough for a clear shot. So, he braced the rifle against his backpack for a good look at the five Ibex billies now in range. He considered each carefully, but the fifth one, the one with the blackest horn curl, took his breath away. This was why Rufet had made the trip – a trophy head for sure.

Like the day before, there was an abrupt drop in temperature, and dark clouds were coming in from the north. The four younger bucks sensed danger and broke downhill towards a covering ravine. But the stately one was unfazed. Rufet realized it was time for him to take a chance, so he made the angle compensations. The shooting light was perfect as he scoped in his trophy at 180 meters, now just slightly below his position. Rufet centered the crosshairs on the buck's shoulders and held his breath.

A single rifle shot echoed shrilly against the stony hills and valleys.

The prize Ibex was startled and bolted downhill to where the others had sought sanctuary only a few minutes earlier.

Rufet Qurb's head had dropped slightly forward against his rifle. Since the First Deputy of House Kedar was already in a prone position, it was the only movement the man with the red mustache could observe. A moment later, he could see that Qurb was bleeding out through a small thorax wound. Whether his quarry was dead or just in a state of shock was unknowable, so the man fired a second time. He hit Qurb again, this time slightly lower, near the abdomen. He methodically checked for any indicators of life once more – nothing.

By now all the animals had fled. The assassin had one more thing to do: somehow hide the body. The killer was positioned on what the locals of Kars Province called the Korluk Ridge, more than 300 meters and at least an hour's trek away from Qurb's body. He could do nothing before darkness fell. Then he noticed a large rock just below the victim's leg. If he took one more shot and shattered that rock, the loose shale would surely send the body off the cliff edge and into the ravine. He aimed carefully, then fired. Instantaneously a small avalanche carried Rufet's body and his backpack tumbling off the precipice. The man stroked his mustache, satisfied. Next, the assassin checked the surrounding hills for witnesses. The sun had set, and a gathering mist had dimmed the panorama, but there was no unusual movement, no out of the ordinary sound. *One fewer Kedar to deal with*, the man thought. Then he picked up his gear and walked to the motorcycle he had hidden below the ridge.

The figure of Qurb dying on the rocky hillside was gone. Only one item was left behind – Rufet's cherished Weatherby. It had fallen forward and out of the assassin's line of sight. For now, that didn't matter. It was the end of a flawed but honorable man.

7

Holiday

Whenn Tali received Conor's text, she was instantly excited. Holiday! She cheered and then began checking flights to Istanbul. Because there were four daily departures from Baku, Tali had no trouble booking a seat on the Turkish Air 2:15 pm flight. The next morning, she packed lightly – her personal items in a carry-on, and a large, empty suitcase for the shopping she would do at the Arasta Bazaar and the Palladium Mall. Once onboard, she sent a text message to Conor: "Will arrive Ataturk International @ 6:05."

Conor replied: "I'll send car for u."

Tali: "Let's dine at Turga's. Love lamb medallions there. You can have your coconut kadayıf."

"Will make the reservation, Conor." The Turga Restaurant was located on the first floor of the historical Cıragan Palace and had a breathtaking view of the Bosporus Strait, the famous waterway that formed the boundary between Europe and Asia.

Tali: "Short meeting w/RG. why?"

Conor: "About that later." Tali understood, and then signed off. TA 3011 left Baku promptly at 2:15 pm; the three-hour flight was uneventful.

It was chilly that late October evening when Tali arrived in Istanbul. The Four Seasons limo picked her up a few minutes after six; it was another 50 minutes to the hotel, where Conor was waiting. As she emerged from the car, Conor smiled, and his eyes sparkled. Then he kissed her. "We've got reservations at eight."

"Great. I'll shower and be ready in a half hour." Then she added, "Let's walk to the Cıragan. I need to stretch out... been sitting since this morning." The Cıragan Palace was only a few blocks from the Four Seasons, and a nighttime stroll along the Bosporus, she thought, would be relaxing. More than anything, Tali wanted a little quiet time with Conor.

The walking path between the hotel and the palace, however, was poorly lit and the shadows and gloominess along the route had a disorienting effect on young Tali Nadirov. The familiar became the bizarre: secluded courtyards, burnt out street lamps, darkened storefronts, and the general absence of other strollers contributed to a growing unease that this way harbored some nameless malevolence. Unexpectedly, Tali conjured up the aura of Vladimir Kos. *I'm just stressed out and all this travel has added more worry.* She took Conor's arm and brought him in closer.

Once they were seated among the great marble columns of the palace, she felt better. Tali knew that a good meal and the spirit of Istanbul would refresh her soul. As expected, dining at the Turga was first-rate. Tali had the medallions, and Conor had his lamb kebabs. They were finishing a glass of wine when Tali leaned over to Conor, and asked, "Do you know that woman at the next table?"

"Where?" Conor twisted to his right.

"No, the other way," Tali replied, "I don't want to point, Conor. She's seated by herself, in the blue tweed jacket." A woman dining by herself in Islamic Turkey was unusual.

"Okay." He thought he'd found the woman, but there was a candelabra between them, and it partially blocked his view.

"Sitting next to... there," she said, "at the moment, she's having tea."

Conor casually glanced her way. He noted that she had an unmistakable manner of discipline and determination: rigid posture, stern smile, hair pulled into a tight bun, cheekbones high on her face. He thought, *Russian, maybe a liaison officer I once knew.* But it wasn't coming to him. *A business associate?* "Why do you ask?"

"She's been watching us, on and off, all evening."

"No. Don't recognize her."

As the waiter was about to interrupt with the Kedar Bey's favorite dessert, Tali changed the subject, "So, tell me why your hunting trip with Guliyev was cut short."

His eyebrows instantly scrunched together, and he put his napkin to his mouth; Conor knew something that Tali did not. He considered the nearby tables fretfully. *Should I be concerned about strangers in a restaurant? Yes!* The Kedar Bey decided to act prudently. After all, the meeting with Rolan Guliyev was about real-life conflict; it was not a Nintendo game. People were going to die. Conor called the waiter to the table, and said, "We'll have the *kadayıf* on the terrace." Tali understood.

Because of the cool night air, none were eating outdoors. The waiter said, "It's quite frosty this evening, Kedar Bey."

"You can bring some space heaters, right?" he asked. The waiter nodded.

Tali added, "And coffee. American, please... decaf."

It took only a few minutes for the staff to set up, and the headwaiter brought Tali a shawl. From the veranda, the splendor of the Istanbul night was unfolding. The waters of the Bosporus glittered spectacularly from the lights on the opposite shore, and Tali noticed a cruise ship docked across the Strait, ablaze with nightlife.

"The hunting invitation was just a ruse," Conor began. "Guliyev was meeting with Turkey's defense minister to finalize plans for an invasion of Armenia."

She sighed deeply. "So, it begins."

"Indeed." For the next hour, Conor explained what was expected of him and House Kedar in the coming conflict.

"Does Mira know?"

"She has had suspicions for a long time. When the oil payments to the families declined year after year, it was obvious that misfortune would soon follow. Guliyev decided he had to do something."

"War is his solution?" Tali scowled.

"Scapegoat is his solution. People like a good scapegoat and Azerbaijan has always relied on the Armenians when it needs to play the victim card."

"So you're going to London as the fixer?"

"Yes. As long as House Kedar can provide a money flow, Guliyev and the families will survive. We will survive."

"Can you do it? Get the money, I mean?"

"I have no idea," Conor replied, anxious to bring the discussion to some kind of end. He waved to the waiter to bring the check. "Let's get out of here."

As they were leaving, Tali stopped to admire the beautiful waters of the Bosporus once again. That's when she heard a band playing. She pointed toward the ocean liner docked across the Strait. "We've got some time before you have to leave. Let's go on holiday before all hell breaks loose."

Conor asked, "Do you think we might get a last-minute booking?"
"I'm sure the new Azerbaijani emissary to London could do it."

Upon entering the Golden Horne Suite, the first thing a guest perceives is a faint yet ubiquitous scent of lavender. After that, one notices the décor: the walls in shades of pale blues, whites, and purples, giving a surreal effect to the spacious rooms; the floors of Adoni Black Slate; the furnishings velvety onyx, metallic silver, and leathers, and the eye-catching oils of the ancient adventures of Odysseus in the land of Troy are everywhere. Truly, an upscale hotel.

For the past five years, the Four Seasons-Istanbul had been Conor's haven from the helter-skelter existence of Baku. And for the past six months, it had been Conor and Tali's escape – a place where they could explore the nature of kinship, dependency, and love, away from prying eyes of judgmental mullahs. The evening at Turga's had been perfect. The long conversation about fate and finality, and the anticipated cruise to the warmer climes filled the heart and mind of both Conor and Tali.

At last, they were in their suite, and Conor was watching as Tali pulled off her shoes and kicked each in the general direction of the closet. She unzipped her dress and let it slip to the floor. Next, she unhooked her bra and found a black satin nighty inside the dresser. Tali then picked up her wine glass and took a sip. She was now dressed only in nighty and matching panties. Taking in the full measure of her beauty, Conor stared unabashedly. Tali was a stunning 25-year-old with a swimmer's trim and taut figure.

He decided it was his turn to entice. So, he tossed his jacket on the chair, undid the two top buttons of his shirt, and then walked to the audio console and found a soft music channel that fit his mood. His explicitly wicked smile was an invitation, and Tali noticed.

Conor snatched her wine glass away, sniffed the bouquet, and then set it on the dresser. He took her hand and gave it an energetic pull, bringing Tali into his arms. He held her tight, his body against hers, and began moving with the music, taking her along.

"I'm glad to see you smiling," she said.

"When I'm with you, Tali, I can breathe, be something of a human once more." The tenderness between them was charged with anticipation. He dropped his head down, stared intently into her coffee eyes, and then traced the tips of his fingers over her face.

Instantly engaged, Tali teased, "What are you waiting for, Conor?"

That was all the encouragement the 26-year-old needed. Conor reached down and grabbed Tali's backside, lifted her up, and then pushed her against the bedroom wall, pinning her there with his hips. Next, he grabbed her face with both hands and kissed her passionately. She moaned mouth agape, leaving an opening for his tongue to penetrate. She responded with an erotic bump and grind. It was only a moment until they were on the bed.

"Do you ever tire of me?" he asked.

Tali rolled on top, then bent down and bit his ear lobe. "Never."

As she kissed his neck, he whispered, "You are a fearless lady, Tali."

"Don't confuse fearless with lust, Conor."

He chuckled roguishly. "Time for making love, then?"

"Yes." It was her warning bell – get moving, Buster. Conor, soulmate and lover, had an exquisite physique, not muscular, but graceful, and his smile was cheeky-delicious. At the moment, his dark auburn hair was tangled and wild on his face, so he brushed it back, still staring down, his blue eyes bold and blazing, and it filled her with desire. Hypnotized, she pulled him into her arms and then bit his lower lip. She tugged gently, and he groaned, muscles clenching, trying to hold back.

They paused momentarily, lying side-by-side, and then Conor traced a hand from Tali's hip to her belly, and then up to the nape of her neck.

"Panties, Conor, panties," she moaned. Tali's breathing had become quite irregular. Faced with what seemed an impossible predicament at a most important moment, he hesitated. Removing her panties seemed frustratingly slow, so he grasped the sides firmly with both hands, and then ripped them off. It wasn't what she meant. "That'll cost you."

Unapologetic, he growled, "I wasn't thinking about cost right then."

Conor and Tali spent the next hour enjoying a beautiful and erotic encounter; all cares and concerns set aside. Afterward, as lovers often do, they cuddled. But neither could sleep and the night was still young.

8

The Bay Club

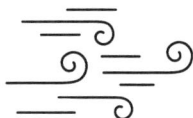

hen Vlad got to the base of the Korluk Ridge, he ripped his weapon apart and tossed the components into separate crags along the mountainside. He had finished his work in Kars and wanted to get out of Turkey and back home as soon as possible. So, he texted the concierge of the Baku Sporting Club: "Will arrive u in 7 hrs – prep my suite, VK."

A few moments later, the BSC desk replied: "The Kos Bey is looking for u – past three days – your brother too."

Kos: "Avoiding them. Notify my boys to be at the Club for wrestling championship on Wednesday." The concierge understood his meaning and messaged Vlad's companions.

When he wished to escape his family, Vlad would stay in the city at the Bay Club. That's what the legacy members called it, and every fourth

Wednesday of the month, the Club held a citywide wrestling tournament. Vlad liked wrestling – more accurately, he liked the violence of the sport – and he planned to be in Baku in time for this last tournament of the year. But the weather was not cooperating. There was only a smattering of light left in the day, and Kos wanted to get off the ridge. So, he put on his leathers and helmet, hit the starter switch of his Ducati SuperSport, and took off down the mountain and headed directly east toward Armenia. Vlad's outbound journey to Kars was a circuitous route that included Ganja and Rustavi. It took two full days because, of course, he needed to avoid any Armenian entanglements. But now he wanted to get home fast, and a more direct route through the heart of Armenia would save him 250 km and almost three hours. It was dangerous – especially at night – but Vlad liked taking risks. When he reached the Armenian border, it was raining, and an impromptu police roadblock was checking all travelers. Vlad wanted nothing to do with the authorities, so he pulled off the road and waited. In fact, he fell asleep, and when he woke some hours later, the border police had moved on. He arrived in Baku at nine the next morning, three hours later than expected.

The Baku Sporting Club was located on the south-central shore of Baku Bay, next door to the Crystal Hall. That venue was the pride of President Guliyev and had hosted major cultural events, including the Eurovision Song Contest and the e-Sports World Championship. The BSC was a partner facility with a hotel. It supported boxing, karate, taekwondo, fencing, volleyball, and most importantly, wrestling. It was built specifically to pamper those Azerbaijani families who governed the nation through crony capitalism. If you weren't one of the historically privileged few, but were wealthy enough to sponsor a national team, you could buy your way in as a benefactor. That's how Viktor Kos became a member of the country's ruling oligarchy. He sponsored the national wrestling program, among other "charities."

But it wasn't easy. Decades earlier, Viktor's grandfather had married the daughter of one of the old Soviet oligarchs. That linkage was the foundation of the Kos wealth – they supplied Russian-made armaments to dozens of central Asian and Middle Eastern autocrats. The Russian connection was also responsible for the Kos family getting a foothold with the ruling elite of Azerbaijan. A generation earlier, House Kos moved in with a large shipment of Russian tanks, which solidified the Guliyev's hold on power. As a reward, Viktor's father was made the Azerbaijani Minister of Oil. After the old man died, Viktor took his place.

When Vlad appeared at the reception desk that late October morning, he was a mess: hair jumbled, boots soaked, leathers mud-covered. The desk clerk was unfazed, "Müserif Kos, your key."

"No interruptions," he said, "not from anyone, even my brother. Understand?"

"Of course, Müserif."

A few minutes later, Vlad was in his suite. He showered, threw on some pajamas, and then drew the curtains closed. He planned to sleep for five hours, and wake up at two, a full hour before his wrestling match with Bhima and three hours before his companions would arrive for the championship and party afterward.

Meanwhile, at his father's house, big brother Vanya was admiring himself in a mirror. He was six years older than Vladimir and physically very different: shorter by two inches, with a receding hairline and lifeless eyes. He had one distinguishing mark: on his throat, a three-inch-long Rosacea stain rose from his left collarbone to just below his chin. So, Vanya often wore turtlenecks to hide the mark.

Vanya was waiting for Viktor to return from a meeting with his Ministry staff. "Well, Misha, what do you think?" Vanya asked the butler. "Do you like my new shoes?" They were Ferragamos, textured leather loafers, black highlighted with horse-bit trims – nothing that Misha could ever afford.

"Most extraordinary, sir."

Vanya replied derisively, "And how do you know they're extraordinary?"

"I just meant..." Misha stumbled for something that would please the future head of the House. "With your… they go well with the outfit."

"I'm glad you admire me," said Vanya. "But it will not bring you favor in my eyes. Is that what you were seeking, my favor?"

"Not at all, sir."

"I will never grant favors to the likes of you, Misha." From early childhood, Vanya had delighted in manners that were cold and manipulative, especially with household servants. Some had suggested that he was just emulating his father, who had always made a game out of exploiting others.

At that moment, the Kos Bey entered the study. "Misha, bring me a whiskey." He then noticed that the fire in the fireplace was burning low. "And get someone to stoke the fire." It was obvious that something was on his mind. "It's freezing in here."

The butler responded, "And you, sir?"

"Wine, Misha," Vanya said, "a rosé, Veuve Clicquot, the one with raspberry and cherry."

"Of course, sir."

Viktor waited for his butler to exit, and then said, "I have been with our associates." The Kos Bey stepped to the window overlooking the courtyard. "The situation is grave, Vanya."

"By that, you mean the others are panicking?"

"It will be impossible to keep them in line."

"How will this end, Viktor?"

"Melania Mirsky says when the Azerbaijani economy crashes, so will our society and our power."

Vanya replied, "Why should we believe a Russian?"

"She has no dog in this fight," said Viktor. "She is an economist, not a politician."

"A woman economist, at that."

"She compared the Azeri economy to a spinning wheel. As long as the wheel is kept in motion, our society is kept in motion. If the wheel should stop, well... our nation would become an unpleasant, violent place, one defined by a struggle over inadequate resources."

"Again, the oil."

"The oil, yes."

"Assuming that is something beneficial to our cause," Vanya asked, "how do we get that wheel back in motion?"

"It is unclear. Azerbaijan has few viable industries."

"Alternatives, then?"

"Guliyev thinks taking us into war with the Armenians is the solution. But how he plans on paying for such a debacle is beyond me."

"That Armenian scam has always been a distraction, meant to stir up the masses, nothing more. No other ideas?"

"Entice a superpower, I suppose, promise a new, glorious empire."

"Iran? Russia?" the elder son speculated.

"Both are running out of oil as well, and neither can control its people. As Mirsky says, 'a struggle over inadequate resources.' A disaster everywhere."

Vanya offered, "What about China or India, then?"

"Rolan has dismissed the idea of soliciting such a partner. One thing is for sure, we must play our cards carefully and not reveal our hand in any overt way."

"Are the Saudis...?"

Viktor interrupted, "Have you seen Vlad? I have been searching for him for days."

"Why would I know Vlad's whereabouts?" Vanya replied. "He doesn't inform me of his plans."

"If he's done something rash…"

"When he wishes to avoid family obligations, he hides at the Bay Club with his boys."

"Go there immediately, Vanya," the Bey commanded. "See what he's done."

In recent years, wrestling had lost much of its popularity to football, but it was still significant to many Azerbaijanis as their time-honored sport. There was a divide between the generations: young Azeris were into World Cup football and the X-Games, while the older generation still held onto traditional sports.

When Vlad was young, he was captivated with wrestling. Viktor made the boy come along for the openings of each national event that the Kos family sponsored. He hadn't wanted to, at first, but then he began watching the matches and was soon fascinated.

When he met Guru Girish, coach of the Olympic team, he wanted to learn the sport. The Guru was the master of Indian style wrestling, and quickly became Vlad's mentor. "But first," Girish insisted, "You must learn its history."

"I have no interest in history," Vlad complained.

"If you want to learn the secret holds and locks, you will have to know about Lord Krishna, who founded the art, and Shri Krishan, the champion of the *Mahabharata*."

Vlad bargained with his teacher. "One history lesson each day, and then one secret hold." The guru agreed.

"In the olden days," Girish began, "wrestling was much more extreme than it is today. It meant crippling or killing your opponent." That was all Vlad needed to hear – he would suffer through history for the secrets of knowing how to kill a man. "In India, wrestling has always been a martial art," Girish continued. "For example, in *Jamuwanti* style, a fighter uses atypical locks to dislocate joints or break bones."

Vlad was hooked by the break bones comment. Who would be his first victim? *Brother*, he thought. *I'll dislocate a shoulder or maybe a wrist, and say that it was an accident.* Fortunately, the future Bey of House Kos had no interest in the art, and only once let Vlad show him how to execute the arm-trap half nelson. It resulted in a separated shoulder that plagued Vanya for a year.

Vanya arrived at the Baku Sporting Club just as Vlad was finishing a match with one of the BSC "jobbers." Mall Bhima was a musclehead, hired as a shill by the Club. He made a living losing to wrestling's big stars, or to the sons of wealthy benefactors.

After his shower, Vlad decided to have a sauna. When he saw his brother waiting, he said, "Join me." The elder son took off his jacket and removed his shoes and socks. There was another man already in the sauna, red-faced and sweating profusely. Vlad poked at the man's shoulder and said, "Get out." Startled, the fellow recognized two of the Dark Triad and exited at once.

"Make it quick, Vanya. I have an engagement tonight."

The elder son got right to the point, "You have done something, Vlad. Father and I want to know what."

"Why the drama? It had to be done."

"What?"

"One of the pillars that prop up the Kedar Bey has been removed from duty."

"Who?" he asked, but then shouted, "You haven't killed Mira Nadirov, have you?"

"The other one, the butler," replied Vlad, "a man of little consequence."

"Rufet Qurb?"

"Yes. Rufet."

"Where?" Vanya was startled. "Did anyone see you?"

"He was alone, hunting on a mountainside," Vlad replied, "He has 'disappeared.' His body will never be found."

"How so?"

"After Azreal left Kars – that's where I found them… can you believe it, Kars, Turkey – after the Kedar Bey departed, Rufet was alone. I tracked him down, shot him, and then sent his body into a deep ravine. There is nothing to worry about."

"That's it, then?"

"Of course not," Vlad replied. "I have sent an assassin after Azreal and his bitch cousin. Alex will report in as soon as they're dead."

Grim-faced, Vanya chastised his brother, "This is a problem, Vladimir. You've put the entire family in jeopardy."

9

Encounter at Ephesus

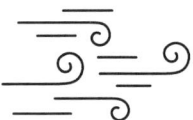

The ship Tali saw docked in Istanbul was the Westerdam, from Holland America. It was a magnificent, Vista-class ocean liner, capable of carrying 2,000 passengers around the world, but its current cruise was full. Try as he might, the concierge at the Four Seasons was unable to book passage for Conor and Tali. But he didn't give up. He found a nine-day voyage on the *Corinthian*, a three-masted gullet yacht that accommodated 137 guests in grand style. It sailed on Saturday, October 21st and returned on the 30th. Perfect timing – Conor and Tali could fly to London after the voyage and be ready to meet with Ambassador Kazimov on November 1.

Tali was delighted. They would avoid the hubbub of 2,000 passengers, and the smaller, wooden sailing vessel was ideal for exploring the shallow, coastal inlets of Turkey. When they stepped aboard the next morning, Tali noticed a distinctive smell – something a fiberglass cruiser, like their Zarifa, did not have. It was hard to pinpoint: mold, turpentine, linseed oil, and a hint of Tung? Yes, the wooden deck definitely had the satiny wetted wood look of tung oil. A few hours later, they were sailing through the Dardanelles and relaxing on lounge chairs they had claimed on the veranda. Tali was reading the Blue Star Line's travel brochure.

"Listen to this, Conor." She read: "Tell me, O muse, of that hero who traveled far and wide after serving his king at the sack of Troy. Many cities did Eternal Odysseus visit while suffering much by sea trying to save his life and that of his men. But do what he might, Odysseus could not save them, for they perished through their own sheer folly, and were prevented from ever reaching home. Homer, 800 BCE."

"Sounds like a new Azeri emissary I know," she said. Sensing that her hero had lost interest, Tali chided the dozing Conor, "Are you listening? This is the story told from the other side… truly, where East meets West."

"I'm listening."

She continued: "Your Corinthian Adventure will follow in the foot-steps of Homer's hero as he strived mightily to save his people. On your 9-day tour, you will experience Trojan highlights on your way to Turkey's wonders in Ephesus and Cappadocia. Then you will spend four days cruis-ing the best of the Aegean in Crete, Patmos, and Santorini. Your adventure ends where it started – Istanbul. Welcome aboard!"

It was early afternoon, and they had reached the turquoise waters of the Aegean. Tali was standing next to the railing, admiring the tranquil sea, when she quipped, "This trip is going to be fun." But her fervor fell on deaf ears. Conor, on a well-pillowed sun-lounger, was sound asleep. She wanted to wake him, but for the moment, she enjoyed watching him. *He looks so different with his eyes closed.* Tali thought she could see Zarifa in him: her delicate bones, her pale skin, and her broad, heavy eyebrows. When Conor was awake, his eyes dominated his face and personality. *Why this heavy burden?* She wondered. *He deserves a young man's distractions: skiing in the Caucasus, shooting wild boar in the highlands, boating on the Caspian with me.*

As she felt the warm sun and gentle breeze, Tali's mind, like that of so many women of her age, drifted to notions of marriage. She imagined a quiet home away from the hubbub of Baku, and children, of course, a boy and a girl. But then she remembered certain discussions with her girlfriends, dreams of the idyllic life of Muslim wives. She thought them nightmares, really: stressful images of confinement, family obligation, and struggles to attain a high-ranking position among the elite families. Tali had rebelled against such ideas. But nagging at her every now and then was the question, *will we ever marry?* It was something she thought about from time to time but kept to herself.

The Corinthian's first port of call was Canakkale, a city on the southern coast of the Dardanelles, made famous by the story of Hero and Leander. Today, it is primarily a tourist attraction for those who wish to visit the archaeological site of ancient Troy. There is even a wooden horse on the seafront. But such adventures require a small vessel like the Carpathian to navigate the shallow coastlines and estuaries along the river. Three thousand years ago, Troy's location near the Aegean Sea, the Sea of Marmara, and the Black Sea made it a hub for military ventures and international trade.

The next day, Conor and Tali signed up for a shore excursion that took them a few miles to the southwest to Hisarlik, the Turkish name for the Trojan ruins. They hired a local guide, a guy named Bart – not his real name, but his customers were mostly English speakers so Barkant would not do in casual conversations. He had an old, banged-up Jeep that made sounds like a mad donkey. "Don't worry," he said, "it's very reliable and perfect for exploring off-road archaeological sites." They were up for an adventure, so they said okay.

Bart first took them inland across the Homeric plain to the place where the Achaeans had bivouacked near the mouth of the Karamenderes.

"This is where they beached their ships and set up base camp," Bart explained. "They believed it would be a short war, maybe take a month, maybe two at the most."

Conor, taken aback by their guide's words, turned to Tali, "Those are the exact words that Guliyev used for the war he is planning." Tali shook her head in disgust.

Bart pointed to the east and continued, "The city stood on that hill, across the plain of Scamander, and that's where most of the battles of the Trojan War took place."

There wasn't much to see. A visitor had to visualize the mêlée that took place three millennia ago: young men around campfires boasting of victories in Thrace and Macedonia; old widows railing at the death of kings; maidens bemoaning vanished heroes who were starved to death in dungeons; the sages of the day grieving for the insane queen, who believed she was formed from ice crystals. Yes, the spirits of the place traveled forward through the ages, meandering, mutable, still elusive.

Tali was somewhat skeptical of Bart's story, "How do you know that?"

"In recent days, archaeologists have been studying the terrain, and have identified the ancient coastline, which has since been filled with alluvial material," Bart explained, docent-like. "We are told the results basically corroborate the Homeric topography of Troy."

Tali was impressed. "You've done your homework."

The guide replied, "Not my work, just repeating what the scholars have reported."

After their day trip, Conor and Tali went back to the Corinthian to clean the dust off their boots and get dressed. They decided to return to shore for dinner, so Conor asked the customer services clerk for a recommendation. She said the Seaside Diner was delightful and had a grand view of the Dardanelles. When they arrived, they asked for a patio table so they could watch the sunset. Like Istanbul, Canakkale was a city that reached across two continents. They could see Europe across the waters to the north, and from their high vantage point, Conor and Tali noticed a spirited ruckus just below. "What's going on?" Conor asked the waiter.

"Hero's Rush," the fellow said. "Young men replicating the legendary swim of Leander across the Hellespont to prove their love." The crowd began shouting when the first swimmer arrived on shore to claim the championship.

Tali asked, "But in the story, didn't Leander drown?"

"No one drowns these days, miss. It wouldn't be good for business." Tali laughed and began clapping with the rest of the onlookers.

Conor, however, was silent, staring intently at the sidewalk below.

Tali noticed. "What is it?" But he didn't respond. "Conor, what's the matter?"

"That woman," he mumbled.

"There are hundreds of people, Conor. Give me a better clue."

"That same woman we saw at the Four Seasons," he said, and then he tried to draw Tali's attention to a sizeable gathering near the sidewalk where the champion was walking. "There, the tall woman in the tweed jacket, hair pulled into a tight bun."

Tali still could not find the woman, and then she disappeared altogether. Frustrated, Tali threw up her hands. "You're concerned? Why?"

"Probably nothing," he said. "I guess I see troubles everywhere."

"It's this thing with Guliyev, isn't it?"

"Yes," he replied. "And what bothers me most is that I haven't heard from Rufet in several days."

"Is that strange?"

"He usually checks in regularly."

"But you said he was hunting."

"Right," Conor said. "Off on a mountain somewhere, and he can't get an Internet connection." Just then, the waiter interrupted with the meal. They forgot about the woman Conor called the Russian and enjoyed a relaxing evening.

After soaking up the sun in Athens and Mykonos, the Corinthian headed for Kusadasi, which was the jumping-off point for visiting the classical ruins at Ephesus. Many vacationers opted for the powdery, white-sand beaches on a low, rocky peninsula that jutted out into the Mediterranean, but Conor and Tali, along with eight other shipmates, decided to take the day trip offered by one of the tour operators. They joined a group of 18, and at 8:30, they all boarded the bus for the leisurely, 40-minute ride from the sea to Selcuk, where the ancient sites were located. Though Conor and Tali had vacationed on the Turkish Riviera many times, neither had visited Ephesus, nor any of the other historical attractions.

As was her hobby, Tali began reviewing the tour pamphlet. "Listen, Conor. The guidebook says: The Ephesus Day Tour includes calls on the ancient city Ephesus, once the economic center of the western Anatolia; the House of Virgin Mary, where Jesus's mother spent her last days, the Temple of Artemis, which is known as one of the seven wonders of the Ancient World, and the famous Library of Celsus."

"Library of Celsus?" Conor was bowled over. "Rufet once told me there was a famous Azeri inscription on the back wall of that library. But he said it was difficult to find. You have to climb the rampart."

"Will they allow that?"

"Don't know," said Conor, "but we can ask one of the locals to help us when we get there." The Kedar Bey liked to break the rules on occasion, liked to find out-of-the-way adventure, liked to see the unusual.

The Corinthian tour group arrived at the Celsus Library at 11 am – when the crowds were at their peak, maybe 300 people jammed into the courtyard in front of the remaining edifice. Tali listened to the guide explain: "The library was planned by the Roman architect Vitruoya, and was constructed on a nine-step pedestal, leading up to the entries. The four sculptures embody the four excellences – Wisdom, Knowledge, Intelligence, and Virtue."

Conor shouted at Tali, "Let's go!" He had found his local, a guy hawking bottled drinking water. For a fee, he promised to take them around the buildings and out of sight so they could climb the outer wall to find the famous Azeri inscription.

As the sun approached its zenith, a lone motorcyclist appeared at the commercial gate behind the Library of Celsus. There were two armed men at the entry, one standing and the other sitting on a bar chair next to the armature that raised and lowered the gate. The standing guard flagged the rider to stop. "You cannot enter here," he barked. He was a private security guard hired by the Ministry of Tourism, not Turkish military.

The rider stopped, flipped the helmet visor upward, and zipped open a bulky, black leather jacket. It was difficult to see the face of the rider, but the voice was that of a woman. She removed a map from inside the jacket. "I guess I'm lost," she said. She spoke crude Turkish with a Russian accent and then offered the map to the guard. *Take it*, she thought, *take it*.

The seated guard turned away momentarily because he saw another group of cyclists coming up the road. The first man reached for the woman's map, letting his Kalashnikov fall to his side. It was a fatal mistake. The rider reached inside her jacket and pulled out a Maxim 9 handgun. Ka-ping, ka-ping. The report of the two shots was almost entirely muffled by the integrated suppressor. Both men were dead before their bodies crumpled to the ground.

The assassin opened the gate as the other four motorcycles, each with a sidecar, approached. There were six men in the unit; the two empty sidecars concealed a cache of weapons. Together, the seven drove to the backside of the historic site, parked their motorcycles, and left them running for a quick get-away. Next, they hustled up the hill that overlooked the Library's courtyard. While the assassin put her Bergara B-14 long rifle together, the other six began assembling other weaponry: AK-12 assault rifles, mortar tubes and shells, and rocket-propelled grenades.

This would be a full-out terrorist attack on one of the icons of Western culture.

"Alex, what are you waiting for?" demanded the gang leader.

After affixing the Bergara's scope, the assassin began searching the packed Library courtyard. "I must find my target," she responded.

"Time is limited, Alex. We cannot execute the attack without you," he urged. "Take out the soldiers, now!"

The plan was simple enough, and the following week, newspaper headlines would read: "Al Qaeda terrorists attack European tourists!" They would be wrong, of course. Only two people knew that it was cover for the assassination of the Kedar Bey.

It was already too late to take out the guards. The terrorists had been spotted, and a volley of bullets came whizzing through the scattered stones where they were hiding. If it weren't for the sun glaring directly into their eyes, the Turkish security would have had clear shots at the intruders.

"Damn it, get moving!" the leader shouted. As rounds ricocheted in all directions, there was a tense scramble of warriors searching for cover along the wall. The fighters had been given a direct order in the middle of chaos and were now engaging targets below.

A moment later, Alex found her target. *Azreal, and there is the cousin too.* They were at the far corner of the Library, in an archway, talking to one of the locals. She took quick aim and fired, but missed. Suddenly, they were on the move.

Behind the assassin, all hell was breaking loose. From the far end of the wall, two RPG operators were ready to launch grenades at the armored personnel carriers stationed at the Harbor and Marble Street entries. Ka-boom, followed by cracking of compressed air, the first one was tracking on target. Ka-boom, the second round was off. An instant later, the two vehicles exploded, roaring into flames and killing the soldiers nearby. The RPG operators dropped their launchers and raced away up the hill toward the others. The trigger flash and the blue-gray smoke gave a clear indication of the launch location, but now the gang's escape was assured.

Next, the ping of a mortar shell leaving its tube and the simultaneous burp-burp-burp… burp-burp-burp of machine gun fire was deafening to everyone close by. Utter panic permeated the courtyard in front of the Library. When the mortar shells crashed into the crowd, there was a whoosh of sparks, like bottle rockets filling the air. No fewer than 50, maybe as many as 75 civilians lay dead or bleeding to death.

It would not be the end of the carnage.

But the assassin had missed her target. Aggravated, Alex shouted, "Keep firing for the next five minutes, then head back to the rendezvous. I'm going to chase down Kedar and his bitch. Meet you there in six minutes."

Conor and Tali followed their new best friend. "Let's get out of here," he bellowed. "Follow me!" Conor nodded, grabbed Tali's hand, and all three raced toward the stone wall at the back of the Library.

"Can you get us out of here?" said Conor. "I'll pay you 1,000 Lira if you do."

Tali stopped abruptly. "Conor, we don't know this man. He could be leading us into out-and-out danger."

"We have no choice, Tali."

"Hurry!" The man shouted. "This way."

As they turned the corner, they saw motorcycles stationed at the back of the Library. Crazy luck. Conor and Tali hid behind a pine tree while the street hustler set off to unravel the mystery. After a minute, he shouted, "They're running!" Then the man motioned for Conor and Tali to hurry. "They belong to the terrorists," the man said. "They left them running for a fast getaway."

"You know the way?" Tali shrieked.

"Yes, just follow me." Conor and Tali chose different bikes, and before he mounted his own cycle, the local man took out a blade and slashed the tires of the other bikes. Then he hopped on, and they were off along the commercial road. Almost at the same moment, Alex appeared at the far corner of the back of the Library. She saw three motorcycles racing for the exit. They were at least 300 yards away and moving fast. It was an impossible shot; there was no use even trying. *There will be another time,* she reasoned.

Instead, she hustled over to the two parked motorcycles. The tires of one were entirely flat, the other, only the front tire. It was decision time, so Alex sat down and waited for the gang members who had survived the bloody skirmish with Turk security. She barely had a moment. Seconds later, three men appeared. With their focus still on the pursuing soldiers, Alex killed them, one at a time. Then she hopped on the bike with the one reliable tire. It was a rough ride, but she managed to escape the carnage and the Turkish military.

When the trio of escapees reached the small town of Belevi, about 15 miles northeast of Ephesus, they stopped. They had been heading away from the Kusadasi port and their ship. Conor said, "We should separate." Tali agreed and then began checking her smartphone for maps and directions.

The street hustler had no argument, "Okay, but you owe me 1,000."

"Not a problem," said Conor, as he reached into his wallet and took out two 500 Turkish Lira notes.

"What is your name, mister?"

Conor eyeballed the man incredulously, "Tartakov... we're the Tartakovs from Grozny, in Chechnya."

The man knew it was a lie, but he didn't care. "I'm going south, into the country." They thanked him, and he was off.

Tali said, "I have texted the pilot to pick us up in Izmir. No response yet."

"How far is it?"

"Best I can tell, about 40 miles."

Conor said, "I'll text Rufet and tell him what has happened. He'll know what to do."

"There's more to this than a terrorist attack," said Tali. "I have a bad feeling."

"Me too. Now we have to get to London as soon as possible."

"Text Mira and Rayna," Tali urged. "Tell her she's in great danger. Tell her to add security for Georghe and Seyfulla."

"This is about the Dark Triad," said Conor, "and the mess it has made... with us out of the way... well, you know."

"Conor, should we warn Jake in the States?" Tali asked.

"Our first job is to get to London safely," he replied. "We can deal with that in a day or two."

Jake

J ake was Catholic, but he often wondered why. Long ago he'd given up
his faith, but not its practice. *Too used to the rhythms and rituals,* he'd
tell himself. His mother was Catholic and Polish, and that meant his
entire family was umbilically tethered to St. Andrew the Apostle Parish and
to the Archdiocese of Chicago. Maybe that's why his father had had to get
out of town. To keep his sanity, Tom Moynihan had spent most of his life in
the Foreign Service, fighting terrorists – at least that's what Jake supposed.
As any kid might, Jake resented his father's absence. Rightly or wrongly,
he imagined that Tom preferred spending time with his other son, and he
fumed about it regularly. Jake had seen his brother's American passport
once; it read Conor Moynihan. Conor had a second one, and it read Azreal
Kedar, Azerbaijani.

When Tom died seven years ago – in Azerbaijan – Jake was filled
with anger. But above all, he was mad at Conor and his alien, inexplica-
ble family. Tom Moynihan was buried over there, and that was a mystery

to the sixteen-year-old. So Jake Moynihan vowed to find out why and to learn more about his brother, his birthright, and the land where his father's bones remain.

10

Jake and Lindy

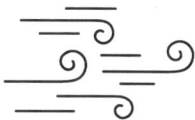

Ahalf a world away from Azerbaijan, Jake Moynihan and
Lindy Bedrosian had boarded the *Amtrak Saluki* at Chicago's
Homewood Station. The train was now picking up speed past
Kankakee, heading south through the fallow cornfields of central Illinois.
Ignoring the bumpy ride and the blurry country scene outside, Lindy
turned to her boyfriend and asked, "So, just where is this ghost town, this
LaRue, Illinois? I cannot find it on any map," she said. "Believe me, I've
tried."

"And so, the meaning of the term, 'ghost town.'"

She wrinkled her nose and curled her upper lip, then demanded,
"Just where are we going, Moynihan?"

"It's near the Mississippi River, a natural wilderness area called Clear
Springs."

It was a weird image for a business class railway carriage – two Chicago South Siders dressed in khakis and wearing tanker boots. Lindy glanced out the window, "Doesn't look like a wilderness to me."

As if discovering a disturbance in the force, Jake peeled his eyes slowly away from his smartphone, "It's in the Shawnee National Forest, another four hours south."

"That doesn't mean a thing to me," she said, and then, frustrated with his never-ending devotion to his new IPhone, snapped back, "I thought the FAA powers-that-be did not allow electronics on this field exercise."

"I'll pack it away once we reach Carbondale, but I have to meet with Sam before we head back home. Just trying to arrange a place to connect."

"Sam Mansour, your father's friend?"

"Yeah, he and his wife live in Carbondale. They're professors at the university, both of them." The 23-year-old looked up and clicked off his phone. "He's always kept a journal, and I want to pick his brain… to get some specifics about my brother and his Azerbaijani family." As expected, Lindy waved a hand for more interaction. Jake wasn't shy when it came to finding fault with his in-laws. "Strange, the whole bunch, that's how I remember them. And Conor is… I don't know, a banker or lawyer of some sort."

"That's not very clear."

"Sorry," he replied. "I just need to know more about them."

"Why?"

Jake did not respond right away, and that frustrated the dark-eyed Armenian beauty. Throughout the summer, Lindy had become more apprehensive about what was driving Jake's moods and their relationship. It had been on and off lately, satisfying during the on-times, yet not quite what she thought it should be. They'd been together for more than a year, and he had told her that she was the love of his life. But Lindy wasn't a fool. She understood what love of my life meant – its fickle duality, its tenuous nature, the promises that might or might not be – however, she worried more about his other passion. In recent days, she sensed that something was driving him in a far different direction.

"Will there be other women in camp?" she asked.

"More than a campsite this time. And yes, there will be other women."

"What's so special?"

"Two years ago, the FAA bought a 50-acre tract of land next to this Clear Spring Wilderness," Jake said. "They have constructed a lodge, a training ground, and a storage facility."

"Running water, toilets?"

"Yes, even hot water."

Naturally, Lindy thought, *Showers.* That made her smile, but she still had another question, "How do we get there? I mean after Carbondale; how do we get to this wilderness area?"

"CS Camp, that's what it's called. The Commanders have built two others, at Panther's Den and Burden Falls. Both camps are to the west of CS but still within the Shawnee Forest." Jake continued, "Mike will meet us at the train station. He's bringing the drone gear, the IEDs, the recons, bug-out bags, and a SnakeRoad Exercise Manual for each of us."

"No sidearms this time?"

"Just what one might carry personally," Jake pointed to the slight bulge in the cuff of his pant leg.

"Snake Road?" Lindy piped up, her head twitching backward slightly. "You're kidding, right?"

"Not at all. Lots of snakes at Clear Springs," Then matter-of-factly, Jake said. "It's why we wear tanker boots. Good eats, you know. Just skin them, rinse the meat with salt water to kill the poison, soak' em in a little egg white and sweet cornmeal, and then fry' em over an open fire. Good eats… tastes like chicken."

"You've been there before, right?"

"Not to CS Camp."

"Then how do you know about the snakes?"

"They are everywhere in the Shawnee Forest," he said. "You could check it out if you had electronics." Without blinking an eye, Lindy retrieved an eReader from her jacket. Jake smiled seeing that Lindy didn't precisely adhere to the rules either, but he said nothing. After a quick eSearch, she was satisfied that Jake had told her more than a few half-truths.

Lindy Bedrosian was a tough gal, raised in an outdoors family with four brothers. Snakes didn't bother her; at least the pictures on Wikipedia pages didn't, so she signed off without making a fuss. Next, the young woman retrieved a pillow from the overhead rack, placed it on Jake's shoulder, and curled herself into a fetal position. She put her head down, made a slight purr, like an unapologetic mouser on a warm couch, and then fell asleep. They arrived in Carbondale four hours later.

The week of camp went by quickly, and subsequently, Mike Bedrosian (Lindy's uncle) had dropped off Jake and Lindy at the home of Sam and Iza Mansour. After dinner that evening, Sam asked, "How was camp?"

Lindy responded enthusiastically, "Real toilets, and showers, so much better for women."

Iza was surprised, "Doesn't sound like the Clear Springs I know."

"And what about the snakes," Sam snickered. "Any inquisitive wigglers crawl into bed with you, Lindy?" Sam knew the favorite pastime of seasoned campers was to place a snake on the bed covers of one waking up newbie.

"No snakes allowed in the lodge," Lindy cackled. "But we saw plenty in the field."

Iza added, "We see a few here on the lake, mostly harmless Black snakes." Sam and Iza lived in a handsome, old rustic house just west of Carbondale. The development was called Lake Chautauqua, 50 or so homes surrounding a man-made lake that had long ago lost its urban panache to scruffy backwoods – just the opposite of Jake or Lindy's apartment in Chicago.

Somehow the house on Lake Chautauqua felt familiar to Jake. Not that he had ever visited before, or even seen a postcard of the Mansours' home. But there were photos everywhere, mostly of family and friends. Sam was a top-notch professional with a camera, and Iza had decorated the walls of every room with his works. Iza and the two girls were the principal subjects, of course, but there were numerous pictures of Jake's father, Sam and their overseas friends from long ago. There was the photo of Sam and Tom on a Nile River showboat called the Mustafa; Tom and a young woman in a hotel lobby labeled Shepherd Belly Dancers; Tom with Captain Azat on a tugboat named the Hazar-Denizi and, of course, the graduation photo of Jake's brother, Conor, and cousins Mira and Tali. The large portraits were in color, but the action shots – Sam's forte – were mostly black and whites. For Jake, it was somewhat unsettling, but by seeing the photos and then talking about them, Jake finally understood Sam's profound feeling for his friend, Tom Moynihan.

Once the dinner dishes were cleared and stacked, the Mansour daughters asked if they could go to town to take in a movie. It wasn't a movie they were interested in, just the going. Natia had just turned 16 and had been driving on her own for a couple of months. Iza worried, of course, but Elene, the younger girl, scolded her mother for being too protective. "We'll be all right, mama," she said. "Don't worry. Natia is a careful driver." Careful, Elene instinctively knew, was a more reassuring descriptor than good. As soon as Iza had given them her okay, the girls said goodbye and hurried out the door.

"Let's have dessert on the deck," Iza said. "Jake, will you help Sam with the ice cream?" Jake nodded. "We'll get a bottle of wine." Lindy followed Iza to the hallway but stopped short of the wine cabinet to view a large, group photo. It was titled The Cairo Gang. As Lindy stood admiring it, Iza had a chance to observe her for a moment. Jake's girlfriend was stunningly attractive. Her ivory skin stood as a stark contrast to her wavy, dark brown hair, thick eyebrows, and long eyelashes. But Lindy's outstanding feature was her Armenian nose – aquiline was the usual term – long and curved, with a prominent bridge, giving it the appearance of being slightly bent. This ethnic nose was the reason why so many Armenian girls go under the knife; it was the reason why plastic surgeons were in such high demand in every Armenian community.

"This is interesting." She recognized Sam and Tom, but not the others.

"That's the old gang at Café Omar Khayyám," Iza replied. Pointing to the man in the far left, she explained, "That's Tom's old boss, J.K. Burke. He was killed by terrorists. Afterward, Tom was appointed to fill his position as the head of the CoC."

"CoC?"

"It means Clash of Civilizations," Iza replied. "The anti-terrorist unit founded by the UN Security Council."

"And the others?"

"The woman next to Burke is Salma Jili, JK's office manager. She still works at the American embassy in Cairo. There's Sam, of course, and his girlfriend, Alesha."

"Girlfriend?" Lindy hooted.

"I wasn't in the picture then," Iza replied. "And that is Tom with his significant other at the time, Zarifa Kedar."

"Conor's mother?"

"Yeah, Conor's mother." Iza face suddenly stiffened, "She's dead, you know," stumbling across the words, "by her brother's hand. It was a so-called honor killing."

"Honor killing?" Lindy recoiled.

"A monstrosity held over from ancient times. It has been banned everywhere in the Muslim world, but some old clans in Central Asia still see it as a tool to control their membership."

There was a sympathetic lull in the discussion, and then Lindy said, "I believe it's why Jake has come to see Sam. He says there's so much he doesn't know about the Kedar family and his brother."

"Not an easy tale to tell," Iza said. "They're a hard family to understand, the Kedars – the language, the culture, and their particular version of Islam – and they're dangerous besides."

From outside on the deck, Sam shouted, "Hey, you two, where's the wine?" Then he added, "And Jake wants whiskey." Iza handed Lindy three wine glasses and a Glencairn, grabbed a bottle of chambourcin and a bottle of Jameson, and then they headed for the sundeck that overlooked the lake.

After pouring the drinks, Iza asked, "How did two Chicagoans survive Clear Springs?"

"I wanted to stay at the lodge, but snake-boy, here," she was pointing at the boyfriend, "would have none of it."

"You're asking about the field exercise?"

Iza spoke up, "Yeah, what was the reason for five days in the wilderness of southern Illinois?"

Sam broke in, "More preppers angst?"

"We're not Preppers, Sam," he growled. Jake and many other FAA associates frowned at the idea that they were preppers or survivalists. "We're stewards."

"Stewards of what?"

Jake couldn't ignore Sam's parry, "The goals of the Founding Fathers, and the coming chaos." But then Jake changed the subject, "Game-training this time. SnakeRoad was all about new forms of combat – drone exercises. Our instructor was a former airman who flew missions over most Asian conflict zones. Only these were petite UAVs, not the big Predator drones used in Afghanistan."

Sam probed on, "Did he ever say how many he killed...in Afghanistan, I mean?"

"I asked one night, but he was reluctant to talk. Maybe it was depression or PTSD, something bothered him about his time there. He said every morning the officers would give each operator a closed envelope with his name written on the outside. Inside was a plain white card with a number. But he said, 'I never opened it. Didn't want anything to do with that.' I guess the burden of knowing how many he had killed was hard to stomach."

Upset by the direction of the conversation, Lindy attempted to steer the group back to the CS Camp, "We were on the recon crew, triangulating targets for strike teams. It was a lot like eGaming, but with real targets. Not people, of course, but wilderness targets."

That's when Iza changed the subject entirely, "So Jake, Lindy tells me that you came to Sam learn about the Kedar clan."

Sam jumped in, "Not tonight, Iza. Jake and I will talk about Azerbaijani issues tomorrow. I'll give him everything he needs to know then."

Iza replied, "Fine by me, professor." Professor was code for her being pissed off. "So tell me, Lindy, how'd you two meet?"

The next day, as they were boarding the train for the return trip to Chicago, Lindy turned to Jake and said, "My goodness, she's a tall woman." They waved goodbye to the Mansours, entered the Business carriage, and found their seats.

"Back in the day, she was called Big Iza," said Jake. "But it wasn't what she was, but who she was."

"Explain, please."

"She was a celebrated journalist in the Caucasus when they met – that's the who. The what – Sam informed me – Iza was once a famous Olympic basketball player for Armenia, I think. She doesn't like to talk about it, though."

"Not Armenia," Lindy chided. "She's Kurdish and a Muslim. She's not Armenian. I'm Armenian. Bedrosian, remember? I would know if she were Armenian."

"Iza saved his life once," Jake recounted the story told by his father. "In the Armenian Highlands, that's where they were ambushed by raiders."

"Patriots, Jake, we call them patriots," Lindy scolded. "So, tell me, what did Sam say about the Kedars? And what, of importance, did he reveal about your brother?"

"He called him a prince, or something like that. He's the head of the Kedar family and the Zebeqi Nation – a cult, seeking its rightful place in the Muslim world."

Lindy asked, "Tied to the Azeri government, then?"

"Like a hand to glove."

After Jake had stored their gear in the overhead, he sat down, and then turned to Lindy and announced, "I've made a decision."

She eyeballed Jake curiously. "Yet another scheme?"

"Call it what you will," Jake replied, "but I'm going back to Azerbaijan."

Lindy moaned, "Why would you want to go back to that goddamn place? We have other pressing work!" For Lindy, Azerbaijan was more than a sore spot in the conversation. She was steeped in the bad blood and the cultural rancor between Armenia and Azerbaijan.

Jake said, "I'm going there to find two men, and wring the truth out of them."

"You know these men?"

"I know them – a guy named Rasuli and a guy named Qurb," Jake said. "After that, I will dig up my father bones, salvage his soul from that heathen ground. I plan to bring him home, and give him a decent burial."

"Seems like a big effort for someone you say you didn't love all that much," Lindy was reminding Jake of his own words, "even if he was your father."

Father. Jake thought of that day seven years ago when he had made a promise to Tom's soul and to himself. Then he said to Lindy, "I also gave my word to my mother that I would bring Tom's body home, that he would have a proper funeral mass, and Catholic burial at St. Andrew Cemetery."

11

FAA

The following day, downtown Carbondale was hectic and loud. Saturdays in the fall were farmers market days, eight blocks of a mishmash: vegetable dealers, fruit sellers, organic egg peddlers, a man sharpening knives, a woman selling ceramics, beekeepers, hawkers of herbal medicines, coffee grinder vendors, and more. Years ago, the city fathers had decided to locate the market not on Main Street, but one block west. That way, the hubbub of activity could easily be noticed, but shoppers and bargain hunters would not obstruct the traffic flow through town. At the market's northern closure, there was a municipal parking lot and a warehouse that served as a swap meet. Visitors could buy collectibles, antiques, toys, kitchenware, cheap perfume, and vintage clothes – junk of all kinds. At the south end, there was a small park and a myriad of restaurants. Mary Lou's was the oldest and most celebrated. Biscuits and gravy and homemade sausage were its long-held staples. Eventually, most shoppers found their way to Mary Lou's, and that's where Sam and Iza were enjoying breakfast today.

Iza wanted to talk about Elene. She was turning 13, and predictable hormone-infused rudeness was rearing its ugly head. *I hate you* was the rant that worried Iza the most. Mother and daughter had already had several conversations about hate. Sam, however, was not paying attention. Jake Moynihan matters filled his head. Frustrated by Sam's silence, Iza decided to shift gears. "So, Sam, what did you and Jake talk about?"

"It was a strange conversation. We talked about the trip we made to Baku for Conor's 18th birthday."

"And about Tom's death?"

"Yes," replied Sam, but then he paused to reconsider the question. "We talked about that, of course, but Jake's memory of what happened and mine were very different."

"Did you talk about that?"

"Not really. It was awkward back and forth. Jake wanted to know about the Kedars: who they were and what they did. He said, 'I hope to understand who the boss is, and what their affiliations are.' And, oddly, he wanted to find out if his father had left any inheritance for Conor. He also had questions about the Zümrə company: how it operated; its military and political connections."

"Sounds like he's planning a visit." At that moment, a server interrupted with coffee and Mary Lou's famous biscuits and gravy. It was a coed Iza thought she knew. "You're Cynthia, right?"

"Samantha," the server replied. "I had you for news writing." Iza smiled, thanked the girl, and then she refocused on Sam.

"It does seem like someone is planning a visit."

"But why?" Iza mused.

"That's the question," said Sam. "Our conversation was one-sided. Jake was the one asking, and I was the one providing the answers, as best I could."

Jake and Conor are so different, Iza thought. *Conor has accomplished so much in so little time.* Then she asked, "Does Jake have the money to make such a trip?"

"His job at the Port of Chicago doesn't pay a lot, but he mentioned something else – an inheritance from grandfather – a treasure of sorts. I think he plans to sell this treasure to finance his trip to Azerbaijan."

"Has he talked to Conor about the treasure?"

"Don't think so."

"Wouldn't Conor have a say in the matter?"

"They don't talk much," Sam said.

"Are you going to let Conor know about this inheritance?" Sam didn't answer, so Iza shifted gears. "What does Jake do, exactly?"

"Security guard," Sam said. "He's a U.S. Customs and Borders inspector."

"That explains a lot."

"I guess. But being paranoid about bombs, terrorists, and refugees flooding onto U.S. shores doesn't explain everything."

"I wonder about his girlfriend."

"Lindy? How so?"

"She mentioned Armenia several times," said Iza. "Bedrosian is an Armenian name, you know."

"That's funny, Iza. Jake brought up Armenian militiamen. I didn't pay much attention; thought it was part of the FAA."

"How old is Conor?"

"Twenty-six, next May," said Sam.

"Jake talk about anything else?"

"More ramblings about the FAA... and the need to return to 'our American values.' More than once, he said, 'My father fought them overseas, now they're invading by the boatload.'"

"Who are they?"

"Muslims, I suppose. I think he really means terrorists. He forgets that we are Muslims."

"He seems to be all over the place, and angry at times, too," Iza said. "What do you think Jake really wants?"

It was the right question. In the past, Jake had talked about his promise, but he had waffled over and over about what action he should take. But Sam sensed there was something more, a secret inside Jake's soul. Then Sam said, "Settling scores, plain and simple. I think that's it."

"Revenge?" Iza was confused, "For what, against whom?

"It became clearer as we spoke. Jake believes Seymur Rasuli and Rufet Qurb were responsible for his father's death, and – this is the crazy part – he suspects Conor as well, thinks he was involved somehow."

Iza was quick to reply, "That's silly and irresponsible. Someone must be feeding him these crazy, angry notions."

"You're right," Sam replied, "It's the FAA, that Martin Mills fellow, and Lindy's neurotic Uncle Mike."

"Mike Bedrosian?" She searched for understanding. "The FAA? I don't get it. Gotta be more to it."

"On the trip to Azerbaijan, Jake told me about the FAA, but I wasn't paying much attention," Sam explained. "I thought he was talking about farmers, you know, FFA. I had it all wrong. Jake has lived his whole life on the South Side of Chicago – farmers, how stupid was I?"

Iza was beginning to see Jake in a different light. In her mind, he had always been just a kid being raised by a single mother on Chicago's sketchy South Side. This new Jake was peculiar, and who was his girlfriend,

Lindy? "I understand settling the score, and I understand the terrorism thing. What I don't understand is the FAA."

Sam reached for a little cup of cream in the basket. He opened it, poured half into his coffee, and then stirred. It wasn't an easy topic to know, let alone to explain. He said, "Freedom Army of America." Sam searched for the right words, and then took a sip of coffee. "They have a hero, a guy named James Wesley Rawles."

"Never heard of him." The name raised more questions than answers. "I don't know a Rawlesian from a Presbyterian," she said.

"Yeah, I get that," he said with an uneven smile. "I didn't know much about them either, but I've been doing a little research."

"And?"

"They're survivalists, Iza," Sam replied. "I read about them on Wiki. The movement began mid-twentieth century during the Cold War Era."

For Iza, the idea of a Cold War and the possibility of a nuclear conflict had a distant ring to it—remote, ancient and unreal. "I thought that craze had disappeared."

"Apparently, the FAA is the latest incarnation of the survivalist movement in the Midwest."

"What set it off?" she asked.

"They have countless grievances: refugees, terrorists, illegal immigrants, but everything is tied to surviving catastrophe. This Martin Mills guy insists that all FAA members train to become self-sufficient, ready for emergencies and disruptions in the social or political order. They see themselves as knights-errant, and that's why they've established so many fortifications down here in the Shawnee Forest."

Iza had endured numerous difficulties in her life. Such grim talk was off-putting, stomach-turning, repellent. She was no shrinking violet, but she now had daughters to consider. Natia and Elene were Muslims; they were all Muslims. "Sam, what kind of beliefs are you talking about?"

"They worry about gun confiscation, of course, but also the end of Christian values, the dissolution of the U.S. Constitution, and the takeover by the forces of One World Government. That's why they hate international treaties. They see such agreements as the precursors of this One World thing."

"Seems like nonsense to me."

Sam waxed philosophical, "When you think about it, it's an old story."

"I think there's more to it than just FAA drivel," Iza replied. "There's something hidden under the surface, maybe a lot of somethings."

"Nonsense to us, but not to them. Out west – Montana, Wyoming, Idaho, and Utah – there are dozens of similar coalitions. And it's not just right-wing nut jobs. There are leftist groups too."

"Sam, you're talking about numbskulls, but have you given any thought to the Armenian connection?"

He looked at her quizzically.

It was late morning, and Iza needed to pick Natia and Elene at the swimming pool. "I've got to go," she said. "You're going to call Conor, right?"

At that moment, Sam's iPhone began buzzing. It was an incoming text from overseas. "It's Conor now," he exclaimed, "on the secure line."

12

Confession

J ake Moynihan always wore tanker boots, cordovan with black heels
    and toes. He wore them summer and winter; to fancy restaurants, to
    Bears games, to the movies; and even at church, there was Kathleen
Moynihan's son in his tankers. At Brother Rice High School there was a
strict dress code, which included gray slacks, white dress shirt, tie, and
black shoes. But Jake still found a way to wear his tankers. To avoid demer-
its, Jake would merely tighten the buckles and slip the trousers over the
boots. Only the black heels and toes were visible, so, strictly speaking, Jake
followed BR Rule #23. Besides, none of the Brother Rice martinets wished
to take on the quick-tempered Jake over his shoes.

Arguments with his mother about the boots were unavoidable. She
would insist, "You cannot wear those goddamn clodhoppers to church!"

Katie was Chicago Polish and all Catholic, a combination that required absolute adherence to decorum as well as dogma.

Jake would laugh, thinking himself beyond such rebukes. "Go ahead, mother, make my day."

Once he was out of high school, Katie stopped trying. Today, she avoided any attempt to scold, and instead, tried to reason with her son. "You'll get a blister, Jake."

Full of himself, the wise-cracking Chicago South Sider snapped back, "Better than Father Wysocki's sermon, Mother." During his on-and-off college years, Jake had figured out that Katie would not fight his stubbornness. This was especially true after the divorce; and when Tom died three years later, mother Katie had settled into a pattern of letting Jake do as he pleased.

There was, however, more to the tankers than youthful rebellion. For members of the FAA, the boots were obligatory. Equipped with steel toes, heels, and sole guards, the Patton-designed tankers were the group's identity. Jake had taken that identity one step further by burnishing the FAA logo, an encircled Liberty Tree, into the heel of his right boot.

Jake was lazy that Saturday morning, and didn't get up until 9:30 am. It was October 14th – the feast day of St. Andrew the Apostle – reckoning day for one Jacob Moynihan. Off to confession. This was the mother-son squabble that Jake had always lost. "You must seek forgiveness at least once a year. Otherwise, it's hell to pay. And I do mean hell!" Jake didn't believe the outmoded mumbo jumbo, but he felt it was the thing he could concede to keep his mother from having an apoplectic fit.

Jake was lazy that day; thought he'd be gone only a short time, so he didn't put on a T-shirt or socks. The no socks thing was a mistake. Something, a small pebble perhaps, had wedged its way between his heel and the boot's inner pad and was hurting like hell. Jake had been seated inside the confessional for some time and was growing impatient and cantankerousness. He reached down, pulled off his boot, and then felt the back of his heel. *Blister*, he cussed. *Mother was right, damnation.*

So he sought someone to blame. His fellow sinner on the other side of the confessional door who was taking so long would do. *He must have something nasty to tell. Guy? Could be a woman*, he mused, and started thinking about her sinfulness: *Sex, lying, had she stolen cigarettes from the drugstore?*

It was 10:30, and with nothing to do but sit and wait, Jake gave his cell the once-over. It was made entirely of wood (*walnut*, he thought) and appropriately cheerless. Only a pin light above a crucifix illumined the confessional box. The priest had closed the sliding partition so tightly Jake couldn't hear anything from the other side. It was maddening. Few Catholics used the old-style confessional anymore. These days, most sinners just sat down with their confessor in the rectory and hashed out their troubles.

St. Andrew the Apostle was the oldest parish in Calumet City, and the Polish people there were set in their ways. Tradition wasn't a burden; it was a blessing. The church even offered a Latin Mass once a month. At long last, the divider slid open, and light flooded into the cubicle. Startled by the unexpected glare, Jake thought, *That's why it's so dark and gloomy in here. It's a trick, a portend that forgiveness is at hand.* "Bless me, Father, for I have sinned."

"How long since your last confession?" With the traditional rejoinder, Jake recognized that his confessor that day was Father Edward Wysocki. He had been Jake's catechism teacher throughout his elementary years.

Jake shifted uncomfortably on the hardwood seat, then wiped a hand across his mouth. "One month." It was a lie, of course, and most of Jake's confession that day would also be an invention. He had no interest in playing the game – no matter how large or small his foibles – to anyone, anytime. Besides, if God were omniscient, as the church proclaimed, he already knew Moynihan's sins. This dishonesty was an audacious act for any Catholic, no matter how devout or indifferent, and Jake secretly wondered if he would one day have to atone for it. *Probably not,* he made his case to no one in particular. Still, Jake suffered from prickly mindfulness about this entire soul-saving ritual. It was meant to get Katie off his back. Then he thought of his mother: daughter of the Kowalski clan, sanctimonious devotees all. One couldn't have a Sunday dinner without hearing the story of Martin Kowalski, the priest who climbed the ranks to become a monsignor under Archbishop Kinsella.

After his declarations, Jake found himself searching for some useful truth, an emotional space he seemingly could never fulfill. He was thinking of that place far from Chicago. Edward Wysocki – an able counselor – recognized the troubled moment and asked, "What's bothering you, Jake?" And then the priest added, "Not your confession, then, something more?"

For all his bluster, there was one thing that bothered Jake, a thing he had wanted to talk about for a long time. "A dream," he said.

Wysocki was quick to recognize the young man's angst. "About your father?"

Now Jake understood why Wysocki's confessions took so long. The priest had an able personal touch. "Yes, about his death. I dream about it sometimes. Can't seem to shake it." That Saturday, in the darkness of the confessional, Jake finally felt the need to tell his story, and the veiled partition between them was sufficient enough to allow Jake to feel secure and open up. It was time, past time, for Jake Moynihan to tackle the anger he held about his father's death.

"Tell me about it, Jake. Tell me what happened."

After a moment, Jake relaxed, leaned back against the cubicle wall, and began, "I was 16, and my father and I had flown to Azerbaijan for my brother's graduation. Sam was with us."

"I didn't know you had a brother." Wysocki had been at St. Andrew for a long time and understood that Tom Moynihan had died in the line of duty. But he knew none of the details.

"Years earlier, my father was married," Jake explained. "Zarifa was her name. She was one of those Muslims, and a member of one of the most influential families in Baku, the Kedars." When he said Muslim, Jake wished he could see the priest's face. Was he surprised? Did he scowl?

Both were silent for a time, then Wysocki spoke up, "Go on."

"I don't know if they were actually married, but they had a son, Conor." In his mind's eye, Jake saw his brother's face illumined by the campfire they'd shared that summer at the cottage. But then, his thoughts returned to Wysocki. He didn't know if he wanted to continue with this confession. He felt the need for some fresh air and cracked open the cubicle door about six inches.

The sound took the priest by surprise. "You're not leaving?" Wysocki asked. "We're just getting started, Jake."

The veiled curtain remained, and Jake turned back to his priest. "She died under mysterious circumstances. Some say she committed suicide; others say Zara – that was her nickname – died in childbirth. I don't really know. I don't really care." Somehow those words rang hollow. "My father wasn't with Zara when she died. Tom was severely injured in a Cairo riot and immediately medevacked to Chicago. He ended up at St. Bernard's Hospital, and he remained there in a coma for a year. He only learned of her death when Sam arrived for a visit fifteen months later.

"It was a heartbreaking time for him. He could hardly cope, but Tom had one blessing that saw him through, my mother. She was his nurse at St. Bernard's. That's where they met. They married a year later." Jake's mind drifted. "There's so much I don't know. I wish I had asked Sam more about it."

This time Wysocki asked, "Sam?"

"Sam Mansour, my father's friend from Egypt. He teaches at a university downstate, in Carbondale. He's one of them."

"One of them?"

"A Muslim."

"That's twice you've mentioned Muslims."

"My mother blames them for their divorce and Tom's death," Jake replied. "She calls them 'that damned overseas crowd.'"

"About your dream, then?"

"Yes, of course," Jake grimaced. "We flew into Baku, and a guy named Rasuli met us at the airport. We got there about three in the morning, so he took us to a nearby hotel. We were drained from the long flight and needed rest. Sam said he was a friend, but I never trusted Rasuli. He led us into a trap."

The priest seemed startled by his choice of words, "Trap?"

Though he couldn't see the priest through the scrim, young Jake Moynihan glared his way. And then he said, "You see, Father Wysocki, my father was murdered."

13

Something's Up

The Pere Marquette Mall was located along the Calumet River on the South Side of Chicago. Before his confession, that's where Jake had dropped off his mother and aunt. They would shop while Jake completed his annual religious duty. "Just an hour, and not more than 90 minutes," Katie shouted as Jake drove away. But she doubted he was paying attention.

For Katie and Julia, shopping was not their preferred Saturday morning activity, and so when Jake was late picking them up, both were predictably irritated. It was now 11:15. Julia pointed at her watch and carped, "The carpet cleaners are coming at noon. Where is your Jake?"

"Big sins, I suppose," replied a smirking mother. "Let's get a Dunkin' Donuts." The shop was at the mall exit where Jake was supposed have been 15 minutes ago.

"So, lots of penance for that one," Julia said laughing, "Want an apple fritter?"

Patting her middle-aged paunch, Katie shook her head, "No, just coffee."

The twin sisters were tall, big-boned Kowalski women and, as they approached the order counter, the clerk was somewhat amazed. After a studied Katie Moynihan glower, he spoke up, "What for you?"

"Two coffees. Leave room for cream in one." It wasn't the snipped off expression that startled Julia, but the boy's appearance. She surveyed his fingerless fishnet gloves and black choker. Odd, but nothing to summon up religious righteousness. The order didn't take long, and then the women walked over to the waist-high counter next to the outside window and found a seat.

Leaning against the wall, Julia asked, "How's the dating going?"

"Going nowhere," Katie replied, then reached for a tissue from inside her purse, placed it on the counter, and set her coffee down. "For 50-year-olds dating is not much fun."

"You're not 50," Julia chided. "If you were, I would be 50, and I've got a year to go before that, sister!"

Katie laughed, "Okay, 49 then." Katie Moynihan had only recently started dating again, and courting the second time around was different. The emotional ups and downs of 20-somethings had long since passed. Now she was looking for a homebody, someone reliable, someone who would take her to church on Sundays. "We're on and off, Rico and me," she said, "mostly off." She poured a little cream into the hot coffee. "He's a pharmaceutical salesman, you know, always on the road." It reminded Katie of her former husband. That one was forever gone. Tom's globetrotting took him overseas for extended periods. Katie resented the travel and the lack of family life. She felt like a single mother, raising an only child. Even in the good times, Tom and Katie's thirteen years of marriage had been rocky.

"Does Rico have a regular route?"

"No," Katie replied, "But it's mostly the Midwest. He drives to Wisconsin and Iowa, but often flies to Memphis, St. Louis, and Kansas City."

"Doesn't leave much time for dating, does it?"

Katie shook her head, blew across her hot coffee, and then took a sip. Before answering, she thought about Tom, and then about Rico. "He is usually home on the weekends, but not always."

It was clear that the romance was going nowhere, so Julia turned her attention to family gossip and their older sister. "You seen Sonia?"

"Couple of weeks ago."

"How's she doing?"

"Sonia is still working at the Jewel on Kedzie," she replied, "but Mike is laid off again."

"Machinists can hardly keep a job these days. Mike's so experienced and knowledgeable. He's done it all – milling, turning, grinding, keyseating, polishing – but robotics has changed everything, and that union is no damn help. What's a regular guy supposed to do?"

"Boeing doesn't hire full time anymore, just temporary if that. It's mostly contract work nowadays," said Katie. "You can't put anything away if you're stuck in the gig economy."

"So, no prospects, then?"

"Sonia says he wants to start his own business," Katie said, and then added nonchalantly, "I invited them to Easter Sunday brunch."

Julia was surprised, and more than a little irritated, "Gee whiz, Katie. They are such bores."

"In-laws, Julia, in-laws." Then she countered her sister's faultfinding demeanor, "What do you mean 'such bores'?"

Julia said, "I mean Mike is a bore. He's always whining: 'the working class gets no respect, gov'ment is no support, Christians takin' the brunt of things.' All that crap, he just won't shut up. Gets tiresome." She looked at her watch again. It was 11:25, and still no Jake. "What kind of business?"

"He wants to open a hardware store." Katie and brother-in-law Mike Bedrosian had recently had a long conversation about life. "He says he knows everything a working man needs to know, but he doesn't have the money."

"What does Mike know about running a business?" Julia asked.

"He's always sayin, 'I understand more than those shit-head college kids.'"

"Just BS."

"Says he has a special way to get the money. At least Sonia is working."

"Special way?" Julia replied, "Sounds unlikely."

"Some scheme with the FAA, I suppose."

"Just what is the FAA?"

Katie wasn't sure, "Jake calls it the Freedom Army."

"And what does that mean?"

"Survivalists. You know, the self-defense crowd."

"Jake still a member?"

"Don't think so, but Jake doesn't tell me much these days."

Julia thought she'd seen the Freedom Army on some watch-list, but didn't want to pursue the rumor. "What about Jake and his girlfriend?"

"Lindy?" She took another sip of coffee. "Jake's love life is like his mother. He's on and off with Lindy."

Endlessly curious about ethnicity, Julia asked, "What kind of name is Lindy?"

"It's Albanian or Armenian, same as Mike's. He is her uncle, you know." She spelled it out, "It's Melinda Bedrosian. That's her full name."

Julia quickly responded, "Makes a big difference."

"How so?" Katie asked.

"Albania is a Muslim country, Katie, and Armenia is Christian. Bedrosian is definitely an Armenian name."

"Catholics then?"

"Not exactly," said Julia. "They have their own church, the oldest in the world."

Katie was insulted by her sister's innuendo, "Can't be older than the one in Rome. Peter's church was first."

Julia again turned to search the pick-up zone in front of the mall entrance, but her nephew was nowhere in sight. "Where is Jake?"

Ignoring her sister's bellyaching, Katie said, "Something's up, you know."

"What?"

"With the boys; they've got something up their sleeves."

"You know this how?"

"I think it's about going to college," Katie said.

"I'll corner Denis," replied Julia. "He can't keep anything from me."

"They're planning to surprise us on Sunday at the brunch."

Julia shrugged her shoulders, and then looked beyond the plate-glass window one last time. It was 11:40. "Where is that Jake of yours?"

14

Crow

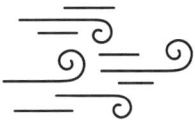

When Crow had left the nest nine days earlier, his mother was doing laundry on the back porch, and his father was at work. It seemed so simple at the time. Wearing a black trench coat and toting a medium-size suitcase, Crow came down the staircase, stepped into the living room, and yelled at his mother, "I'm outta here."

Alice Duda rushed through the kitchen, ready to argue with her son. But she could see that he was in a fidgety state. She worried that something she might say would set him off, or make him angry, so she said nothing. When he finished his unfriending speech, he placed a small piece of paper on the hallway bureau, turned away and walked out of the front door for the last time. He was pleased with himself.

Alone in the house, Alice glanced back toward the kitchen where her husband often sat drinking coffee. She blamed him for everything. *Why wasn't he here?* she thought. Carmen was the one who had all the answers. *Let the boy go, Alice,* she remembered the sound of his castigating wails. *He's 19, and he's got a job.*

Finally, she said out loud, "Troubled boy." Typically, she had never said that to her husband or anyone else. Then Alice walked to the bureau and picked up the slip of paper expecting some sort of an explanation: a lament for lost love or a rant against a neighbor, something he often did when he was fidgety. No, it was only an address. She imagined walking there in the night, and it sent a shiver down her neck. After thinking that, she folded the paper neatly and tucked it into her dress pocket. Alice Duda was a mother in need of comfort, and so she walked to the front room window and looked outside to the street. But there was nothing there to ease her pain.

These days, he called himself Crow, but Alice didn't know why. He tried to explain it once, "A raven is beautiful, the cleverest of all birds."

"Cleverest of all what?" she questioned. The odd logic didn't make sense. Alice continued to stare at the street until Mr. Czasik, who was walking his dog, came into view. *The boy is gone,* she resolved. So, she let the window curtain fall back in place, then looked at her hands. They felt sweaty and dirty.

Sometime around seven pm, Alice Duda decided to call her husband. The phone rang over and over, and just as she was about to hang up, someone picked up. Inexplicably, there was no voice at the other end. "Carmen," she said, "Carmen?" Then she heard him talking, "Carmen, you there?" But there was still no response. She began talking anyway, "Carmen, the boy is gone."

"Alice… What?" The man on the other end growled. "Who's gone?"

"He left about an hour ago. Didn't say a word," Alice Duda glanced down at her pocket, "just handed me this piece of paper."

Carmen Duda, Sr. had an inkling of what she was talking about, but he did not understand the details – he never did, never wanted to.

"What paper?" You're not making any sense, Alice." There was a moment of silence, "You there, Alice?"

"I am," she slurred. "Carmen's gone, moved out. He came down about an hour ago – dressed in that outfit he wears, that damn black outfit he wears. He gave me this paper. He didn't say anything."

"For Christ's sake, Alice, I thought something was really wrong... like he hurt you or something. Why do you get so worked up over this crap? Stupid."

"I was worried, and I thought you should know."

"You don't see me flying off the handle," he said. "You've got to be calm and logical. Now, tell me again. Where's he gone?"

Alice wanted to explain, but she didn't think her husband would listen. "What's the address, Alice?" She read it aloud. "For Christ's sake, that's only eight blocks away. You'd thought he moved to Alaska. Hell, quit worrying. He'll be back in a few days. You're being stupid, Alice."

It was hard between them nowadays. Maybe Alice and Carmen no longer loved each other, or perhaps they were just too old and had forgotten how to care. Whatever it was the Dudas no longer tried to understand, let alone comfort each other. Maybe it was the city, the damn city, the accursed South Side.

"You don't think it'll happen again, do you?"

"Hell no. He's all right. The doctors said he was all right. They released him, didn't they?"

Alice persisted, "But he's on that list."

"Stop worrying, will ya," said Carmen. "I'll be home in an hour. Make some supper, will ya? Do something to ease your mind. Give it a think."

After a moment, Alice heard a busy signal. Her husband had hung up. *Ease your mind,* that's what he said. She stopped at the hallway mirror to check her hair and makeup. *Quit being stupid; that's what I'll do.* As she entered the kitchen, she pinned the note onto her magnetic board, and then went to the coffee maker. There was a half-cup left from the morning pot. *It'll be okay.* Then she pressed the one-minute reheat on the microwave, and said out loud, "Quit being stupid. That's what I'll do."

Like her son, the 55-year-old was a frail soul and dealing with stress was not easy. She put a hand to her mouth as if that would, somehow, ease her worrying. Next, she turned back toward the hallway where her husband would be arriving soon. "Supper," she said, "I'll make a nice supper for Carmen."

Guns! She agonized, *had he taken any with him? That is silly*, she fussed, *he would have hidden them under that damn, black trench coat he always wore.* For the past year, her son had been stockpiling guns. *Why?* She stewed. But she had no know idea why. Alice replayed the boy's exit. Was there something she'd missed? Under her breath, she cursed, "Goddamnit, Carmen, it was your idea: make him responsible, make him a man."

Then the unthinkable crossed her mind, *would he harm that boy?* The thought didn't last long. "Supper, I've got to make supper for Carmen."

Ten days had passed; so many days to think about all the things that bothered him. Crow had made a resolution. It was time to confront Greg.

He had skipped two full shifts of work to make his plans. *H&R eGames doesn't matter,* he thought, *I will never work there again.* He detested everyone who worked there because he was the butt of their jokes, day after day. "Goth boy," they would squeal, "darkwave wannabe." They hammered away, driving him into the back alleyways of his mind.

Crow's apartment that Saturday morning was entirely gloomy. He had pulled down the window shade, and the door to the bathroom was closed. Still groggy, he propped himself on his elbows, straining in the blackness. The only light in the room was his clock on the nightstand. It was flashing on and off, red PF, PF. The PF signal didn't process; nothing was processing. Then Crow fell back onto the pillow and remained still for a long time. But he could not get back to sleep.

"Power failure." He reached over and hit the reset button, and the alarm began its annoying buzz-buzz-buzz. Next, he started slapping wildly in the darkness, but he could not find the snooze button. Finally, Crow sat up, the old bedsprings shrieking at his repellant flailing. In frustration, he reached over, grabbed the clock, and yanked it out of the electrical socket. The riling shrieking stopped.

Still groggy, he wondered, *why so dark?* The commotion had ruffled the window shade, and a crease of light streamed in. Crow could see his "stakeout chair" a few feet away and thought of the boy. Suddenly angry, Crow ran a hand through a gnarly head of hair, threw off the bedcover and scuttled to the window. He raised the blind and then strained to see. The light was so intense that Crow had to cover his face and squint. He was an odd sight: a smallish figure in white briefs, framed in the 10 o'clock morning glare. Reinforcing the peculiarity of the moment was the ink design on Crow's back. As the light evened out, the tattoo, a torso-length raven perched on the threatening thorns of a rose bush, became visible.

Below was dingy Chicago. Here, hundreds of factories and foundries had once pounded out industrial steel, machine parts, and cars, but now it was mostly abandoned. A haze had settled in. An early winter rain had stirred up decades-old rust and soot and stink. The gutters of the street were choked with black waters, newspapers and old winter cinders.

As he stared down from his four stories high studio apartment, Crow seemed to be the only player in this silent movie scene. There were no people or cars or buses on the move. Apparently, the 19-year-old was searching for someone he thought would pass by. Time passed. "Goddamnit, I must have missed him," he cursed.

Everything in Crow's world had changed. As he returned to his nightstand, a lone fly buzzed in front of his face. It had been drawn to the outside light. Irritated, he batted twice at the creature. Crow watched quietly as the fly banged against the windowpane over and over. But there was no escape for it.

Then Crow spoke to it, "My precious, I accept and so must you, that there is no way out." Slowly, steadily, he moved an open hand toward the annoying pest, and then with a nimble snatch, jerked it out of the air. When he opened his fist, the fly was dead. He brushed it away and then walked to his closet to dress.

Crow's mind had turned to the Pere Marquette Mall. It was only a short walk away. Today, he would go to the donut shop where the boy worked, and challenge his Gregory face to face.

15

Nightmare

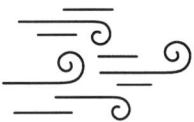

"**M**urdered?" Father Wysocki stumbled over the word. "That's a serious charge, Jake."

"Murdered, I'm sure of it," replied Jake

"Go on."

"Rasuli said he would pick us up the next day about 10 am, and then we were supposed to drive to Gobustan. But he was late. No one knew why."

"I thought you were in Baku?"

"It's a suburb of Baku. The Kedars have a summer cottage in Gobustan," Jake said, "and that's where the party was being held."

"Okay."

"It was cloudy that morning, but the rain had stopped. As I said, Rasuli was late. Once we got on the road we hit a traffic snag, a military convoy blocked our way. Rasuli got out of the car. I think he was searching for a route around the blockade. After he got back inside, I could see he was upset, as if being late was a big problem."

"Did your father say anything?"

"Tom and Sam were preoccupied," Jake described. "They were chatting about an old tower we had just passed. I think it was Old Town Baku. After the traffic cleared, Rasuli started driving like a maniac until he got to the Gobustan turn-off. We slowed down at the light. Suddenly, there was an accident. We were rear-ended, and I hit my head on something."

The priest interrupted, "Anyone else hurt?"

"I don't know. I was groggy." Jake leaned forward toward the priest: "Rasuli started to pull off the highway, and my father said something like, 'Why are you getting off?' Then I noticed a delivery van in front of us. It started backing up. At least I think it was backing up. Maybe we were traveling forward. My recall isn't precise."

Out of the blue, there was someone gently rapping on the confessional door, "Father Wysocki, it is Sister Justine."

"Yes, sister?"

"There's a long line of people waiting."

For a brief moment, the priest was baffled. Then, "Go get Father Maris. Explain that I need help." There was no immediate reply. "Sister Justine, did you hear?"

"Yes. I was just telling those waiting that I will fetch another priest."

"Okay, woman, go." Wysocki waited for an answer, but there was none. He turned back to his charge and said, "Sorry, Jake. Your story is important to me, go on."

"We crashed into the rear of the van, or maybe it crashed into us. I can't be sure. It was so long ago. I screamed, 'Look out.' But it was too late. In lockstep, the three vehicles paraded off the road. I thought that unusual.

I wanted to get out, but my father told me to stay inside. Something was wrong. That's when they launched the attack.

"Two men were coming our way, angry. I remember someone yelling, 'You bastard!' My father was in the front seat. When Tom got out, he was facing the men coming from the front. I don't know why, but I turned to the rear and saw a boy approaching fast. He had a knife in his hand. I screamed, 'Dad, behind you.'

"The boy shouted, 'Murder, or something like that.'

"He was after your father, then?" the priest surmised.

"Next, there was the sound: pop-pop, pop-pop-pop, pop-pop-pop. It was Rasuli firing an assault pistol."

"At the boy?"

"No, at the two men approaching from the front. Curiously, he was shooting at the ground, not at the cutthroats. I could see the splat of shells hitting the gray and dusty gravel at their feet.

Wysocki cut in again, "I thought you said he was a seasoned security man."

Jake's head fell back, his forehead creased. "I have tried to figure out why our 'so-called minder' was not aiming at the assassins. Now I know."

"Yes?" Father Wysocki demanded.

"Rasuli was one of them," Jake said coldly.

"You don't know that."

"After seeing it in my mind over and over, puzzling it for seven years, there is no other explanation."

"So, what happened next?"

"At the front of the car, Sam was shooting. He hit one, maybe both of the assailants. I don't know because I twisted around to check on my father. He was fighting off the kid with the knife. It was long, almost a sword. Tom had taken a fighting stance but had no weapon. He was blocking the assassin's thrusts with his hands and feet. It was the first time I knew that my father was skilled at hand-to-hand combat. Then the boy made several countermoves, prodding, and thrusting. One caught my father in the chest. I could see blood spurt from his rib cage. Then the assassin smiled, judging that one final lunge would end Thomas Moynihan's life. But my father blocked it cleanly, and then he hammered the boy's wrist with a breaking, karate chop. I caught the sounds clearly: the crunch of bone and the blade clattering to the pavement."

"And then?"

"The assassination had failed – Mansour had taken care of the two in front, and Tom had disarmed the boy – the attackers fled the scene. Tom fell back against the car bleeding. My father was weak from his recent chemotherapy treatments, and the unexpected struggle had taken its toll. Sam helped him into the rear seat. I found a blanket in the trunk and wrapped him up as best I could. I bellowed, 'Who were those bastards?'

"'No time to explain,' said Sam, and then he shouted at Seymur, 'get us to the nearest hospital now!'"

Unexpectedly, Jake's story was interrupted by the ding of his iPhone. It was Katie texting: "Where are you?"

He answered: "Still in confession."

She typed: "Get your penance and go... been waiting forty-five minutes!!!"

"Who is it?" Wysocki asked.

"My mother. Got to go, Father."

"Finish this, Jake," insisted the Jesuit. "You've got to hash this thing out." Jake didn't respond. But Wysocki didn't hear any groaning wooden panels either. Jacob Moynihan was a big man, not fat but stocky, maybe 220 pounds. If he had moved to get up, the old confessional would have made an announcement.

After a brief moment, Jake said: "The doctors told us, and I remember the exact words: '... everything is fine, the wounds are superficial, and we have cleaned up the other scrapes. We'll keep him overnight just to be sure.'

"Mira said we should go back to the house for a meal and a good night's sleep."

"Mira?" asked Father Wysocki.

"She's Azreal's aunt. She and Azreal came to the hospital later. Mira Nadirov was the one hosting the party for my brother."

"Sorry, I get a little confused," said the priest. "Azreal... that's Conor, right?"

"Right, his U.S. passport identifies him as Conor Moynihan, but in Azerbaijan, he's known as Azreal Kedar – can't use his Christian name there. Kedar is the clan name.

"Azreal?" Father inquired. "Strange name."

"My brother hates it," replied Jake. "It means 'angel of death.'"

"I can understand why," replied Wysocki. "Tell me more."

"The next day everything changed," Jake continued. "First, Azreal... I mean Conor, disappeared right before the party. Nobody knew where he went. We were supposed to bring Tom back to the Gobustan that afternoon, but we got a call from the hospital – something was wrong – come immediately."

"Your father died that night?"

With his jaw clenched and lips knotted, Jake said, "They claimed it was sepsis. But I suspected poison. I'm sure of it now." What none knew at the time was that the 16-year-old Jake found his way to the morgue... to see death for the first time, to stare at his father's lifeless face. It was not enough to be told the cause was poor hospital care or a weaken immune system. Something or someone had taken my father's life.

Wysocki was puzzled, "Poisoned by whom?"

"Rasuli, I suspect, and Qurb had something to do with it too," Jake replied. "But I think, no, I'm sure Conor's uncle planned it. Elshan Kedar and my father had been mortal enemies for years. Tom hunted him down, arrested him, and put him in jail."

"Was there an investigation?"

"'No time for an investigation' that's what they said. My father was buried the next day. They said it was their tradition, their religious practice, but I have questions about that."

"Did they ask you about it; the burial, I mean?"

"I had no say in the matter. It was the Kedars who made the call."

"That seems peculiar."

"Peculiar, indeed," said Jake. "So, I phoned my mother. Tom and Katie had been divorced for years, but in a certain way, she had never let him go. Katie wanted Tom brought back to the States for a Catholic burial.

"As I said, it was unusual, this Muslim practice. Tali brought a brass vase from home. It was filled with water, holy water, I guess. She poured it over the hands of the Azerbaijanis, but not over my hands, nor any of the other Christians. Her father then turned to me and said, 'You cannot pray with us. You are not Muslim.' Unclean is what I suspect he meant. 'You must sit behind us.' When I got home, I told all my friends in the FAA about this.

"The FAA?" Wysocki asked.

"My associates, comrades-in-arms, the Freedom Army of America," said Jake. "After they finished praying they lowered my father's body – Thomas Moynihan, the UN head of worldwide counterterrorism – into the dirt of Azerbaijan. There was no coffin, just a shroud covering his body. I felt utterly helpless, useless, but I said nothing. Then they all celebrated. They had a picnic and celebrated. It was disgusting."

"You don't think your brother was complicit in the matter, do you?" asked the priest. "Why would Conor want his father killed?"

"I don't think he was part of the plan, but I suspect he knew something; a mystery that I will unravel soon enough."

"That's it, then?" said the confessor.

"One last thing," Jake remembered, "on the morning that I left for home I made a promise."

"Yes?"

"We had already left the cottage. A driver was taking me to the airport in Baku. But before we were out of sight, I asked him to stop for one last look. I wanted to remember the place where my father was buried. I noticed a large landscaping truck carrying two tree saplings. The men had already planted one and were just getting to the other. It was shaking vigorously from side to side as it was being lowered into the ground. The uppermost limbs and leaves were shifting back and forth. I got the distinct impression of someone waving. It was as if my father was waving to me, his spirit saying goodbye."

"And the promise?" asked the confessor.

"That one day I would return: to consider what the Kedars had done to my father, to learn more about my brother and his ways, and to rescue Tom Moynihan's bones from that heathen place."

What Jake didn't tell Father Wysocki was that he planned to kill Rasuli – poison him if he could – and Elshan's right-hand man, Rufet Qurb as well. That would settle the score.

"It does no good, Jake, to brood over past wrongs and forget to live," rebuked the priest. "That way leads to folly."

"You, church, purveyors of debauchery," Jake growled angrily, "you dare to chastise me?"

A minute of silence past between them, and then Jake's phone dinged again. This time it was a text from Julia: "Got to get home N-O-W."

Jake replied: "On my way."

"Got to go, Wysocki." This time the door to the confessional slammed shut with a bang. It was 11:50, and the mall was more than ten minutes away.

16

Defender

Crow had many bizarre preoccupations. One was lying. Lying is nothing unusual, of course, but the frequent rehearsal of it is. On the inside closet door of his Wilson Avenue apartment, Crow had nailed up a small mirror. He had stolen it from his parents' house because, the young man thought, he needed it to improve his facial expressions when he was telling a lie. Crow had been practicing this skill since he was 15. Lately, he'd settled on a dogged face and a gravelly monotone, "Alice, you've been a good mother. None of this is your fault." Every so often, he would try adding something personal to his act, like reaching out and touching her forearm, "Why concern yourself about my friends?"

His mother complained about such friends, "These boys are so young." Crow would invariably respond, "I'm just trying to keep them from harm, Alice." Keep was probably the right word for the evolving pedophile, who had not yet perfected his skills.

When Crow left his apartment that Saturday morning, it was 11:30. He planned to stop, but only shortly, at H&R eGames. That's where he had worked off and on throughout high school. Crow wanted to check on Hal. His plan included Hal, but Crow had decided to deal with that one after he had dealt with Gregory. Time was crucial. He knew that Greg would return from lunch precisely at noon, so his visit to the game store had to be brief.

H&R's was located behind the Pere Marquette Mall. The old, stand-alone building had been many things over the years – a grocery store, a pool hall, and hardware retailer – now its shelving displayed eGames and trading cards. In a backroom, old men played rummy, smoked, chewed tobacco, and complained about everything that came to their sloth-ful minds.

As he approached the store, Crow felt no moral qualms related to what he was about to do and utterly confident in his plan. When he entered, a bell sounded. "Carmen Duda, the saints be praised," said Steve, the clerk behind the counter. Besides manning the register, Steve did all the workers' schedules. *Perfect*, Crow thought, *he will know when Hal would be there.*

"Where the hell have you been, Duda?"

"It's Crow, stupid." For the first time that day, the young Carmen Duda was unnerved by someone, so he reached into his inside pocket. The gun he had loaded and holstered at the apartment was still there. "Is Hal around today?"

"Be back at one," replied the testy co-worker. "But he's not giving you back your job. You're done for here. Nobody wants your kind around here, Duda."

Crow reflected, *it would have been better if you had not said that, Steve.* Then, "Tell Hal I need to see him. Let's say quarter past one." He smiled cold-heartedly, and afterward, "Will you be here at one o'clock, Steve?"

"What's it to ya?" snapped the clerk. "Want to take it to the street?" The last thing Crow needed at that instant was a fight, so he turned around and walked out of the shop.

As he neared the mall, Crow's mind turned to the boy named Gregory, his Gregory. The boy had not been as accommodating as Crow had wished, and had recently told him "to fuck off." When Gregory said that, Crow bit his lips, and then reached out and grasped the boy's shoulder. "Why so cruel, Greg," he offered. "I've only been good to you." The lie did not work, and Greg insisted that Carmen Duda, Jr. leave him alone.

Crow looked at his watch. It was 11:55. The closest access to the mall was on Plummer Street, next to Dunkin' Donuts. He knew that Greg would be filling orders at the display case, so he planned to arrive a few minutes before noon and then waited for the next shift to begin.

Meanwhile, after escaping from St. Andrew, Jake jumped into his Sierra. It was timeworn, but well cared for, a customized 4-door that he used for his FAA work. Julia and Katie griped about the high step-up on the old truck, but they were always glad to have a chauffeur.

When he opened the door, he came face to face with a blazing hot cab. He'd forgotten to crack a window. *I'll hear it from the sisters if I don't get this oven cooled down.* So Jake turned on the air conditioning full blast and headed out. By the time he reached the mall intersection, there was a traffic jam at Plummer, and he was just inching forward. With each passing moment, Jake knew Julia would grow more impatient, so he texted: "Traffic hevy... will be there ASAP."

Julia texted back: "We're at the Dunkin' Donuts. Just drive by. No need to park. We'll look for u and come out." He returned a smiley face. Jake finally got to the left lane at Plummer and entered the mall parking lot.

It was bumper to bumper. He searched for the pickup zone, but nothing. At least the cab had cooled nicely. It was 11:55.

At the same time, Carmen Duda had taken up his position at the front window of the donut shop. Two tall women blocked his view inside. They were apparently searching for someone beyond the entry, but he imagined they were staring at him. Unnerved, Crow spun away, trying to avoid eye contact. He moved away quickly and found a better angle. When he turned back again, Crow spotted Gregory – the thing he had come to claim. The boy was slipping on an apron behind the counter. It was time, so Crow started forward, unbuttoning his trench coat as he walked forward.

As Jake neared the pickup zone, the mall traffic was still a tangled mess – pedestrians strolling across the street and drivers frustrated at being strung out. He began searching for his mother and aunt. The clock was ticking, almost noon, and he knew he wasn't going to get there on time. So, he rolled down the passenger window; maybe he could listen for Katie yelling. That's when he heard an earsplitting bang. *Metal on metal,* Jake reckoned, *like the lid of a dumpster slamming hard against a garbage truck.* He rolled the window down trying to figure it out.

What happened next was utterly out of the blue at the crowded Pere Marquette Mall. Shoppers were racing from the entrance. Several fell. One man stopped, looked back as if he were searching for someone, a wife or child. *What the hell?* Jake thought. Then he pulled his truck onto the sidewalk and threw the Sierra into neutral. There was a second bang. He recognized it this time – a gunshot, high velocity, high caliber – probably a .357 or .38 revolver.

Jake jumped out of his truck and reached under the dashboard for his Ruger 9mm pistol. It was small, suitable for concealed carry, and held

17 rounds. He checked the magazine, then stuffed into his ankle holster, and ran toward the mall entrance.

When the Dunkin Donut manager heard the first gunshot, he snapped around in disbelief. Then he saw a man in a black trench coat muscling his way through the shop. He was heading straight for the donuts case. The man knocked over a food tray and pushed his way behind the counter, next to one of his employees, Gregory.

Hearing the thundering second bang of the .357, everyone inside the Dunkin' Donuts froze in place. Their safe world had suddenly been terrorized, and no one knew how to react, least of all the 16-year-old named Gregory. When he saw Crow coming his way – with a gun – he wished he had talked to someone about this crazy man.

Then Crow shouted, "See!" He held his gun-hand high. "I've come for the boy," he said. "We'll be gone in a moment. Don't do anything stupid."

The one person who didn't panic was the Dunkin' Donuts manager, a middle-aged guy named Leslie Jones. He'd had some training about how to handle a robbery. But when he saw a real live gunman rushing toward the counter, he felt all the air racing out of his lungs. It only lasted a moment, then Leslie regained his composure and some of his nerve.

There was the gun hidden under the cash register. *Can I find the key,* the manager fretted. *Is my life worth this?* His mouth went dry as he fumbled for the keychain. Leslie Jones had lied during his job interview about having firearms training. He had scarcely ever touched a gun but needed the job.

Crow put the barrel of the .357 against Gregory's neck and said, "You're coming with me, baby boy."

At the mall entry, right before he ducked into the donut shop, Jake did a quick look around. He was facing a shooter, who had a gun at his victim's head. *Not a robbery*, he reasoned, *something personal.*

Most of the store patrons had dropped to the floor. To his right, Jake spotted his mother and Aunt Julia huddled against a pillar. It was no protection from stray bullets. To the left, a man stood next to the cash register, guarding it. He had one hand raised and with the other, he was fumbling with a set of keys. *The store manager,* Jake guessed, *and he's got a gun... under the counter.* Jake could see his trembling hands and instinctively knew that if the manager decided to use his weapon, his mother and aunt would be in the direct line of fire.

Jake pulled out his Ruger, moved inside the donut shop, and then he shouted, "Don't shoot!"

Crow's warning shots were intended to panic the public, but a confrontation with a loudmouthed bystander was not part of his plan.

Jake could see the gunman's hand starting to quiver, a sure sign of an adrenaline spike. Moynihan understood the danger – a nervous perpetrator with fine-motor control out of whack – the .357 he was waving around had a hair trigger, and the hammer was already cocked. Jake knew that was a mistake. The culprit had grabbed his victim's neck and had shoved the gun under his chin.

When he turned away to see who was doing the shouting, the .357 cannon went off. The gunman felt a gush of hot air from the shockwave. It shook the entire room and everyone in it. This was not his plan. When Crow turned back to Gregory, the left side of boy's face was blown away, and with it, an eruption of blood and viscera covered his hands. Then, as if it were a distant echo, he heard the second command, "Drop the gun."

From the front of the shop, Crow saw a stranger approaching. He suddenly froze. *Why was he stopping?* Crow wondered. *Why was he raising his arm?*

The Ruger – a precision pistol of blued alloy steel – was now being carefully aimed. Crow looked into the eyes of the other but only for a moment. Crow did not drop the gun, and he never heard the discharge of Jake's weapon.

The red diode laser that was fixed on the bridge of Carmen Duda's nose was the last thing Crow ever saw.

17

Deceiver

I ndian summer was gone, and there was a bite to the air as clouds of blackbirds gathered over the Wentworth Forest Preserve. The mad wheeling and swooping in the gray sky was an annual affair – a portend that winter was coming, a Chicago winter, which was always long and hard. It had been eight days since Jake Moynihan killed the culprit named Crow. Jake had become a Chicagoland hero. There were YouTube interviews, media engagements, and a lengthy feature in The Trib about the valiant South Sider who saved his mother, aunt, and a half dozen other shoppers at the Pere Marquette Mall.

Lindy Bedrosian was giddy about her boyfriend's celebrity, and fellow FAA members were thrilled by his bold action in the face of a lunatic, sex predator. Jake, however, had some reservations. The distractions had postponed the Sunday brunch where he and Denis were supposed to make their pitch about their college plans. Jake had not seen his cousin for some time and was worried about Denis' commitment. He had never been entirely sold on Jake's scheme. Denis knew his older cousin had something more in mind than just going to college overseas, and he wanted to know what that was. Jake, on the other hand, worried that the delay might lead his spineless cousin to back out entirely. But finally, events seemed to be coming together; today, the de Barras family was hosting the Moynihans for Sunday brunch.

The brunch had always been Julia's idea. After Tom's death, Julia thought her sister needed some family support to shake off her gloominess. Katie just could not get over it, and Julia thought her sister's grieving abnormally long. "Three years is more than enough time," she'd say to her husband. "Besides, Katie and Tom had been divorced for years." Sean de Barras, however, paid little attention to Julia's carping.

But Katie felt a strong obligation about Tom's soul. "Why did we abandon him there? Katie complained every time they were together. When Sam and Jake returned from Baku, Sam explained the sepsis issue: that there were dangers, and that Tom's body would have to be cremated to be shipped home. Katie, however, remained unconvinced, and cremation was out of the question for the passionately devout Katie. Jake was no help. He had his own account of things, and it was different from the official report. Most of the family had moved on, but Katie found it easier said than done.

This was Chicago, and the Kowalski sisters and the men they married were from typical, working-class families. Going to college was never a given. If a family member did go on to school, it was to earn a certificate or maybe a two-year degree. They enrolled at city schools like Roosevelt, Rush, DePaul, or the Illinois Institute of Technology. Tuition was cheap, and living at home helped defray the costs. Julia had a business degree from IIT and Katie a B.S. in Nursing from Rush. If Jake or Denis wanted to pursue a college degree, the city option was what was expected. The boys, however, had a different idea, and it wasn't Notre Dame or Georgetown.

Jake had proposed the scheme to Denis a month earlier. They were eating at Hardy's on 154th when Jake said, "You start the talk."

"Why me? It's your idea."

"They pay attention when you talk." Although Denis was five years younger, everyone considered him more trustworthy.

"Okay," said Denis, and then he hesitated knowing Jake would not react calmly to his next sentence. "I've told my mother."

"You what?"

"I have spoken to Julia about going to Ireland for school." Jake threw a French fry onto the tray and then turned his head away in a huff. "You've got to trust me on this," said Denis. "She'd be livid if I hadn't told her. Then we'd be nowhere."

"What'd you say?"

"'That I want to see Dublin,' that's what I told her," Denis said. "'I want to take a gap year and see our ancestral home.'"

"Gap year, ancestral home, that's good, de Barras."

"I added, 'that will give me time to think about college here, or maybe I'll just come home after a year, and go to IIT.'"

"Give her a way out. Pretty smart for a kid." It was smart, and Jake knew it. But Denis wasn't entirely forthcoming. He wanted out, out of Calumet Park and out of the stifling Polish culture and its sanctimonious claustrophobia.

"'Fair enough,' I'll say."

Then you talk about staying with Sean's sister, Maggie; pay her a small stipend for room and board, it will help three families all at the same time."

"'It would save a lot of money,' I'll add." It was set, then, the gap year plot. They had constructed a scheme they thought unassailable.

For most of his high school years, Denis had dreamed of Trinity College in Dublin, where his grandfather had graduated. He thought he would study the classics – unheard of in his family – and then, if his grades were good enough, go on to graduate school. For Jake, however, Ireland was just stopover. He had a promise to keep, and he was determined to get to Azerbaijan. But this he kept to himself.

No one could recall an instance when the de Barras didn't live on Wentworth Avenue. They had a second-floor apartment above the Nowicki Grocery. It was a spacious apartment with a front-room, which had a bay window overlooking the busy thoroughfare. The brunch was going as planned, except for one problem. Katie had invited the Mike and Sonia Bedrosian the week before so Julia couldn't uninvite them this week. Sonia was the elder Kowalski sibling and forever felt duty-bound to mother her little sisters. The twins, of course, didn't appreciate being bossed around. But that's what Sonia did, even at this late stage of their lives. Her husband, Mike, had some irksome faults as well. Like Jake, he was a member of the FAA and had an opinion about anything and everything. Sean said he would argue with a stump, particularly if the stump was one of those "damn downtown Democrats."

Today, Katie and Jake were late, and for Sean, the tardiness took on a sense of prickly anxiety. "I'm not certain they'll turn up," he said.

"Calm down," Julia said.

"Born late those Moynihans. Like Tom, he was always late." Before they had married the Kowalski sisters, Sean de Barras and Tom Moynihan were family acquaintances, but not chums. Both were from a long line of expat Irishmen – Sinn Féin families – and that was often the subject of heated conversations. But they had no mutual acquaintances or core interests. Sean was a stevedore at the Chicago docks; Tom's father, Gerry Moynihan, got Sean his job, just as he had for Mike. As Harbormaster of the Port of Chicago, Gerry had lots of influence.

"Why think ill of them?" Julia said, "They'll be here."

"They're just a last-minute family," Denis commented.

"They are not going to turn up, I think," said Sean with an air of exasperation.

"Denis and Jacob have important matters to discuss today. They'll be here."

"Why would you be callin' him Jacob," demanded Sean. "It's Jake, Mrs. De Barras."

"It's a boy's name," she complained. "He's a man, and we should use his proper name, Jacob, like the one in the Bible." It was more than the name, of course. It was about Julia getting her way with her husband.

Denis' father was cold and aloof. Sean de Barras seemed to purposefully give the impression that he was indifferent to any father-son relationship. At least that's the way Denis saw it. As a youngster, Denis never felt he knew his father. Knew is not the right word, but understood or appreciated were not right either. He was somehow apart from his son. Sean was around as the boy was growing up, but he was not in Denis' life.

But Julia was there. Mothers are like that, ready with affection or attention when needed. It didn't really matter what kind of attention, a kiss, a little pat on the back, or a scolding. When Jake was ten and Denis five they would scream at each other, fight over who got to cling onto to their mom's dress or pant leg. Jake remembered being disgusted by such petulance on his cousin's part. He was in fifth grade and thought Denis immature.

At that moment, Julia heard a knock on the back door. Katie opened it, and shouted out, "Yoo-hoo, the Moynihans have arrived." Five minutes later they were all seated for the Sunday brunch. After they had finished, cleared off the dirty dishes, and put away the leftovers, Julia invited the family to the front room for coffee and tea. Everyone was surprised. Rarely did the de Barras use that space for anything. The new sofa was still wrapped in a protective plastic covering.

Julia began the discussion, a purposefully casual chat about Denis taking his university degree next year. When the idea of going to Ireland came up, Sean and Mike were understandably taken aback. "And what would be the trouble with DePaul or Loyola?" Sean asked.

"Both fine Catholic schools, and here on safe American soil," Mike added.

By nature, Denis was not confrontational, so he let Jake take the lead arguing with Uncle Mike. "I'll be going with Denis. We want to experience our Irish heritage."

"Will ya now," Katie said sarcastically. "After all the years of in and out, Jake'll be goin' to college again. That's funny."

Jake countered, "Well, someone's got to look after the boy."

Out of the blue, Denis said, "I'm done with Newman and Jesuit schools."

"Don't be sayin' such a thing," Katie cautioned. "Newman's a saint."

"It's a venial sin, for sure, Denis," Julia added.

Sonia piped in, "There'll be no pleas from the saint when the daars of the purgatory are slammed on ya, now will there?"

Jake laughed at Denis' predicament, moral outrage by three Kowalski sisters was a tough thing to face. Working to get the proposal back on track, Denis said, "I meant to say 'I'd like to have a gap year to see if I really want to spend four years in Ireland.'" It was a perfect dodge.

"We could live with the de Barras cousins in Dublin and save a lot of money."

Everyone joined in the discussion except Mike. Quietly fuming, he was trying to stay calm knowing that Jake and Denis were up to something.

He just didn't know what. *A different deal,* he thought. Jake had made a pledge. What was he doing? *Was this a double-cross?*

That's when Mr. de Barras came to the crux of the matter, "And how, saints be praised, would either household pay for such an education?" The room turned silent. No one wanted to be the next to speak.

Katie looked at her sister, simmering with resentment. Julia knew something she didn't. Then, with an air of certitude, Julia said, "It's hangin' in the Moynihans' hallway, the boys' future is." She meant, of course, Papa Martin's treasure. The document – the original draft of the 1937 Constitution of Ireland, signed by Éamon de Valera – greeted every guest that entered the Moynihan household. It hung next to a picture of de Valera, Papa Martin, and his brothers. It was Martin's last and most precious gift to his grandson, Tom. When Tom died, Papa Martin insisted that Jake have it.

"If we sell Martin's treasure the boys will have money enough for college and the gap year," Julia said.

"It'll bring a million dollars, it will," Jake insisted.

"Not a million," Sean said, "but several hundred thousand.

"If it were ever brought to auction in Ireland, it would fetch a fortune."

There it was... the scheme unfolded. "Would anyone take another cup?" Julia asked. It was a lot to understand, but the final decision was Katie's to make. If she agreed to the plan, it was a done deal.

Katie Moynihan was dazed by her family's spirited back-and-forth. But her face told a different story. She put a soft hand to her mouth, recalling of all those sad years when Tom was overseas. Then she turned to Jake, took a small breath, and then asked, "What would you have me do, Jacob?" She searched for a sign in his eyes, "Do you want to go to Ireland? Is that what you want, Jacob?"

There would be no sitting on the fence now, and Jake reassured her that it was his heart's desire. Afterward, he said something entirely unexpected, "I want to take Lindy with me." That was a surprise. Jake and Denis had never talked about Lindy coming along. But no one put up a fight – Lindy was in.

And so, it was settled. Jake would put Papa Martin's Treasure up for auction. Sean said it would be best if they used a London auction house, "Sotheby's would bring in clients from all over the UK, and get the best price."

With everything agreed, Sonia began clearing away the last of the dishes. Katie rose from the couch and hugged her son. All seemed satisfied, except for Mike Bedrosian. He stood next to the bay window facing Wentworth Avenue, unmistakably in a black mood. Once the others had gone from the room, he grabbed Jake's elbow and escorted him outside. "Just gettin' a smoke," he said to Sean who had already turned on the TV for the Bears pregame.

"What the hell, Jake! This is not the promise you made."

"There have been adjustments, Mike. I had to make Denis and Julia happy. I don't care about throwaway promises."

"I'm not talking about the Freedom Army," Mike shouted. "I'm talking about the others… you know who. If they get a hold of this news, there will be trouble." He stopped for a moment, then added, "I have no idea what Tadesian and the Alliance will do. No one can control them."

Jake, needless to say, knew what Mike meant. "I've got this, Mike."

Unable to calm himself, Bedrosian went on, "We set up Clear Spring so you could become an expert at drone tactics." Hoping to get the upper hand, he added, "This is not over, Moynihan. I'll be talking to Katie. The treasure, by law… she's the rightful owner.

"It will all work out," Jake reassured Mike, "as we have agreed."

But Jake had a plan of his own. He had quit his job and purchased three, one-way tickets to London. The treasure was already scheduled for auction at Sotheby's on Tuesday, October 31st. "Nothing has changed," said Jake, "You'll see." He was lying, of course.

18

Tad Tadesian

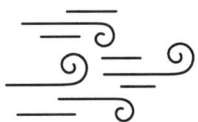

Four days later, Jake Moynihan and Lindy Bedrosian were driving through Pennsylvania on their way to Boston. The long trip from Chicago was not merely for business, but also for pleasure and discovery. The previous day, they had stopped at Fallingwater to see the famous Frank Lloyd Wright site. Presently, they were several hundred miles further southeast. The plan was to visit three Revolutionary War battle sites: Brandywine, White Marsh, and finally, Valley Forge, where family legend had it, one of Jake's ancestors had wintered in 1777-78 with General Washington. Afterward, they would meet with Tad Tadesian in Watertown, Massachusetts before heading to the Sotheby's auction of Papa Martin's Treasure.

To fill in the time, Jake said, "Tell me about Tadesian."

"I've only met him twice," Lindy replied. "He was one of the founding delegates of the Vartan Alliance."

"Does that mean he's Armenian?"

"Armenian-American. Both of his parents were part of the Armenian diaspora that came to the States about 60 years ago."

"What does he do for a living?"

"He's a publisher. Runs Saroyan Weekly, the Saroyan Review, and the Armenia-America website called Voices from Ararat." Tali continued, "Watertown is a tiny suburb of Boston. It is the center of Tadesian's operations, and his media outlets are nationwide and very profitable."

"How does he have time for the Vartan Alliance?"

"Sees it as his patriotic duty, I suppose."

"A fanatic then?"

"Dedicated, political, and clever," Lindy replied acidly, "Yes, he is a fanatic, just like me. It's a just war, Jake."

"Quoting Saint Augustine, are we?

"Quoting Vartan, the warrior. He was first to explain what justice meant in war." Lindy was wrong, of course, but like partisans of any ages, mythos was more important than the facts. Vartan the Brave was the legendary, fifth-century hero in the Armenian war with Persia. The Vartan Alliance was an expat movement of diehards that supported greater Armenia against evil others, especially those of Shia Islam. Lindy and her Uncle Mike were members.

"It's simply that Sam told me this thing between Armenia and Azerbaijan has been going on for years, decades, each party playing the victim card when it suited them."

"The 1.5 million dead by forced labor and death marches give credence for us to say otherwise, Mister Moynihan."

"Ah, the Armenian genocide. But wasn't that the Ottoman Turks?"

"Same people, Turks and Azerbaijanis," Lindy replied.

Jake lamented, *how quickly the woman forgets that my brother is Azeri, a bigshot Azeri.*

That night, Jake and Lindy stopped in Strasburg, a small town in Lancaster County. It was Amish country: rolling hills, working farms, horse and buggy, all that. They found a cheap motel next to the Strasburg rail road. They had hot dogs, chips, and Cokes at the depot café, and then took a ride to Paradise aboard a historic steam train.

It was an entertaining tour until 40 Amish men boarded the train, speaking German. Jake and Lindy had never seen real Amish and didn't know any German. One old gentleman sat next

to Jake, and said, "We're going to Paradise. How about you?" It was a joke, but Jake didn't appreciate it; Paradise was the next town along the Strasburg Line.

The next day they arrived at Valley Forge mid-morning. This was the place where Jake's ancestor bivouacked in the 1777-78 winter with the Continental Army. John Potts was his name, and he was a member of the 11th-Regiment in the Virginia Line, which was commanded by Colonel Daniel Morgan of the famed Morgan Rifles. It was a sacred place to Jake, and to all members of the FAA. *Here,* Jake thought, *are buried the patriots of our America.*

Another relative, Isaac Potts, owned the house where General Washington headquartered that fateful winter of the war. From that plain, stone farmhouse, the General and his staff received government officials, foreign dignitaries and coordinated the daily operations of the Continental Army.

"There's a famous painting of Isaac Potts with General Washington," Jake said.

"Where's that?"

"In Philadelphia, and I want to see it."

"No time, Jake," Lindy insisted. "We've got more important issues with Tadesian."

"More important to you, not me."

For many Armenians, assimilation into mainstream American culture had always been challenging and was the primary reason why the link to their homeland remained so strong. More than half continue to speak the Armenian language, and most live in US Armenian enclaves. Watertown, Massachusetts is one – not the largest, but it is a significant Armenian gateway. And for generations, the Tadesian family had played host to those arriving from or returning to the homeland. This had been particularly true in recent months, as the Vartan Alliance had been amassing a corps of fighters in Watertown.

In the second-floor headquarters of Saroyan Weekly/Saroyan Review, Tad Tadesian sat on a lounge in his private office, which was next to the main production floor. He took a sip of tea, and then opened the storage compartment of the couch and took out his iJournal. He toggled through the headings, found the section titled VA Training, and began writing again:

October 27: Captain Mike Bedrosian left for the Carpathians two days ago; other allies are headed for the gathering place as well. Romania's mountainous and volcanic countryside, with rapidly flowing rivers and limited forests is perfect for acclimating our troops to the Armenian terrain. The climate there is highland continental, which means hot summers and cold winters – same as Armenia. Our men will be well prepared for anything that may come their way.

Lieutenant Lindy Bedrosian and FAA freelancer Jake Moynihan are scheduled to arrive today. Mike, Lindy, and this Moynihan fellow will lead the VA training program at the gathering place.

Mike and Lindy Bedrosian were lifelong members of the Vartan Alliance, but Jake was not. He had been hired as its principal drone-trainer – on loan from the FAA. VA security vetted Moynihan a year ago. It was an often-used strategy of the Alliance to utilize other groups for training and for cover. Its international operation was frequently under suspicion.

Mike reports that the micro-drone demonstration at Clear Spring was a great success – will ship 5000 units to the Carpathians next week. Our new technologies will counter-balance – no, exceed – the enemy's oil wealth.

Having finished his report, Tadesian turned to the iJournal section titled civil disobedience. Tad Tadesian considered himself the historian-philosopher of the Vartan movement, and began writing once more:

Civil disobedience in the pursuit of justice is laughable, though laudable. But what should follow when civil disobedience predictably fails to achieve any meaningful results; when peaceful protests and parliamentary pleas are ignored? What should be done if corrupt authorities and a compliant citizenry pay no attention to righteous actions?

Militancy, of course, but morally acceptable militancy, those actions that draw attention to demands and put pressure on the government, but cause no harm to people. The inevitable question becomes what to do when further action also falls flat? When politicians have been corrupted beyond redemption or reconciliation? Duty requires action– we will be prepared for such action within a few weeks!

The registration clerk at the Revere Hotel said, "Check-in begins at three pm, Mr. Moynihan." It was ten minutes past noon when Jake and Lindy arrived in downtown Boston.

"Can we get into our room any earlier?" Lindy asked. She was tired of life on the road and was ready for a long, hot shower.

The clerk checked his computer screen for the progress of the cleaning staff, and then replied, "Sorry, they've just now entered that room." Afterward, he turned away to answer the house phone.

Jake had saved enough money from the week's drive to Boston to splurge on a hotel. The Revere was expensive but was also only a few blocks from the Charles River and the Freedom

Trail. For those who could afford it, the Revere was the ideal spot to stay for exploring American patriots' heritage – it overlooked Back Bay and Boston Common.

Jake said, "We can leave our bags, and then head for the Trail." It was Friday, the 27th of October. They planned to explore the Freedom Trail in the afternoon, have a nice dinner that evening, and then meet with Tadesian in Watertown the next day. Everything was now on target for their Sunday departure to London.

"Okay," Lindy replied, "but I want some time to soak."

"We'll leave our bags. Can you make a dinner reservation for us; say, 7:30."

"Eight," Lindy urged.

"No problem, Mrs. Moynihan." The clerk rang the bellman's station.

Jake asked, "How do we find the Freedom Trail?"

"Yes, of course, Freedom Trail Players tours begin every 45 minutes. The next one will begin at 12:45. Great fun, featuring tales of high treason, mob agitations, revolutionary actions, and partisan fights of the American Revolution." The clerk was reciting straight out of the tour brochure. "Just watch for the red arrows on the sidewalk, across the street on Boston Common; you'll see the signs."

Feeling a bit grumpy, Lindy asked, "How long does it take?"

"The distance is less than three miles, but if you spend some time at each of the sites you will be gone for several hours."

"And the Liberty Tree?"

"That is not on the Freedom Trail, sir, but down Boylston Street. There's a large bronze plaque on the sidewalk where the great elm tree once stood."

For members of the Freedom Army of America, the Tree was the Holy Grail of pre-revolutionary America. It was the focal point for rallies by the old secret society known as Sons of Liberty, and it became an essential symbol for the struggle against unlawful government rule. Jake had the logo burnished into the heel of his right tanker boot.

Jake and Lindy spent the afternoon on the walking tour and returned to the hotel at five o'clock. Jake was still energized, but Lindy was exhausted and headed straight for the room. Meanwhile, Jake stopped at the concierge desk to check about dinner reservations. "Moynihan, at eight," he said.

"Yes, here it is," the woman answered, "dinner for two in the lounge."

Jake frowned, "I asked for a reservation at Rooftop Revere. We need some private time."

"It is a seasonal restaurant, Mr. Moynihan. Management is closing it down for the coming winter months." Looking out over Back Bay's famous Victorian brownstones, the restaurant was one of the most coveted rooftop dining spots in Boston and usually closed mid-October.

"There are cabanas, right?" Jake said, then handed the woman a fifty-dollar bill. "If you could arrange a patio heater we will be fine."

"I'll see what I can do. Check back with me when you are ready for dinner."

Three hours later, Jake and Lindy appeared at the restaurant entry. It was a fabulous way to cap off the day of exploring. The sky was resplendent: great billowing clouds of slate and silver, sapphire and ultramarine. They could see the Charles River in the distance and a smattering of high-rise buildings on the far shore. A man came up to the table, "I'm Padraig. I will be your server tonight." He was at least 65, bent over at the waist, with a ruddy complexion, and a full head of gray hair.

As they approached their cabana, the twinkling cityscape disappeared. An overhead canvass had been closed and two intersecting partitions placed at the front to keep out the brisk night air. Inside the brightly lit cabana were a welcoming, well-pillowed couch and coffee table, a carafe of water, a dinner setting for two, and menus. Lindy said, "Can we draw back the overhead slightly? I'd like to see some sky."

"Not a problem, miss." He struggled to reach the pull, so Jake lent a hand.

After they had ordered dinner and the waiter had disappeared, Jake said, "I want to visit Minute Man Park tomorrow, before we see Tadesian. Google says it's only a few miles from Watertown."

The idea of another history excursion aggravated Lindy. She turned up her nose, cocked one eyebrow, and said, "We've been doing this stuff for a week." She waved one hand in the air, "Haven't you had enough?" The 21-year-old had a goal, but it had nothing to do with eighteenth-century minutemen.

"When would I have another chance to…"

"Mike said you'd get hung up with the patriot stuff."

"Leave Mike out of this."

"We agreed to a schedule," she said, refusing to accept the idea that they had all the time in the world for playing tourists. At that juncture, Padraig entered with two Sam Adams, glasses, and a plate of cheeses.

Once he was gone, Jake said, "So tell me about Tadesian."

At last, happy to be moving on from the "sacrosanct" American Revolution, Lindy replied, "He will want to know about the drones… how they work, how you will train the troops for what's to come."

"And the recruits Mike is gathering in Romania?"

"It's a global phenomenon," she said, "but the flow of foreign fighters is neither steady nor even."

"From where?"

"They come principally from the States: Armenian hotbeds like Glendale in Los Angeles, Queens in New York, and Waukegan in Illinois. There is a large contingency from the Baltic States, from urban populations in Tallinn, Riga, and Vilnius. But there are many from neighboring Abkhazia and Georgia."

"Not Russia?"

"Gaghut leadership does not trust the Russians. They change sides on a whim, whenever it suits them."

"Gaghut?"

"It's an Armenian word," Lindy explained, "what the indigenous folk call the diaspora, meaning us."

"Do I need to understand anything special about Tadesian?"

"He's president of the Vartan Alliance, of course, but most importantly, he's the money-man." Lindy shifted on the couch as Padraig returned with the entrée. "Let's talk about this tomorrow on the way to Watertown."

"Good idea," said Jake, then added bluntly, "tonight is for relaxing, enjoying dinner, and making love."

Lindy replied cheekily, "Which do you prefer first, Jake Moynihan?"

The next day, Jake and Lindy left for Watertown in the late morning. Lindy had won the agenda battle – no Minuteman Park. They headed straight for Watertown for the big powwow with Tad Tadesian. After lunch, they found the Saroyan building. A short, middle-aged man stood guard in the foyer. After identifying themselves, and the guard escorted them to the upper floor.

Tadesian was waiting. "I see you have met my aide, John Josef."

He offered a hand. "Everybody calls me JJ."

Lindy introduced Jake, "This is Moynihan, our drone specialist." Afterward, they entered Tadesian's private office and then sat down.

"So, Lindy, you and Jake are headed for London?"

"Right. We have some business at Sotheby's on Monday."

Jake said, "A family matter."

"Afterward, we are meeting with Jake's cousin. We have planned a little vacation in the Cotswolds, then we'll take off for Ireland."

"I have cousins there, they live in Dublin." That was the end of the small talk.

"So, tell me about the drones," said Tadesian.

Jake began: "At Operation SnakeRoad we had a drone pilot. He had lots of experience, mostly in Asia, but also in Afghanistan. He had been an Army airman, and flew the big Predators as well as petite UAVs."

JJ interrupted, "But these are micro-drones."

"Let me explain," said Jake. "Drone tech has changed a lot. They are not actually the same equipment used a decade ago. Initially, those were for surveillance only. But after 911, the CIA started exploiting some Predators to strike at the enemy. They were trying to kill Osama bin Laden. But on that nascent mission, they were too late. Apparently, he had left the kill site two days earlier."

Lindy filled in: "Just the same, they got three kills. It was a new tactic – drones had been weaponized – but the technology was at its initial stage, not ready for primetime, so to speak."

"In the decades that followed, pilots flew Predators and Reapers from military bases hundreds of miles from the action. It was nothing more than a video game, and the targets were bug splats on their computer screens."

Tadesian interrupted, "So just how far has the technology advanced?"

"It's not a straight line, Tad," said Lindy. "The old tech was abandoned when civilian casualties mounted to an unacceptable level."

"Private corporations have entered the game. AI and drone miniaturization are the norm. It's called swarm tech, and it's now quite inexpensive."

JJ asked, "So our guys will not be flying drones?"

"That's right," replied Lindy. "Perdix drones don't need humans telling them where to go, or even how to get there."

"Don't need maintenance crews either."

"But how?"

"Perdix communicate independent of any operator, and often utilize shared decision-making to find the best way to a target.

"It's the AI – miniaturized."

Tadesian interrupted again, "So, you're telling us that the 5000-man army that Mike is assembling in Romania is useless."

"That's right," Lindy said. "Useless!"

"The original Vartan-Armenian plan was simple: equalize the equation – 50K + 20K = 70K. Azerbaijan's armed forces required recruiting at least 20K fighters from the Armenian diaspora."

JJ interjected, "… or reduce their numbers below ours."

"You're thinking is entirely outdated," said Jake. "Old Soviet tactics."

Lindy added, "We should press our advantage ASAP."

"So, Lindy," Tadesian insisted, "just how many troops do we need?"

It was finally the right question, and they had the answer. "500! 500 well-trained operators, and five million Perdix drones."

Jake added, "And a different strategy."

Moynihan's Dream

om Moynihan had spent his career fighting terrorists. When he died, his eulogy was a grand litany of praise about his successes. Ridding the world of radicals and diehards, however, was not Tom's real goal. From a lifetime working against the global menace, he knew that cutting off one head of the Hydra only meant two rising in its place. Taking down Islamic Jihad, Boko Haram, Abu Nidal, the Shining Path, or any of their evil incarnations would not solve the genuine problem. No; they all were merely symptoms of the dilemmas facing the civilizations of the twenty first-century.

Moynihan's dream was more about bringing an end to global tribalism – specifically, the escalating and coalescing hostilities between the West and the East. Tom knew the misunderstandings were more than religious; they involved cultures, economics, morals, and mores of vastly conflicting sorts.

So now, two knights take the field – one as victor, the other as victim – to face the dragons perilous, and history's jesters play on, to no good end...

19

Old Mr. Chubby

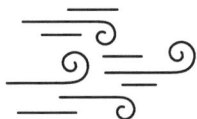

Londonwas cold, cloudy, and damp that last day of October. In fact, at the London City Airport, it was snowing: big flakes, falling straight down. For the pilot and passengers of the business jet about to land, the mantle of pristine whiteness masked the true character of the city below. LCA is unique among London airports. Its short runway and 5.8-degree glide path make for white-knuckle landings. Most pilots relish the test, but for passengers not used to the sudden weightlessness and steep dive, it is stomach churning, often evoking a moment of terror. So, the pilot of the Zümrə XLS-4 flipped on the cabin intercom and announced, "Hold onto your hats, folks, the landing will be something of a plunge." The Azeri private plane was the last to arrive at LCA that wintry day.

Conor was used to the unusual maneuver, but not Tali. She tightened her grip on the armrests as the nose of the Cessna dropped down, and the plane began falling out of the sky. Trying to reassure Tali, Conor said, "London City is closest to central London, just a short ride to the hotel." The Four Seasons was home base when Conor was in London. It suited his tastes, had excellent security and was halfway between the airport and Foreign Secretary Kazimov's Ash Park Mansions in Chelsea. "It's handy, and there are no long lines at Customs." For Tali, Conor's words were no comfort at the time; but he was right about the convenience. It only took 45 minutes from touch down to get to the hotel.

Jake Moynihan and Lindy Bedrosian, on the other hand, had arrived two days earlier and were staying at a small boutique hotel near Eccleston Square. The Premier Inn suited their needs and was only 15 minutes from Sotheby's auction house. They could have walked to the auction if they had wished. It was also close to a bus station, and there they could find day tours to all the great sights where England's monarchy was eternally on display.

As for the meeting arranged between the two brothers and their significant others, the goal was to hook up at Secretary Kazimov's party mid-week. With their pressing matters behind them, the brothers could introduce Tali and Lindy to each other and then enjoy some long-awaited family bonding.

Aleksandr Kazimov never held his grand parties at the Azerbaijani embassy. Frankly, the Kensington Court space was too small to host all of the friends and sycophants. Kazimov and his business partners had to lease the first floor of the Ash Park Mansions for such events. What attracted the Foreign Secretary to the Mansions was not the fame of Victorian writers Dickens, Tennyson, or George Eliot, nor the nearby royal dwellings of Henry VIII and Elizabeth I; no, Aleksandr knew nothing of English literature or British history. What brought him to Chelsea were football and the trappings of a top-drawer sporting club: the hotels, restaurants, and nightclubs. He loved the glitz of the game and the glamor of the moneyed patrons who trailed after the heroes of the pitch.

By late afternoon that second day of November, the Ash Park Mansions was ready for a party. A genuine, brass-railing bar – stocked with all forms of liquors, wines, and cordials – had been installed a few feet from the entry. The heavy wooden buffet tables had been adorned with a flashy painting of hors d'oeuvres, mulled hams, tart sausages, and cheese pastries. The odd five-walled parlor had been set up with barstools and tavern tables, perfect for chatting, drinking, and enjoying appetizers and snacks.

It was a Thursday, which was odd for a London party. But the UN Asia Conference was scheduled to begin the next day, and Kazimov wanted his diplomatic associates to be in a good mood, pliable to his arguments about Azerbaijan.

The guests began arriving shortly after eight. Courtyard security guards checked invitations, IDs, and ladies' handbags. Afterward, the guests were escorted through the entry to the welcoming line. Once beyond that, they found themselves in the parlor, greeted by a flotilla of tuxedoed servers offering cocktails. The piano man was already playing, but the rest of the band was still setting up under a small nook framed by the staircase to the balcony. As always at these kinds of affairs, formal introductions quickly turned to petty chatter and the casual innuendo about others not present – all forgotten immediately as the partygoers moved from group to group.

Jake and Lindy weren't used to such affairs nor the banality. They felt very much out of place. Lindy asked, "Do you know any of these people?" It wasn't really a question, but a general plea against the obvious.

"How would I know anyone?"

"Maybe someone we met at the auction house, or someone from the bank?" She searched the room but had no luck, and the few lines of trivia they had rehearsed for the occasion seemed a waste of time. Feeling awkward in the center of the parlor, Lindy dragged Jake off to the side, where she thought they wouldn't be so noticeable.

For a while it worked, but then, "Ciao!" a woman in her mid-thirties bellowed out, and a wave of over-here followed. As she arrived, she said, "I knew you would be here." She was alone and unmistakably looking for company as well.

"I don't think we've met, Miss…?"

"A month ago, you remember?" the woman insisted.

"We were in the States last month," Lindy responded.

But the woman bullied forward, and said, "You've cut your hair since." Lindy reached a hand into her hair as if she couldn't remember whether or not she'd been to the stylist. "It was at the Turkish Ambassador's party."

Trying to find common ground, Jake asked, "You often come to these things?"

"I like to have fun. Any party will do." Realizing she had made a first-class blunder, the woman searched for a way to end the awkward conversation. "Have you seen Kazimov?"

"The Secretary?"

"There's Carla Stempfeld. I'll bet she knows Kazimov's whereabouts." Waving goodbye, the woman rushed off. "We'll talk later," she shouted. Jake and Lindy were relieved at her departure.

Taking her arm in his, Jake promenaded Lindy among the late-arriving guests, still looking for a recognizable face. As a server passed by, Jake replaced their old drinks with fresh ones, and then found a quiet table at the back of the hall. "Glad to get out of that."

Lindy had moved on. "What time did Conor say he would arrive?"

"Didn't. Just said to meet up at the bar."

Lindy glanced toward the cocktail station where three barkeeps were feverishly serving drinks. Nothing. She was nervous, not knowing what to expect in this first meeting with Conor and Tali. Then she noticed a portly, pink-cheeked man at the next table. He had trouble getting seated because of his cane—a walking stick, actually. It was a beautiful accouterment, cut to a length to suit his frame, and shod with a steel spike to help with traction. The handgrip, with a lanyard attached, was made of fine woven leather. Demonstrably, he was a person of another age, and alone. There was something about him that was unsettling. He was ruffled and seemed quite unsteady, but it was too early to be drunk. Had something happened earlier in the day? Then he took to staring at Lindy over his old-fashioned Roosevelt glasses. He must have thought they complimented his very plump face, but they didn't. Next, he pointed to several photos on the wall, and said, "I think they stink."

Taken aback, and not really knowing how to respond, Lindy said, "The photos are very nice." She was hoping to avoid an engagement.

"Not the pictures, the Chelsea Footballers. I think they stink." He waved his hand through the air, somehow trusting that his gesture would wipe away the football club's latest failure in the Premier League.

"Oh, the soccer team?" Lindy replied. "We don't follow soccer."

"Soccer?" he said acerbically. "It's football! You must be…." Out of the blue, he changed the subject, "Do you know Kazimov?"

Jake said, "Don't know him."

The old man was surprised by Jake's brusque demeanor and punched back. "Then how the hell did you get in here?" Afterward, Old Mr. Chubby – that's what Jake and Lindy called him from then on – ranted on rather incoherently, "He tells of the debaucheries of Sheikh Ajani, who sailed the Caspian under the standard of the new Shah, and of his three wives, all daughters of the Sturgeon King."

Eyes narrowed, Lindy gave him the once-over, "What are you blabbering about?"

"These are ancient rumors, you see," Old Mr. Chubby continued, though he seemed to be speaking only to an evasive ghost in the room. "But some people, we must never forget, do have confidence in the veracity of such rumors."

Lindy cut him off, "You're speaking of the Secretary?"

The googly-eyed ancient one then vulgarly attacked her: "You're a Jew, right?"

"I beg your pardon?!" Ms. Bedrosian was suddenly riled.

"The nose," he snorted, "it's so big you gotta be a Jew."

"You've got some nerve!" Jake roared. "It's none of your business—either her nationality or religion." He rose off his chair. Old Mr. Chubby grabbed his cane and thrust it forward in a defensive move.

Lindy, seeing what was about to happen, extended her arm, holding Jake back from doing something he would later regret. "I'm Armenian if you must know."

"Armenian?" His face screwed up mysteriously. "How'd the two of you get in here? This all ends tonight, but I suppose you know that."

Jake was confused by the rant and could take no more. But before he advanced on him, Lindy grabbed his hand and pulled Jake away from the table. She moved forward quickly, her form-fitting, gray satin evening dress accentuating her purposeful sexuality. At first, he trailed reluctantly, then, a few man-melting strides later, he followed quite willingly.

As they crossed the dance floor, bursts of laughter rose from the crowd, and Jake and Lindy soon forgot the chance meeting with the old fool. They were bouncing about for only a few minutes when the music unexpectedly stopped. Above the din of confused dancers, the band leader's voice rang out. "Ladies and gentlemen," he said, "at Secretary Kazimov's request, we bring you Gadir Mammadov's latest Muğam composition." From behind the bandstand, the composer appeared and took a gracious bow. "Please stand back as the wait staff clear a space for the performers."

Jake and Lindy hustled to the wall. Then the impresario announced, "From the Land of Fire and Wind, I give you The Legend of Bul-Bul."

Few Londoners were familiar with Azeri music. Unlike European classical compositions, there is no long overture to either the music or the dance. Muğam is a sudden burst of the lute, drum, fiddle, and a rush of movement and costume. Tonight, the musicians began playing double-quick, and a split-second later, eight dancers in full Azeri dress leaped onto the floor. The traditional whine and whir of the first tune were so enchanting, so hypnotic, that those present began dancing, clapping and snapping their fingers. It didn't last long, but it was a big hit with all the partygoers.

When it was over, there was another round of applause. After that, Jake took Lindy in his arms and kissed her. "Thanks for the cover," he said, "the old guy was just a dope."

Lindy said nothing but wasn't so sure that Jake was right. There was cunning in the man's demeanor, and she was still angry about the ethnic insult. That's when Lindy spotted Conor at the bar. There was a woman with him, had to be Tali. For Lindy, it was a relief to see someone she knew. She had never met Conor in person but recognized him from the photos at Sam and Iza's house in Carbondale. For the moment, however, she was paying attention to the woman on his arm. She was turned away so Lindy couldn't see her face. But she wore a black lace Maxi dress, with an open back, which accentuated her powerful swimmer's shoulders and slender hips.

For Jake, however, it was a different matter. He was filled with apprehension about seeing his brother for the first time since their father's death. He worried, not about what to say, but how to say it. He wondered, *will he still think of me as a kid?*

How could he? Back then, Conor had his own demons to fight. Only days earlier, he had become an orphan and then was suddenly saddled with the crown of one of the ruling families of Azerbaijan. *Will Conor remember how I felt?*

More importantly, Jake remembered the matter of Seymur Rasuli and Rufet Qurb; the two men that were involved in his father's murder. He had promised to confront Conor about this, but now that the moment was at hand, his resolve wavered.

As they neared, Conor smiled bigheartedly, "Good to see you, Jake." He offered his hand, and afterward introduced Tali, "This is my cousin, Talia Nadirov."

Though most Americans are comfortable with hugging, Azeri Muslims are not. The woman shook Jake's hand. "Call me Tali. I am the daughter of Mirana and Seyfulla. Maybe you remember them?" For the moment, he did not, though there was something about the names that triggered a memory. But Jake couldn't quite recall what.

"Did you like the Muğam?" Conor asked.

"First time for me. Found it interesting, though."

Not wanting Jake to go abruptly sullen at the long-anticipated meeting, Lindy jumped in. "I'm Lindy, the girlfriend."

Conor took up her cue, "I'm Conor, the elderly brother." They laughed.

"Conor," said Tali, touching his arm. "There's Alexandr. Shouldn't we say hello?"

The Kedar Bey turn to his brother. "Do you mind, Jake?" Moynihan shook his head, and they all paraded off to the head table where Kazimov was holding court.

As Conor was speaking with Kazimov, Lindy noticed that Old Mr. Chubby had moved to a table behind Kazimov. She tapped Jake's arm and pointed. He wasn't acting crazy like before, just drinking a cup of tea; but his proximity to the Secretary was somewhat troubling.

Jake, however, was paying no attention. He was trying to remember the connection to the Nadirovs. Then it came to him. It was at his father's funeral, and he blurted out, "The water girl!"

Tali was bowled over. "Water girl?"

"It was seven years ago; you were the one who anointed everyone with holy water – everyone except me."

The corners of her eyes crinkled, and Tali replied, "I'm not sure I understand."

For Jake, it was a defining moment. The Markirovs and Nadirovs had taken over the funeral proceedings, and Jake felt abandoned. Only Sam Mansour recognized his torment. Jake recalled the exact phrase Sam used as he prayed his father on to the next world: *Praise the one who breaks the darkness.* The 16-year-old did not appreciate what it meant, only how he felt at the time: profound loss, betrayal, confusion, and loneliness. Over the years, when Jake felt morose and alienated, he would think of the incident and know that in that place, he was a stranger in a strange land.

Out of the blue, Jake asked, "Your bodyguard, Qurb, he's not around?"

"On holiday," Conor replied. "Hunting goats in the Armenian Highlands."

The offhanded comment piqued Lindy's interest, but she divulged nothing. Grasping Jake's arm confidently, she looked at Conor and said, "Lead on."

The library was a small room, just off the parlor, where the Kazimov-Kedar strategy meeting had taken place the day before. It had been repurposed and redecorated. It was now a reception room for the Secretary's meetings—not embassy business, but other business. It had been debugged, sealed off, and secured with bulletproof windows and doors. Kazimov had given the Kedar Bey the entry code for the evening.

Conor walked to the liquor cabinet, and then asked, "Lindy, what will you have: wine, beer, whiskey?"

"White wine would be nice," she replied. Conor poured one glass for Lindy and one for Tali.

"Jake?"

"Whiskey."

"He's got Johnnie Walker, Glenkinchie, and Jameson."

"Let's have Jameson. That was Papa Martin's favorite whiskey." Unwittingly, Jake had opened the door to the secret he so wanted to keep hidden. But in that split second, Conor was unwilling to confront his brother about the treasure.

Conor persisted with the casual exchange, "Jake, are you still working at the Port of Chicago?"

"Quit last month. I decided to go back to school. I plan to finish my education at Trinity in Ireland."

Conor squeezed his eyes shut and mulled over his thoughts before speaking again. "I think Papa Martin and his brothers went to school there."

Jake replied, "Maybe so. I'm not sure."

"Trinity is expensive. I can help if you need some money." Conor's words were offhanded, but his thoughts were: *Is that why you sold Papa Martin's Treasure... to go back to school? Doesn't sound right. The treasure belonged to our father, Jake. I only wanted a say in the matter.*

Hoping to avoid an embarrassment, Jake said, "I've got it covered." This first brotherly encounter wasn't going as expected.

There was a long pause in the conversation, so much so that Tali felt she had to change the topic. "Bedrosian, that's Armenian, right?" The question was disingenuous. Tali knew the answer. Nevertheless, her entrenched Azeri cultural bias was rearing its ugly head.

Lindy was taken aback by the pointedness of Tali's interrogation. "Armenian-American," she replied. "My family has been in America, in Chicago, for generations."

But Tali went on the offensive, "So, Lindy, tell me what you do in Chicago."

It was the nastiness of the way she said, "do" that made Lindy cringe. Tali's emphasis was clearly discourteous, her tone off-putting. But Lindy had a stock answer, which usually satisfied most in a casual chat, "I'm a technical planner," she said.

The response was meant to be evasive, though it only piqued Tali's curiosity. "In what field do you do this planning?"

Lindy replied, "I work at UAVtech."

The acronym didn't clarify anything, so Jake jumped in, "Drones. She means drone technologies."

"For the military?" The temperature in the room was rising.

"Mostly business applications, you know: pipelines, electric transmission lines, those kinds of things. But yes, our hyperspectral pod system is one of our latest military apps."

Knowing that their secret links to the Vartans might suddenly be exposed, Jake jumped in. "Don't get her started. She'll bore you to death with analyses." Lindy knew what Jake was doing, and she didn't like it. She could speak for herself. But she needed to cool down, so Lindy stood up and walked to the far wall, to the window there, to see if anyone was still coming in from the courtyard.

Seeing the friction building between the two women, Conor attempted an intervention. He turned to Tali and said, "Jake and Lindy know nothing about the old culture wars between Armenia and Azerbaijan."

But Lindy responded instantly, "Oh, I know all about those tensions."

"I'll bet you do," Tali replied. The cooling down period hadn't lasted.

Conor's eyes widened, and then he frowned at his now tough-talking cousin. "What about your mother, Jake; how is she doing?"

At that propitious moment, Secretary Kazimov and his butler burst through the door. An entourage followed closely behind with desserts. The butler made a short presentation about the Azeri dessert called Shekerbura, and then the servers continued with the table setting. "Can I refresh the drinks?" one of the waiters asked.

"I'll have another Jameson. Make it a double, will ya?"

Lindy objected, "You've had enough, Jake."

"Anything else, sir?" the butler asked.

"Thanks, we're fine," Kazimov responded. "Please close the door when you leave."

"Glad you could join us," Conor said. After a few minutes, the tension in the room subsided nicely, and the balance of the evening was spent enjoying casual conversation and the shekerbura.

The following morning, Conor and Jake met for brunch at the Gillingham Street Grill, a small kitchen near Eccleston Square. The food was good, but the service was terrible. In hopes of avoiding more arguments about Armenia and Azerbaijan, the men carried on alone. Tali went shopping; she had a suitcase to fill. Lindy decided to take out her frustrations by exploring Westminster on foot. More than ever, she wanted to visit the Abbey where all the dead English kings were on display.

In stark contrast to the women, the issues that Jake and Conor faced were not nationalistic, but personal. Though they didn't really know one another well, nor understand each other's worlds, the same elephant-in-the-room had burdened both men for a long time – Tom Moynihan. For Conor, it was about guilt. Growing up under Mira's didactic custody, he felt the stifling yoke as the heir apparent of House Kedar. But even more onerous were his feelings about the loss of his father, and strangely, about the death of his Uncle Elshan.

For Jake, it was different. In the past few years, he had bent his memories of Azerbaijan to suit his beliefs. Jake was convinced that his father was murdered by Muslims, and maybe by the Kedar family itself – Rasuli and Qurb for sure.

No longer saddled with the need for polite chitchat, Conor struck the first blow. "So, Jake, tell me about Papa Martin's treasure."

"So you know?"

"Sam Mansour told me. He said you wanted to go back to school."

"That's right," Jake insisted. "My cousin, Denis, and I are headed for Trinity in Dublin. I told you that last night."

"I don't believe the 'going to school' story for a minute."

Jake replied stiffly, "And I don't believe you have any say in my business."

"It was Tom Moynihan's estate," Conor said, "don't I have a say in that?"

"Why do you care? You have plenty of money… big Muslim money."

"This is about Tom's funeral, isn't it?"

"It is about my father's murder," Jake insisted, "and I want to know if you or your family had anything to do with it."

There it was – the wound finally exposed. Conor felt deeply offended, but Jake had unwittingly stumbled onto Conor's long and gloomy guilt. Elshan Kedar had killed Tom Moynihan, and Conor bore the burden not only of his father's death but also of his brother's hatred.

When the waiter finally brought the luncheon fish and chips, both Jake nor Conor were thankful for the intervention. They pawed at their food for a time, in silence. Then Conor's phone pinged. It was Kazimov with a message: "President wants to talk – urgent. Meet me at Ash Park Mansions in one hour."

Conor was relieved and troubled at the same time. He looked at Jake, eyes darting anxiously, "I've got to go. Aliyev business."

Jake tipped his head to the side, not wanting to face his brother. "Me to," he replied. "I promised Lindy I'd take her shopping before we left for Ireland."

It was a lie, of course. But a way to end a tense family conversation. By six that evening, both couples had left London.

20

Carpathian
Rendezvous

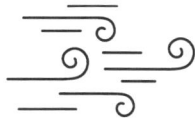

"Not Romanian, she's Roma," Mike Bedrosian said. "Calls her-self Della; says she's married to the King of the Gypsies." Uncle Mike was speaking of the woman who was serving dinner to members of the Vartan Alliance.

"King of the Gypsies, who's that?" Jake asked.

"Name's Johnny Gann. The guy we do business with… he's the guy who set up the campsite." For all intents and purposes, the 40-acre lay-out at the Rendezvous was similar to Clear Spring Wilderness in southern Illinois, minus the snakes. Mike had seen a few European Adders, but they were tolerably shy and typically vanished into the undergrowth at any hint of danger. Since it was now winter in the Carpathians, all the wiggler species were now in hibernation.

Lindy said, "I doubt it."

"Doubt what?"

"That 'King of the Gypsies' thing," she said. "I know a guy in Chicago that calls himself King of the Gypsies."

"What's that got to do with our guy?"

"Nothing, I guess," Lindy said indifferently,

Oblivious to the trivia pursued by the others, Jake had been chasing a no less trifling question of his own. "What's the difference between Romanians and the Roma?" Jake asked.

Surprisingly, Mike had an answer. "Big difference. The Romanians are Slavs. The Roma people are originally from India. Their languages, traditions, and laws are very different, and most importantly, the Roma were slaves of the Romanians until the mid-19th century."

Lindy, bemused by her uncle's tidy chronicle, questioned its authenticity, "How do you know that?"

"My guy, Johnny Gann, has schooled me on such things."

Lindy laughed, then asked, "Can they be trusted?"

"As long as we pay them," said Mike. "They keep to themselves... avoid government entanglements, and that suits us."

The rendezvous site was located about 70 miles northeast of Bucharest. The camp was not actually in the Carpathian Mountains but was situated in the foothills just below. Most importantly, the Buzau River was nearby, which has always been the conduit to a free port at the mouth of the Danube. That was where the Vartan Alliance would launch its effort to cross the Black Sea before heading to Armenia.

After their hasty retreat from London, Jake and Lindy headed for Ireland to see Denis and the de Barras family. They had been in camp for two weeks but hadn't mentioned that side trip to anyone. But Mike Bedrosian was curious. He wondered why Jake and Lindy had not come directly to the training facility as scheduled. "Did you see your cousin in Dublin?"

"Yeah," Jake said, "Denis met us at the pier with his aunt, Maggie de Barras."

Lindy added, "I don't know how he does it, but he was driving, and already used to the wrong side of the road." There was something different about Denis. Jake and Lindy both noticed it after a few days. He was a changed person; saw himself as a Dubliner. He'd been living in the city with his relatives for almost a month. The de Barras family lived on St. Augustine Street in a flat near the Liffey River. Less than 30 minutes away, his commute to Trinity College was uncomplicated, and getting out of dreary Calumet City clearly did him a lot of good. The limp that Denis had been afflicted with most of his life was now barely noticeable. Maybe that's what Jake and Lindy really noticed.

To Denis, the infirmity was a drain on his soul. When he was a little boy, he told his father he wanted to be the harbormaster of the Port of Chicago, same as Jake's grandfather, Gerry Moynihan. But Denis had a clubfoot, which made his early years more traumatic than they should have been. Chicago's South Side was a tough place to grow up with a clubfoot, and the neighborhood boys tormented him habitually and without shame. Jake was no help. He often sided with the bullies. All the mothers scolded the boys about this, but they did it anyway when no adults were around. Deny had surgeries, of course, and they allowed the foot to grow correctly in the coming years. But he wore a brace until he was seven, and that was the spoiler to his dream of being a man of rivers or lakes or seas.

Lindy followed on, "When Jake told him that he wasn't going to stay in Dublin and attend school at Trinity, they had a big fight."

"I gave him enough money for two years of college. He didn't put up much of a fuss. We left after a week."

After the meeting with Conor and Tali, Jake and Lindy knew they had a few days to kill before hooking up with Denis. So, they decided to rent a car and tour the rolling hills and lush meadows of the upper Thames. They headed for the famous Cotswolds, but they stopped first at Winchcombe to visit Sudeley Castle. The next morning, they traveled north to Birmingham, and then followed a western route into Wales before turning north again. The plan was simple; catch the ferry at Holyhead and then cross the Irish Sea in the late afternoon.

"So you sold the treasure?"

"Fetched a great price in London," Jake replied.

Mike cussed, "So you say."

"Don't worry, Mike. When I'm finished with what I have to do in Azerbaijan, I'll turn over the balance to Tadesian." Derisively, Mike thought, *Minus the money to Denis de Barras!*

Lindy narrowed her eyes at Jake, and said, "Never mind that. We've got work to do here."

"How do we deal with all the volunteers we don't need?" Mike asked.

"We need engineers, mechanics, and maintenance personnel, not foot soldiers."

"Cull them out," Lindy said tersely. "1000 is the most we can handle."

Weeks of AWS training flew by quickly, and then it was time for the boss to arrive. Tad Tadesian, along with his trusted aide JJ Franks, showed up at Coandă International Airport in Bucharest. Johnny Gann and the woman called Della were waiting for them at the arrival hall. After clearing Customs, the foursome quickly found their way out of town and into a frozen, late December in Romania. Winter's clutch had choked off much of life as they motored northward on what geologists called the Carpathian Uplift. The world of the Carpathian rendezvous was gray, chilly, and entombed by snowy stillness. The drive to camp took a little more than two hours.

At the guardhouse that evening, Mike Bedrosian and two armed Vartan militiamen were searching the distant highway for the man to arrive.

It was almost eight pm when they spotted the lone headlights headed their way. Five minutes later, the SUV pulled up, and Mike stepped to the passenger side window, "Welcome to CR Camp, Mr. Tadesian." He clapped his gloved hands together to ward off the cold, and said, "Let's get you inside. It gets really cold after sunset." Tadesian nodded, and after that, Mike turned to Johnny Gann, "We're having a late supper at the mess hall. You and Della are welcome to join us."

It was ten o'clock when they finished dessert. Everyone was milling around having a late cocktail when Lindy pulled her uncle aside. "It's getting late," she said, pointing at locals. "We've got to get the show on the road before the wind comes up."

Mike understood. He strolled over to Johnny Gann. "We're happy to have you stay for another drink, but tomorrow we have a tight schedule, so we'll all be going to bed soon."

Gann recognized the message. "Thanks for dinner, but it's time for us to be going home." The King of the Gypsies and his wife stopped to say goodbye to Tadesian and then were escorted to the CR gate. Once the lights of their car had disappeared down the hill, one of the guards called the mess hall, "All clear, Mike."

The captain banged a tin water goblet on the table to get everyone's attention. "Okay, CR," he shouted, "let's head for the staging area."

The contingent of ten VA commanders, Tad Tadesian, JJ Frank, Lindy, Jake, and Mike Bedrosian, followed a well-worn trail some 200 hundred yards into a clearing above the camp. "A perfect night to put on a show," Lindy said. The moonless, slate sky was ideal for "night flight," as the operators had named it.

"Let's hope everything works. I'm troubled by what effect the cold air may have on the drone systems."

"We've made the adjustments, Jake. You're such a worrywart." The staging area was outdoors, a raised, wooden platform two feet off the frozen ground with 20 folding chairs. Though she didn't say anything to the others, Lindy was grateful that the weather wasn't the windy bone-chilling freeze of a Chicago winter. The Vartan Alliance had chosen the Carpathian Uplift because its weather closely matched that of the Armenian Highlands.

For the next hour, Jake, Lindy, and the control team synchronized an outdoor light show, employing a fleet of 1000 LED-equipped, fire-star drones. Four operators had programmed a demonstration of 2 billion color combinations that illuminated the night sky with captivating 3D shapes overhead. The highlight of the demo was two groups of larger-than-life soldiers engaged in mock battle. Standing at side podium, Mike explained, "Neither team is aware of the other's action plan. They are reacting in real time."

"We have had to adjust for freezing temperatures and wind gusts. It has been a real challenge."

"It's incredible," said JJ Frank. "Watching it, you get a real sense of the future."

"We've had our work cut out for us. The drones are pre-programmed for on-the-fly solutions – setting and adjusting flight paths, countermeasures, even when partner-drones have been "killed." We've run multiple tests under multiple conditions to ensure peak performance."

Tadesian asked, "So, each team is being controlled by one computer and one pilot?"

"A dangerous flaw in that strategy," Grigor Davidian, liaison of the Armenian Armed Defense, interjected.

Tad saw the flaw, "Eliminate the computer…"

"… or the pilot," Davidian added, "and you eliminate the fighting unit."

Jake was ready for just such a concern. "Tonight, that's what's happening." He looked at Mike for backing. Mike nodded, so Jake carried on, "As you can see, this performance is just an old-fashioned, fireworks display. Tomorrow, we'll lay out the battlefront blueprint."

When it was over, the software engineers, hardware engineers, drone technicians, and pilots put away their equipment. "Watching battle animation light up the sky is one thing," Tadesian's aide said. "But to think that it's done with drones astonishes me."

Not everyone within range was so stirred as JJ Frank. About a half-mile below the staging area, Johnny Gann was observing the display through binoculars. Once out of sight, he had pulled his car off the road and turned off the headlamps to spy on CR events. Della asked, "What do you think they're doing?"

The king of the gypsies put down his field glasses for a moment, turned to Della, "Well, I don't think it's about selling fireworks to the Romanians."

At CR camp, there were three rows of barracks where the recruited and volunteer militiamen bunked. There were no segregated quarters for women. For privacy, they simply partitioned themselves off from the men with metal storage cabinets. On the highest ridge above CR, there were a few private cabins for the VA leaders. Jake and Lindy had claimed a cozy shack at the back. It had a private bathroom, plenty of hot water, and even a tub. It was a saddle-cut design, steel with a porcelain-enamel coating. A cheap tub, but large, and likely "borrowed" from one of the fancy houses in Buzau City along the river. The Roma often scrounged for such things. "I'm going to take a bath," Lindy said. It had been a tiring day. She put on a warm robe and turned the hot water facet full on.

"I may join you."

Lindy assumed he was kidding. "Sure, the tub's big enough for two." Next, she searched her duffel bag for some bath oil. She poured a small amount of coconut-scented unction into the water and watched it gurgling up almost instantly. Lindy always took a bubble bath when she wanted to unwind after long, bureaucratic meetings at UAVtech. But her work there seemed to be a thing of the past. *This is my work now*, she thought, *this Vartan Cause*. Afterward, Lindy let the robe slip off her back, took a deep breath, and then stepped into the water. Her legs throb at the hotness, so she sat on the tub's edge and splattered a bit of water onto her legs and up her thighs. Slowly she eased in, letting the warmth flow over her body. As the stress of the day started to abate, Lindy leaned back against the tub and closed her eyes.

Her thoughts soon turned in a different direction… to Jake, not to his usual crankiness or his stubborn quarrels with others, but to his superb physique and unbridled sexuality. A funny vision unfolded in her head: Jake standing before her naked, except for his tanker boots. Gads, she hated those tankers. Jake was tall, cut, and an attentive lover. In need of more than a vision, she cried out, "Get in here, boy-toy!"

A moment later, Jake appeared at the door. He threw off his t-shirt and shorts, and said, "Slide up, and I'll jump in."

As he tumbled in, the water splashed against the walls of the bathtub. "What's that smell?" Jake asked as he reached around to pull Lindy into his arms.

"Coconut bath oil."

"Smells like home," he said while pointing to the bottle of body wash at the front of the tub. She passed it back, and he emptied a tiny measure into his palms. It lathered quickly, and afterward Jake began massaging Lindy's tight shoulders and then her neck. She closed her eyes again, relaxing instantly in his firm, vigorous hand rub. She no longer had to conjure up Jake's image; her boy-toy was right on the job.

Next, he pulled her closer and with her head resting on his chest, he began rubbing ever so gently against her breasts. She inhaled deeply, and her chest bowed upward naturally, pushing her now erect nipples above the water. He reacted intuitively, kneading first one and then the other – all gentleness at that point set aside. He cupped her left breast with one hand and glided his other down her chest, lingering momentarily, playfully on the sternum. She exalted in suspense. But then Lindy began tensing, her long legs stretching out together, her toes pushing up against the wall of the tub. As she felt his erection rising between her buttocks, Lindy could sense her heart rate accelerating unchecked.

Jake stopped for a moment, reached down and firmly grasped her knees, and pulled her legs apart. She took in a mouthful of air. Next, Jake wrestled his legs over hers and pinned them to the side of the bathtub. Although her hands were free, Lindy felt willfully powerless to move. Jake squeezed more of the bath oil into his hands, reached down to her belly, and then worked his palms between her legs. Lindy grabbed the sides of the tub with both hands and groaned passionately. Vagina opened fully, his fingers began a stimulating dance against her clitoris. She stiffened suddenly as the pressure grew. "Wait, wait, wait!"

He understood – the demon bastard – and paused for her to quiet down before resuming once more. After a short breather, his hands started moving in a widening circle around her sex, pushing and pulling. Against intrusive hands and fingers, Lindy's hips began a rhythm of their own. Her body screamed as she struggled to keep her hands on the tub. Then a wholesome orgasm seized her entire body, repeating its potency over and over for the next few minutes. She could no longer hold back, and let out a long moan from her core.

Once Lindy caught her breath, she leaped out of the tub, water sloshing everywhere. She turned around and reached out her hand to Jake and pulled him from the bathtub. "Your turn," she screamed, and they both raced toward the bedroom.

When Jake opened his eyes the next morning, he heard the sound of a coffee pot percolating, and, in the background, the creaking of cabin logs as the winter winds found their voice. At least, there was no clamor of Chicago traffic, no racket of televisions, not even a sunrise chorus of Carpathian birds on this daybreak. Jake and Lindy had enjoyed each other's company for the night, but soon the CR Camp would awaken, and both had to prepare for the business meeting with Tad Tadesian and commanders of the Vartan Alliance.

Jake looked at his watch. It was eight am, December 24th. "Christmas tomorrow," he said.

Lindy was dressing for their big day ahead. "What did you say?"

"It is Christmas Eve, Lindy."

She frowned, "Armenian Christmas is two weeks away."

"Oh, yeah, I forgot."

"We had this discussion last year. The Armenian Church was established two centuries before the Roman Church and never felt the need to change the date. The Armenian faithful have always celebrated Christmas on January 6th – it's called Asdvadza-Haydnutyun – meaning the Revelation of God."

"Couldn't we at least have a candle or something?"

"Let it go, Jake. We've got more important things to think about." Lifestyles, poles apart and contradictory; Lindy wondered if they could ever work out such matters. Lindy knew that Jake was stubborn about religion, even though he claimed he was not.

An hour later, Tadesian opened the session with a crucial question, "Initially, the Armenian powers-that-be asked the VA to supplement its defense forces with 5,000 volunteers. The Armenian military, they told us, was undermanned and needed additional troops."

"Balance of power," said JJ, "that's what they said would deter the Azerbaijanis."

Mike Bedrosian was flabbergasted by Frank's naive remark, and responded, "This isn't World War I, JJ."

Jake added, "Even the Russians have moved beyond counting tanks and troops." It was easy to see that Tadesian's aide was embarrassed by the off-handed comment.

"Artificial intelligence and robotics have changed the nature of modern... future warfare," Lindy said

"Autonomous weaponry."

Tadesian, the man who had raised millions from the Armenian diaspora and paid for the unproven armaments, was unconvinced and nagged, "Drones, you mean?"

"Drones 4.0," Lindy corrected.

"The technologies have come a long way," said Jake. "The big Predators were first used as eyes-in-the-skies; after that, they were weaponized."

"Military technocrats imagined a vastly different future: AI, miniaturization, and robotics made it possible."

"It?"

Mike said, "AWS, Autonomous Weapon Systems – third-wave weapons – after gunpowder and nuclear missiles."

Colonel Davidian, who had always been skeptical of diaspora forces, was not persuaded, "Boots on the ground; that's what wins wars, not toys."

Knowing the high likelihood of skepticism, Lindy had developed a Videopoint presentation: "As you can see, an alternative to inspecting electrical power lines, AUVs can be utilized to monitor troop movements and find mobile targets.

Frank asked, "AUV?"

"Unmanned Aerial Vehicle," she said. "Instead of delivering parcels, some AUVs have been designed to drop ordnance; instead of spraying crops, drones could broadcast nerve agents."

Tadesian interrupted, "Hasn't the U.S. military developed lasers and microwave guns that can blast drones out the sky?"

"True," said Jake, "the larger Predators and Reaper drones, flown by pilots at air force centers hundreds of miles from the front line, are vulnerable to such advanced countermeasures."

"But our UAVs are different," said Lindy. "They are self-directed. Autonomous Weapons Systems means they fly and make tactical choices independently. Think self-driving cars."

"Is that possible?" asked Tadesian.

"This afternoon, we will demonstrate the capabilities of our new AWS for everyone to see."

Jake added, "It is based on swarm technology – think 10,000 weaponized micro UAVs."

Tadesian was impressed, but he had a concern. "The timeframe is critical," he said. "Captain Bedrosian, if we approve the new tactics, equipment, and weapons, when will the AWS team be ready for action? When will we be able to deploy to Armenia?"

Mike turned to Jake for the answer. "We'll have to weed down the present contingent to 500," said Jake. "But we can be ready in ten weeks; no later than the first week of March."

That was enough to convince most of the doubters in the room. Tadesian said, "Good enough, we'll gather up after lunch, see the demo, and then strategize about our next move."

21

Novruz

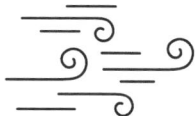

It was late February, and the frigid winds of the north Caspian Sea had finally settled down. It was the season of expectancy when Azeris looked forward to planting the flower buds they had nourished through the winter, going to the market to find fresh vegetables, and seeing their neighbors on the street. Most importantly, however, was *Novruz*, the spring festival when all Azeri citizens get a five-day holiday to celebrates the beginning of the new year.

On Baku Bay, where the Caspian bends against the shore like a crescent moon, city workers were already busy putting up placards and streamers along the main thoroughfares and squares. They always begin on the hills of Upland Park, where the elite families have built their estates. The view there, more than 100 feet above the bay, is spectacular.

Viktor Kos's Victorian manor house sits at the end of Lemontov Street, about a block above the funicular railway. At its grand entrance, the mansion has a panoramic view of the bay below, and from his personal study at the back, Viktor can scrutinize, verify, and record all the comings and goings on Parliament Square.

It was eight minutes past 11 pm, and the leader of the Dark Triad was putting his long-deliberated scheme into action. Rolan Guliyev had arrived 20 minutes earlier, and the two men had been ensconced in Viktor's study finishing tea and cakes. The Oil Minister and the President were sitting on the couch in front of the window that overlooked the courtyard. "I see you have many Russian icons, Viktor," said Rolan.

"An inheritance from my grandmother, a daughter of House Gusin," Viktor replied. "She was an Orthodox Christian, and she loved her icons."

"Are they valuable?"

"Some. The ones of Jesus from the Hagia Sophia image are valuable... and the originals of Mary too."

"Yes, the Virgin."

There was an urgency to this late-night meeting. Two days ago, the President had faced and barely survived a no-confidence vote. Kos and his alliance had abstained, and Rolan realized that Viktor's "Russian bloc" could make or break him in the next ballot. A deal had to be made; Guliyev's adventures for the Armenian war depended on it.

"You would be a fool, Viktor, to oppose me," said Guliyev. "Only I can steer this nation through the troubled waters we will soon face."

"Fool that I am, Rolan, I intend to keep my options open." Viktor's sarcasm was a clear message to the President that his alliance's support would not come cheaply.

Guliyev stood up and walked to the window. Though it was very dark, the Parliament building stood out distinctly against the hill. Rolan said, "You have an extraordinary view of the government here."

Meanwhile, in his second-floor bedroom suite, Vanya was finishing a communiqué for his committee meeting the next day. The one job where Vanya Kos performed actual work was as the Director of the Novruz Festival. The day of the vernal equinox varies, of course, but throughout the Caucasus, the festival begins on day one, month one of the Iranian calendar. Westerners are usually surprised that not everyone uses the rule-based Gregorian system, but the observation-based, Iranian calendar makes a lot of sense. In Central Asia, the New Year starts the moment the sun crosses the celestial equator and equalizes night and day. For the coming year, that date in the western world translated to the 21st of March.

Vanya treasured Novruz because it was seven days of spectacle: the folk song jubilee, medieval warriors' parade, wheatgrass cookouts, boat regatta, wrestling tournaments, and horseracing were just a few of the events planned during the pageant. Most importantly, Vanya would be at the center of the attention, and that suited his vanity perfectly. This year, he planned to add a new element to the festivities: every night, a thousand burning campfires on the hills above Baku. They were meant to be symbolic: the fires signified a final purification of the people and the elimination of past Azerbaijani failures. He would see to it that all media would cover his lighting of the torches. When Vanya finished the communiqué, he walked to the mirror and began rehearsing his introduction.

There was a knock on the door. "Müserif," Kos's butler announced, "The Kos Bey would like you to join him in his study."

"I have important matters here. Tell the old boob I cannot be bothered." Vanya knew the butler could not deliver such a message, but he delighted in the conundrum he created for the man.

"He said to tell you that it is a most consequential government matter." With that, the butler exited. Viktor had instructed the man to deliver the same message to his younger son, but the whereabouts of Vladimir Kos were unknown.

Fifteen minutes later, Vanya entered his father's study. He was startled when he saw Rolan Guliyev. Viktor signaled for Vanya to pull up a chair. "I'm sure you remember my firstborn, Vanya Nikolayev." Though he did not rise, Rolan offered his hand. As he did, he thought, *this House is steeped in Russian custom, politics, and blood.*

"Vanya, President Guliyev is here to discuss a most consequential government matter."

"And you asked me to moderate?"

"To listen," his father scolded. "And where is your brother?"

"Am I my brother's keeper?"

"He is not in the house, sir," said the butler.

Guliyev could wait no longer. The President turned to the Oil Minister and said, "Viktor, let's put our cards on the table."

The next day, the Kos household was awash with activities. The kitchen staff was busy preparing for a banquet that afternoon – Madam Aydan in charge. Viktor Kos had two wives. Aydan, four years his senior, was his first wife and the taskmaster of the household. Their union was a marriage of convenience. She was a daughter of House Bagirov, which controlled the Agricultural and Fishery industries. Dina, the second wife, was 15 years younger than Aydan, the love of Viktor's life, and the mother of Vladimir. Needless to say, the two women did not get along.

The animosity traced back to the days immediately after Dina entered Kos family life. Aydan insisted that the new wife read the lessons of the Obedient Wives Club. Aydan's lectures followed. According to the book, it was Dina's job, as the second wife, to provide all kinds of sex to

Viktor as a first-class prostitute would. Dina didn't object to the sex part, but she did to the prostitute part, calling it the objectification of women, disrespectful and degrading to wives. She fought back, "Islamic marriage is not merely a sexual exchange."

When Vladimir was born, Aydan began complaining to Viktor that "the prostitute and the boy she had produced" were hell-bent on supplanting her rights as the first wife and Vanya's position as the next Bey of House Kos. For the next five years, Aydan threatened Viktor relentlessly; she would go to her clan and charge Viktor with breach of contract and with maltreatment of a dutiful wife. Frustrated by the constant bickering, Viktor finally settled the matter: he threatened to ship them both off to his Russian relatives in Chechnya; they would remain there permanently, and then he would look for a third wife. The open warfare ended quickly after that, but not surreptitious battles between the wives and their sons.

For dinner that afternoon, Aydan had prepared a menu she thought befitting the clan's rising social position: rare roast beef, mushroom soup, bitter greens and zucchini with a dash of pepper, noodles in a wheat-grass sauce, and for dessert, rhubarb crème brûlée. Present were several Kos allies, but mostly, it was a family affair. One distant relative had been invited, though, a man named William Gusin of Chechnya. As they were finishing dessert, he said, "I have never enjoyed such an exquisite meal, Madam Kos." Aydan smiled at the Bey of House Gusin, but then her gaze fell unkindly on the woman sitting next to him, his wife. In these troubled times, it was unusual that he brought her along because she was the daughter of an influential Armenian family. Her name was Susan, and she was the sister of Tad Tadesian, the leader of the Armenian diaspora in America. Soon afterward, Vanya told the gathering of his plans for the coming Novruz Festival.

Then it was time for tea and cordials. The servers placed Waterford crystal at each guest's plate, and then the wine steward presented the Grand Marnier Cuvee 1880, an exquisite cognac with hints of dried apricot, hazelnut, and a subtle fragrance of orange for a finish. Vanya rose up and said, "Our father has an exciting announcement."

Viktor Kos first acknowledged his appreciation to House Vidadi, House Bagirov, and especially to William Gusin, and then said, "As you know, there are difficult days ahead...."

A deal between Rolan Guliyev and Viktor Kos had been struck. Kos would throw his team of allies behind the President in the next vote. In return, Viktor would become the Azerbaijani Vice President. Vanya would take Viktor's place as Minister of Oil, and Vladimir would be named as the chair of the newly formed National Security Council.

Later that evening, the Dark Triad had retired to Viktor's study for a nightcap. Vanya paced back and forth in front of the fireplace. "I am curious to know what the duties and responsibilities of this new Security Council are." He was speaking to his father, but the words were directed at his brother, who was smoking a cigar on the sofa.

As he picked cigar bits from his mustache, Vlad guffawed, "Why concern yourself, big brother?"

"Such a Council has powers over the Secret Service, powers to spy on Ministers."

Viktor added, "And what the Azeri President is doing." It was an undeniable sign that at some point in the future, Viktor Kos had ambitions grander than just being vice president.

Vanya wasn't pleased, "You've given him power over me."

"Nonsense, Vanya, the position is the tool we need inside. Remember, Guliyev has his plans, and we have ours."

From across the room, Vlad had another question, "What about the Kedar Bey? He has been quiet for many months."

Viktor did not hesitate, "With Rufet already out of the way, and despite your clumsy efforts at Ephesus, everything is falling into place."

"And what of Mira Nadirov? Has she recovered from her injuries at Istanbul?"

"She can barely walk these days," said Vlad. "She is recovering in Gobustan."

Then Viktor added vindictively, "We will deal with Azreal next."

22

Bəla is Coming

I n the meantime, at Warsaw's Chopin International Airport, LOT Flight
2525 had just lifted off, heading east for Tbilisi, Georgia. For the past
few minutes, Iza Beggs Mansour had been gazing out the window of
the Boeing 757 as it climbed to cruising altitude. When the plane entered
a cloudbank at 12,000 feet, she pulled down the window shade, turned to
Sam and asked, "Did you message Conor... tell him we are on our way to
see Mother?"

"I did. But he said he couldn't talk very long, a business meeting or
something." It was the first week of March, and the university was on spring
break. Sam and Iza had left Chicago for New York the previous night, and
then, to avoid peak-hour traffic, they took the red-eye flight to Warsaw.
It was a long ride – 22 hours altogether – but the Polish Airlines fare was
cheap enough that both could make the trip.

"What did he have to say?"

"That the London meeting last fall with Jake was a disaster."

"The business about the treasure?"

"Yeah. Conor said Jake claimed he never got the text about not selling it."

Iza was puzzled. "But Jake needed the money, right?"

"Conor told Jake he would loan him the money for school, but that just made him mad. There's always been a problem. You heard what Jake said when he and Lindy visited last fall."

"Worse now?"

"Conor is frustrated; he doesn't know how his problems with Jake can be resolved."

"Too bad." Iza frowned. Then she changed the subject. "Natia has a new boyfriend."

"I didn't know that."

"You've got to get closer to the girls, Sam. Before you know it, they'll be out of the house, and you'll be wondering what in the world happened." It was true. He loved Natia and Elene, of course, but too often it was hard for him to maintain a wholesome father-daughter bond.

Sam said, "I don't know what to do."

"You don't have to do anything, just talk to Natia." It wasn't only his daughters; Sam Mansour was reticent in most social situations. He got worse after Tom Moynihan died; felt lost, and had a hard time making new friends.

"What happened to Bobby... what's his name?"

"You mean Bobby Hiller," Iza said. "That's done. At their age they get into a fight, then it's over as quick as it started."

"What's his name, this new boyfriend?"

"Nathan Shrock. Professor's Shrock's son. You know, the English Department chair."

"Should I send her a congratulatory note?"

"Don't be a smartass."

"What about Elene?"

"There you go again. You've got to get closer to both girls," Iza said, then, "All the 14-year-olds just go out together, boys and girls."

"They're pulling away from me, you know," Sam complained.

"Welcome to the club." Now that they had reached cruising altitude, the clouds were gone, and the sky was an enveloping pale blue from western horizon to deep indigo at the zenith above. It would take the travelers a little more than three hours to complete the journey from Warsaw to Tbilisi.

Changing the subject, Sam asked, "So what does your mother say these days?"

Iza replied, "She tells me that she is dying."

"A little exaggeration, wouldn't you say?"

"Don't be dismissive, Sam. She's an old woman, and to her people, she's a saint." Chira Beggs had just turned 80, and Iza was getting more and more concerned about her health, so Sam and Iza had moved up their annual visit to spring break.

A moment later, the flight attendant interrupted, "Hard roll or bran muffin?"

"I'll have the muffin."

"Me too, and coffee with cream."

Sam looked across Iza's shoulder and out the window. Off in the far distant east, Sam could see an occluded front appearing on the horizon. "Bad weather over there," he said.

"How do you know that?"

"An old friend, JK Burke. You remember him?"

"Of course, Tom's old boss."

"Yeah, he used to school me about the weather when we traveled. He was a nervous flyer, and wanted to know everything that might bring down a plane, especially the weather."

"An omen, then, this gathering storm in the east?"

Sam wondered about it, "Just weather." And then he changed the subject again. "Never understood this business of saints your mother is always talking about."

Iza offered a reason, "Most of her people were either Sufi or Alevi… you know, mysticism, the blending of religion, mythology, and culture."

"Not theologians, then?"

"In the wild country that was the Kars Province of her youth, mullahs and imams were few and far between. She grew up with a simple belief in Haji Veli, the most famous of the Alevi saints."

Alevi Muslims stand apart from most others of the Islamic faith. Alevi men and women are treated as equals in all ways, even worshiping together. Alevi women have no dress conventions, and, more often than not, wear modern clothes. Alevi parents encourage their daughters to get the best educations they can, and that they are free to go into any profession they choose.

"A sacred person, then?"

"Not exactly sacred; that's a Western notion," Iza replied. "As you know, I'm not an expert when it comes to religion, Islam or otherwise." She was trying to find the right words. "Custodian, helper, friend… a person chosen by God – supposedly – who is endowed with special gifts. Chira can heal, you know."

"Your mother, a doctor?"

"A faith healer."

Sam Mansour was dumbfounded by this revelation. "Why have we never talked about this?"

"Communication, Sam, communication," Iza nagged once more. "But no, it's never been part of our lives. Don't forget the worlds from which we came. Growing up in the United States is very different from growing up in the Caucasus. It makes a difference."

"You don't consider it real, do you?"

"For many Kurdish people belief is more important than facts."

"You don't believe that!"

"I don't, but her people do. You should ask her about her skills to cure when you see her. She'll talk your ear off."

"I'd like to hear what she has to say," Sam replied, "I just might do that."

Chira Beggs lived in Kojori, a small village 20 miles west of Tbilisi. It was not by choice that she lived in Georgia, but because her old homestead near Kars, Turkey, had been subjected to Turk-Armenian skirmishes for more than 40 years. Tbilisi was easier these days, and Chira made a modest living as an Alevi saint—a minor saint, of course.

In the Kurdish language, the name Chira meant the bringer of light, which suited Mrs. Beggs' remarkable personality. She was much like her daughter: tall, dark-skinned, clear-eyed, stout, now a little tubby, but she had beautiful, long white tresses that fell to her waist. Outside of her home, she covered her hair, not for religious piety but because that's what was expected of a faith healer. In the West, she would have been called a spiritualist.

When she was 22, she married John Beggs. He was an oil worker, one of the men who helped build the Baku-Tbilisi-Ceyhan pipeline. Chira and

John had loved each other dearly, but their time together was chaotic and stressful. Mainly, Alevi elders did not approve of a marriage to an outsider, let alone to a Christian. Chira foresaw troubled times ahead… and loss. She was right. The marriage didn't last long: not because of marital differences, but because John died in a gas explosion a month before pipeline construction was completed. Iza was a kid, just 14 when her father vanished from her life. It left a mark deep within her big, beautiful, charismatic self, an everlasting rage against feckless fate.

At lunch the next day, Sam decided to follow up on his promise to ask Chira about her gifts. "Iza tells me that Kurdish people don't use modern medicine?"

Chira was surprised by the question. No one had ever questioned her about that. She responded sheepishly, "Some do, some don't. In Kojori, a goodly number don't trust doctors, so they come to me." Iza was ignoring the discussion. She was happy to be home, but exhausted.

"Why are they fearful?"

"Because it has limits, Western medicine that is."

"That's not logical, Chira."

Cheekily, she shot back, "I don't believe in logic, Mr. Mansour." Sam laughed, knowing that his mother-in-law was fearless in an argument.

"Okay," he reconsidered, "what's wrong with Western medicine?

"It has a mixed record," said Chira. "For many, such practices often fail to examine the connection between physical illness and spiritual affliction." Chira's customers came to her for what they saw as a redeeming encounter.

"Okay, what's the connection?"

Chira rolled her eyes and raised an index finger to indicate that she suspected sarcasm. "If you wish to understand why the cures of saints are more helpful than those of Western doctors, you will have to first rethink your unschooled attitude about folk medicine."

She had thrown down the gauntlet. Nonetheless, Sam countered, "I cannot refute what is not science."

"You see me as a shaman, a reader of tea leaves, but parlor magic is not what saints do, or how Alevi mysticism works."

"Go on."

Iza watched the jousting between her husband and mother. "You're not going to win this argument, Sam. Not on Chira's turf."

But Sam didn't back down, "Faith healing has no...."

She cut him off. "The ablest doctor can only put folks back into their previous physical condition. Doctors know nothing about remedies for longstanding ill health, let alone the essential aim of all healing."

"Which is?"

The old woman didn't hesitate. "Redemption, of course."

Iza was amused, and chimed in, "There it is – a saint's view of the Western world."

"We have alternative ways," Chira said. "I am a student of history, and history is a living thing, not something dead in a book. You just have to be smart enough to read the signs, and project into the future."

"Iza, you didn't tell me that your mother was both healer and soothsayer."

"Tell him about Aslan, mother."

"The lion of Derbent?"

Iza said, "She foretold of a man rising to power in the north, but that he would be struck down by a great power, and his people would be swallowed up."

"Not much of a prediction, Iza," Chira cautioned. "It has happened over and over in this accursed land."

"So, Chira, tell me something I don't know."

Chira paused before speaking again, worried that her words might be misunderstood. She shifted uncomfortably in her chair, then looked into her daughter's eyes and said, "Bəla is coming." Iza was taken aback. Bəla was a word not used lightly by the Kurds.

"Bəla?" Sam had no clue.

Eyeing Sam impatiently, Iza said, "It means menace, peril, a great evil." She turned back to Chira. "Seriously, mother, how do you know this?"

Neither Sam nor Iza had a chance to follow up. Sam's iPhone began its annoying ringtone. It was the Kedar Bey calling from Baku, and he had a request.

Three days later, Sam, Iza, and Chira Beggs were traveling west on the M80 highway and were now about 75 miles west of Tbilisi in the Lesser Caucasus Mountain Range. They had crossed the top pass and could see a massive lake to the south. "That's Lake Panavani," Chira said, "and Mount Samsari is to the west. It has a huge caldera, but it's hard to see because the floor is hidden by debris from the last volcanic eruption."

Chira sat in the front seat. Iza thought it might be a more comfortable ride for the 80-year-old. "How are you doing, mother?"

"Fine," she replied. "Don't worry about me. I'm not a baby doll."

"In November, you said you were dying."

"Well, I am dying... just not today."

The son-in-law chimed in, "Not for a week, at least. You're our guide. Who else could get us through the wilds?" Sam had rented a Land Rover.

He knew the terrain would be challenging, and felt confident that the 4x4, turbocharged SUV would get them across any mountain and through most streams on their way to Kars Provence in Turkey.

"When we get to the southern end of the lake," Chira said, "we'll need to avoid the village at Highway 11. It's an Armenian listening station."

"More Alevi magic?"

Chira took him seriously, "When I was young, our family had to flee the fighting between the Turks and Armenians. This is the way we escaped the carnage."

"Ninots? Is that the village?" Iza asked. She had googled a map of the region.

"Yes," Mother Beggs replied. "And Highway 11 is the key access road between the Black Sea and Yerevan."

"So, Sam, tell us again what Conor said."

"He was very concerned about Rufet," Sam began. "Said he hadn't heard from him in several months."

"Is that unusual?"

"Very. They usually text two or three times each week if they aren't in touch by phone."

"Did he check in with Rufet's family?"

"Conor asked Mira's husband to search there and in the mountains, but Seyfulla found nothing. Rufet was supposed to meet Conor in London, but after the attack at Ephesus everything blew up, and he went missing."

"What's going on?" Iza asked. "Why all this subterfuge?"

"He hinted that Azerbaijan was about to explode… something big at hand," Sam explained. "He asked us to keep everything hush-hush. Maybe you're right, Chira. Maybe Bəla is coming our way."

"Not just here," Chira said. "It's bigger than that."

Two hours later, they had crossed the Georgia-Turkey border, caught the main highway south, and headed straight for Kars. If there was any possibility that Rufet was still there, they were confident that Chira's local knowledge would be the key to finding him.

23

The Brothers Kos

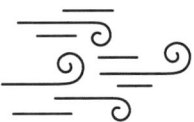

The educational system of Azerbaijan during Soviet times, was, by design, schizophrenic. On the one hand, all Azeri language instruction was forbidden: Azeri script was banned, textbooks were burned, and teachers could not speak their native language, not even on the playground. On the other hand, Russian instruction was encouraged: Russian schools were free, Cyrillic was the script, and Russian was the standard prose for all textbooks.

Some Azeri citizens, nevertheless, did have a choice other than the government-run Russian system – the British school. And that's where the vast majority of the ruling Houses of Azerbaijan sent their kids. And once they had completed their primary and secondary education, it was off to European universities for most.

The exception was Viktor Kos. He was so steeped in Russian history and heritage that he selected the Russian schools for his sons. But it was more than tradition that persuaded the newest of the ruling elites not to follow the other Houses. Viktor was shrewd not just in politics, but in all things where he thought he could acquire an advantage. He knew that the Kos boys would dominate the vast majority of common Azeris who attended the Russian schools. "Always remember, Vanya," Viktor would intone, "in this world, there are elites and serviles, and you must be the winner of the huggermugger game."

Utterly oblivious to his father's schemes, the six-year-old Vanya reacted hostilely to what he thought was an affront to his playmates, "But I like Cid and Nico, Papa."

"Like them for what they can do for you," Viktor would discipline, "otherwise, they are just life's losers." After many such lessons, Vanya accepted his father's advice and acquired his ways. It suited him. The future Bey was well-liked, at first. He was, after all, one of the privileged few, and his chums would often scramble frantically to find their place among his chosen friends.

His mother, Aydan, encouraged the self-absorbed behavior. She would throw elaborate birthday parties for her son, the sole purpose of which was to show off Vanya's collection of scooter cars, fancy clothes, and latest Nintendo games. In subsequent weeks, Vanya would hand out pictures of himself receiving presents, followed with, "As you can see, I'm the most popular boy in school." In those early years at school, Vanya found intimacy difficult, realizing that he had little empathy for others. In fact, his lording over his classmates became a testing ground for his life-long egotistical behavior.

By age nine, Vanya took to taunting others who had to work to support their families. He would often offer them the clothes he no longer wanted, and then laugh behind their back when they accepted his charity. Vanya became more and more antagonistic, particularly toward younger boys. His teachers regularly marked him as a bully. His mother, however, could not imagine that Vanya might have a character disorder and paid no attention to the school reports. Viktor, on the other hand, approved of such behavior, and even complimented his son, saying, "I see that you have learned, Vanya, how to apply the lessons of those who rule." The boy relished the praise.

Everyone in the family thought they knew how his personality would develop in the coming years. But Vanya was, in fact, acutely insecure about his standing outside of the family situation. His grandiosity, need for attention, and belittling others were merely cover-ups that made him feel powerful and relevant when he really was not. He was always in need of motherly encouragement, but sometimes Aydan's affection was a muddle to the boy. An overly strict woman who suffered from neurotic tendencies, she could be cold with family, friends, servants, and sometimes with Vanya himself. Viktor, on the other hand, did little to inspire the boy's confidence. As a result of these very mixed messages, Vanya's response to even mild criticism was to become wildly unhinged and pout for days. All this was before the arrival of a second wife six years later and her son a year after that.

For Vanya, little Vladimir was entirely unexpected – a world-altering complication for which Vanya had limited preparation and absolutely no understanding. So, he dealt with the wrinkly pooping-peeing thing the same way he had dealt with his schoolmates. He turned to aggression, meting out taunts and tantrums on his new rival. By the time Vlad was four, Vanya's verbal and physical abuse was unrelenting.

As the boys grew older, they had adjoining bedrooms on the second floor, and at least twice a week, Vanya would invite Vlad to his room to play. It was odd seeing boys of such different ages taking part in make-believe. It regularly ended in some form of torment: Vanya telling Vlad how stupid he was, yelling at the boy for childish behavior until he cried, or squeezing Vlad's ears to see if he could stand the pain like a man. Vanya would laugh, taking pleasure in the agony he caused his brother. To say the least, the boys never bonded.

At the sound of her son squealing, Dina would rush in and unload thunderous admonishments on Vanya. Of course, such rebuke was unacceptable to Aydan, and the two women would quarrel until one or the other would walk away in sheer exhaustion. Just before Vladimir reached his teenage years, Vanya settled on harassing the boy about his appearance. The older brother would regularly convey how ugly Vlad was to everyone in the neighborhood. Once puberty arrived, such activities intensified, and Vladimir was exposed to almost daily abuses about his looks.

Vlad, however, if not a quick study, was a cunning apprentice to his brother's cruelties. By the time he entered high school, Vladimir had understood the nature of his brother's behavior. He recognized that what Vanya said was nothing but bunkum, and most importantly, that his older brother was a person who was insecure and vulnerable. Vlad cleverly turned the tables. When friends began drifting away because of Vanya's vanities, Vlad would echo the acerbities. It worked. Soon the brothers Kos were on equal footing. Eventually, they formed a non-aggression pact that suited both – Vanya continued to live in a fantasy world of self-aggrandizement, and Vlad was set free to explore a nasty track of his own.

In due course, Vladimir was seduced by the pleasures of pain. It started when he was eight, and it grew as he grew. Foremost in his neurotic hierarchy was the misery of others. When the squabbling mothers decided to separate the boys, Vanya remained upstairs, while Vlad moved to a little room next to the garden house on the first floor.

Because of all the plants, flowers, and wiggly creatures nearby, he developed an interest in insects. He was especially fond of dragonflies, those that a cousin brought back from camping excursions in the Talysh hills, where creeks and ponds drained from the highlands into the Caspian Sea. Over the next few years, Vlad collected, preserved, and mounted more than 30 species. But the real reason for his being a collector of Anisoptera was odd. It wasn't their carnivorous nature or the science of taxonomy itself, but a perverse fixation with afflicting agony on the poor creatures that he enjoyed.

Vlad once asked the gardener, "Does it feel pain?"

"They're not human, Müserif," the man said. "They can't have feelings." The gardener thought he was saving the boy from some heartfelt anguish. But Vlad had no remorse for such creatures; in fact, he relished in their suffering. Vlad began experimenting with a variety of cruelties. He pulled off a wing or two to see if the creatures could still fly. They could not; they just fluttered frantically in stillborn circles on his table. On the Internet, he learned that dragonflies had 24,000 eyes... they don't, but Vlad decided to see if could pluck out an eye or two or 20, so to speak. In the end, Vladimir settled on pinning each captive dragonfly alive to his mounting board, and then watch it die. It was his first deep dive into sadism.

At school, Vlad was a prankster. His shenanigans always involved biting and stinging creatures: wolf spiders, vampire bats, bees, wasps, and especially snakes. The pleasure he took from seeing a classmate recoil in fear was Vlad's second dip into deviance. But it wasn't just physical sadism that excited Vladimir Kos; emotional cruelty was equally stimulating, chiefly when his victims were girls.

In his teen years, he grew expressly fond of two-timing girlfriends. He dated a series of enthusiastic ladies, and his callous and non-committal attitude was apparent even after a few short weeks. When he was tired of one, he didn't fret over hurting his castoff. Vlad openly attacked the poor girl during the break-up, citing her looks or behavior or status as being unsuitable to the House of Kos. One of Vlad's chief means of exerting authority over them was to select very young girls who were far beneath him on the social pecking order. He opted for girls he could dominate, control, and, punish.

"You know, Leyla," he would say, "your sister has asked me to take her out on my boat."

"She's a bitch," said the incensed Leyla. "She already has many boyfriends."

Vlad responded stingingly, "She is prettier than you, you know... and more mature." He drew out the words as if they were an affront to his dignity, "Don't you think I deserve the prettiest one in your family?"

"I'll fix her," Leyla shouted as she stomped away. "You'll see."

That night, Leyla brutalized her sister with a wooden meat mallet. Afterward, she took a picture of her sister's face and brought it to school. "See, I told you," as she threw the photo at Vladimir. "She's not so pretty now!"

To his surprise, the photo of the bloodied woman pleased Vlad – no, thrilled and aroused him. "Leyla, you did this for me?" Now he knew what was missing in his burgeoning sex life. He gave the little girl a hug, and while doing so, began working out a plan to bring his sexual cravings to a much-needed climax.

"Anything for you, Vlad," she pined, wholly unaware of the debauchery he was intending.

Later that day, Vlad had some misgivings about the upcoming encounter – not about the things he would do to her, but about her willingness to obey. But he quickly settled the matter in his mind, *if she does not agree, I will force her. Yes! That would be even more fun.* She was only 14, but Vlad didn't care. *No one will care,* he argued to himself. *After all, she is servile, and I am elite.*

But the tryst didn't go as he planned. Vlad had a problem – a problem of which he was not yet fully aware. His sexual proclivities did not readily spring forth with women. Oh, he had no problem battering women emotionally, but, as he would learn in the coming years, his sexual gratification would come only with men.

Leyla had come to the Kos mansion that night, prepared for heavy petting. She had borrowed her older sister's high heels, one of her fashionably short, tight-fitting skirts, and a frilly blouse. The young woman had even discarded her bra, and her nipples were excitedly visible. After just a few minutes, Vlad realized that Leyla did not arouse him as he thought she should. He was confused, and soon infuriated, and then he summarily rejected her. "Get out of my house," he shouted. But as Leyla left his room, he added, "Tell your sister I want a real woman, and will be coming for her next." It was pretense, but Leyla felt relieved.

After a few years, Vladimir moved out of his father's house and into an apartment at the Baku Sporting Club. It was caused by an argument with Vanya, which erupted into violence and an injury. By the time he was 20, Vlad had outgrown his brother and had a working knowledge of *Jamuwanti*, the fighting techniques taught to him by Master Girish. The robust younger man had convinced his brother to tussle for a bit; he would show Vanya a few wrestling tricks. But when Vlad applied the arm-trap half nelson, he dislocated Vanya's shoulder. He claimed it was unintentional, but neither Vanya nor Viktor was convinced.

Dina was unhappy that Vladimir should be kicked out of the house, but there was scarcely anything she could do to stop it. Viktor, Vanya, and Aydan demanded the move, and her son did not object. So, after a few months of renovations at the Club, Vlad moved away. He was happy there. Vlad could gather his boys together, and they could practice their lifestyle without further family interferences.

24

Ghost on The Hill

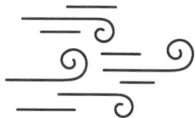

Spring was still two weeks away, and the winter winds had suddenly returned to Azerbaijan. There was a storm howling across Baku Bay. Mira Nadirov stared out the car window, "Khazri will not give up; hope it doesn't ruin Novruz." She was sitting next to Conor in the back of the Zümrə limo, which was stopped at a light on the access road to Heydar Aliyev Airport. She watched intently as the cavalcade of flags was blowing straight out against the overcast skies.

Conor replied, "Very intense… more than the usual spring squall." Each was thinking of Tali, who had just boarded Flight 233, bound for Istanbul. They were concerned about the gale-force turbulence the plane might encounter overhead.

The limo driver said, "She will be all right once the plane gets above the clouds." It was David, Rufet's long-time chauffeur. Ever since Qurb had gone missing, he'd been reassigned to drive the Kedar Bey. In any case, Conor wished that Tali had taken the Zümrə jet. It was nimble and able to avoid dangerous cumulonimbus clouds. But in his subconscious, he knew that the massive Boeing 757 was the safer plane.

David was driving southward on Neftcilar Boulevard, taking Mira and Conor back to the Zümrə Estates when Conor said, "After we drop off Mira, you can take me to the residence. I will be staying there tonight." The chauffeur acknowledged his boss's request.

Currently, everyone associated with House Kedar was on edge. Throughout the winter months, a restless people, economic instability, and rumors of war had alarmed the Azerbaijani population, especially the ruling elite. Undercover agents were everywhere, watching. Any clan meeting in Baku was now out of the question, so Conor had decided to move the Kedar strategy session to Gobustan. Tonight's plan was simple enough: Rayna would drive Mira to the Nadirov home in Gobustan, and she would wait for Conor and other allies to join her there.

Conor was checking his iPhone when he came across an old text. "I forgot to tell you. Sam sent a reply."

"What did he say?" asked Mira.

"That they would be on the road to Kars in a day or two. Iza's mother is going with them."

"Old Chira?" Mira was puzzled. "What can she do besides tell fortunes?"

"She lived in Kars Province as a kid. It's hostile territory now, as it was then, and they thought she might be helpful in the search for Rufet."

Mira glanced upward at the roof of the limo, then turned to look at Conor face-to-face. "Rufet is dead, Conor, probably lost in the mountains or fallen into a gorge. You cannot put off finding a second-in-command any longer."

Mira Nadirov had no formal standing in House Kedar, but she was Conor's personal confidant and life-long surrogate mother. There was an urgency to her message. Political alliances had shifted. The Kedar-Kazimov faction had lost much of its power, and Viktor Kos had just recently been named Azeri Vice President.

It wasn't the first time that his cherished aunt had badgered Conor about her husband, Seyfulla. "Mira, I am not going to name him First Deputy." There was a curtness to his tone as he continued, "Seyfulla is a good man, but he has no interest in business or political machinations."

"True, but he is someone you can trust."

"He better serves us as the head of the Nadirov family in the Outlands."

Mira knew when to quit badgering, so she changed the subject. "What is the name of this conference that Tali's attending?"

"It's called Inshallah… like Davos, only for Islamic Asia and the Middle East."

"'If God wills it.' That is a good name." Tali was not only representing the Zümrə companies but also would assist the Foreign Secretary. She had wanted to do this on her own and decided to go unaided on commercial air. "Who else is going to be there?"

"Secretary Kazimov, of course, and several others," said Conor. "Most troubling is Vladimir, the nastiest of the Kos."

"Can you explain the new position he's been given?"

"National Security Councilor," Conor harrumphed. "Rolan says the crisis with Armenia required someone to coordinate all security agencies. But it's obviously a reward to Viktor for voting with Guliyev against the latest no-confidence initiative."

"Sounds fishy to me."

After passing through the electronic access gate, the limo headed for the closest building, which was where the business offices were located. David pulled into the cul-de-sac, where he found Rayna waiting with

Mira's car. David jumped out, opened the passenger door, then fetched Mira's bags from the trunk and handed them over to her bodyguard. But before Mira could switch cars, Conor called her back. "I may be slightly delayed... getting to Gobustan, I mean."

"Why's that?"

"I'm going to visit with an old friend, Mo Chinske."

Mira nodded, "A good friend to have these days. Give him my regards."

"If all goes as planned, I'll bring Mo to the strategy meeting in Gobustan."

She gave the Kedar Bey a thumbs-up, and said, "When we're finished with the business of the retreat, I want to show you my ghost on the hill."

Conor crooked his head and chuckled. "You ridicule Chira Beggs for being a faith healer and fortune teller, and now you're telling me you have a ghost to show me?"

"Yes. A ghost dear to my heart and yours."

Conor loved his aunt profoundly but did not understand so many of her ways. She waved goodbye and rushed off to the other car.

What all employees called the residence at the Zümrə Estates was actually a multipurpose building complex between the business center and the boat dock. It housed a storage facility, a large garage, and four apartments. Two were occupied by maintenance and housekeeping staff, a third was used for Kedar guests, and then there was Conor's garden apartment, which had a beautiful southern view of Baku Bay and the Caspian Sea. That's where Conor and Tali lived most of the year.

The next morning, Conor sat in the sunroom adjacent to the kitchen, having tea. He was watching last night's clouds clearing on the eastern horizon when he received a text from Mira: "Tali landed safe; now at Four Seasons registering for conference."

"Good news… waiting for the storm to end."

"Wish I had sent Rayna with her. I worry when Tali's by herself."

Conor's return words were somewhat snarky: "She's 25… a woman thoroughly competent to take care of herself. You are such a worrywart!"

Mira replied sharply: "I'm her mother, remember? Don't tell me when I can or cannot worry."

Sometime around 11 am, the foul weather had subsided, and the winds had calmed, so Conor decided he could make the sea voyage to meet Mo Chinske. He dressed warmly and then walked down to the boathouse, where the Zarifa was stored for the winter. He exchanged batteries and gassed up the Fairlane 62-footer. After letting the engine idle for 10 minutes, he engaged the power doors and headed out to sea – alone. Once he passed the breakers, he dialed in the coordinates, and the cabin cruiser's navigation system took over. He sent a secured message to Captain Azat on the Hazar-Denizi that he was on the way, and estimated his arrival at 12:30 pm.

Somewhere in the middle of the Caspian, the Hazar-Denizi had been moored throughout the night at Exxon Oil Platform-5CS. The captain and crew were also waiting out the storm. A minute or two after Azat received Conor's message, he dialed Chinske's room. "The Kedar Bey is on the move," the Captain reported.

"How far?" Mo asked.

"He says a little more than an hour. We can be underway in 30 minutes; then, depending on the seas, it's 50 to 75 minutes to the meeting place." The Hazar-Denizi was a commuter tug that shuttled workers to and from oil platforms in the middle of the Caspian. Exxon-5CS was a regular stopover, so no one paid attention to the lone passenger on the

Hazar-Denizi. More importantly, no one cared even if he was the chief field agent of CIA-Central Asia.

"Tell him we'll be there at one, or 1:30 pm at the latest."

At the Gobustan cottage two days later, Mo Chinske began his briefing to the Kedar Bey and his ever-diminishing band of allies. He had their undivided attention.

"As you well know, for decades – centuries, really – the battle between the Shiites and Sunnis for the heart of Islam has been fierce, fraught with disaster, and always conducted under the table, so to speak. We refer to them as proxy wars: the Bader Gang versus the Khorasani Brigade, Peshmerga versus ISIS, Al-Qaeda affiliates clashing in Africa, Asia, and the Middle East, just to name a few. The clandestine services of many nations have tried intervention in many forms, but none has ever been successful. In fact, we now accept as truth that sectarian fighting is the very thing that has prevented the battle from exploding into total warfare."

Seeking to bring a bit of levity to the room, one of the Nadirov cousins interjected, "In Azerbaijan, it is Kedar versus Kos." Mira frowned at the boy.

Chinske took a sip of coffee, paying no attention to the comment, and then brought up a PowerPoint slide. "But things have changed. Both the Saudis and Iranians now have nukes. Small tactical weapons: dirty bombs, SAMs with lightweight nuclear warheads, nuclear artillery shells, and land mines… stuff like that."

Mira asked, "Are they building these weapons?"

"Or just smuggling them into the region?" Rayna probed.

"Buying them, mostly from China, North Korea, any rogue regime that's in the business," Mo replied. "But they are both developing the infrastructure for a munitions industry."

Secretary Kazimov's son followed up, "Just how does Azerbaijan fit into the picture, Mr. Chinske?" Paul Kazimov was a serious student of international politics and had a profound concern for his native land.

"Good question. Most analysts see the Caucasus as the hottest spot, the most dangerous place on the planet."

Conor asked, "Why is that, Mo?"

"We think…" Mo hesitated, remembering Conor's father and his struggles, "Tom Moynihan always thought the battle between Shiite and Sunni must be settled," he said, "but the Azerbaijan-Armenia struggle is critically different; it's between Christians and Muslims, the West versus the East, the clash of civilization that Tom sought to avoid all of his life."

"If you Americans had kept your word…"

Another shouted, "Crusaders invade, Muslims react!"

"True enough," Chinske said. "But that doesn't alleviate the immediate problem."

Conor said, "Guliyev is ready for war right now."

Chinske added, "We know, and so are the Armenians."

"So, what can we do?" asked Mira.

"Stop Guliyev Bey," Mo said. "And Viktor Kos too. We think he's planning to assassinate Rolan and assume the Presidency."

"How do you know this?" Rayna demanded.

"We've been monitoring the activities of each member of the Triad for some time now."

By late morning the next day, they had worked out a strategy, and everyone had been given an assignment. After that, the retreat ended and everyone scattered. Mo Chinske headed for Baku to speak with David. Mira and Conor remained in Gobustan – there was a ghost to see.

After dinner that evening, Mira began explaining about her first encounter with the ghost. "I told Rayna I was going for a walk. She objected, of course, but I insisted… I was just going to find some youthful memories, I told her. Rayna stipulated that I should take a walkie-talkie and a flashlight. It was October, and the daylight was fleeting."

"Did you have any wine that evening?" asked an accusatory son.

"This was not about the wine, Conor."

"Sorry, Mother. Please go on." They stepped outside and then headed upward toward the Rock Garden. There was plenty of sun above the horizon, and as before, there was a sweet scent of honeysuckle on the trail.

"When I got to the jingling stone, I heard a door slam back in the direction of the cottage. When I turned, I saw a flash of blue, like a strobe light in the night sky. I imagined it was just Rayna and dismissed it.

"Here is the jingling stone," she said, pointing. "Want to hear it sing, Conor?" He agreed, naturally. Mira knelt down at the base of the rock and found two hammering rocks. A moment later, a beguiling Muğam rhythm echoed against the Gobustan hills.

"Your music is still so wonderful, Mira," a smiling Conor whispered.

"I wish you could have heard Zara play. She was a gift to all of us."

"I just wish I had known her."

"I wish that too," Mira said sadly.

"I have no memory of Zara, you know?"

"I know."

After that, Mira showed Conor the ghost dancers. She took his hand and placed it gently on one of the figures, and said, "Zara always claimed that she was a ghost dancer. From the time we were children."

"And you believed her?"

"Conor, there was no arguing with your mother."

"I guess not."

Mira continued: "I decided to head back down. But about halfway to the cottage, I turned the flashlight off to admire the sky and stars. That's when the blue glow caught my eye again. It was coming from the top floor of the cottage and seemed to be moving, like a living thing. I raced to the cottage. The door slammed behind me and startled Rayna."

It was already dark when Mira and Conor returned to the cottage. They were standing between the garden gravesite where Zara and Tom were buried and the two noble plane trees that stood with them. Mira gazed upward toward the top floor of the cottage, searching for the specter to appear again. But nothing happened, and she continued her story: "I asked Rayna if she had been upstairs. She said, 'No.' But our always-on-duty Rayna was troubled. We searched each room carefully but found nothing. Rayna thought it was a motion-detector light outside... just a bird flying by that set it off."

Conor meandered to the graves, looking at the freshly planted flowers. "I cannot tell which is Zara's and which is Tom's."

"It's impossible now," Mira replied. "Zara's grave is more than 25 years old, Tom's about eight. But there's no marker to tell which is which."

Conor asked, "Should we buy a headstone?"

"It's not our way," Mira replied. "They are with God, not here."

Conor turned back to face Mira. "Go on."

"Rayna was satisfied that there was no intruder upstairs, so she left to check below. I stayed behind. Next, I heard something outside, so I turned off the light, and walked to the window. That's when I saw the blue presence again. In the beginning, it was only a shimmering, but almost immediately it took shape – a figure of a woman, standing near the garden. It was Zara. And then, to my horror, I witnessed the murder play out once again."

Conor wrapped his arms around Mira, "I'm so sad that you had to go through it again. But Mira, it was nothing, a recalled memory, perhaps."

"But there is more, Conor. There was another phantom nearby, a child – you! As your mother lay dying on the ground, Elshan snatched you up and stole you away. Then everything vanished.

"The moment passed, and I was alone again. The leaves were rustling through the trees; not leaves, but Zara. Her fading voice spoke to me: 'Protect the child... protect the child.' That's when I called you... *Protect Conor*, I thought, *I must protect Conor*."

They had gone inside and were sitting at the kitchen table when Conor said, "About this episode, I have one last question."

"Yes?"

"When this voice said, 'Protect the child,' why did you think it meant me?"

Mira was taken aback and sat up, "Who else could it be?"

Conor responded instantly, "Well, 'by child,' this ghost could have meant your natural child, Tali, not me."

Mira was horrified at the thought. It had never crossed her mind that Tali might be the one in danger.

"It is most likely nothing to worry about, Mira. Tomorrow, we can sort everything out."

The next morning, Conor rose early and made a pot of tea. That's when he spotted a note on the table. It was from Mira: "I cannot wait on this, Conor. I must go to Istanbul and bring Tali safely home."

25

Dinner at Turga's

C hasing after Tali was a nerve-wracking experience because protecting her daughter had never been Mira's job. That was the duty of the men of her family. When Tali was a kid, it was her grandfather and father who protected her; and of course, in recent days, it was Conor who was her armor and shield. This was the Azeri way. It had nothing to do with Mira's strength of character or self-reliance or even her role under Shia traditions. But somehow, this felt different – this sudden and wholly unexpected upheaval brought about by Zara's ghost – and Mira knew she had to act. So, she woke Rayna at six the next morning and then texted David in Baku: "Get the Zümrə jet ready. This is urgent; call for pilot to meet Rayna and me at airport. We leave for Istanbul at 8 am."

Mira and Rayna arrived in Istanbul at 12:15 pm. It was the 10th of March, and the scheduled sessions of the Inshallah Convention

L'Internationale had concluded. All that was left was the banquet that evening. When Tali received Mira's text, she was bowled over: "Tali – Rayna & I arrived Istanbul today. Are you OK? Wanted to hear your talk this evening... so proud."

Tali replied: "Am fine! What are you doing, Mother?"

"Just want to be with you tonight."

"Cant talk... busy. See you in morning. I'm in Golden Horne Suite."

Mira insisted: "I will send Rayna to check on you tonight."

"No need! See you in am."

The next morning, the three women met at the hotel coffee shop. After ordering rolls and jam, Mira said, "We were there last night, and saw you speak."

Tali looked at Rayna, searching her eyes for a sisterhood of sympathy. "Thank you for the praise. But why are you really here?"

"This assignment has been such a great honor for you."

It was time for some straight talk. "Mother, has something happened?" Tali demanded. "Stop stalling. Did Conor come too?"

"No, he stayed in Baku. He had much to arrange after our Gobustan strategy meeting."

Tali looked like thunder. "I don't have time for this."

"We can go shopping today," Mira said. "I want to pick up some things for the family at the Grand Bazaar." She could not bring herself to say that a ghost had issued a warning and that she had freaked out over her daughter's welfare. The white lies were easier.

"Stop, stop, stop."

Not wanting to get involved in the confrontation, Rayna picked up her breakfast and stood up. "I'm going to the gym. Haven't worked out in days." It wasn't true, of course, but Rayna had the good sense to know when it was time to leave mother and daughter alone.

Mira and Tali understood and were relieved. Mira said, "I'll text you when we're ready."

"Fine." Rayna nodded, then left.

"You can pick up junk at the airport, Mother."

Mira replied snootily, "We commandeered the Zümrə jet; no trinkets at the Sabiha terminal."

"Okay, we'll go to the Grand Bazaar," Tali said. "But I have a dinner slated tonight at Turga's with Alexandr Kazimov. We have to be back by seven pm."

"Promise. But we're coming with to you to Turga's."

"Okay... So, what's up?"

Mira hadn't planned on using a diversion, but at that instant, she thought it the easiest way to begin an odd chat about a ghost. "I have some worries," she said, "about you and Conor."

"We are fine, Mother."

"You should get married."

Tali's eyes widened, "You said the mullahs would come after my head."

"I know," Mira replied.

"That's a huge change of heart," said a surprised daughter.

"He is so vulnerable, so breakable, you know." There it was – blurted out and unvarnished. "Conor just cannot live without you."

"Conor is not breakable, Mother," Tali replied. "He is tough, resilient and measured, not fragile." It was evident that something had set off Mira in a strange direction, but what?

"He worries, you know. Especially since Rufet disappeared. We have to be his anchors – you and I – his advisors and advocates."

"This is about the Kos, isn't it?"

"About them… and others. It's hard to determine these days who is on your side and who is not."

"Are you worried about Secretary Kazimov?"

"Not Kazimov, but other Houses." Next, she added, "By the way, I sent Conor a message last night; that all is okay, and that we'd be home sometime tomorrow."

"Good. Tonight, I'll tell Alexandr that I'm going home with you."

What followed was the intimate conversation about life and love that mothers and daughters have from time to time. What they did not talk about was Zara's ghost, and the strange and ambiguous warning it had delivered at the cottage. Mira considered the time not right, and she decided to bring it up later, maybe at dinner that evening. If not then, then on the plane ride home the next day. She had time – or so she thought.

At the heart of their tête-à-tête, Tali revealed that she had thought about marriage and children, but also that she and Conor had never had a serious discussion about such a commitment. It was something they both recognized would happen sooner or later, but they had never set a date or even announced the possibility of it to the family. Both women agreed that they should address the subject sometime soon, and promised that when they got home, it would be on their long agenda with Conor.

Both night and day, the waters of the Bosporus Strait are heavily traveled. Boat traffic is large, small, and everything in between: commercial freighters and tankers, cruise ships, ferries, fishing boats, dinghies, and private yachts.

This March evening was no different. Sightseeing cruisers were everywhere, and water taxis were exceptionally busy picking up and dropping off tourists at the elegant restaurants along the banks of the Strait. It was just after dusk, and a slight breeze carried the fresh, salty air in from the Sea of Marmara. The sky over the city of 17 million was tranquil, and the only sound that stood out was the muezzin calls from the minaret of the Blue Mosque on shore.

It was almost nine o'clock, and Tali, Mira, and Rayna were late for dinner with the Azeri Foreign Secretary. Traffic on the street outside the Four Seasons was still busy, so they decided to take a water taxi to the Ciragan Palace. It was a short ride on the Bosporus, and the evening was exquisite.

Halfway there, the driver chose to stop momentarily so his passengers could admire the star-filled heavens overhead. Evidently an amateur stargazer, he pointed out the constellation Gemini. "There," he said. "The two bright stars are the twins, Castor and Pollux."

Tali found the image high in the night sky, nudged Mira, and said, "Like Conor and Jake."

Mira laughed. "Brothers, but certainly not twins."

Another passenger complained, "We have reservations at nine. Let's move on."

But the taximan continued, "Pollux is the brighter star. It has a faint orange tinge. The other, Castor, is actually a six-star cluster, but they look like one." After that, the driver resumed his route, dropping off the Azeri ladies a few minutes later at the Ciragan Palace Pier.

It was only a brief walk from the landing to Turga's restaurant. "The darkness made for perfect stargazing," Rayna remarked.

"Perfect indeed," Mira replied. "I could actually see that constellation."

Their comments may have been trivial, but for Tali the darkness brought back anxious feelings. The last time she was here, Tali had been traveling all day and was dead-tired. The unfamiliar surroundings had frightened her, and the shadows of the night seemed to mask a menace and pose a risk. Once again, she noticed the secluded courtyards, the darkened storefronts, and that's when the image of a stalker, lurking, crossed her mind. But there was a difference this time; she was with a crowd of tourists heading for Turga's. Besides, Rayna was there, and she was a reckoning force.

Tali had fallen behind, and Rayna yelled, "Let's go, girl. Keep up."

A moment later, the Azeri women entered the restaurant from the patio. They immediately spotted Kazimov sitting at a large round table only a few feet away. He was holding court with friends from other embassies, and apparently hadn't noticed that Tali and Mira were late for dinner. Tali was relieved.

There were two men – bodyguards – standing next to the marble columns nearby. Rayna spoke with each momentarily, and afterward, one of the men went to the restaurant entrance to stand guard there, and the other to a post next to the kitchen. Rayna remained with the group, knowing that security was now tightly triangulated.

By 10:30 that night, most of the showboat and sightseeing traffic on the Bosporus had ended, and that's when two Turk naval boats advanced on the Ciragan pier from the Asian side of the Strait. It was not the regular patrol rounds, so the two men working at the dock that night were surprised and a little startled.

After docking, a dozen heavily armed SWAT officers approached the workstation at the end of the pier. The captain found the headman and said, "We've gotten word of suspicious activity on the Ciragan Road. We're closing down access to the Palace for the night."

The two men inside didn't argue. They grabbed their jackets, turned off the beacon light, signaling that the pier was shut down, and left. In the meantime, at the Ciragan Road access point, three Turk riot vehicles closed off the front entrance to the restaurant. This activity was also out of the ordinary. It was now 10:45.

The attack began with a tremendous explosion at the maître d' stand. It shattered the archway entrance to Turga's and killed two waiters and the Kazimov man who was stationed there. The other security forces immediately braced for action. One of the restaurant security men and Kazimov's other bodyguard took cover against the assault they knew would be coming their way. The firefight broke out within seconds, killing or wounding several of the diners nearest the entrance.

Rayna reacted instantaneously. Seeing the attack coming from street-side, she gathered Kazimov, Mira, and Tali and herded them out of the dining room and onto the restaurant patio. In the helter-skelter of the moment, it seemed the best route for escaping. Once outside, Rayna scanned the perimeter for other assailants. The way looked clear, but the bodyguard was suspicious. It seemed too easy.

Then Rayna spied a tall, granite statue of Ataturk about 50 feet across the courtyard, and motioned for Kazimov first to make a run for it, and then afterward the two Nadirov women. Her improvised plan was to steer her little group toward the Bosporus, find a boat, and whisk them off to safety. At least, that was her intention. But when Rayna saw that the light at the pier was off, she recognized she could not send them into the darkness. In fact, all lighting between the restaurant and the dock had been extinguished. Rayna held her breath, but it was too late. Kazimov was on his way when Rayna realized the danger.

The assailants from the bogus Turk cruisers were waiting. Two sharpshooters with night-vision gear were positioned just beyond the statute, hidden by the darkness. Naturally, when Aleksandr Kazimov reached the statue, he crouched behind it, waiting for the others to arrive. The Secretary didn't have a chance. The shooters at the dock unloaded, and Kazimov fell to the ground in a pool of blood.

Suddenly, Rayna realized they were caught in a crossfire, and now she could see others coming from Turga's patio. So, she reasoned their only escape was to head along the street toward the Four Seasons building, hiding in the darkness of the alleys along the way. Rayna sent Tali first. "There," she pointed, "next to the storefront. Hide in the alley. We'll be right behind you." Tali raced off, but another volley of bullets shattered the plate glass window at the store and diverted her away from the alley.

Rayna turned to Mira, and yelled, "Run fast – now!" But Mira was not nearly as agile as her daughter and fell after only 20 feet. As she lay exposed, one of the sharpshooters took dead aim and fired a bullet into her left hip. It shattered bone and opened a gaping wound. Mira would not be going further, so Rayna – the loyal and ever-courageous bodyguard – raced to Mira's side. She placed her body between the shooters and the woman she so admired and then began firing back. She was an easy target in the crossfire. First, a barrage from the landing and then another from the patio peppered her body.

Without bothering to think about the consequences, Tali raced back to her mother and Rayna. As luck would have it, someone had ordered the attackers to stop firing. "Mother!" she cried out as she slid to Mira's side.

Mira responded in full distress, "I'm hit, my hip, my arm." There was blood everywhere, but it was mostly from Rayna's bullet-riddled body. Then Mira Nadirov passed out, her head hitting the concrete with a thud.

As Tali had feared, there was a man in the shadows, a tall, slim man who advanced on the fallen women. His hair was combed to one side, and he wore a mustache, thick and bushy, that completely covered his upper lip. "All dead, Tali," It was an Azeri voice, in some way familiar, but she could not place it at this moment of panic, "except for you."

Then one of the fighters grabbed Tali, pulled her up, and held her while another injected her with a mixture of Fentanyl and Propanol, a drug cocktail that had a rapid onset. Tali would be out cold for several hours.

"Get her to the cruiser," said the shadow man. "I will return to the hideout in a week, maybe ten days. Make sure she cannot escape."

The first soldier hoisted Tali's limp body onto his shoulder, and then they all scurried for the Ciragan pier. A few minutes later, the Turkish police arrived on the scene, but the kidnappers had entirely disappeared.

The following morning, the Istanbul newspaper headlines read: *Armenian Terrorists Attack Ciragan Palace – Azeri Foreign Secretary Killed.* All told, 25 people lay dead in the aftermath. Two were identified as Armenian nationals. The investigating officer said that it appeared to be an assassination and that the perpetrators were looking for a second target. But nothing else was found.

26

The Many Roads to Ninots

Mone of the Vartan Alliance commanders, 400 miles north in the Romanian outback, saw the headlines announcing the assassination of the Azerbaijani Foreign Secretary. It didn't matter, a decision had been made – the new team was ready for a test. After many weeks of training and culling, Mike, Lindy, and Jake had reduced the Armenian diaspora force to a few hundred AWS operators and support staff. The more than 4,000 others were paid, asked to sign a pledge of secrecy, and then sent home.

Nonetheless, in the back of his mind, Tad Tadesian understood that he could recall his stand-by volunteers any time if the drone strategy failed. But everything had changed. No longer ground troops, members of the reconstituted unit saw themselves as flyers. Accordingly, Tadesian rechristened his team the Vartan Defense Wing. But nobody liked such long awkward moniker; instead, everyone used a shorter handle. They called it the d-Wing.

The commanders of the air company divided the d-Wing into five flights of 40 airmen plus support staff, with a captain in charge of each flight. Then, as many combatants often do, the men and women of the force nicknamed their units to their liking: the California group was called d-Wing Glendale, the Boston association d-Wing Watertown, and so on. Tadesian was the commander, while Mike and Lindy were colonels in charge of logistics and technology. Each flight managed an air regiment: 50,000 weaponized micro drones. But none was sure the d-Wing could perform on the battlefield as it had on the practice fields, so it was time to put theory into action. But how? Was Tadesian's overriding concern.

"Something will come up," said Mike.

One of the commanders who knew the trek from the Georgian coast to the Armenian frontier said, "Once we reach Batumi, there are several valleys where we can set up an exercise."

Another added, "The Turks often use the region for training. We might engage one of their units on the ground."

"Too risky," Tadesian said. "We don't want to be discovered too early." No one had an answer, so the idea of a test was put on the backburner.

For the past two days, the Carpathian rendezvous contingent had been shutting down the campsite and preparing for the Black Sea crossing. All records, equipment, and munitions had been loaded, and everyone was ready to make the voyage to Georgia and beyond. Lindy and Jake were in their tiny hovel finishing last-minute packing. In a somewhat ornery mood, Lindy said, "I don't understand why you didn't take Tadesian's offer."

"To join the TDW?"

"To be a Wing captain," she barked.

"I can't be tied down. You know I have other plans."

Lindy closed her eyes and fell back against the wall of the cabin. "That again?" she mumbled. "We've worked on this project for more than a year. You can't quit now."

Jaws clenched, Jake raised his voice, "Didn't you hear me? I have plans."

She opened one eye and glared, ready—if only she had the super-power—to vaporize Moynihan's stubbornness on the spot. "We. Where, in perdition's name, is the we in that plan?"

"Go away."

"Go away? This dump has a bath, a bedroom, and a coffee pot. Where in the name of Christ am I supposed to go?"

Jake said, "You know what I mean."

Lindy paused for a moment as a picture of Jake's scheme materialized in her head: *Dig up Tom's bones and steal them away... God, that sounds crazy.* Frustrated by the bickering, Lindy reached across and touched Jake's shoulder, "I understand," she said, "and want to be a part of that, trust me."

"Then why all this bitching?"

"Look, crazy boy, I'm not asking you to give up your plans." She turned back, looked searchingly into Jake's eyes, and tried to nudge him gently to levelheadedness. "Just not now."

"Crazy or not, I made a promise."

She thought to herself, *Yeah, yeah, the fucking promise.* After that, Lindy clammed up, knowing that nothing more could be accomplished this morning.

By two pm, the entire d-Wing was on the move. It was an eighty-mile trip to the launching point at the Danube delta. Avoiding Romanian authorities was essential, so the convoy didn't use the main port, but a private facility at Tulcea, some five miles to the southeast. Tadesian had retained three commercial hydrofoils for the 90-minute trip to the coast. Each high-speed riverboat would have to make two round trips through the streamlets and channels, and then unload the airmen, munitions, and equipment to the cargo vessel waiting on tenterhooks offshore. They hoped to finish before nightfall.

At the same time, across the Black Sea and some 170 miles inland, Sam and Iza Mansour and Chira Beggs had just entered Kars Province in far eastern Turkey when it began sleeting. A spring storm had rendered many of the access roads to the city impassable. The first turnoff to Kars was closed, so Sam was forced to drive further south on the main highway, and then turn west to enter the city. Locating their hotel would now be more difficult. It had been many years since Chira had lived in the area, and she was familiar with only a few of the local landmarks. Chira said, "I know that… it's the Kars mosque." She was pointing to a domed building with a conical roof. "It was a museum when I was a kid, during Soviet times."

"Just one mosque?" Sam asked.

"There are several," Chira replied. "But that one used to be a Russian Orthodox church called the Church of the Holy Apostles. If you look closely at the exterior, there is a bas-relief of twelve men. The Alevi elders thought they must be the Twelve Apostles of Jesus."

Iza asked, "Why did it change hands?"

"Like everything here, when outsiders take over the city, they change things up," she explained. "An Armenian church it once was, then back to Russian, then a warehouse, then a school gymnasium, and so on. I suppose God gets confused about what we silly humans want."

Sam was more concerned about their destination than the city's landmarks. "Where's our hotel?"

"By the river. Look for the Castle on the hill, then keep going west." It wasn't a direct route; many streets were mud-packed quagmires, rendered impassable. Then they saw the Castle, high above the Kars. As they drove nearby, they were surprised to see an armed checkpoint, manned by guards, assault vehicles, and a thoroughly controlled entry gate. Further up the road, they recognized what looked like a military bivouac just below the walls of the Castle. It was the Turkish military. "That's odd," said Iza. "Why would the Turkish armed forces be stationed here in Kars? It's a nowhere town."

"Armenia," Chira said. "Something is up, and it can't be good."

"Now which way to the hotel?"

"Hotel Katerina, yes." Chira paused to remember the way, but it had been so long ago. "Keep heading west, I think. Look for the river."

Fifteen minutes later, the little band of travelers found their hotel, tucked between the river and Castle Hill. It was an old hotel – Russian panache with over-the-top gilded fixtures and furnishings, and thermal-insulated burgundy drapes. "Your rooms are on the upper floor," the clerk said. "Would you like some help with your luggage?" Iza nodded, and the woman motioned for the bellhop. She called him TJ.

"We're searching for a friend."

"Yes?"

"He was here a few months ago," she said, "hunting."

"Did he have a guide?" the clerk asked.

"Yes, I believe his name was Ali."

"Ali Tabak," the receptionist replied. "He doesn't live here, but in Sarikamis."

"How can we contact him?"

"I'm sure the desk at Katherina's Mansion would have his number. It is an hour away."

"Katherina's Mansion?"

"It's the ski resort and hunting lodge at Sarikamis."

Sam commented, "Everything here is named Katerina."

"Yes," the clerk replied, "after the Russian Czarina. She lived here, you know."

After a 60-hour voyage across the Black Sea, the cargo vessel carrying the Vartan Defense Wing arrived at Batumi in the early afternoon of March 9. It docked inland at a commercial port near the mouth of the Chorokhi River. A convoy of trucks was waiting as planned. That's where Jake Moynihan said goodbye to Lindy Bedrosian. "Once I secure my father's remains," he said, "I'll rejoin the VDW as soon as possible."

Lindy didn't believe him. "Stop lying, Jake. Just go back to Chicago and forget about us."

"I can't forget about you."

Lindy looked directly into his eyes and knew that this might be the end of their relationship. They hugged without affection, and then Jake picked up his duffel and left. Lindy watched him intently for a few minutes, a few tears welling up. But when he was out of sight, she caught her breath and turned to the obligations she had waiting in Armenia.

After a night's rest, Sam, Iza, and Chira left their hotel in search of Ali Tabak. Because Sarikamis was 1,000 feet higher than Kars, the road was still frozen, and traveling there was less complicated. Once they arrived at the resort, they quickly found the concierge, who knew the hunting guide. "I have his number. Would you like me to text him?"

Sam replied, "Yes. Please tell him we are looking for Rufet Qurb." A few minutes later, Ali replied: "No problem. Tell them to come to my cabin. Rufet is here with me."

Ali lived in a small house above the city. The simple pinewood cabin was first owned by his uncle, who raised him and a cousin there, but now he lived alone. His uncle was dead, as were his parents, and he had no siblings. The one luxury of Tabak Chalet was the magnificent view of Mt. Aladag; it was the highest peak in the district.

Ali made a living as what Americans would call, in an earlier century, a mountain man. He worked various jobs. In late fall and early winter, he guided hunters in the lower Caucasus. The Russians forever wanted to hunt wolves, brown bears, and the Caucasian lynx, but such species were rare nowadays, and the hunts often ended without seeing any game. Ali preferred to hunt the Ibex, and there were plenty of Europeans and Middle Easterners who sought a trophy for mounting at home.

In summers, Ali would guide birdwatchers in the Aras-Kura Valley wetlands. In recent years, he and one group of ringers and observers had identified a bird species new to the area, the raptor commonly known as the Little Banded Goshawk. When not hunting or guiding birders, Ali hired out as a scout for the Turkish army. To make such a living, Ali needed a keen sense of the territories, a knowledge of herbal remedies, and, of course, the skills of an expert marksman.

When the two university professors knocked on Ali's door, they didn't know what to expect but were delighted at the prospect of seeing Rufet again. "Mr. Tabak!" Iza shouted out. "It's the Mansours."

A moment later, Ali appeared. "Welcome," he said. "Come in. I've made tea." The interior of the cabin was a surprise. Each of the visitors expected to see a variety of taxidermy mounted on the walls, but there was none, just a few photos of Ali with friends. Everything was natural white pine, which was plentiful in the area. All the furnishings were simple, rustic, and were painted a pale blue, a nice compliment to the aged wood.

"Have a seat," said Ali. "I'll bring the pot." Ali was short, stocky, and sported a military buzz-cut. He was 28 years old, poised and affable.

Sam said, "Very kind of you, Ali, but we're anxious to see our old friend Rufet."

Ali was taken aback, "See Mr. Qurb?"

"Yes, he's been missing for months."

It took a moment, but Ali gradually understood, and his face fell. "When I said, 'Rufet's with me,' you thought..." He paused and heaved a sigh. "Let me show you. Come with me." Ali led Sam, Iza, and Chira into a bedroom at the back of the cabin. It was empty, but Sam recognized Rufet's old Weatherby rifle sitting next to the bed. Ali walked to the window that looked out toward the mountain and pointed. "He's there," he said. "I buried him next to the path that leads to the high ridge. See that pillar of stones? I thought I should mark his grave."

"Rufet's dead?" Iza asked in a whisper.

"He loved looking at Mt. Sarikamis," Ali replied. "He spent his time in this bedroom longing for one more hunt on the mountains."

Sam said, "No one knew what happened."

Chira recognized what to do next. It was the custom of the people of the region to convey the story of how a loved one died. "Tell us about it, Ali... tell us what happened, and how you saved him."

Ali nodded humbly and then escorted his guests back to the great room of the cabin. They sat down at the table, and Ali said, "I'll bring the tea now."

Once everyone had been served, Ali began: "Straightaway I knew Rufet Qurb to be a righteous man, a man of the mountains. I joined him in the lobby of the ski resort. He said, 'I want to hunt for an Ibex trophy; 50-inch horns, nothing less will do.' Rufet told me he had four days, and wanted to hunt alone as he did in his youth on Mount Sheki."

Sam said, "Rufet and his boss, Conor, had had a meeting with President Guliyev at Kars Castle."

"Yes, he told me about that. He told me many things about the Kedar Bey."

"So, you know that war is in the offing?" said Iza.

"Rufet had a strong sense that he was dying, and said he had vital information about the Kos family… that I needed to relay things about them and what was happening in Azerbaijan."

Chira interjected, "Finish your story first, Ali. We can talk about Bəla later."

Ali looked at Chira Beggs enigmatically, "You're Alevi, right?" She affirmed his reading. "A soothsayer?" Chira nodded again.

Ali continued the story of the rescue: "I was concerned about his age, the rugged terrain, and a snow squall that would soon blanket the region. But he was adamant: 'I'll take my satellite phone; I'll just call you in case of trouble,' he said.

"I didn't argue. The next day, I packed camping gear, bought provisions, and rented two good horses for the trip up-range. After several hours, I discovered what I thought to be an excellent location for hunting Ibex, on a rising slope just below the two ridges, the Torluu Ridge and the Korluk. It was late afternoon when I found a suitable spot for his base camp. It was level ground, so I dug a pit in case he wanted to start a fire. He was set. He had an old Weatherby rifle; bolt-action with a Swarovski scope. You saw it in the bedroom. Rufet knew what he was doing, and I was okay with that. 'Be back in three days,' Qurb said. I agreed, spiked out the tent, and then left.

"The following day, there was a sudden drop in the temperature, and on the Anatolian Plateau, that often means a storm. I became worried… that I couldn't get back to him on time, so I decided to head out in the morning. When I arrived at his camp at noon, I was a day early, and Rufet was missing. At first, I thought nothing of it. *He's on the hunt. I'll just wait until he returns.* But then I noticed the snow on the ground around his tent was undisturbed, and there were no warm ashes in the fire pit. I realized, *no one was in camp last night.* I had four or five hours before sunset, so I set out with both horses to track his movements.

"About 90 minutes later, I arrived at the grazing slopes where a large herd of Ibex was usually found. There was no snow there, and that was good news, so I searched up and down the range but found nothing, no clues. I dismounted, sat down, and reached for my canteen. Just as I began sitting, there was a flash of light that startled me. I thought it might be a signal. I reached for my binoculars and searched the area. It happened again, and I marked the location with my rangefinder. It was 100 yards or so below.

"When I arrived there, I quickly understood what was causing the flash of light. It was sunlight reflecting off the lens of the scope of Rufet's Weatherby. It had been abandoned on the ground. *What the hell?* I thought. *Qurb would never leave his rifle.* But he was nowhere in sight. That's when I noticed the loose shale on the precipice just above. It was dangerous, but I peeked over the edge and saw Rufet's body about 20 or 25 feet below."

Iza interrupted, "How in God's name did you rescue his body?"

"Let him finish, Iza."

"Good question," Ali replied. "I always carry a rope on my hunts, and I secured one end to my lead horse, then rappelled to the ledge below. Once I secured Rufet's body, I climbed back out and then walked the horse away until he was out of the crag. I had no notion whether he was alive or dead. Once I got back to the base camp, I carried Rufet inside the tent. He was alive… barely. He had two wounds, one in the chest and the other in the leg. The chest wound looked grave, but the ribs had stopped the bullet from penetrating any vital organs. It must have been a very long shot. It severed veins, and there was a lot of bleeding at first. The cold temperatures probably saved his life. The leg wound was much worse.

"When we returned to my cabin, I was able to nurse him back to reasonably good health. Rufet was mostly unconscious for the first two months. After that, he was bedridden, but we had many long conversations. They were mostly about hunting, but then he started telling me things he thought I should know and convey to the Kedar Bey. He made me promise I would do so.

"But then, last month, the skin around the leg wound began to change, first red, then bluish-gray, then rotting black, and there was numbness, swelling, and pain. Gangrene had set in. I cut out the dead tissue and finally had to remove his left leg entirely. I had a few antibiotics, but it wasn't enough to treat the infection long term. We were snowed in – six feet, maybe eight – so there was no way of getting more medicine. It was three weeks ago; Rufet, as usual, was sitting up in bed, watching the mountain. He didn't say anything, he just died. I felt rotten. After all my efforts, and his too, I could not save him."

Chira said, "I'm sure he was grateful, Ali. It was better than dying alone on that horrible crag."

"You did all you could," Iza added.

At that moment, Ali received a text message from TJ, his friend at the hotel: "Turks are looking for the foreigners who are staying at Hotel Katrina."

Ali looked up and said, "Not good news."

"What do you mean?" Sam asked.

"The Turk army is searching for you. I don't know why."

Chira was adamant, "I told you. Bəla is coming, and they don't want us interfering."

"You must leave," Ali said. "I know them. They will eliminate any threat in front of them."

"But how?" asked Iza. "We can't go back to Kars."

Ali said, "I'll take you. There is another way that the Turks don't know about."

Sam was glad he had rented the 4x4. The other way was slow and treacherous. Before they headed north, Ali sent a message to the concierge at Katherina's Mansion that he had taken a hunting gig, and would not be available for two weeks. He didn't know if the Turks would buy the ruse, but it gave them time to escape. Ali had plenty of provisions, of course, and thought they had enough gas to get to Ninots.

Twenty-four hours later, they arrived at Highway #11 and were heading east for the village of Ninots at the border. Ali knew that if he got his new friends past that village and into Georgia, they would be safe. When they arrived at Ninots, they stopped to top off their tank. Sam thought it would be enough gas to get them home. The attendant at the station asked if they had been detained by soldiers. "The Turks?" Ali asked.

"No," replied the man, "not Turks. They said they were Armenian… called themselves the Vartan Defense Wing."

"So they were heading for Yerevan?" Chira asked.

"No," the attendant replied. "They turned south. They said they were setting out for Kars to test their mettle."

27

Bone Thief

Whation. he told Lindy "I can't forget you," Jake was being deceitful. They had had too many fights, and he had grown tired of Lindy, disillusioned with her and the Armenian cause. The promise that Jake had held to so tightly for the past seven years could only be fulfilled in Azerbaijan, and he was determined to find his father's bones and return them home for a proper burial. Once he achieved that, he would turn to his cause – restoring America's patriotic past – and maybe even seek an office in the FAA. The decision had been a long time coming, and in the middle of the Black Sea crossing, Moynihan had settled on a course of action. He would leave the d-Wing after they reached Georgian shores, and then put Lindy Bedrosian out of his mind.

After a short walk along the Chorokhi River Port, Jake found himself outside the main gate at a transportation kiosk. He inquired about a taxi, and the clerk pointed to the stand 50 yards down the sidewalk. The ride to Batumi's Kartveli Airport was uneventful and took less than 30 minutes. After searching several local carriers for a flight to Tbilisi, he found one that would work, Ural Airlines #16, leaving in three hours. It was the best he could do. The good news was, he was already within Georgian borders and flying domestic, so there was no customs inspector to complicate his life.

The trip to the capital was short, only 40 minutes, and by eight pm he had cleared the TAV domestic terminal. But the next leg of the journey, he knew, would be complicated. Crossing the Georgia-Azerbaijan border would be tricky for the very American-looking Jake Moynihan. He was roughly a head taller than any Georgian man, with steely blue eyes and a broad Irish brow, so he would likely not pass for a national of any nearby Caucasian country. The best way to sidestep Azerbaijani customs, he decided, was to take the BTK Rail Line. There was an overnight train to Baku leaving at ten, so he booked private sleeper accommodation. It had a bed, a toilet, a snug bench seat with a pull-down table, and a wardrobe.

Jake assumed a generous bribe to train personnel would be enough to avoid any border entanglements. When he arrived at his compartment, he unzipped his duffel and removed a small, black-and-silver shoulder bag with a lock attached. It was perfectly sized to hold his Ruger 9mm and two magazines. Jake said to the conductor, "Would you place this bag in a secure locker, please?" and then handed the man a $50 bill. The man nodded, acknowledging Jake's intent.

His sleep didn't last long. At 11:30 pm, Jake was awakened as the train braked hard once, twice, and then slowed to a stop. Right away, he realized he had made a mistake; the train would not be an easy escape from the customs authorities on the frontier. After 15 minutes of waiting anxiously, Jake heard the officers enter his sleeping car. He had no plan now, only the hope that the conductor he bribed could somehow divert the Azeri inspectors.

When Moynihan opened the cabin door, he saw the border-enforcement officers approaching – two women and a man, all uniformed, all armed. One of the female officers approached and said indifferently, "Identification and passport." She inspected it against Jake's data and photo, then uttered, "Wait here for the inspector."

Afterward, she returned to the corridor and spoke with the male officer. As was his custom, the chief inspector took his time. He snatched the passport away, gave it a quick look, and then entered Jake's cabin. "Good evening, Mr. J. Monahan."

"It's Moynihan," Jake said calmly, then started to reach for his wallet. Making only the slightest movement, the conductor shook his head. Jake understood.

"My apologies, sir," said the inspector. "You're traveling to Azerbaijan?"

"A family trip. I have a brother in Baku. I haven't seen him in some time."

"Please step out of the cabin," the policeman ordered. Jake had no idea if this bumpkin had gotten word of the Vartan militia on the march or was just being a typical bureaucrat, but he followed the inspector into the hall. Glancing back tentatively, he could see the two female officers ransacking the interior of his quarters. He was reasonably sure they were looking for contraband: drugs, weapons, or illegal cash.

"Your bag, sir, will you please open it?" Jake obliged, unpacking the clothes, toiletries, a new iPod, and his tanker boots. After rummaging through everything, the inspector searched the duffel bag for hidden pockets or slots. "The boots," he intoned, "you are a military man, then?"

"Not really, officer," Jake replied. "I expect to do some hiking in the mountains while I'm here. I love hiking."

"Okay, Mr. Monahan. You may pack everything up."

"Moynihan," Jake insisted.

One of the others handed Moynihan a pen and a 5x8 card. "Please fill out this customs form." Once he had finished packing, Jake sat down at the desk to complete the form. For a second time, the woman checked the information card against his passport data. Afterward, she handed it back to Moynihan, saying, "Have a good trip." By 12:45 am, the border guards had left, and Jake was able to breathe again. Ten minutes later, the train was rumbling its way eastward.

Gobustan was the next-to-last station on the BTK route to Baku. Ordinarily, a transnational train wouldn't stop at such a tiny village, but Gobustan was on the Caspian seacoast just three miles west of the main dock, and that's where BP oil workers boarded commuter tugs to their off-shore rigs. The BP work-shifts were monthly, and the changeover always occurred on day eleven. Among the 40 or so young men who got on and off the train that Sunday in March, Jake Moynihan went unnoticed.

"Taxi, mister?"

Jake was taken aback by a stranger speaking English. "How'd you know I was…"

"British?"

"Yes, British," Jake smiled.

"I smart-assed man in village." Moynihan laughed at Mr. Malaprop, but the would-be taximan went on with his broken English, "All forengers in Gobustan is BP mans."

"Okay, okay," an amused Jake said, and then he asked, "You know where Georghe Markirov lives?"

"Of course, the Markirov Bey is my grandfather! I am Shahin. Twenty pounds and we go anywhere."

"Too much. I'll pay $5 US if you take me to the Markirov Bey."

It was a short ride. Ten minutes later they pulled up to the only two-story house in the village. Shahin got out and waved to Moynihan to follow. "Let's go." As he stepped through the front door, he shouted, "Ana, is Georghe Bey here? This man wants to see grandpa."

They had met only once before – at Tom's funeral. Nevertheless, during a long and leisurely lunch, Jake and Georghe Markirov reminisced about Tom's career fighting terrorists, and about the few weeks after the funeral when they all worked to clean up the cottage grounds and begin rebuilding the lodge. The American dutifully asked about Tali and Conor, and said he planned to see his brother in the coming days. "You just missed him," said Markirov. "He was here with Mira and others this past week."

Then Jake asked if he could visit his father's grave. "I'd like to see the cottage," he said, "maybe spend the night, if that would be all right?"

"Everyone is at the cottage this week," Shahin commented.

The Markirov Bey thought Jake's request odd, but could not deny a guest's request. "Yes, it would be okay. Shahin will take you there. It is already open. We must simply unlock the gate."

Shahin laughed, "Critters, you know."

"Shahin can stay the night if you like."

"Thanks, but no thanks. I'd like to be alone."

The cottage was nothing like he remembered years ago; at the time, it was a mess. The great Oriental plane tree that dominated the grounds had been struck by lightning and had fallen, entirely obliterating the dilapidated structure. The only thing uncluttered at the time was the garden. The workers had put out a few blooming azaleas to make it more presentable during the interment. Jake thought, *that's where they buried my father – in an*

unmarked grave. Standing at the kitchen window, Jake was looking directly at a spot in the far corner of the garden. It was different now, a beautifully manicured yard of azaleas.

What Jake also recalled was anger: a malevolent, concealed anger. He wanted revenge, then and now. Muslims had killed Tom Moynihan, director of a worldwide antiterrorism task force, and Muslims were entombing his American father in unholy ground. He'd felt impotent, isolated, and betrayed. His only friend then was Sam Mansour. He remembered Sam scooping up a handful of earth from the gravesite and then tossing it into the air, saying, "Praise the one who breaks the darkness." A swirl of wind caught the dust, and it blew upward and away, but not out of Jake's memory. Jake Moynihan had held that memory close to his heart for most of his adult years, and now he sensed that a settling of scores was at hand.

That's when Jake noticed a lightning storm offshore, and coming his way. The trees next to the garden caught his eye; they and the three-story cottage were the tallest structures in Gobustan District. If lightning were headed his way, the garden would be a dangerous place. It was now or never – if he were ever to discover his father's bones, he would have to do it pronto.

He found a shovel in the utility room next to the kitchen. It was not yet dark when Jake reached the garden, but he was immediately confronted with two problems: the absence of any kind of grave markers for either Zara or Tom, and a thick growth of flowers and shrubs everywhere. He took a chance and began digging at the place he guessed was the burial site. Jake knew there would be no coffin to uncover – Azeri Muslims traditionally buried their dead with a simple shroud – so he expected to find only bones, no flesh. Zara's remains were decades old and most likely irretrievable, but Tom had died less than eight years earlier, so his bones should be somewhat intact. After 30 minutes, however, he had uncovered nothing but dirt and roots.

As Jake sat down to rest, he heard the rumblings of thunder. Up to that point, it had been a clear day. *Still far away,* he thought. The bellows rolled on, becoming louder as darkness grew. The cracklings arose from the Caspian, so Jake turned to see what was coming his way. That's when he felt the cool breeze on his face. It was sweeping over and bumping into the warm earth of Gobustan Hill, and Jake recognized an abrupt atmospheric imbalance. *Something different about this storm,* he believed. *A lightning show will assuredly follow.*

The storm began as spider lightning – blinding shocks of whiteness zigzagging from cloud to cloud – flashing, cracking, hissing like a creature searching to escape. Jake thought he might have to stop digging and move inside. If it rained, there would be no retrieving the bones this night. He would just be dealing with a pool of mud.

But as the thunder grew raucous and the lightning more frequent, Jake became fascinated with the display. Now he could see white-hot bolts attacking the shoreline and then moving up the hill toward the cottage. Without intending to do so, he counted the seconds between the lightning and the thunder. *Closer,* he calculated. But then everything abruptly stopped, and there was stillness all around. It reminded him of the silence of the confessional and his lengthy chat with Father Wysocki, an ecclesiastical debate about the very act he was now committing. Jake thought it very weird.

That's when the ghosts became visible – fire ghosts.

The first appeared as a single flame of soft blue light at the apex of the chimney. It lingered there momentarily, divided in two, and then rolled along the peak of the roof in opposite directions. They stopped at the gables. *Lightning rods there,* Jake imagined.

He thought he heard sizzling and popping, and the distinct smell of sulfur as well, but he wasn't sure of any of it. *Thunder again?*

"That doesn't make any sense," he said aloud. After ten seconds, the flames disappeared, and the utter blackness was a shock. Jake couldn't find anything on which to focus. It was intensely pure, as if he had found another existence, a place without light. He felt something, but he could not see, only sense. Moynihan wondered wildly about what was happening.

Sprites playing with my mind, he thought.

Next, the fire ghosts emerged at the tiptops of the trees that framed the yard. Again, they lingered – two teardrop flames, growing ever larger. After a few seconds, they abruptly plummeted to the ground and exploded. A 1,000 delicate, dazzling blue lights lit up all the surfaces of the garden. It was overwhelming for the most part, but there was something out-of-place. Jake noticed an object a few feet away that did not naturally belong in a garden. He rose, walked over, and picked it up. That's when the blue, brilliant flames faded and disappeared, and the security lights came on. Jake could see once more.

As he brushed away the dirt, he recognized the object as a belt buckle, and it seemed to be familiar. When Jake scrapped away more of the debris, he uncovered the image of the Irish Harp, the traditional symbol of immortality. That's when it dawned on Jake. It was his father's belt buckle, an heirloom given to Tom's grandfather by the Ancient Order of Hibernians.

Jake was completely puzzled. *How could this buckle emerge from six feet underground?*

Shifting ground, of course; earthquakes, erosion, and earthworms; somehow, some way, over the years, the belt buckle had worked itself to the surface. It struck him like a clap of thunder. He'd been digging in the wrong place. Tom's grave was at his feet!

After that, it didn't take long to find the bones. Zara's and Tom's remains, like the belt buckle, had been on the move for years. But it was now impossible to tell any difference between the two sets. He conceded, *this is not going to work.* He wished he had done more thinking than digging.

But Jake kept tunneling through, and eventually, he discovered every gravedigger's prize: a large skull with an ample brow like that of many Irish men. He sat on the ground, brushed away the dirt of the years, and slowly but surely realized that he had found his long sought-after trophy: his father's bones. Holding it up toward the sky to measure the worth of the thing, he boasted, "What crown is this that I have come so far for?"

Jake Moynihan had always been a man of resolve. But this night, with its mysteries and surprises, had challenged his sense of order and control. So, he set aside his new trophy and then filled the holes he had made in the garden. He picked up the skull and went to the cottage. He sat down on the front stoop, his mind full of questions. But would there be any answers? *Only if someone writes a story about this*, he mused.

The night magic did not fool Jake Moynihan. He recognized the blue flames for what they were. His grandfather was Chicago's harbormaster, after all, and men of the sea relish telling stories of St. Elmo's Fire. On more than a few occasions, Jake had heard tales of the Pentecostal flames flitting about on topsails and masts. But the experience of it transcended his grandfather's telling of it. And Jake Moynihan knew that because it happened in this place and at this time, it was more than a coincidence.

A miracle, then? Not likely.

For Jake, religion had always been about ritual, not faith nor fanaticism. But he realized that he would now have to make some adjustments to his thinking. His world would not be the same. And as he sat on that cottage stoop in the middle of Azerbaijan, he finally understood that his brother was not his enemy. They had both suffered, deep wounds that were hard to shake off.

Then Jake glanced at the thing resting beside him. *Tomorrow*, he decided, *I will talk with Conor and test this animosity between us.*

28

Who Was He?
She Wondered

ied up, gagged, and blindfolded, Tali awoke from her drug-in-
duced stupor several hours later. Immediately, her head exploded
with a throbbing pain like nothing she'd ever experienced before.
Nausea and difficulty breathing followed. Clearly, she'd been sedated to
keep her still and compliant. She wondered, *How long?* The question only
made her head ache more, this time right behind her eyebrows. Her eyes
burned, and she wanted to claw at them unceasingly. She couldn't help herself, *where am I?* Her eyes longed for light, but there was only blackness,
shades mutating in bizarre colors and shapes. "Bastard!" she screamed, but
she knew that no one would respond.

Then she heard the sounds of engine and propeller – no, twin engines
– and realized she was in an airplane and shackled to a seat, probably a

window seat. It was hard to make sense of it all. Tali had no recollection of the order of events, just scenes of terrible violence. It slowly became clear, and then she remembered: the explosion at the maître d' stand, the terrifying sprint from Turga's, the wind welling up from the Bosporus, the blood splatter as Kazimov lay dying at the statue… and, most terrifying of all, her mother going down in a hail of bullets. *Dead?* She weighed, *but I can't know for sure!* Tali's head pulsed painfully.

Next, she picked up the sound of voices from the back of the plane. Oddly, it was reassuring. *I'm not dead.* Tali's hearing took over where her vision was stymied. She twisted her head upward, and pushed hard against the seatback, stretching out to understand what was being said. She recognized three voices, their cadence and pace rising and falling in an agitated conversation. One thing was for sure: *they were speaking Armenian.* But the shadow man who'd stood over her at the ambush site had spoken Azerbaijani. For the time being, Tali had no way to solve the puzzle.

Next, she tried to relax, hoping to restore rhythm to her breathing and to calm the pounding of her aching head. A few minutes later, she heard her kidnappers coming her way. She pinned her ears back, hoping to detect that Azeri voice, but it wasn't among these villains. Then she heard someone say, "We'll be landing soon." The sound was high-pitched, almost squeaky – a woman, perhaps. The voice had a distinctive mountain dialect. Tali had known such people. They lived along the Armenia-Azerbaijan border, and she would remember that.

"Time for another nap." It was someone different, a man's voice. What Tali couldn't see was the hypodermic syringe, half full of a milky green liquid that the person was holding. "Take off her sock. I inject her foot this time."

"Don't you dare!" Tali screamed through the suppressor in her mouth. She began squirming against their restraints, and when one of the men grabbed her foot, she kicked at him as hard as she could.

"Hold the bitch down."

Once she was subdued, the brutalizer inserted the needle into the fleshiness just under the nail of her big toe. "Be still, Tali Nadirov. We don't want to leave any scars for the boys, do we?" Then pushed the plunger down until it emptied. Because Tali was agitated and exhausted, the drug took effect instantly. She wouldn't reawaken for three hours.

"Serge, will Kos be at the lake hideout when we arrive?" asked the one with the squeaky voice.

"He said he wouldn't be there for at least a week."

"What does the man intend to do with this bitch?"

"Have his way with her," said the third kidnapper, laughing. "Take her flower, and then send her back to Kedar with a bastard child."

Day 3. It wasn't really the third day. There was no way of knowing if 72 hours had passed, but it was the third event in a blurry sequence that Tali used as a reference: the kidnapping, the plane ride, and now this – the prison where she was being held captive. It was a great room, of sorts. There was a dining table with six chairs, a study with dozens of books shelved in one corner, and a queen-size bed next to a massive potbellied stove. Understandably, someone had removed the living room furniture to make room for the bedroom set. There was an en suite bathroom at the far corner of the room, and next to that was the only door. Because it was an interior room, there were no windows, which was meant to keep the captive disoriented.

Upon returning from the bathroom the first time, the female jailer failed to immediately secure Tali's ankle bracelet to the 20-foot chain that kept her from escaping. Tali had tried twice to kick her way to freedom. The first was on the plane, and the second as they stripped her naked earlier in the day. As she was being restrained, Tali waited for the opportune moment, and then viciously kicked at one of the men. They all scuffled and went to the floor. One held her down while another handcuffed Tali to the large potbellied stove. Stubborn, she soon tried a third time. But the kidnappers had learned their lesson. They brought a billy club to the fight and slugged her repeatedly until she fell unconscious on the floor.

When Tali woke, she thought, *that was asinine. I need a different tactic.* She was naked except for panties, so she decided to appeal to her female captor. "What is your name?" she asked.

"Karun."

"Is this your home, Karun?"

"No questions, Nadirov," she barked. "I am your keeper, not your counselor."

"I am well aware of what you are," Tali replied. "My face has the bruises as proof. I just thought you might have a little kindness for a woman captive."

"The chain and padlock will remain."

"No, no," Tali said. "I know you must keep me shackled. I just wondered if I could have a robe. I'm cold, and… you know, embarrassed."

The next day (the fourth?), Karun brought a silk dressing gown for Tali to wear. It wasn't useful as a bathrobe, but it did cover her nakedness as she paced like a restless tiger in the cage that was her bedroom. Tali was pleased with her new approach, *It's a start.*

That night, Tali was slammed with nightmares about the attack at Turga's. Rayna was dead, she knew that, but what about her mother? She had witnessed Mira's collapse and her gaping hip wound. She had rushed back to help and had seen the pool of blood, but was Mother dead? The assassins had stopped firing. After that, there was a man speaking – a shadow in the darkness – he said, "They are all dead, Tali." He was lying, Tali knew. She had just heard Mira's cry for help. Others quickly came and injected her with a sleeping agent. But before she passed out, Tali remembered that voice of darkness saying, "Take her to the hideout. Make sure she cannot escape. I will return in a week." *Who was he?* she wondered.

I must find an escape, Tali thought. *Tomorrow!* So, to help alleviate her ever-present anxieties, Tali devised a course of physical and mental therapy. She wished she could swim her way to fitness, as she had as a young girl. But Karun wasn't going to let her swim in the nearby lake. So Tali worked out, hour after hour, day after day, on her muscles, stamina, and flexibility.

She became tougher and more determined as time passed.

29

Battle at Kars Castle

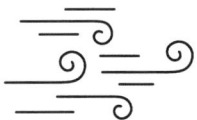

After Ali said goodbye to Sam, Iza, and Chris at Ninots, he hiked to Javak National Park and stayed the night. The next morning, he crossed the Georgia-Turkey border and then found the main highway. At that point, Ali had a choice to make: retrace the long way home or head south towards Kars. Ali decided on the southern route, not because it was faster, but because he was curious about this Vartan Defense Wing and the test it was planning.

Ali was lucky that afternoon. It was sunny, but the early March air was still crisp and excellent for hiking. A truck farmer picked him up after only 15 minutes. "My place is off the highway, just a few miles from the outskirts of Kars," he said. "I can drop you there."

"That would be great," Ali replied.

"Where are you going?"

"I live in Sarikamis. Ever come that way?"

"Only a few times a year."

It was a slow trip. The farmer's truck was shabby and probably on its last legs, but Ali was glad to have the ride. Home was still several hours away, and he thought he might have to stay at Kars for the night. When they reached the cutoff, Ali said, "If you're ever down my way, I'll buy you lunch." He thanked the man, waved, and then headed south once more.

It was getting cloudy, and he worried that it might snow, or worse, start raining again. He knew Kars was a muddy mess, and he hoped to find transportation as soon as possible. There was a bus service to Sarikamis, but Ali almost certainly would miss the last one scheduled that day. Worst case, he knew he could stay with TJ, a friend. TJ had an apartment on Takuu Street, just below Hotel Katarina, where he worked as a bellman.

Ali had been walking about two miles when he sensed change on the highland terrain. Stillness hung in the air. But it wasn't a calmness that brought relief; it was one that conveyed alarm. A small rise in the road ahead blocked his view, and the sight of scavenger birds circling overhead startled Ali. He jumped off the road instinctively, and, ducking low, began a steady trot down the embankment. When he popped up on the other side of the hill, he stopped. A Turk ZPT patrol car was sitting on the side of the road. Ali thought he recognized it as one of the scout vehicles he'd seen in the past. He couldn't be sure, however, and no soldiers were visible, so he proceeded cautiously. When he went around to the other side of the ZPT, Ali found three Turkish infantrymen on the ground – dead.

Beads of sweat dripped from the young man's brow, stinging his eyes and temporarily blinding him to the blood splatter, the splintered bones, and the missing left arms of Scout Team 2023. The clamor of the skirmish had died away, and all that remained were the empty eyes of the unburied. At that instant, Ali thought of the vultures above. His mouth felt parched and his tongue sour. The taste of bitterness filled his core. He knew these men.

Ali wondered if history would record such a minor clash of men. *Somewhere*, Ali thought, *a mother will weep, and a father will ask about his son.* Nevertheless, Ali gathered himself and searched the grounds nearby. The 2023 had been firing RPGs. Five or six spent powder boosters were evident, and two other RPGs were ready to be launched. He looked in the direction that the rockets had been fired and saw several plumes of smoke rising in the distance. Without a doubt, it was the Vartan Defense Wing convoy. They had parked their trucks, offloaded equipment and personnel, and had set up some sort of encampment.

Not more than three hours ago, Ali reckoned, *this Battle of Kars.*

Not wanting to be seen, Ali ducked low, found a vantage point, and then abruptly fell to the ground. He retrieved his binoculars, and in the prone position, began checking out the situation.

There had been five lightly armored 18-wheel transports, but three had been wholly destroyed by the RPGs. Further up the road, troops of the Vartan force were loading two X-65 Marauder drones and one Krunk-3 onto the undamaged carriers. Now Ali understood what wing meant in the name Vartan Defense Wing. They could call it anything they chose, but it was *not* a defensive force – it was a striker team, utilizing the latest drone technology.

They did a recon of the Turk's base camp with the Krunk-3, he said to himself, *then launched the Marauders.* He saw that there were no missile systems attached to the wings of the Marauders, only large carryalls on the belly of the X-65s. *They must have used militarized micro-drones for the attack.* The real damage would be at Kars Castle. The 2023 patrol just happened to have spotted the intruders and fought back.

Six hours earlier, the Vartan programmers had completed their work and were ready to fly their drones. The encoded target for the engagement was not man or machine, but the red insignia that all members of the Turkish Armed Forces wore on the left arm of their uniforms – al bayrak, the Crescent Moon and Star of the Turkish flag.

The battle at Kars Castle started with a speech. Tad Tadesian reminded his men they were sons of St. Vartan, and that the plateau upon which they now stood was formerly part of their Armenian homeland. "It is your sacred calling to take this land back from the Turks," he cried out, "and your duty starts today!"

The raid was intended to be something of a kamikaze mission, a bolt from the blue, and suicidal if need be. But Tadesian and the commanders wanted to degrade the Turk garrison, not destroy their arms and equipment. That was a central benefit of drone warfare – kill the men, keep the munitions. Tadesian, however, had no way of knowing if 20,000 swarm drones, equipped with high explosive ordnance, was enough to subdue the enemy. This would be their test.

At precisely 11 that morning, two X-65s lifted off the highway and flew directly toward the Castle. At the halfway point, the aperture of one carryall opened, and 10,000 Perdix drones fell out of the sky like a swarm of angry hornets on the hunt. Once they deployed, each drone was self-directed, programmed to find the encoded target and then explode. If the first drone didn't get the job done, a second would strike, and then others would follow until the kill had been completed. There were 20 Perdix drones for each Turk in uniform, and another X-65 Marauder waiting on the wing.

Ten minutes into the assault, Tadesian heard three loud explosions coming from the direction of the VDW encampment. He shouted, "Us or them?"

"Can't be us," Mike Bedrosian replied. "We don't have…"

Commander Davidian, who was also on the observer team, interrupted, "RPGs! The enemy is fighting back!"

"Commander, we're taking enemy fire at base camp." It was Tadesian's aide, JJ Frank, on the encrypted walkie-talkie.

"Who?"

"Don't know," JJ replied. "Turk patrols, I'm guessing."

"Send counterforces immediately," Tadesian ordered. "Must protect the convoy."

Gregir Davidian sneered caustically, and afterward said, "I told you they would fight back. This isn't a DC comic book."

"We've got to get back there!" Lindy screamed. No one objected. When they returned to the convoy, the firefight with the Turk patrol was over, but three of the five operational VDW Flights had been destroyed, and 40 men killed.

The first-timers in charge of the VDW had not bothered to think about Force Protection. Everywhere within the camp was a whirlwind of dust and disorder. The souls of the dead had long since renounced the scene, and the wounded were being loaded onto the trucks that were still intact. Because the forward observers had abandoned their positions, no one knew the damage the drone swarm had caused to the garrison at Kars Hill.

"It's over!" Tadesian shouted. "We're outta here!"

What was left of the convoy – the heavy vehicles at least – headed north on the main highway. They hoped to escape to Turkey, then flee to the east, to Armenia. The others, the commanders who had not been injured, headed directly across the Highland Plain to Ani. It was the closest point of entry to Armenia.

Ali Tabak watched the VDW convoy split up and then leave. He walked back to the ZPT to see if it was still functioning. It was riddled with bullet holes, but when Ali hit the starter, the engine purred. He took the patrol car and headed straight for TJ's apartment.

Fifteen minutes later, Ali found TJ outside his apartment on Takuu Street. He was helping two soldiers into an ambulance. "TJ!" he yelled.

When TJ saw Tabak, he waved, "Let's get inside."

Later, as TJ was making tea, Ali asked, "What has happened here?"

"I was walking back from the hotel when I heard a very strange sound."

"Something in the sky?"

"Yes. At first, I suspected it might be an ultralight or a model plane," TJ said. "But it didn't sound right, and there was no airplane in sight."

"Drones."

"Yes, drones… thousands of drones."

"Attack drones," Ali explained. "From an outfit calling itself the Vartan Defensive Wing."

"Armenians, then."

"Foreign fighters, I think. But definitely warriors for Armenia."

TJ continued: "The previous day, Turk lookouts had discovered the intruders, and the command had deployed a parameter defense at the base of Kars Hill, while others manned the parapets of the Castle, and the balance of the troops were scattered out along the roads of the city and the access points at the river."

"Those guys you helped into the ambulance, they were stationed on your street for security?"

"Right. Nice guys," TJ replied. "They said they didn't understand the threat. Said an attacking force against Kars Castle should be no less than three times the size of our 500-man contingent, and that the group coming down the highway was less than 100. They just didn't see the convoy as dangerous."

"But it was a grave danger."

"I watched the drones scatter and attack the men below the Castle. There were no detectable sounds of combat, only hundreds and hundreds of low-level flashes and arcs across the hillside. I didn't appreciate what was going on."

"It seems the drones were programmed to strike the insignia on their uniform."

TJ was amazed, "Yes! The soldier's left arm!"

"Al bayrak," said Ali, "the Crescent Moon and Star on the field of red."

"Most men had bullet-proof vests," said TJ. "But the drones sometimes came in twos and threes, and the men had no chance."

"How many dead?"

"I have no idea. About half of the garrison, I guess. There's more. Worse."

"More casualties?"

"Eight schoolkids were killed," the bellman said. "Some of the drones lost power and fell on a playground. The kids thought they were toys. The damn things exploded when they picked them up." There were other fatalities as well. All told, some 30 civilians had died that afternoon. The VDW's ideal technology and perfect military tactics weren't so flawless after all.

To Tad Tadesian, the drone strike seemed to have little risk and a big reward. When it was over, however, the battle of Kars Castle looked just like any other war to the experienced fighters of the Vartan Defense Wing.

30
The Brothers Moynihan

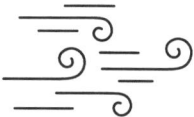

It was morning, half-past ten when the black limo pulled up to the parameter gate at the cottage on the hill. The driver entered the code and then proceeded to the parking area.

Jake was waiting. It was finally time. He picked up his duffel bag and carried it to the kitchen table. Next, he removed his black-and-silver shoulder bag, and then his Ruger 9mm and the two magazines of ARX bullets. The ARX rounds were unique, designed to inflict immense shock and tissue damage to fleshy targets. He shoved the automatic in his ankle holster under his right pant-leg and then hid a second magazine inside his waistline.

The priceless trophy that Jake had uncovered the night before, a half-rotted skull, was securely packaged in a container on the table. The shipping address was marked: Jake Moynihan, Port Authority, Chicago,

USA. *I'll send it priority UPS,* he thought, *and if all goes well, it will arrive about the same time I do.* Then Jake placed the box into his duffel bag. He was ready. He threw his duffel over his shoulder and left via the kitchen, locking the cottage as he departed.

"Moynihan," the driver shouted as he got out of the car, "over here!" It was Shahin, but he was in a different car, his grandfather's Mercedes Maybach S700. "The old man said, 'Take my car.' It has diplomatic plates, and no one questions or stops us."

"Are you expecting problems?" Jake asked.

"Troubled times. Don't know what to expect." Taking Jake's duffel, he opened the backseat door for Jake. Afterward, he tossed the bag into the trunk. Jake winced.

"How long's the trip?"

"Just 60 kilometers to the Zümrə Estates. That's where Kedar Bey lives," Shahin said, "about 60 minutes if traffic isn't backed up." Jake was leaving the cottage for the last time; or at least, that's what he thought. But a few minutes down the road, Jake recognized the place where he'd made his promise years before. "Stop here, Shahin, will ya?" There was no traffic, so it didn't matter whether Shahin pulled off the road or just came to a stop.

"What's a mistake, Mr. Jake… remember something?"

"This is where we stopped. Seymur was driving me to the airport."

"Seymur Rasuli?"

Jake stepped out of the car to gaze back at Gobustan Hill. He remembered the moment; it seemed so long ago. *The carpenters were working on the walls, and a truck was unloading the two saplings.* Jake looked intently at the now fully-grown trees. They stretched upwards against the sky and were as tall as the cottage. Jake was satisfied – he had fulfilled his promise to rescue his father's bones.

But he had also sworn to challenge his brother about Tom's death. He felt unsure of his next step. He knew little to nothing about Conor or his clan, or Muslims in general. Then there was the matter of Rufet Qurb and Seymur Rasuli. They were free, as best he knew, and their crimes had been forgotten. *Revenge*, he mused, *but how?*

"Yes, Rasuli. Do you know where he lives?"

Shahin Markirov glanced into the rearview mirror. He was uncertain of Jake's motives. "He's not a man you trust."

"But do you know where he lives?"

"Yes, near the Baku Shipyard," Shahin replied. "It's on the way."

"Take me there, Shahin," Jake demanded. "I'll pay you $50." Ten minutes later, they were on the main highway speeding towards the little town of Tanta, where the Baku Shipyard was located on the Caspian Sea.

When Georghe Markirov called Conor earlier that morning, he told his nephew that Shahin would be dropping off Jake no later than 12:30. "Shahin can pick up Mira and Tali if you like," the old man said.

"I've already sent David to the airport, but thanks anyway." Actually, Conor had no idea when Tali and Mira would arrive. They had said they'd be home sometime Sunday. If they decided to go shopping, David might have a long wait. It had happened before.

"Parliament opens this afternoon, right?"

"Yes, six pm."

"I'll text Shahin and tell him to stick around," Markirov said. "Besides, he would rather be in Baku than here in Gobustan."

"That sounds fine. Shahin can hang out here or at the Bay Club."

It was early afternoon when Sam Mansour sent a confidential text to Conor: "Arrved Tbilisi this PM. Got out of Kars jst in time."

Conor replied: "Just in time???"

"Spotted foreign fighters headed to Armenia. Ali says something's up."

"Who is Ali?"

"Ali Tabak. Rufet's hunting guide last autumn."

Conor explained:" I met Tali for holiday in Istanbul, Rufet stayed behind in Kars."

There was a long pause at Sam's end, then: "I have bad news… no easy way to say this. Rufet Qurb is dead."

Conor closed his eyes. It was not surprising, though he had not allowed the notion of Rufet's death to enter his mind until that very moment. He then asked the critical question: "How?"

Sam: "Assassination!"

"Assassination?" Conor was puzzled. "Why?"

The Bey of House Kedar had much to think about, but his two life-long counselors were not on hand to help. *Maybe that was it*, Conor guessed, *to isolate me from Mira and Rufet*. Now he hoped Mira would be home soon. Conor replied: "You know this how?"

"Two bullet wounds found – .30 caliber cartridges. Ali alleges from a Dragunov sniper rifle."

"Where?"

"Hunting on the mountain. Ali fond Rufet alive, but in bad shape… nursed him back, but he died 2-3 weeks ago in Kars. Buried there."

"Does he know who did it?"

"Ali thinks it was House Kos. During his short recovery, Rufet revealed many secrets about the Dark Triad, their motives, their plans, and their hideaways."

"Bastards," Conor typed. "Sam, FYI, Jake is here, says he wants to talk."

"About what?"

"Don't know, exactly."

"Be careful, Conor. Could be trouble. I'll call you soon… after we're settled in."

Then Conor relayed the good news: "Tali's coming home today, or maybe tomorrow. We'll be at the Zümrə residence for the next few days. Call anytime."

"Will do. Much to discuss."

Conor felt he needed something to settle his nerves, so he walked to the kitchen to make tea. But as he was filling the pot with water, he was startled. Outside his garden apartment window, he was bowled over by the sight of thousands of dark red flower petals swirling across the yard. He didn't understand, so he stepped through the connecting door into the sunroom. At once, he faced a stout wind blowing away the entire season of delicate puffs of the Persian ironwood trees.

There was a sound to it, a whirling swish. In Azerbaijan, from childhood onward, most residents develop a keen eye and a natural concern about the arrival of such winds. When the Khazri reaches 90 mph, not only can it destroy hearth and home, but it also can peel off skin or blind a person if coarse desert sands are part of its fury. The high-pitched howl is a warning to all: take shelter now.

For Conor, the untamed winds had always been an obsession, particularly the strange whirrs and shrieks they made. There was something profoundly moving about the sound of Oriental hornbeams in the wind, or the whistling hullabaloo of jingling stones on the desert uplift, or the soft sighs of Gilavar as summer overcame the wild moods of winter.

Suddenly, Conor heard a limb breaking. His eyes darted upward to the high boughs of the Cappadocian maples. They were swaying and rolling in uneven circles, the big branches moaning and cracking. Then his attention turned to the boat dock. He could see the Zarifa rocking up and down in the choppy waters.

Got to move her inside, he decided. So, he stepped outside, went around the corner, and raced to the caretaker's apartment. Conor banged on the door, but there was no answer. *He's out, cleaning up after last night's storm*, he thought. Now what? *Got to do it yourself, city boy*.

As he reached the dock, the side gusts had turned into a steady blow. Just getting aboard the pitching and bucking cruiser would be difficult. He decided to jump the gap and catch part of the rigging, hoping not to break a leg in the process. It worked, but not without injury. When he sprang across, he missed the first hold and scraped his hand and wrist against a cable. It left a raw ten-inch abrasion on his wrist, something like a rope burn. For the moment, however, the adrenalin rush was enough to mask the pain.

Next, he scrambled up the ladder to the pilothouse and started the engine. It roared to life, as angry as the surrounding sea. After he cast off the lines, Conor eased the Zarifa away from the dock and into the Caspian. The boathouse was only 20 feet away, but he'd forgotten to open the automatic roll-up door. *Stupid!* He cursed himself, *back to the pier*. But the sea had a different idea. Without warning, the wind shifted and pulled the cruiser out to deeper water. Off the shoreline, an outcropping of massive barrier rocks loomed. The choppiness made the boat hard to control, and because Conor still had the gear in reverse when he gunned the engine, the Zarifa crashed into one unusually large boulder. "Goddammit!" he cursed. He struggled to get the driveshaft into the right gear, and a moment later, found forward and cleared the rock field. But the cruiser had already begun taking on water.

"Kedar Bey, Kedar Bey!" screamed a man on the dock. It was John, the caretaker. He had already raised the sea access and was motioning for Conor to bring the Zarifa into the boathouse. Ten minutes later, the men had engaged the hydraulic hoists, and the cruiser was safe but badly in need of repair.

"Glad you spotted me. I was just about to lose her."

"It was the damn winds, Kedar Bey, not your fault."

"The squalls are always after me," Conor mused. "It wasn't the winds, John, but my own stupidity."

"You go back to the residence. I'll close up and make everything safe and sound." Conor nodded in agreement.

But before he started back, he turned to face the sea again. The winds howled, and Conor thought, *you old devil.* His cheekiness lasted only a second. He was exhausted, so turned away and headed for home. "John, I will need you in about an hour. Come to the apartment when you are finished." The caretaker shook his head, okay.

Ninety minutes later, John drove up to Conor's apartment, parked the car, and waited. It was late afternoon, and the Kedar Bey could no longer put off his departure for the opening of Parliament. Conor got in and slammed the car door behind, then the caretaker asked, "Government House, sir?"

"Right," Conor replied. "I will need you tonight, John."

"No problem, sir, I'm free all evening."

"My brother will arrive here sometime soon, but I'm not sure exactly when. Shahin Markirov is bringing him in from Gobustan."

"Understood."

"When he gets here, I want you to bring him directly to the Milli Majlis Assembly Hall. He doesn't speak Azeri, and you will need to help him to get through security."

"How will I recognize him?"

"The eyes, John, cerulean blue like mine. He's American, tall, broad shoulders, about 220 pounds."

"And he'll be with Shahin."

"That's right." Conor reached over the front seat and handed John a ticket. "This is his seat in the front row," he added. "It's right next to the podium. Make sure he finds it."

"Understood."

Vanya Kos, the newly installed Azeri Minister of Oil, walked into the Assembly Hall with a stranger. Obviously, a guest, he seemed quite elderly, and moved totteringly, using a cane. Vanya explained, "This is where members of our Parliament meet on opening day."

The portly visitor peered over his old-fashioned Roosevelt glasses, and asked, "Will your father be seated with the President?" It was a curious question.

"The Vice President is the acting head of the Milli Majlis, and therefore sits with the members on the other side with the assembly." The two men passed the security guards at the base of the stage. An officer approached to ask for IDs, but Kos waved him off and began helping the older man up the three steps to the platform.

"Good," the man replied. "And you?"

"I will be seated with the other ministers two rows behind the President. The row directly behind Guliyev is reserved for his guests and special dignitaries."

"And where will I be seated?"

"Directly behind me, in the honored visitors' section."

At room temperature, polonium-210 is solid silver metal, and one of the most lethal materials known in the world of assassins. Oddly, it isn't hazardous to transport, because any thin barrier can easily impede its high-energy radiation; even 24-pound paper will do. Furthermore, it is almost impossible to detect, because only a microgram is required to kill a man. These are valuable advantages for any would-be poisoner to have.

Delivering a fatal body blow with Po-210, however, isn't so easy. The poison must be introduced to the victim's body by inhalation, ingestion, or through a skin abrasion or puncture wound. Because the killer must get close to the victim, the assassin must also be a crafty stalker or must employ some ruse that would make the killing event seem normal.

After Vanya's guest had been seated with other guests, one of the aides came by and asked, "May I take your cane, sir?" The young woman was reaching for it as she spoke.

"Don't touch it!" the fellow reacted, snatching it back quickly.

Vanya looked at the young woman, "He may need it later. He's an old man; you know, to go to the bathroom."

At that split second, Vanya glanced over the aide's shoulder and saw the Kedar Bey approaching. Kos extended his hand, "My friend, Azreal." Conor's eyes turned steely cold as he passed. Then he noticed the chubby man seated at the end of the row. He looked familiar. The round, black-framed glasses struck a chord, but nothing came to mind in that instant. Conor walked to his seat behind the President. Still curious, a few minutes later, he twisted around to eyeball Kos's guest one more time. *Yes*, he recalled, *At Kazimov's party in London. Jake pointed him out*, and then Conor wondered, *What business does that man have here tonight?*

Shahin and Jake arrived at the Zümrə residence at precisely 5:35 pm. John was waiting as instructed. "Markirov," he said, "the Kedar Bey has asked me to take Mr. Moynihan directly to Government House."

"Why not me?"

"I have his ticket," the caretaker replied, "and the Kedar Bey's instructions."

"I will take him!" Shahin demanded. "I have régime clearance and can get right through the security gate."

John didn't argue. "Yes, Mr. Markirov." He was just a caretaker, and Shahin was family.

"You stay here and wait for Tali and Mira," Shahin said. "Bring them to Milli Majlis if they arrive in time. Otherwise, get the apartment ready. They will be tired, and maybe want something to eat. "

Disguised as maintenance staff, two men approached the entrance to the catwalk above the Assembly Hall. They carried a replacement light fixture and a bag of tools. A single security guard, patrolling the mezzanine hallway there, stopped them at the door. "Just where do you think you're going?" he demanded.

"The president's spotlight has failed," the taller man said. "We have instructions to replace it." Then he showed the officer the work order.

The military guard called his supervisor and got the go-ahead. "Okay," he said, "but you must finish before Guliyev comes on stage." Both men nodded and then proceeded to the access. The officer clicked on his walkie-talkie and reported, "They said it should be a simple repair and be done in five minutes, over and out." After the access door closed, the shorter of the men reached over a large girder and found a hidden case of armaments. Two minutes later, one of the repairmen walked up to the spotlight operator stationed 30 feet above the main floor, "My friend has hurt himself, can you help me?" They walked the catwalk back out of sight, and that's when the operator felt a pistol pushed against his kidneys.

"Take off your shirt," the man demanded. They exchanged shirts and caps, and then the second man said, "If you want to live, do as you are told." The spotlight operator was entirely compliant. Three minutes later, two repairmen left the catwalk. "We're done," said the same tall man as he turned to the security officer.

"All clear up here," the officer messaged his supervisor.

Shahin and Jake entered the floor of Parliament at 5:55 pm. After finding Jake's seat, Shahin caught Conor's attention and signaled that Jake had arrived. Conor acknowledged Shahin and then sent a thumbs-up to his brother. Shahin said, "I cannot sit with you, Jake, but I'll be in the hallway during Guliyev's address."

"Thanks, Shahin."

"I'll find you and Conor after it's over."

As was his practice, before he sat down Jake surveyed his surroundings for any tactical vulnerabilities. He was seated at the corner of the stage and had a perfect view of the presidential podium. Two armed guards were stationed up front, but no others were nearby. There were four entrances, and each was secured by military police. The ground level was secure.

Next, he looked up at the mezzanine level. There were guards posted at the entrances there as well. Lastly, Jake checked the ceiling and noticed a lighting grid, but saw that no one was manning the center spot. Jake thought that odd because he recognized it to be the president's spotlight. But at that instant, Guliyev entered the hall from the back of the stage, and the entire assemblage stood up and offered a warm reception for the man of the hour. He walked forward, shaking hands and smiling. Everything seemed routine, but in the back of his mind, Jake's sixth sense hung on the spotlight operator who was absent from his post.

When the Azeri president passed Conor, Jake's eyes lingered on his brother, impressed. *He has position and respect here in Azerbaijan*, he thought. But Jake also worried about how their meeting would go. *Will it be a repeat of London?* Naturally, Jake's studied the others seated next to his brother. Nothing unusual. But when he explored the honored visitor's section behind Conor, he noticed an old man sitting two rows back who looked familiar, but somehow different. Then he saw the cane, and Jake knew it was the vile character that he and Lindy had encountered in London – the one they'd called Old Man Chubby. Jake was shaken to the core, and instantly suspicious. *What's he doing here?* He intuitively glanced upward to the lighting grid, to the vulnerability there. A lurking figure was now in position. He had focused the spotlight on the podium and was stepping away and reaching for something that had been placed on the grid.

The Dark Triad's plan for seizing the Azerbaijani government depended upon simultaneous attacks in Istanbul and Baku. Four opposition Houses would be eliminated in a single evening: the Guliyevs, the Kedars, the Nadirovs, and the Kazimovs. Once Guliyev was dead, VP Viktor Kos would immediately take over as head of the Azeri government.

As always happens, such plans are often tossed to the wind as events unfold. The assassination of Mira Nadirov and Alexandr Kazimov at Turga's had occurred 90 minutes too early, so the assault on Rolan Guliyev and Azreal Kedar at Government House required fast action before anyone got word of what had happened in Istanbul. Consequently, the killers in Baku were forced to strike faster than they had planned.

President Guliyev had already shuffled up to the microphone and had pulled his speech from his inside jacket pocket. The assassin on the catwalk crouched low to pick up the thing he'd left on the grid – it was a high-powered rifle. Jake recognized the situation. "Assassin!" he cried out, pointing upward to the catwalk and the man in shooting position.

The guards next to the presidential podium reacted instantly. They followed Jake's hand pointing upward, saw the man with the rifle, and fired. The assassin hadn't been able to aim his weapon accurately, but he returned fire, though it was entirely unfocused. Every eye in the Assembly Hall fixated on the catwalk as the assassin was hit several times, and then tumbled off the grid and into the air. In the same moment, Guliyev's bodyguards rushed onto the stage to pull the president out of harm's way. They began by shielding him from the shooter above and pushing him toward the rear stage exit.

That's when Old Man Chubby stepped forward. He was the second assassin, meant for Conor, but would now have to take out the president. He jumped in front of Rolan Guliyev as the president came his way, his cane thrusting out like a sword at Guliyev's chest.

Jake shouted at Conor, "Baol, baol!"

Only another Irishman would know the Gaelic word for danger. Seeing Old Man Chubby advancing on the president, Conor understood the menace at once. He rushed between Guliyev and the would-be hit man wielding the polonium-tipped cane.

Chubby – no longer aged and infirmed, but quick and agile – lunged forward. But Conor was faster. He grabbed the cane with his right hand and spun Old Man Chubby around directly in front of Jake.

The sudden plunge into nonstop action was something Jake had prepared for these past months in Romania. His mind, and more importantly his physical reaction, was swift and precise. Jake's breathing drew out long, and his heart rate steadied – everything before him was taking place in slow motion – then Jake pulled the Ruger 9mm from his ankle holster.

When Conor forced the assassin to twist around, presenting his full torso, he was an easy target. Jake fired three times, the first striking the man's shoulder. The bullet shattered the assassin's arm and forced the release of the weapon. The second and third tore into Old Man Chubby's torso, and the stopping power of the ARX rounds put him out of action instantly. The firefight ended abruptly when the assassin tumbled off the stage.

Conor was relieved. Both he and the president were unharmed. At least, that's what he thought as he watched as the guards wrestled Old Man Chubby to the floor below. But then he stared at the cane, realizing it was likely the delivery method for some kind of poison. It appeared that the release mechanism at the tip had been activated. Conor tossed the cane to the floor, and then looked at his hands for a puncture wound. Nothing – God be praised. Then he realized that the abrasion he'd suffered on the Zarifa earlier in the day had been exposed. But now was not the time for worry as the crowd surrounding the president began cheering wildly for the brothers Moynihan. "The Kedar Bey has saved the president!" a man shouted.

Pointing at Jake, Rolan Guliyev responded immediately. "Who is that man, Azreal?"

"My brother."

"Have him come to my house," Rolan commanded. "We will celebrate, and then find the culprit behind this murderous plot!"

But Conor was unable to respond. Out of the blue, he felt dizzy and nauseated. He lost his balance, crumpled to the floor, and then began shaking uncontrollably. Guliyev shouted, "Get medics, now!"

Shahin, who had rushed from the hallway, grabbed Jake's arm, and said, "Let's get out of here!"

"Not until Conor is safely in an ambulance." The medics had arrived and saw the convulsions. They quickly cleared Conor's mouth, but vomit began spewing from the edges. Within a minute, Conor had lapsed into a coma.

"Where will you take him?" Jake asked.

"Central Clinic is only ten minutes away," the medic replied.

"I know it," Shahin said. "It's on Parliament Prospekti, good care."

"Follow the ambulance, Shahin. I don't want to lose him." They watched intently as the paramedics wheeled Conor out of the Assembly Hall.

Central Clinic had a reputation for providing healthcare to special persons – ranking military officers, government officials, and foreign diplomats. It was the best Azerbaijan had to offer. But as the men neared the hospital, Jake recognized it as the same hospital where his father had been treated, the same hospital where Tom Moynihan had suddenly died seven years earlier.

Jake's face paled, and this time he was unable to control the panic that flooded his soul.

31

Return to London

Conor had been in the isolation ward for more than an hour when Georghe Markirov showed up at the Central Clinic. "The Kedar Bey?" He asked the receptionist.

"Isolation ward," she pointed down the corridor, "first wing on the right."

Georghe found Jake and Shahin standing alone at the nurse's station. "What the hell has happened?"

"Terrorist attack," Shahin replied. "Two heroes – Conor saved the president's life, and Jake killed the assassin." Jake said nothing, his face expressionless.

"And Conor?"

"Just collapsed a minute later," said Shahin, "and started throwing up."

President Guliyev, with his entourage in tow, arrived ten minutes later and demanded that he see the head of emergency care immediately. The receptionist gathered everyone together and herded all into a small conference room next to emergency care.

When Dr. Yusif Hasanov entered a few minutes later, Guliyev insisted on an explanation.

"What the hell has happened?"

"It's a nerve agent," said the doctor. "We think VX, ricin, or maybe even Po-210. We don't know for sure."

"Don't know? You're supposed to be the expert."

"It's not that easy Mr. President," Hasanov tried to deflect the President's fury.

Jake intervened, "I know about VX and ricin, but what is Po-210?"

"Polonium, a rare and extremely radioactive metal," the doctor replied. "It was probably the element that killed Marie Curie. You know, the scientist."

"How do you treat the poison?" Markirov asked.

"We can give him supportive care. But without knowing what exactly has caused Azreal's condition…"

"Supportive care?"

"Helping Azreal breathe, giving him intravenous fluids, flushing the stomach… things like that," Hasanov said.

"This is life-threatening, then?" Guliyev bellowed.

"We don't know for sure."

"Don't know much, do you, Hasanov?" Shahin yelled. "Bull shit!"

The president turned to Georghe, and asked, "What would you have us do, Markirov Bey?"

"If Mira were here, or Tali," Georghe mused. "We could…"

"Where are they?" Jake asked.

"Returning from Istanbul," said Shahin.

Rolan explained, "Tali was my delegate at the Asian conference."

"They should have returned by now. Something's wrong."

"Could be a coordinated attack," General Aslan suggested.

"Without Mira and Tali here," Markirov stated, "the decision falls to Jake."

"What about Rufet?"

"Rufet is dead, Mr. President," replied the Markirov Bey. Jake was startled by the comment but said nothing for the moment.

"Hasanov, where is the best treatment center for such poisons?"

"London, Mr. President. University College Hospital, they have treated numerous similar cases."

Jake agreed, "Alexander Litvinenko, for example." *Get Conor out of this damn hospital, out of this damn country*, that's what Jake thought and wanted to hear.

"Then it is off to London if that's your decision, Jake." The President glanced at his military attaché.

"We can have a plane ready in one hour."

At eight the next morning, the Lear 65, with Conor, Jake, Shahin, Georghe Markirov, and the airborne medical staff onboard, was less than three hours from London. President Guliyev had ordered a medically configured aircraft from MedAsiaEvac. The Lear 65 had a max cruise speed of 520 mph and range up to 2,113 km, so it had to refuel in Istanbul. They now had another 1900 km before reaching England so the jet would be landing on fumes when it arrived at London City Airport.

"You said Rufet Qurb was dead," Jake asked, "how do you know this?"

"Conor received a message from Sam."

"Sam Mansour?"

"Yes," replied Georghe. "Sam found Qurb in Turkey. He said he was assassinated."

Jake reacted callously, "Good, it will save me the trouble."

Georghe Markirov, who had known Qurb for more than 30 years, was taken aback by young Moynihan's crudeness, "You are wrong about Rufet," he said. "He saved Conor's life more than once, and your father's life as well."

"Not the way I saw it seven years ago," Jake insisted. "He and that damned Seymur Rasuli were part of the plot."

"Rasuli is a different matter," Georghe insisted. "That one has always worked for the clan or gang that paid him the most."

"I visited him today," Jake said, "not worth killing. He's crippled and confined to a wheelchair."

"A gunfight with Chechnyan henchmen last year. I know of your visit, Jake. Shahin told me."

"Did he also tell you that I dug up my father's bones? I found the skull."

"Of course, he told me," Georghe said. "Desecration, Jake. Why do you so shame the dead?"

"I plan to give my father a Christian burial, Markirov."

"Will you shame your brother at the same time?"

"Don't know him that well."

"It is a betrayal of family, whether you know them or not."

Jake was startled by the Markirov attack. Unfazed, Jake followed on, "You sound like an American politician. Treason is their preferred policy."

"No House can endure treachery from within," Markirov declared. "That is the greatest message of last night's attack."

"You know the culprit, then?"

"The villain from within moves freely, his hand close to the seat of power, encouraged by a gathering of miscreants and ambitious fools."

"Then only a purge will do," Jake concluded.

"Better we face the Armenians. We can survive the enemy outside the gate, but not the man with the sly tongue and vile purpose," said Georghe Markirov. "The infection within is the Dark Triad, and it has made its move. But thanks to you, Jake, it has failed."

"What will Guliyev do?"

"General Aslan watches everything. He took notice of the assassin with Vanya Kos last night. The attack on Guliyev was supposed to be subtle – just a pinprick, no one would suspect an old man – but he botched the job."

"My brother would say otherwise."

"Guliyev will have his revenge. If Vanya has survived the night, he will face Aslan's men and their enhanced interrogation in the coming days."

At that moment, the nurse entered the cabin, "The Kedar Bey is awake." Georghe and Jake dashed for the nursing station at the front of the Lear 65.

"Conor," Markirov said. "Awake at last." The medical cabin was filled with equipment, so it was a tight fit for the men, besides the doctor and nurse.

"Dr. Hasanov tells me we are traveling to London." Conor's normally healthy, suntanned cheeks had turned pale, his eyes swollen, and crusty splotches of dried blood were evident inside his nose. The nurse was swabbing away the scabs and moistening his lips as he spoke. "I don't remember what happened, just hearing gunshots."

Dr. Hasanov intervened, "Not too much detail, we've got to keep him calm."

"Assassins tried to kill Guliyev," said Markirov. "But you and Jake stopped them."

"I want to talk to Jake alone. Everyone out." Before Dr. Hasanov left, he advised Jake to make it short. They had to monitor his vitals and make sure his liver and kidneys were functioning properly. Jake understood.

"They're gone," he said as he pulled up a chair next to Conor's bed.

"Look, Jake, Hasanov says I have all the symptoms of radiation poisoning."

"Yeah, he mentioned Polonium-210. Bad stuff that."

"Did Tali get back from Istanbul okay?"

"Don't know for sure. We left ASAP. But I expect she's back by now. Your driver guy…"

"David."

"Yeah, David. He was waiting at the airport," said Jake. "As soon as we land, I'll check on it, and let you know."

"Thanks, Jake… I love her you know."

"I get that."

"Dr. Hasanov says this poisoning could be bad, really bad." Conor was having breathing difficulties, so he had to speak in spurts. "He said it's fatal in most cases, even with the best of care."

"But that's why we're heading to London. They'll pull you through. It's not like that goddamn hospital in Baku."

Suddenly, Conor realized what was on Jake's mind. "I know what you're thinking. That's where father died. I've always felt guilty about it; should have gotten him to a better place for better care."

"What do you mean, you felt guilty?"

"I was absent when I was needed most," Conor replied. "I was in the wilderness, confronting my Uncle Elshan. You didn't know him. He hated Tom Moynihan fiercely. Tom chased him down, arrested him, and then sent him off to prison."

"So, it was the Kedar family that killed father."

"It was Elshan, not the family," Conor choked out the confession. "I killed Elshan for what he did to Tom and my mother.

"You killed the head of your House?"

"Actually, it was Rufet Qurb that wielded the knife. He had always loved Zarifa, and was happy to end the evil man's life on my behalf."

At that moment, the nurse interrupted again, "Mr. Moynihan, we have got to check his vital signs."

"Not now," Conor yelled. "I will let you know when I want you."

"You have to forget that episode, Jake. It's water under the bridge." Then Conor changed the subject. "As I said, I may not survive this. The doctor says there may be bone marrow loss, DNA problems, immune deficiencies, organ damage; all kinds of bad things."

"You are not going to…"

"Listen, Jake. I need your help."

"Okay, I'm listening."

"You must take care of Tali."

It was the last thing Jake expected, "Doesn't seem like she needs my help."

"Well, not in the Western sense. But in Azerbaijan, it is different. A woman cannot lead the clan."

"We are from two different worlds," Jake said.

"Muslim men are permitted to marry four wives. But it doesn't happen very often these days. One or two are always marriages of convenience. Even I may have to marry for political reasons, one day."

Starting to feel differently, Jake smiled at his brother. "In case you haven't noticed, I'm not Muslim."

"Neither was our father, but Tom loved Zara, and he married her."

"You're asking me to marry Tali?"

"Yes, marry her if need be," Conor implored. "It will give her the status she needs. She will do the rest. She has the ear of President Guliyev."

"I am not going to marry your cousin, your girlfriend, your lover."

"Why not?" Conor asked. Jake had no concept of Shia sensibilities or Azeri cultural norms. He thought of Lindy, and what she might say to such a proposal. It was an explosive idea. "You have to promise me, Jake. It's the only thing I ask of you."

"I promise to ensure Tali's safety and good health."

"Will you keep your word, even if I am dead?"

"I always keep my word, Mr. Kedar Bey."

"I can rest easy then."

Wanting desperately to move on, Jake changed the topic, "I was at the cottage earlier."

"Yes?"

"I found father's grave. I was never happy with leaving him here. I was angry with you and your family."

"I know."

"I promised myself that I would one day give Thomas Moynihan a Christian burial."

"I expected something like that."

Jake went on, "I found his bones, a skull actually. I have long planned to take something of him back to the States."

"Yes?"

"Steal it from the earth, you might say."

"Yes, I understand."

"You don't object?"

"I object, Jake, but…" Conor sighed, and then he offered a compromise, "Take the head, but leave his heart here, in Azerbaijan, with me."

Those were the last words Conor would utter that day, and for many days to come. He began convulsing; his eyes falling back under his lids, his legs stiffening, his hands trembling. Jake rushed to the door and shouted, "He's having a seizure."

A half-hour later, Jake was sitting in the passenger cabin when he looked outside and noticed the lights of a large city below. Then the plane suddenly fell out of the sky, causing Georghe, Shahin, and Jake to feel something of a panic. Conor would have laughed, and told them, "It is only the circus plunge to LCA runway." But he could not tell them anything. Dr. Hasanov had determined that a medically induced coma was required if they were to save the Kedar Bey's life.

The next morning, Jake, Georghe, and Shahin were enjoying a light breakfast at the Four Seasons' restaurant. They had delivered Conor to the poison center at University College Hospital, and there was nothing any of them could now do that would make a difference in his care. "I must get back to Baku as soon as possible," said the Markirov Bey. "Guliyev and the investigation, you know. Shahin will stay here to monitor Conor's progress."

"So, what's next for you, Jake?" Shahin asked. "It's going to be a long recovery for sure."

"There's a United flight leaving this afternoon," he replied. "I have some unfinished business in Chicago."

"To bury some demons, yes?" Georghe asked.

Jake said, "And other business."

"Then we will say goodbye for now. We'll let you know as soon as Conor is well."

Jake next wrote out his U.S. telephone number and address, and then handed it to Shahin. "I can be reached here at any time." They all exchanged handshakes, and then Jake went back to his room to pack.

What Georghe Markirov hadn't told Jake spoke to the mistrust of not only the man but also of the West. Georghe's son-in-law, Seyfulla Nadirov, had texted Georghe earlier that morning: "disaster in Istanbul, Kazimov dead, Mira wounded terribly, Tali missing!"

Markirov replied: "Tell no one. Shahin and I will return immediately. You and I will lead the clans now.

Seyfulla: "Guliyev suspects all members of the Dark Triad."

Markirov: "Careful who you trust. We must take care of this problem ourselves!"

32

A Christian Burial

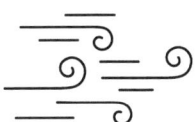

American flight #91 from London to Chicago seemed to take forever. There was a 20-minute ground delay at Heathrow, and after that, a strong headwind put the airliner another 15 minutes behind. But it gave Jake time to reflect on recent events in Azerbaijan.

He thought about the trophy he had shipped home: *would it arrive in one piece; would Katie be pleased?* He had never considered the righteousness of his actions, just his duty and the promise he had made. Jake also weighed his shameful breakup with Lindy. *Hope she's all right*, he reflected on more than one occasion.

But most of all, Jake thought about his newfound relationship with Conor. The life-flight from Baku was the first time that he and Conor had a chance to really learn about one another. For several hours during the flight, Conor had been unconscious – he had the look and reek of sickness and mortality – antiseptics, chloroform, and disinfectants. Maybe it was just the smell of the medivac plane, but it left a nauseating taste in Jake's mouth. *If he dies*, he thought, *I will never know his mind, his intentions or his feelings about me*. But then Conor woke up, and the brothers had a chance to talk, something they had never done before. His world and Conor's were so different, their childhoods so different, their futures diverging. Jake did not know if things could be worked out. Conor even had the confidence in Jake to take care of his beloved should he die from the poison. That was wholly unexpected. But then Conor had another seizure, and many things were left unaddressed. But still, things were different now.

All that was for another time; Jake had reached his journey's end. He gazed out the window of the 777 as the jumbo jet banked against the westerly horizon on its final approach to O'Hare International. He had to squint; the sun was a fiery spatter of reds and oranges in a cloud-laden sky. When the plane leveled off, Jake could see the entire expanse of the city against Lake Michigan. He was glad to be home.

True to his mulish self, Jake hadn't let anyone know that he was returning. He just didn't want the hassles. *Too many questions and too few answers*, he thought. So he decided to get a room downtown and spend the weekend recouping before he contacted the family or tried to restart his life in the city of the Big Shoulders. He was lucky to get a place to stay. It was the St. Patrick's Day weekend, and with the parade and all the other activities, most hotels had been long ago booked. The Conrad Hilton, however, had a cancellation, so he grabbed the reservation.

After getting through customs around 11 pm, he took the Metra train to downtown and then walked to the south Michigan hotel. It was chilly, probably in the high 30s and dropping, but Jake didn't mind. The brisk air felt good. He needed a bit of exercise to keep him awake, trying to acclimate to the different time zone. He was hungry, but most of the restaurants were closing, so he stopped at Fontano's Subs and bought the Big Italian and a bag of chips. After checking in, Jake stopped at the hotel gift shop and bought a bottle of Jameson. Then he headed for his room. By 1:30, he had feasted on the Big Italian, watched a little late-night television, and then passed out.

Partly because he was still on a distant time zone and partly because he was exhausted, when Jake awoke the next day, it was already getting dark. Jake had slept for 15 hours. It was a disorientating feeling, made more so by a strange, kelly green glow in his room. *What the hell?* He searched for something to right the spinning ship that was his head. So, he turned to the clock on the nightstand. It read 4:30 pm, Friday, March 16.

Okay, he understood the kelly green mystery – the street lamps were all lit green for St. Patrick's Day. Jake had experienced the changeover to all things Irish many times. Taverns everywhere in the city would be packed with revelers, jovial crowds would jam the city streets, and tomorrow the Chicago River would sparkle in celebrated colors of orange and then, with a bit of leprechaun alchemy, turn emerald green. He felt good, refreshed. So, he shaved, showered, changed clothes, and headed down to the hotel lobby.

On the ground floor of the Hilton, there was a raucous swarm of people at Kitty O'Sheas. But it wasn't his sort of crowd, mostly tourists, businessmen, and pub crawl types. So Jake headed for an old haunt nearby, Kasey's Tavern on Dearborn St. It was a mere six blocks away; he could get some comfort food there, and, hopefully, see a few old friends. Fifteen minutes later, Jake had ordered a burger and fries and was enjoying a green beer at the bar.

"Jake Moynihan," a voice from behind boomed. "Where the hell have you been?"

Jake swiveled around to see Martin Mills. "Marty, good to see you." Mills was the head of the FAA Midwest and was just the familiar face Jake had expected to see at Kasey's.

"There are a bunch of us in a private room," Marty said, pointing to the back of the tavern. "Come join us?"

"I'll get my food and be right over."

The bartender interrupted, "Go ahead. I'll have Judith bring your food over." Jake thanked him, and then he followed Mills. "Hey guys, look who found his way home." Everyone in the room was wearing tanker boots, and that's when Jake Moynihan knew he was really home.

After a round of handshakes, Jake sat down with Mills, "I was going to come and see you next week."

"That'll be great."

Marty reached inside his vest pocket and pulled out a pack of Marlboros. "What about?" he asked, then lit a cigarette.

"I'm all finished with my overseas gig," Jake replied, "and need a job."

The waitress interrupted Jake with his food. "Run a tab, honey?" He nodded.

"What about the Port Authority job?"

"Quit that before I left. I'm sure it's been filled by now." Jake really didn't know whether that was true or not, but he had decided not to resume his tedious relationship with family at the docks.

"You know, Mike's position is still open," Marty replied. "With your reputation, you'd be an asset to the FAA. You interested?"

"Maybe so."

"Just part-time – as recruiter and facilitator – doesn't pay much," Mills said, "but it's a start."

"I just got back last night and have lots to do this week. How about I come and see you the week after next?"

Marty pulled out a business card and handed it to Jake. "Here's my number. Call me when you're ready to talk. We'll work something out."

On Monday morning, Jake left the Hilton shortly after nine, walked to the CTA station at Harrison Street, and then took the Red Line L south. He was headed for the Port of Chicago, where he had worked for three years as a security guard. At 95th street he boarded a bus that brought him to the Calumet terminal, which housed the transit sheds. That's where the overseas package from Azerbaijan would have been delivered. But Jake was worried. No one knew him there; he'd always worked at the Lakefront Terminal. He agonized, *if someone asks, how do I explain a skull from Azerbaijan?* When he spotted the security checkpoint, he knew he was in trouble. The guard stopped him and asked for an ID. Jake opened with, "I'm here to pick up a transit package from overseas."

"See da clerk in da office," said the guard. "Then bring your Port Clearance and ID back to me."

As fate would have it, a cousin of Sean de Barras, a fellow stevedore, was passing by on a skip loader. "You're Gerry Moynihan's kid, right?"

Jake smiled, "Grandson."

He yelled at the guard, "He's Gerry Moynihan's kid, Ed. For Chissake, let him in," said the man, "He works at Lakefront, he's okay."

The security guard got the message, nodded, then motioned Jake through the checkpoint. "No more than 30 minutes," he said. "Otherwise, ya gotta get da ID."

Jake wanted to avoid any entanglement, so he quickly hustled across the warehouse floor to the transit desk and handed the clerk a claim slip. "It's a small package," he said, "about 12 by 12 inches."

The clerk read the manifest. "You Jake Moynihan?" he asked. "I need to see ID." After he showed his Illinois driver's license, the clerk handed a retrieval number to one of his runners. "It'll take some time. You can have a seat in the office."

"I'm okay. I'll just wait."

After a half hour of pacing, Jake began to have doubts. *They've lost it*, he thought. *Maybe an inspector had it x-rayed… believes it some kind of bomb.* But nothing nefarious happened. The runner appeared shortly after that and placed the package on the clerk's desk. It had been crushed during the overseas flight; a quarter of it flattened, probably by a careless freight handler. "For Christ's sake," Jake yelled. "What have you done?"

"Sorry, man, but there was no order for special handling. Was it valuable? You can make a claim."

"Time, effort, and maybe ten-grand," Jake complained, then, "No. No value, just a family heirloom." He could only imagine what the fragile skull looked like now.

It took an hour to return to the Hilton and was a dreary trip. He set the package on the coffee table in front of the TV, got a knife from the mini-kitchen, and then sliced through the packing tape. The bubble wrap he had placed around the inner box had cushioned the outer jolt, so Jake hoped the skull inside had been protected from any real damage. When he opened it, Jake recognized the trophy he had recovered a week earlier. It appeared the only destruction to it occurred at the topmost of the parientale bone, where the impact had been greatest. But Jake really didn't know if it was old or fresh damage. Only God would know that.

That afternoon, Jake called his mother to tell her he was home. She insisted he come to the apartment and stay with her, but Jake said no. "At least, you must come to Sunday brunch," Katie said. "Julia will be terribly disappointed if you say no to that."

"When?"

"After church, what else?"

"Okay. But I'll be busy all week with other things," Moynihan said. "I can't have them fussing just because I'm back in the States, agreed?"

"What other things?"

"Just other things. I'll call… let's say on Thursday, agreed?"

"Okay," Katie replied. "I'll make kielbasas, dinner at 7:30, agreed?"

Jake was quiet for a moment, and then Katie asked, "Something else?"

"Yeah," he broke off, then. "I've brought him home."

"Him?" Katie Moynihan was puzzled. "Tom? You've brought Tom home?"

"Well, I've brought part of him home… his skull, or what left of it."

There was a long, awkward moment. Katie grimaced and sucked at her teeth. Afterward, she said, "I want to see it, Jake."

"Mother, it's only the remains… of the dead, why would you have to see it?"

"My husband, he was," Katie replied. "Bring it Thursday when you come."

Jake checked out of the Hilton on Sunday morning. One of his FAA buddies had offered him a temporary room in his apartment until he found full-time work. He would head there after brunch at the de Barras. Once again, Jake took the L south. Wentworth Avenue, where the de Barras lived, was parallel to the Red Line tracks. He would hop off at 87th Street, and then walk the rest of the way to Sean and Julia's place above Nowicki's Grocery. Gazing out the window at 72th, Jake noticed the upscale buildings on Lake Michigan, just north of the South Shore neighborhood. The Freedom Army had often visited there – it was the home of the Nation of Islam and the headquarters of the National Black United Front. Jake considered Conor and the Shia Muslims of Azerbaijan. *At least, they're not a bunch of racists.* He questioned how people of the same religion could be so distinctly different, but then he remembered the Republicans of Northern Ireland and their brand of Christianity. It was only a passing thought. He arrived at the de Barras apartment at 10:30, and the families were eating by 11 am.

Sonia had been invited to the brunch that day, and she immediately asked about her husband, who had been absent for months. "Have you seen Mike?"

"Not for a few weeks. I left the Vartans in Georgia," Jake replied. "He, Lindy, and the other expats were headed for Armenia."

"To do what?" Sean asked.

"Help defend the motherland."

Julia asked, "Why did you leave?"

Katie interrupted, of course, "To find Tom's remains." She felt she had to defend her son's actions.

"And did you?"

"Yes."

Julia pressed on, "And?"

"He brought the remains – body and soul – back with him from that God forsaken land," said Katie. "We're planning a burial at St. Andrew."

"You brought back the body?"

"Just the head... his skull, actually," Jake replied, "and his belt buckle, the one he received from the Ancient Order of the Hibernians."

"Nothing else?"

Jake skipped over the details of St. Elmo's Fire, and went on to explain, "There were many bones at the grave site, and...," he gazed at his mother dolefully, "Tom was buried next to his first wife, Zara Kedar. I couldn't tell the difference among so many bones, just this skull was obvious. It was my father." Katie looked sadly away, remembering that her husband had chosen to be buried with that other woman. "I'll be talking with Father Wysocki tomorrow," Jake concluded.

"Twill be a full funeral service he'll have," insisted Katie. "Extreme Unction, and finally, a Christian burial."

"And who'll be payin' for all this?" asked Sean.

"Jake, of course," Katie insisted, "out of the money got from Papa Martin's inheritance."

Everyone at the table was anxious to hear about London, the sale of Papa Martin's treasure, and Denis' school days in Dublin with Aunt Maggie. But Jake refused to talk about the Vartan Alliance or his encounter with his brother, and so for the rest of the day, conversations centered on chit-chat about White Sox baseball and Chicago politics.

The next morning, Jake met Father Wysocki at his rectory office at St. Andrew the Apostle. Sister Justine knocked on the door and said, "Father, Jake Moynihan is here."

"Show him in," said Wysocki, and a moment later, "Come in, Jake, and take a seat."

"Thanks."

"So, you've been to the funeral home?"

"Yeah, Wozniak's on Archer Avenue."

"Kathleen still insists on a casket, then?"

"Yeah, says it will bring some dignity to his memory, Father Wysocki."

"You can call me Ed," the priest replied. "We'll hold off on the Father business until your next confession."

"Not likely, Ed. I'm finished with religion."

Edmund Wysocki shook his head. He'd been through such moods many times. "Okay, Jake," he said. "About the cemetery costs, a double plot at St. Andrew is $4,000, and perpetual maintenance is another $1,000, so five grand, altogether."

"I'll make the check for $7,500.," Moynihan said. "My donation to the church."

"Not quite finished with religion, then?"

"Honorarium for my mother and father. That's all."

"By the way, the entire parish heard about your exploits in Azerbaijan," he said, "saving your brother and all."

"Thanks," Jake mumbled. "It seems I'm good at killing."

The priest shifted uncomfortably in his chair, "Last fall, when we spoke you talked about killing those men who murdered your father, did you kill them?"

"Didn't have to," Jake replied. "One was dead, and the other was all banged up, crippled and in a wheelchair."

"You have fulfilled one of your promises, to bring your father back home for burial. What about the second?" Wysocki asked. "Did you find out who was behind Tom Moynihan's murder."

"I had a long talk with my brother about that. Conor had nothing to do with it. In fact, he is the one who killed the real killer – Elshan Kedar, a relative of sorts."

"Circle closed, then?"

"Yes, closed. Just this burial left, and then all the promises I made are fulfilled."

"What about that Bedrosian girl," the priest asked. "You two were so close."

"Had a falling out," Jake replied, "and just broke up."

"Maybe you should reconsider," said Wysocki. "Don't give up so easy, Jake. Maybe there is another promise to be made."

Jake laughed, wondering how Lindy was getting along within the male-dominated VDW.

He was unsure about the reason for their breakup, *did she understand why he abandoned the VDW cause, really understand?* He brooded, *does she know that I still love her?* It was probably too late for such considerations. *If I ever go back*, he thought, *I will, at least, try to visit with her... so we can talk about things.*

33

Wind Rising Up from the Sea

D ay-10. In the deep recesses of her mind, Tali suspected that something dreadful had happened in her world. She could feel it closing in – the assault in Istanbul must have been part of a coordinated attack on her family, her House, or even a conspiracy against the Azeri government itself. Otherwise, Conor and Georghe and Seyfulla would have been breaking down the damn doors of this prison. *Where were they?* she asked repeatedly.

Day 17. Twice each day, Karun came to bring Tali food and unlock her chains so she could use the bathroom and shower. It was Tali's only respite from the long hours of weighing fear against hope in her struggle to know what might be coming next. She enjoyed a few minutes of chit-chat with her keeper while loathing her at the same time. In the afternoons, a man named Serge came along with an armload of firewood for the stove. Tali believed it was April, but it was still cold in the cabin at night, a sure sign that they were likely in the mountains. Long after Tali had finished her afternoon workout, and Karun and Serge had disappeared, Tali would sit close to the stove and let her imagination run wild. Mostly, she wondered about Conor and their future together.

But those dreams would have to wait. Tali was in a fix and all alone. So, she had made up her mind. There was no other conclusion – it was up to her – time to find an escape plan and put it into action.

At University College Hospital, it had been weeks since the Kedar Bey had fallen unconscious before arriving at London City Airport. The doctors did not know whether the young man was in a coma or merely suffering from the strange condition known as locked-in syndrome. In either case, to the outside observer, he seemed to be vegetative. But that opinion wasn't entirely right. To none other than himself, Conor was now detecting human activity just beyond his ability to communicate.

His greatest pleasure, however, was not seeking that world just beyond, but his escape to recurrent dreams of an alternate reality. For the present, it was impossible for Conor to know which was genuine and which was not.

I was seven and already in the second grade; my brother was five, but for some reason, not yet in school. After I came home, he would want to play in the yard. He was such a pest.

"Conor," the man on the porch said, "don't tease your brother."

I looked at the man strangely, not because he called me out, but because he always wore a green belt with a gold harp on the buckle.

"He's so dimwitted," I yelled. "Stupid, stupid, three-times stupid." Then this Jacob thing began to cry.

"Baby!" I teased. And so he ran onto the porch and jumped into the man's big welcoming arms. I stared at my brother disgustedly, and then wondered, "Why does that man coddle him so?"

The man with the green belt was a marvel with Jacob, and could always trick my stupid brother into smiling. "Itsy, bitsy spider," he'd sing, "went up the water spout." Jacob would walk his hands up the man's arms, his fake tears disappearing as the game went on.

"Not really a part of the family, that boy," I said. After that, a woman appeared from the house, picked up Jacob, and took him inside.

The next day, I heard a distant voice calling, but I had no interest in what it had to say. I asked my cousin, "Where did that boy go?"

"You mean Jacob?" the little girl said. "You sent him away."

"He was chasing me," I said, "and wouldn't let me be alone."

"He just wanted to play," the little girl replied.

Then I asked, "Why did the man with the green belt with the gold harp on the buckle leave?" The girl shrugged, having no answer to that old question.

Day-24. One night, just after she had finished her exercise routine and was getting up to go to bed, Tali noticed that one of the oaken floorboards behind the stove had been slightly dislodged. When she walked to the back of the stove and stepped on a board there, it gave way. Rotten! Tali immediately stepped back, not wanting to reveal her surprise to any of the kidnappers. She had no idea what to do with her secret, but it was some-thing to ponder.

The next day, after Karun had left the bedroom, Tali checked the floor carefully. She thought, *not built on a concrete slab. There's a crawlspace below.* The owners of the cabin had placed the potbellied stove on a 4-inch chunk of fire-resistant stone that rested on the floor. Through the years, something had rotted the wood. *Termites*, she guessed. A layer of ash per-manently covered the stone slab, so the casual observer would not know its poor condition.

Day-30. One week later, Tali had carefully removed the layer of ash and found that the slab was cracked into several large pieces, the largest, which was approximately a 20-inch square, fell directly under the belly of the stove. For the currently very muscular Tali, it was not hard to remove. Beneath, two boards were almost completely rotted out and only hanging on because of the tension against the others. If she could somehow remove another two boards, Tali could squeeze through the opening and find the crawl space below. Tali had no idea what she would stumble upon in the darkness under the cabin. Whatever she discovered would be better than facing endless confinement, and the fear of violence and rape in the form of the shadow man that she expected at any time.

Meanwhile, in Baku, Georghe Markirov grew increasingly worried about Conor's safety in London. It was no place for the Kedar Bey. He decided that Conor could be protected at home with family, more so than in a for-eign land, wholly a continent away. The doctors at University Hospital had flushed away all the effects of the Polonium, and the patient was getting stronger. One of the nurses, moreover, had noticed a change in the Kedar Bey's bedside mannerisms. He could not yet speak, but she had observed some marked facial movements. She was sure that Conor now had mental cognition and would be communicating within a few days.

"Probably mid-stage locked-in syndrome," the doctor told his staff. He then reported his diagnosis to Georghe Markirov, who took it to heart and called his daughter. "He'll be better off in Baku."

Mira agreed, "I'm ready to come home too." Two days later, the Zümrə jet left London with Conor on board. It stopped briefly in Istanbul to pick up Mira, but they were all home by eight that night. Yet, Conor still dreamed.

The young girl asked, "Where are all the adults, Conor?"

"We are safe here," I replied, "and I can build a fire to keep you warm." I really had no idea how to build a fire – I was ten. It was just something I thought might reassure my cousin.

We had been in the juniper forest but had gotten lost. So, we headed up a rugged ravine and found a craggy overhang. A leopard was chasing us, a big one, maybe 150lbs.

The nine-year-old Tali said, "We need an adult, Conor." Then I heard the leopard, hissing, and growling. It seemed very close.

"Run, Tali," I yelled.

She took off down the canyon, and I followed close behind. When Tali got to the bottom, she turned past a large boulder. "Wait for me, girl," I shouted.

But I hesitated and then twisted around to see if the leopard was on my heels. Surprisingly, I saw nothing. So, I listened – again nothing. Confident that our hungry pursuer had given up the chase, I hiked slowly to the bend where Tali had fled. When I rounded the bend, she was nowhere in sight.

I shouted over and over, "Tali, where are you?" But like the leopard, she had vanished.

When they arrived in Baku, Mira and Conor were split up: Conor to his residence on the Zümrə Estates, and Mira to her home in Gobustan. The arrangement was adequate for a few days. Georghe, Mira, and Seyfulla spent much of their time assessing their political situation and planning a survival strategy. They thought they were safe, but there was no way of telling for sure. Conor had around the clock care at the residence but was comatose most of the time.

It was a joyous day when Conor was finally able to speak. Mira had come to town for the day and was in the kitchen when the nursed called out. "Mrs. Nadirov, the Kedar Bey is awake."

When Mira entered his bedroom in a wheelchair, Conor was bewildered. "I know," she said emphatically. "I have much to tell." Though she had had plenty of time to prepare for the moment, when it finally happened, Mira was at a loss for words. She had put it off, hoping against hope that Tali would find her way home before Conor awoke.

"Tali?" he mouthed. The nurse used a wet cloth to swab his dry, cracked lips.

"Yes, yes, Conor, I'll get to that in a minute. Nurse, will you please find Georghe and Seyfulla. Tell them that Conor has awakened, and ask them to come ASAP."

Day-49. Tali had been into the crawlspace below the cabin twice. It had taken her two weeks to chip away enough floorboard space under the stove so that she could squeeze through easily. The first time, it was during the night, after Karun and Serge had made their rounds and disappeared for the evening. The descent into darkness was terrifying, and she learned nothing. Tali had better results the second time, but she had to take a chance during the day. Once below, there was enough daylight seeping through the cracks that she could see the four walls and two air vents at opposite ends of the cinder block foundation. The light coming through at the nearby wall was substantial, and she had enough length in the tethering chain to reach that wall. So, she crawled through the smelly ground debris and realized that the vent had been partially dislodged, probably by one of the wiggly forest creatures that now likely inhabited the crawlspace with her. Satisfied, Tali felt she had discovered the means of her escape.

When Georghe and Seyfulla arrived at the residence, there was a feeling of relief – the Kedar Bey was on the road to recovery. But for everyone involved, the next few hours would be gut-wrenching. How would they put into plain words the predicament they were in, let alone explain that Tali had been missing for almost two months? The sum of their fears, however, had to be revealed – one thunderbolt after another. Upon learning the truth of things, Conor's face went ashen and his eyes vacant, returning to the corpse-like state that had plagued him throughout his time in London.

But the depression only lasted a short time, and Conor was no longer bothered by dreams or hallucinations, so he asked the nurse to move him to the sunroom next to the kitchen. There he could see his garden, his Cappadocian maple trees, his azaleas, and the dock where the Zarifa was moored. He cheered up quickly and made a request for Mira, "Will you please ask Mrs. Nadirov to join me?"

Minutes later, Mira wheeled herself in. "Conor, you're feeling better?"

"Where is Sam?" he asked.

"Sam Mansour? By now, he's back in the States."

Still having trouble with his parched throat, he asked for paper and pencil. *He knows how to find Tali,* he wrote.

Mira glanced at the note, and then asked, "How is that possible?"

When we spoke in March, he said a man named Ali might be able to help.

"Who is Ali?"

Conor stumbled across a few words, "Hunting guide…" He took a drink of water, "the guy who saved Rufet and nursed him back to health."

"Go on."

"Rufet told him many secrets about the Kos," said Conor. "Ali might have an idea where the Dark Triad is holding Tali."

Mira's eyes brightened, and she smiled gleefully, "It's worth a try."

Conor felt the spark of hope and lifted himself to the side of the bed. "I'll call Sam tomorrow," he said raspingly. "He'll know what to do."

Mira was startled by Conor's sudden turn for the better. "Do you feel up to it?"

"I have no time for any more of this," he replied. "Mira, please find Mo Chinske. Tell him I need to see him right away."

With that, Conor motioned to Mira to help him from the bed. With her support he found his land legs, and they walked to the windows facing the garden. One of the windows unexpectedly blew open, and Conor could feel a red-hot wind rising up from the sea.

34

Iza and Ali

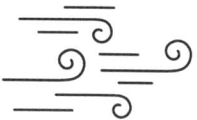

Mo Chinske asked, "How's your mother, Iza?"

"She has home care now. A nurse comes to the house every other day."

"What happened?"

"Crohn's Disease. You know, diarrhea, anemia, fatigue," Iza explained. "Chira has had it for years. It's just gotten worse as she's gotten older."

"Manageable, then?"

"As soon as I got here, we put her in the hospital," said Iza. "She will be okay with time; just got to keep her stress level down."

Chinske continued, "So, you can get away for a few days?"

"No problem."

"I talked to Conor, and he has asked me to help in the search for Tali, but I'm tied up with this hunt for Viktor Kos and his sons," the CIA officer said. "President Guliyev wants them caught immediately. I'm headed for Ganja right now."

"So, it was the Dark Triad behind the murder of Secretary Kazimov and Tali's kidnapping."

"Absolutely. The assassin that Jake shot at Parliamentary Hall didn't die right away. He implicated Viktor, and General Aslan saw Vanya with the hitman. They disappeared sometime after the Hall was cleared."

"So, why Ganja?"

"The Kos is directly tied to Kirovabad."

"Kirovabad?"

"It's the old Russian term for Ganja. After Perestroika, the city regained its original name. Lots of Russians there and a small Armenian community as well. The Kos have relatives there. More importantly, Kirovabad is the code word they've been using for their cabal."

"Do you know of any secret sanctuary there?"

"Not in the city," Mo replied. "But likely somewhere outside, maybe in nearby Goygol National Park."

Iza thought for a moment. "Ali said Rufet talked about Lake Goygol. He believed the Dark Triad might have a hunting lodge there."

"Qurb would know about hunting lodges."

"Then we'll head straight for Lake Goygol; it's a place to start. I'm at the airport right now, waiting for Ali."

Mo asked, "How long will it take you to get to Lake Goygol?"

"Never been there before. But Ganja is a little more than three hours, and then Lake Goygol is another hour away according to Google Maps. Ali's been there. He's guided birdwatcher tours everywhere in the Aras and Kur Valley region."

"We're headed in the same direction. I've got a contingent of 20 men in the field. I can spare a few if you get into a bind."

"Thanks, Mo. Let's keep in touch."

"Right."

Day-52. For almost two months, Tali had fought off fear and loathing, but now she was just angry and ready to explode. Last night, she had descended into the bowels below the cabin with two, fist-sized stones that she would employ as hammer and chisel to knock out enough cinder block around the vent opening to escape. But Tali also thought they might be a useful weapon should her wiggly friend appear suddenly. The only matter now remaining was getting rid of the chains that bound her to this prison. She was ready.

That night, after he had finished loading logs into the firepot, Serge noticed that a sizeable pile of ash had accumulated on the stones. "I'll clean up the mess tomorrow."

Realizing that he might uncover her escape route, Tali felt her heart racing, and her tongue going thick. Panic at this moment would be a bitter adversary. "Not in the morning," she insisted. Serge looked at her suspiciously. "Let the fire cool down. It gets too hot nowadays."

It was a good comeback, so Serge nodded in agreement. "I'll bring the ash bucket tomorrow night."

"Thanks," Tali said.

Day-53 – Fight or flight. Karun arrived at nine am as usual. She was wearing a raincoat and rubber boots. *A storm outside*, Tali surmised. The middle-aged woman took off the cloak and tossed it across the chair next to the door. Then she sat down and pulled off the boots. Tali was already out of bed and pacing. "Karun, I have to use the toilet right away," she said. "I'm having some diarrhea problems."

Not wanting to deal with an unseemly mess, Karun eagerly unlocked her prisoner's ankle bracelets, freeing her from the chains. Tali raced to the bathroom. As she passed by, Karun didn't notice the pockets of Tali's robe were bulging, heavy-laden with stones. "I'll set your meals for the day out on the table," she said, but Tali didn't respond.

Ten minutes went by without a sound. "You okay, Ms. Nadirov?" Curious, Karun went to the door and knocked. Still nothing, so she opened the door and peeked through the crack, "Ms. Nadirov?"

When she poked her head sufficiently inside, Tali barked, "Surprise, bitch!"

As Karun looked up, Tali struck down on the woman's skull with one of the stones. Next, full of rage, Tali leaped at Karun and forced her to the floor. She was about to strike again, but the woman was out cold, her right temple bleeding freely. Instantly, Tali found a towel, tore it into several three-inches shreds, then wrapped Karun's head. She didn't want to kill the woman.

After that, Tali took a long breath and then did a mental check of her escape plan. Karun was a hefty woman, but no match for Tali's new-found strength. She dragged the woman to the bedroom, found the keys to the locks, and fastened one bracelet around Karun's left ankle. Next, she stripped the woman of all her clothes, leaving her with only panties. Tali took a moment to reflect on the irony of seeing Karun naked, *how do you like that, bitch!* It was all she could manage to hold back a primal scream. Tali was unsure of Serge's whereabouts, but she thought that he was proba-bly in the next room. Silence was a friend at this crucial moment.

Tali quickly dressed, using most of Karun's clothes; her bra was too big and would just be an annoyance on the trail. Everything was too big, but she cinched up the pants and shirt as best she could, and then pulled on boots. Lastly, Tali gathered up the packaged foods on the table and stuffed them into the pockets of the raincoat. She heard a thunderclap, and took it as a warning – *get moving now!*

Twenty minutes later, a mud-soaked Tali Nadirov had found her way through the crawlspace, had knocked out a gap around the vent, and had wriggled her way outside. For an instant, she thought about surprising Serge with one of her stones, but then she remembered that there was sometimes another thug guarding the cabin. She decided to take flight, but which way?

At the very same time that Tali was escaping into the forest, Iza Beggs and Ali Tabak were on the road from Ganja, traveling to Lake Goygol. A little more than an hour earlier they had hooked up at Rustavi: Iza had taken the train from Tbilisi, and Ali had driven in from Kars.

"You didn't have a car when last we met," said Iza. "Where'd you get this one?

"I confiscated it. Used to be a Turk ZPT Patrol Car."

"Confiscated?"

"After seeing you guys off at Ninots, I headed back to Kars," he explained. "There had been a battle, not more than 90 minutes earlier. That VDW crew and a Turkish army unit had skirmished ferociously; all the Turks had been wiped out."

"My mother foresees Bəla coming."

"Great evil, indeed," Ali remarked. "No one was ever going to use this ZPT again, so I borrowed it. If we run into any trouble, it will be a useful vehicle to have... armored and four-wheel-drive."

"Okay," Iza was changing the subject, "What about this Lake Goygol?"

"It's not just one, but many, maybe 18, 20 altogether."

"We can't search them all," Iza said. "How do we choose?"

"The biggest lake is the one they call Goygol. That's where I've guided the bird-watching tours, lots of tourists there. The others are smaller lakes up in the mountains."

Beggs was analyzing an area map on her iPhone. "There's just one road leading from Goygol to the others."

"That's right. The lakes at the highest elevations are connected to ski resorts, but Rufet told me that the mid-level lakes are where the hunting lodges are located."

"We should start there."

"Exactly." So, they turned away from the big lake called Goygol and headed up the mountain road where they thought they might find the Kos hideout.

The cabin where Tali had been imprisoned was located in the riparian woodlands of the Goygol Nature Reserve. The ancient Celts, who once lived there, saw such woods as the natural meeting place of two magical realms, one of water and the other of forest.

The first thing Tali saw, as she raced from the cabin, was the forest – a stand of Cappadocian maple trees. It reminded her of the trees in Conor's garden at the Zümrə Estates. It gave young Tali Nadirov a feeling of confidence as she raced down the mountainside to the waters of Lake Goygol. *He's okay*, she thought, *I'll be with him soon.*

But Tali was not yet free.

35

Flight to Ganja

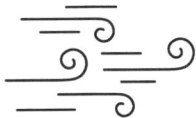

It was a sunny spring morning in Ganja, and the men of the Dark Triad were resting quietly inside a boathouse that sat beside the windswept, cobblestoned esplanade of the Ganja River. The facility looked out over the water and the dock where most of the local ruling families moored their yachts. It belonged to Alexandre Kos, Viktor's cousin.

Viktor was still dressed in his official Azeri VP regalia, but his coat lapel had been torn, and his pant cuffs were mud-splattered from the muck he'd stepped through next to the pier at Baku Bay. "Don't think we're free and clear," he rebuked his sons. "Guliyev will send his army after us."

Vanya agreed, "That CIA bastard will lead. He's been after us for years."

"Chinske?"

"Yeah, Mo Chinske." The Kos Bey looked frazzled. It had been an exhausting 11-hour getaway through the night. "He's a pal of Azreal."

After the failed assassination and unrelenting chaos in Baku, the Dark Triad had successfully cut and run. Knowing the highways, rail lines, and airports would be blocked, Viktor, Vanya, and Vladimir made their way to a secluded dock on the Caspian coast and boarded the 1605 oil-crew transfer vessel they owned. They fled five hours south on the Sea to the city of Lankaran, near the Iranian border. It was the stronghold of House Vidadi, one of Viktor's closest allies. There, they procured a fast car – a Porsche Turbo S, sapphire blue – and drove nonstop to the house of their clan relatives in Ganja. After securing food, water, and a cache of small-arms, Alexandre Kos escorted them to the boathouse, where they had been hiding since early morning.

Viktor was staring out the window at an ornate white-stone building across the street. It served as a library and archives for maps and charts of the lakes and rivers of the region. The Kos Bey had made an evaluation. "I'm going to call our friends in Armenia; tell them we need assistance in getting across the border."

Vanya's eyes lit up, and he scowled, "Do you think that's wise? I assume that Guliyev; no, I assume everyone is listening." The elder Kos son was worried about his father's judgment, which seemed to be getting worse as the crisis grew more complicated.

Viktor said, "I'm going to call just the same." The collaborators in Armenia were the ones that hired Old Man Chubby and the other assassins. "You two, step outside so I can hear."

Vlad shot back, "But we agreed to contact them by courier only."

"I still make the decisions for this House," Viktor howled. "Step outside."

A few minutes later, the brothers were alone at the end of the dock. Vanya opened a cryptic dialogue. "Sometimes I believe we would be better off without that old man. He's been leading our House to destruction for a long time."

"Agreed."

"I would do things differently," said Vanya.

"Agreed."

"If he were out of the way, we could plead our case to Guliyev."

Vlad grinned broadly, then added, "Before it is too late."

By nine am, Mo Chinske and his unit had run into a dead-end. They had chased the Kos 1605 cruiser to Lankaran, knowing that Vidadi clan would harbor Viktor and his sons, or at least supply them with a means of escaping. The logical assumption was that they were headed to the Iranian border, but President Guliyev had ordered all border crossings closed and issued an arrest warrant for the Kos leaders and their allies.

The senior officer of the Azeri State Police turned to Chinske, and said, "My lieutenant tells me that the Kos men are nowhere in the city."

"And what about Vidadi?" Mo asked.

"All the Vidadis have disappeared."

"Rolan should not have closed the border and issued the warrants," Chinske replied. "All the rats have fled the barn."

The officer continued, "However, we have found the pilot of the 1605 vessel." He took out a cigarette and lit it. "They have just now finished with his interrogation."

Mo squirmed at the thought, but he said nothing. "And?"

"The lieutenant reports that the Vidadi had supplied the Kos with a car and weapons."

"Did the man indicate anything about direction?"

"Only that the Kos knew that the Iranian border was closed, Chinske, sir."

"That leaves Ganja."

The State Police officer took another drag on his cigarette, then flipped it away, "Or the Black Garden."

"Right," Mo agreed, "that's the only way into Armenia."

"I'll order up the helicopter. We can get to the Ganja airport in 90 minutes."

Back at the Ganja River, Viktor walked out of the boathouse, and waved to his sons, "Vanya, Vladimir, let's go."

The brothers hurried back to the shed, and then Vlad asked, "You've talked to Kirdenbad?"

"Yes, they will send two SUVs to meet us at the Lake Goygol lodge," Viktor replied, "The Porsche will be useless off-road. We'll change vehicles and then head overland to a wilderness crossing called the Sotk Pass."

"We can be at the cabin in about an hour," Vlad said. "Our captive is still there, Tali Nadirov."

"Perfect," Vanya said. "We can utilize her as a negotiating tool if anything should go wrong." At precisely 11 am, the Dark Triad stopped at a gas station at the outskirts of Ganga. Any Porsche Turbo S would draw a few gawkers. The Dark Triad's sapphire blue one attracted a half dozen. But the Kos men had no time for such trivialities, so an angry Vlad chased the them away. It was a mistake. One of the panhandlers at the gas station would remember the fancy car and the wrathful men it carried.

36
Showdown at Sotk Pass

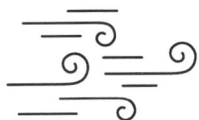

Goddamnit, goddamnit, goddamnit!

Silent screams between gasping breaths and burning lungs.

Just don't trip, just don't trip.

Tali's prayer as she entered the unfamiliar forest outside the cabin.

… and what do I do now?

After 15 minutes of rattled racing down the mountain, it was inevitable. Tali tripped.

Goddamnit, goddamnit, goddamnit!

She tugged off her left boot and rubbed her ankle. Tali looked for swelling to begin, then frowned in disgust, as if it was the fault of the boot.

Just a wader without ankle support. Now what?

A fallen branch, a boot too big, a twist, a tumble – Tali sat on the damp forest floor with a throbbing foot, wanting to shout out, but knowing she could not. Out of the blue, she heard another branch breaking and then another – sounds from somewhere behind, menacing and foreboding – pursuers pressing near?

Serge, goddamnit.

She thought of his brutish, bad-tempered, sour face and remembered the beating he had given her on that first day.

It won't be a beating this time, not after...

She had crushed in Karun fat head. For the moment, Tali's pounding heart had calmed, her aching thighs eased, and then the sounds, which had seemed nearby only a moment ago, moved off in a different direction. *Not here yet.*

She looked around for some clue, but nothing spoke to her. There was no transcendental revelation.

I cannot just run. Run? Not likely now.

Tali had nothing to wrap her ankle tight, so she quietly pulled on her boot. Moving forward at this point would be painful and slow.

I have to have a plan. I, I, I... have to have a plan. Where is my sweet forest fairy to point out the way?

That's when Tali noticed a trail. City girls don't typically detect game trails, but there it was, crossing right in front of her.

Wild boars? Wolves? A Panther perhaps? Deer? Yes, deer, a deer trail... and that's what I heard, a deer.

Stealth, hide and seek... something to put Serge on the wrong track. Tali stood up and moved to examine the imprint the creatures had made. It was narrow, no more than 12, maybe 15 inches wide.

Whatever it is it's going somewhere for food, water, or safety.

She had to take a chance. So, Tali limped another 50 feet in the same direction she had been traveling, retrieved and unwrapped a power bar that Karun had brought that morning, and then tossed the wrapper into the brush. Afterward, she retraced her steps to the game trail and carefully entered.

He will be coming for sure, but this will give me some time.

Meanwhile, Iza and Ali were parked on the side of the road that led to the smaller Goygol lakes above. "What can you see?" Iza asked.

Ali was scanning the switchback road above with his field glasses. "An old farm truck about 20 minutes ahead, nothing much else." Tabak, the consummate tracker, was used to measuring distance as time, instead of miles.

"That fellow at the gas station said he recognized the oil minister," Iza said. "He was sure of it."

"What kind of car?"

"He didn't know what kind, but said it was bright blue, navy, something like that."

"There it is!" Ali shouted. "About an hour ahead of us, and moving fast." He could not exactly identify the color of the car, but he could see a cloud of dust rising behind. "Whoever it is, they're desperate."

"Got to be the Kos. Let's go. Tali is surely close at hand."

"Wait, Iza, let me check the surroundings and possible escape routes."

"Okay. But I'm going to let Mo Chinske know that we've found the Kos and probably Tali too."

"Give me a minute, and I'll get the coordinates for you."

Fifteen minutes later, as Ali was making the turn at the mountain road's first switchback, Beggs received Mo's response. "He says they are in helicopters, heading our way."

"I think I know how the Kos plan to cross into Armenia... an old, abandoned border crossing called the Sotk Pass. Tell Mo that."

Iza waited a moment, then read Chinske's reply: "He says he has a State Police officer with him who knows the place. They will head directly for the Sotk Pass to block off any escape."

"I told Mo that we'll be searching for the hunting lodge and Iza." Another few minutes went by, and then Iza frowned. "He says we should wait for backup,"

Ali shouted, "The hell with that!"

After 30 minutes along the deer trail, Tali heard the sounds of something completely out of place in the woods – the high-pitched revving of a four-stroke engine.

ATVs – two, maybe three. I thought they'd be on foot. I thought I'd have a chance.

Eyes wide with panic, Adrenaline surged through her body. Without regard to the pain or consequences, Tali began running again.

They're coming. I thought I'd have more time.

With every footfall, jolting pain spurted through Tali's now very swollen ankle. Then she heard the ATVs roar at full throttle. She could feel them closing in.

It's not just Serge. He is coming... the shadow man... beating, smashing, rape, torture... Tali was in a tight spot, her mind a tangled mess. Fail, and the sum total of who she is or will ever be will in the balance – run, and the damage is limited to shins, ankles, and knees.

When the Kos men had reached the cabin and found that Tali Nadirov had escaped, they were incensed. "How long ago?" Vlad demanded.

"Not sure, Müserif," Serge muttered.

Vlad burst open the door to Tali's prison and quickly spied the hole under the stove where Tali had made her getaway. Eyes in a rage, Vlad returned to the outer room. He began grinding his teeth, then railed against the man in charge, "You and Karun had one job – keep the bitch here until I returned." Vlad walked to the fireplace, picked up a poker from the rack, and then struck Serge across the back."

Viktor Kos was unmoved. "Never mind that, Vlad. We have to leave now."

"Don't be a fool, old man," Vanya shouted. "She's insurance. Besides, once she's found by Guliyev's forces, they will know our location."

"I'm still in charge, boy," Viktor retorted, then struck out a fist at his elder son's cynical face.

Vanya reacted violently, catching the old man's hand in mid-air, and twisting it sadistically until Viktor cried out. Next, he forced his father to the floor, showing the old man who was really in charge.

Serge broke in, "We have three Honda TRXs in the back. She's on foot, and we can catch her if we hurry."

"But how do you know where she's headed?"

"Karun knows the forest. She will find her."

"Get the guns out of the car, Serge," said Vlad. "If we cannot catch her, I'll kill the bitch, so no one will know where we're headed."

"Okay," Vanya replied, "We'll wait here, and try to contact the Armenians. They should be here within the hour."

Tali's breathing rose and fell in short spurts, red-hot and edgy; her heart beat madly, in and out of rhythm. Besides the roar of the ATVs, she could now hear the splash of the deep-treaded tires navigating through the mud puddles and root covered terrain. Then,

Blue sky!

Tali unexpectedly stopped to stare at an opening in the forest canopy ahead. Next, she heard what she thought was a car engine coming up from somewhere below. A few minutes later, Tali burst into a clearing, and then glanced over the edge at a 20-foot precipice overlooking a large lake.

Trapped! Goddamnit!

Iza yelled, "Stop the car, Ali!" As the Turk patrol car screeched to a halt, Iza grabbed Tabak's binoculars and stepped outside. As she did, two Azeri military helicopters shrieked overhead.

"What are you looking for?"

"Just above and to the right about 200 yards, someone is running."

Ali jumped out of the patrol car, opened the liftgate, and retrieved Rufet's old Weatherby rifle. It had an excellent Swarovski scope that he could use to identify the person on the side of the hill. "It is a woman, and she has pursuers."

Iza raced over to Ali. "Let me look," she screamed. Ali held the rifle steady against the roof of the ZPT. "Tali," Iza said in a hushed tone.

"Al Hamdallah!"

"Thank God, indeed."

Without warning, there was the report of small arms fire on the hill. Iza saw Tali quickly duck behind a rocky mound.

"I can see them, Ali. Two… now three ATV chasing after Tali. What can we do?"

"Iza, give me the rifle. You run to the edge of the lake. See if you can get Tali's attention. I'll distract the pursuers."

The roof of ZPT provided a perfect mount for Ali to steady the Weatherby. He fired three times in rapid succession, and the ATV riders came to a screeching halt, hopped off, and began searching for the unanticipated sniper. It was a lapse in judgment more experienced thugs would not have made.

Next, Ali began a detailed scan of the three targets on the ridge. There was one who seemed to be in charge. Tabak, a marksman of the highest order, had decided to target him first. Because he was kneeling beside his four-tracker, he made for a small target. But Ali was determined, so he steadied his breathing, took careful aim at the pursuer's contorted upper body and fired.

After a two-count, the cartridge struck the man a little right and a little high on the chest, missing the heart altogether. It was a severe wound and put the man down for the time being. Another man raced to his side.

In the meantime, Iza had reached the edge of the water, and began shouting, "Tali! Tali! Over here."

Because the small arms fire had stopped momentarily, Tali was able to hear the frantic calls from below. She peered over the edge of the cliff at the water. It was crystal clear and deep – her final escape from Serge, Karun, and that forest prison. So, Tali took a half dozen quick steps to the edge and then jumped as far as she could, hoping to get away from the sharp edges of the rock face.

At that same moment, a second shot rang out from the direction of the ZPT. Ali had made the compensation for the old Weatherby's pull to the right, and the bullet struck the second man dead center. He was a brutish looking man and died without making a sound.

Tali's punch into waters of Lake Goygol was like the crack of thunder, and it took her down far lower than she had thought possible. It seemed like a lifetime of plunging into the cold depths of the lake. *Would she ever slow down, stop?* she wondered.

Then she did, and afterward, for some odd reason, she began counting the seconds to the surface: one thousand and one, one thousand and two, one thousand and three, upward and struggling for a few last bits of breath. After what seemed like an age, Tali roared through the surface, gulping great buckets of air.

Water! This was her element. Refreshed and invigorated, Tali dipped under the surface, and Dolphin kicked away from the direction she thought bullets might come. Another twenty yards and she surfaced again. That's when she heard the voice from the shore crying out, "Tali, Tali." She stopped swimming for a moment to look. That's when she recognized her friend Iza and waved exuberantly at the most welcomed sight.

While Iza was helping Tali out of the water, Ali was driving the ZPT toward the shore. Within a few minutes, all were on board. Iza said, "Tali, this is Ali Tabak, our friend from Kars, Turkey."

"I'd kiss you Ali Tabak, but I haven't brushed my teeth in two days."

"Well," Ali mused. "At least you've bathed." It was a relief to laugh, if only briefly.

A moment later, there was earsplitting explosion up-range. "Chinske and the airships attacking the Armenians."

"Listen," Ali whispered, "rocket launcher." A second afterward, there were two additional explosions. "Air-to-surface weapons; they're called Mighty Mouse rockets."

A distracted Tali was not paying any attention to the distant battle. "Did you kill Kos?" she asked. "I heard you shooting. Did you kill Kos?"

Ali replied, "One is dead for sure, and the other is wounded. But I don't know how badly."

Tali insisted they check, and after a ten-minute ride up the mountain and another few minutes off-road they found the ATVs. There were three, parked in a protective triangle at the edge of the woods. Suddenly – ping, ping, ping… ping, ping – a round of cartridges splattered against the front window of Ali's ZPT. "There's your answer, Tali, still alive," shouted Ali. At least someone is still alive."

"Thank God for the armored vehicle."

"Iza, see if you can determine how many are shooting." Then Tabak jumped out the door and retrieved the Weatherby.

"Just one. It's a woman behind the first ATV."

"That would be Karun, my kidnapper. Give me a gun," Tali insisted. "I'll keep her busy while you circle around."

Iza was surprised. "I didn't know you could handle a gun."

"Sixty days in hell changes a lot of things," Tali said. "I'm never again going to stand by and allow others to run my life." Iza was impressed by this new Tali Nadirov.

Two minutes into the firefight, Iza and Tali heard a single shot from a high-powered rifle ring out, and all went quiet. Then they saw Tabak cautiously approaching the small fortress in the woods. Everything was secured, so he stood up and signaled for the women to advance.

As the two women neared, Tali shouted out, "Is he dead?"

Vladimir Kos was lying with his back against the ATV engine. "No, Nadirov cunt," he said, dripping with sarcasm, "I am not dead. This Kos is planning to live forever."

Eyes glowering, brows knitted, jaw clenched, Tali countered, "Not likely."

"I've just got a message from Mo Chinske," said Iza. "He says Vanya Kos has surrendered," and after a moment another, "says Viktor Kos is dead… committed suicide."

"I didn't think Vanya could do it," said Vlad with a snicker.

Tali had had enough. She handed her pistol to Iza, limped over to Tabak and asked for Rufet's Weatherby. There was no resisting Tali Nadirov at the moment. "Cartridge," she demanded. Ali was surprised, but he handed her one of the Nosler hunting cartridges. She loaded it resolutely, and then there was the famous double-click of the bolt-action that places the shell into the firing chamber.

The last thought that crossed the Kos second son's mind was, *like me now*. Then the 180-grain bullet smashed through Vladimir's skull.

Tali said aloud, "And that's the end of the vile beast who had been masquerading on the earth as a human."

37

BTK-57

It had been almost a year and a half since the Dark Triad coup d'état
had failed, Viktor and Vladimir had been justly dispatched from this
Earth, and Vanya had been convicted of numerous crimes against the
state and sentenced to prison for a seven-year term. One way or another,
in spite of all the high-profile security, Vanya had escaped. Some say a large
bribe was involved. Whatever the case, Vanya was no longer a threat to
Azerbaijan or House Kedar, at least not in the foreseeable future.

Tbilisi, Georgia – autumn – a time for moving cattle down from the mountain range, gathering grapes from upland slopes for wine-making, and
basking in the warm afternoon sun. The people of the Caucasus everywhere

were happy to put the hot and humid days of summer behind them. This was especially true in the Georgian capital, where the hillsides had already turned into a grand panorama of maple reds, oranges, and yellows, and the mornings were often frost-covered. For many, it was the most marvelous time of year.

Tbilisi's Central Railway Station, however, stood in stark contrast to the fall splendor: an aging relic of raw, cast concrete and the Brutalist architecture of long ago. But that's where Sam and Iza were boarding the train for Baku. Their younger daughter Elene, a slim dark-haired beauty with coltish legs who threatened to be as tall as Iza someday, was with them. The Mansours had flown in from the States two days earlier to pick up Chira Beggs, and now they were all traveling to Azerbaijan for Conor and Tali's highly anticipated wedding.

There is something romantic about overnight travel on a train: the hubbub of finding the right track and boarding, the hectic search for your cabin, and the strident whistling off that all are leaving on a long journey. For Elene, it was magic, but she wasn't going to say that to her parents.

Train 57, the newest on the Baku-Tbilisi-Kars route, left promptly at 6:15 pm and headed southeast to the one place in the Lower Caucasus where Georgia, Armenia, and Azerbaijan found a common border. The crossing was less than an hour away, but the customs inspectors there were notoriously slow, so the train would be stopped for at least 90 minutes, maybe more. It didn't matter. No one on board BTK-57 was in a hurry this splendid October day.

Sam had secured two first-class sleeper compartments, which had private toilets, face-to-face window seats, two sleeping berths each, and even a television. But it was Russian TV, and none cared to watch Russian propaganda trolls. After they had all settled in, Iza knocked on Chira and Elene's cabin door, and announced, "We've got dinner reservations at seven, so we need to leave in five minutes."

Elene replied brusquely, "Izolda, I'm texting Mary back home. I'll be ready when I'm ready." Like many her age, Elene was a nervy teenager, testing her boundaries. Calling her mother by her full given name was her way of asserting her place in the world of adults. It was the first time Elene had visited the Caucasus, but naturally, her friends in Carbondale were far more important than her mother's dinner announcement or her family's homeland.

Besides the wedding, the Mansours planned to stay in Baku for the Independence Day festival. There was much to celebrate. October 18th was the day the new Azeri government would be installed. Guliyev had been re-elected president, of course, but there would be a new foreign secretary – one Azreal Kedar – and the first female officer of the Azeri Security Service, Tali Nadirov. At 29 and 28 respectively, they were the youngest to ever be so honored in Azerbaijan.

Half an hour later, after the family had ordered dinner, they were enjoying coffees, teas and watching a magnificent sunset as BTK-57 picked up speed beyond the city limits. It was the first time Elene had visited Georgia, let alone Tbilisi, and she was curious about everything. She asked, "Chira, why do you live in Georgia?"

Chira beamed, amazed by such a question from her 16-year-old granddaughter. "When Izolda was a child we lived in Kurdistan, in the farthest northern province of Kars. The Turks and Armenians were always fighting over our land, and when my husband died, I had to move. There was no fighting in Tbilisi, and I had a cousin there. It's been a good place for me."

"But they are Christians," Elene continued, "Why didn't you move to another Muslim country?"

Sam said patiently, "Your grandmother is Alevi, Elene."

"Is that different from us?"

"Alevis are Muslims like us," Sam replied. "But they are mostly Kurds, who come from eastern Turkey and northern Iraq."

Iza eyed her mother and frowned. "The Alevis don't get along with Sunnis or Shias."

"Why's that?"

"Theological differences," said Iza, her brow now wrinkled.

Chira snapped, "You know that's not the reason, Daughter."

"Well, what is the reason, Mother?"

"It's culture, not religion," Chira defended. "Sunnis are mostly Arabs, Shiites are mostly Iranians, and Alevis are Kurds. Our traditional ways are too often at odds… and then there's the persecution and subjugation, of course."

Iza put it in plainer words, "Alevis do not recognize Sharia as God's word. Chira calls that culture; I call it religion."

"Keeping our pre-Islamic culture alive is not a sin, Daughter."

Elene was puzzled and looked to her mother for an explanation, "Mary Shoemaker says the Bible is God's word."

"One more misleading Western notion," Chira Beggs hooted.

"God speaks to many peoples, in many discrete ways," Sam said. "Declaring one way better or more accurate than another just leads to trouble."

The punch-counterpunch was interrupted when the servers brought the meal. Sam and Iza were both relieved that good food had suspended a tedious argument.

Twenty minutes after they had finished their meal, the train began to slow down. Iza glanced out at the landscape and said flatly, "The border." These were new tracks on the Baku-Tbilisi-Kars route and were perilously joined to the Azerbaijan-Armenia war zone.

"Elene, look," Iza was pointing to the crossroad, just beyond the station. "See that sign?"

"Ayrum, 18 km south; Nagorno-Karabakh, 200 km southeast. It has no meaning for me, Izolda... what?"

"Ayrum is a small village across the Armenian border, but the other, Nagorno-Karabakh, that's the Black Garden," said Iza.

A cynical Chira added, "What the Azeris and Armenians have been fighting over for decades."

"Doesn't look like anything to fight over."

Iza snorted, "It's not."

"Then why," asked the 16-year-old, "do they fight?"

"Men will fight over whatever," Chira declared sarcastically. "Pigs, hairy cows, women, whatever. If you have it and they want it, they think it's worth the fight."

Sam started to explain, "Historical issues..."

But Chira interrupted, "Don't let him confuse you, Elene. It's simple. Men get bored," she raised her eyebrows and pointed at Sam, "and need something to do. To touch a bit of glory is always tempting. Planting potatoes and herding cattle are not matters poets write about." Sam laughed. Obviously, Chira was not familiar with David Dill's Texas cowboy poetry.

"I'm tired," Iza said. "I'm heading back to our cabin."

The three adults got up, but Elene remained in her seat. "I'm going to stay awhile," she said. Picking up her iJournal, she flashed it at her mother, "I want to make a few entries." After they left, Elene set the device down and stared out the window as the last slivers of light disappeared below the western horizon.

Sam Mansour woke up at six the next morning, expecting to see their final destination, the low rising, saltbush hills of Gobustan. Instead, the train had come to a complete stop, but he wasn't sure where. So, he dressed quickly and walked down to the dining car.

"Would you like a table, sir," asked the steward.

"Why are we stopped?"

"A detour, sir," replied the steward. "There have been several incidents."

"Incidents?"

"We are very near the conflict zone," he said, "and Armenian insurgents have crossed into Azerbaijani lands. There seems to be some fighting at the Agcabadi Station just ahead."

"Yes, I'll take a table," Sam replied, "one next to the windows."

Half an hour later, Elene burst into the dining car, plopped down next to her father, and asked, "What's going on, Sam?"

At first, her father did not reply, his head craning so strenuously against the window pane of the dining car that he knew he would not be understood. He was staring outside at a scene Elene could not yet see. "Skirmish up ahead," Mansour replied. "I think the fighting has stopped, but I'm not sure."

Elene jumped into the seat across from her father and searched for any commotion ahead. Gazing along the length of the train along the tracks in front of her, Elene could see a group of men meandering back and forth, and the station just beyond. "Why are they fighting?" she demanded, if not from God then at least from her father. "Really, Sam, what's it all about?"

Before he could answer, there was a loud hiss of airbrakes releasing and then a second as the train lurched forward bit by bit. Next, the whistle sounded three shorts, a long, and another short, signaling the station ahead of the BTK-57's approach, however sluggishly. The station master indicated to the engineer that he should move on through without stopping, and so the train proceeded forward. Elene peered out the window anxiously as the train crept along at a snail's pace.

It was an odd moment, and Elene felt out of sync with the world. A lone fly buzzed past her face as it sought an exit from the dining car. Her attention slipped from the scene outside to the little creature banging over and over against the windowpane, eager to be outside for some reason; but there was no escape for it. "You want out," she whispered and then cracked open the window latch.

It was an action she quickly came to regret. The fly got out, but the putrid stench of rotting flesh seeped in through the opened window, like an evil ghost.

The train's forward motion didn't last long, and Elene sensed that something was wrong. As it neared the station, she could see a man in a military uniform of some kind shouting at the train engineer to stop. Everyone inside the dining car could taste the stench in the back of their throats – rot, body fluids, stale urine, and fecal matter. All searched in vain for a breath of clean air. Maybe it was the reek that confused her, but nothing was clear in Elene's head. She could see several men picking up large white bags, and then loading them into the back of a truck. *Sleeping bags?* she wondered. *Why would they need sleeping bags?* One man was slashing a marker across each one before it was tossed onto the truck-bed.

As the train inched forward, and she could see that there were bodies laid out in front of the truck to be bagged. Elene's mouth turned suddenly dry, her face pale. She bit her lips, but her eyes could not turn away from the carnage.

"The ravages of war, Elene," said her father. "That's the cliché."

"Is this for real?" she looked on.

As the train slid to a stop, Elene saw two soldiers just below her window carrying a body toward the truck. It was a young man, Elene's age, and he had a horrific wound. His left arm had been blown clean away, and a large chunk of torso was exposed under his rib cage. What flesh remained on his face had turned gray, and his eyes were open to a sky he would never see again. As gravely as it played on her mind, that's when Elene knew his soul had moved on, and that all that was left was the pitiless disposal of a boy's body.

"Is this the reason you take photos, father?" she asked, proud that she kept the trembling out of her voice.

"Sad, sensational, and provocative – all equivalent emotions banging against your brain at the same time," Sam responded.

"Bela is coming!" Chira rang out. Elene turned to see her grim-faced grandmother staring out the window.

Iza followed on, "Let's go back to the sleeping compartment. The air is better there, and we can talk." It was agreed, and they all returned to their sleeping car post haste. But there was little talk. Iza opened her iPad and began searching for news about the incident. Chira picked up her history book and started to read. Sam pulled out his camera and took a few photos through the glass, but he knew the quality would not be up to standard. Elene watched him closely, followed his techniques and mannerisms, and she searched his face, knowing that she had found her future at last.

They would be in Baku in less than two hours.

38

Phantom

L ater that morning, as BTK-57 was entering the Hajigabul district along the ancient Silk Road, Jake Moynihan was landing at the Stepanakert airport, the capital of the disputed Nagorno-Karabakh territory. It was just 250 km west of Baku. He had told the Mansours, Tali, and Conor that he would be flying directly from the States. But he had altered his travel plans slightly. It wouldn't be absolutely direct – there would be a detour to see Lindy Bedrosian. It was something he had to do. He wanted to know how she was doing and how the VDW was fairing after the disaster at Kars. Colonel Davidian would undoubtedly use the misadventure to advance his personal agenda.

Meanwhile, Lindy and her Uncle Mike were waiting impatiently at the terminal's egress gate for their former VDW comrade to show up. "Can we really trust him, Lindy?" Mike Bedrosian asked.

"Jake has promised me he would always be on our side, and you know that Jake keeps his promises." It wasn't unerringly true, of course, but the recently promoted Vartan lieutenant commander had convinced Tadesian and others that they could use this nascent American politician as an ally if or when war came to Armenia.

"I can't believe that Jake Moynihan is running for the House seat back home," Mike said. "What does he know about politics?"

"He's a hero twice over. It's all you need, and that speaks to the people of the South Side."

"Yeah," said Mike Bedrosian, "redistricting has made a big difference. It's no longer a minority-dominated district."

Lindy answered back, "Sonia says he has a chance with more Polish and Irish populations now added to Illinois's 1st Congressional District."

"Sonia?"

"Yeah, Sonia," Lindy snarked. "You remember your wife, right?"

"It's that Nation of Islam thing," Mike groused. "The Farrakhan crowd has had the welcome mat out for years, and the Black Muslims moved in by the thousands. People are frightened."

"We'll see." At that juncture, Lindy turned her attention to the crowd coming their way and recognized the dark hair and broad Irish forehead of Jake Moynihan popping above the rest. "There he is," she announced. But this was a different looking Jake Moynihan. He was wearing a custom fit black blazer, gray slacks, and a white dress shirt, but no tie. He had a garment bag draped over his shoulder and was carrying a briefcase. But what knocked Lindy for a loop were the shoes – charcoal gray suede loafers. The tanker boots were gone – a new Jake Moynihan, indeed!

"Jake," Lindy shouted out, "over here."

Moynihan hesitated for a moment, then smiled no holds barred. When she offered an embrace, Jake set his attaché on the ground, put his arm around her waist, and then kissed her unreservedly. "I've been considering that for a year," he said.

Taken aback at first, Lindy stared at Jake quizzically, then responded, "That took a year of considering?" Jake beamed at her good-humor.

"Car is this way," Mike grunted.

Jake nodded and acknowledged his old rival. A moment later, they were off to the Stepanakert airport auxiliary barracks. It was a half-hour away, and that's where the Vartan Defense Wing had been stationed ever since it had entered Armenia.

Thirty-six hours earlier, after the firefight at Agcabadi had come to an end, the lieutenant of the Azeri unit was congratulating his second in command for holding off the Armenian invaders. "How many casualties, sergeant?"

"Eleven, sir," replied the man. "Four dead and seven wounded; Quliyeva is critical, bad chest wound."

"And the enemy?"

"We have counted 16 dead so far," said the sergeant. "Looks like they have gathered up their wounded and scurried back into no man's land."

That wasn't true, exactly. There was still an Armenian presence, just not a human one.

None of the Azeri military personnel recognized the low hum of the Phantom-7 drone as it surveyed the scene just beyond the Agcabadi train station. The Zenmuse X7 camera lens zoomed in on the defense parameter at the outskirts of the village, transmitting vital information to headquarters about the defensive tactics employed by the Azeri unit. The DJI Phantom 7 was the best surveillance drone on the market. It was also a smart-flyer, equipped with an intelligent flight system, which included a satellite positioning system and enhanced visual capabilities.

The man operating the drone was a member of the Vartan Defense Wing, and he had been dreaming of this moment for months. He understood full well what the Azeri lieutenant did not: the purpose of the incursion was exploratory, not a confrontation to take ground. Tadesian and Lindy would not let the failure at Kars be repeated. Force protection would be assured in any future battle between the Armenian and Azeri troops.

As the camera got closer, a row of houses came into focus – stone and concrete, two stories – the enemy had stored supplies there, and there was a sniper's perch. The drone orbited, allowing the operator to explore every angle inside. There was a soldier lying three feet from the window, dead, his limbs folded at awkward angles, his head twisted in such a way that no one could conclude that he might be sleeping. The drone paused; a moment of insight, or perhaps just data collection? Who will come for him? Who will weep for him? Who will pray him forward?

"Move on," came the command. And the Phantom-7 hovered at the window opening to view the landscape beyond. Across the street, there was an apartment building. Laundry was fluttering in the breeze outside the windows, so it was not possible to get any view of what was happening internally. "Move on," repeated the voice from headquarters.

For the next half hour, the VDW operator continued mapping the village fortifications. "Mostly dry holes," the operator reported.

"We've got what we need," said headquarters. "Vulnerabilities have been mapped. Return to base."

That evening, after supper at the VDW mess hall, Lindy invited Jake to her private headquarters. It wasn't much, just a sparse, two-room apartment with a personal bath. The sitting room, however, had two lounge chairs and a table. Tonight, sitting on the table, was a bottle of Jameson and two whiskey glasses. Jake smiled, "You remembered."

"Well, it's the best I could do for an old boy-toy."

Jake beamed, "Does this mean I'm forgiven?"

"For leaving us at Ninots?" She sneered. "Don't be too sure… and don't read too much into this bottle of whiskey, Moynihan."

Jake had really wanted to talk about their lost relationship, but Lindy's command was something he couldn't ignore.

She began pouring a generous dram into his glass. Jake added a splash of water, and then sat back. Lindy had changed. She had picked up weight – muscle mostly – and cut her hair, leaving a short bob with a smart side-swept bang. Then she changed the subject. "Tell me about this run for Congress, Jake. What made you decide to take up politics?"

"It was Marty Mills and others at Kasey's place," Jake replied.

"Oh yeah, the South Side watering hole."

"Yeah, Marty gave me Mike's former job as FAA recruiter."

"Doesn't explain the political connection."

"Right," Jake acknowledged. "Lots of guys recognized me from that Crow thing. It was so long ago."

"Two years have come and gone," Lindy reflected.

"I thought they would have forgotten, but no."

"Nobody forgets something like that, Jake."

"One of the guys was a Chicago alderman," he continued, "and the Democrats were looking for somebody new in the Illinois First. I had lots of success recruiting; they thought I knew how to speak to South Siders."

Lindy put forward the real question, "Can you win?"

"Some think so. We'll see." Then he added, "The election is next month. I've got to get back soon."

Unexpectedly, there was a loud fist-bang on the door. "Bedrosian!" Without waiting for an invitation, an Armenian army regular burst into the room. "We've got a mess," he shouted. Moynihan knew the man from the Carpathian rendezvous: Colonel Davidian, the liaison officer of the Armenian Defense Force. Jake remembered him as the man who always opposed the VDW forces for interfering with professional military planners.

"What's the problem, Gregir?" Lindy demanded.

"Your recon mission at Agcabadi has come to a bad end," he shouted, "Twenty plus dead, twenty plus wounded!"

"But did they get the information?"

"VDW reports yes, but the Azeris are closing and re-enforcing the border everywhere!"

"The information is all that counts," Lindy insisted.

"Ground counts too," Davidian huffed. "Toys on the wind mean nothing!"

Bedrosian replied, "We have everything in place, sir."

As the Colonel retreated to the door, he shouted back, "Force protection lieutenant commander! Remember your mistake at Kars, and get to your forward position now!" Then he left, slamming the door behind.

"I don't like that guy," said Jake. "He is out for himself."

Lindy put down her glass. "Listen, Jake. He is right about one thing. We've got to protect the drone fleet. It's our tactical advantage against the Azeris if this comes to war."

"Where?"

"Fifty percent of our forces, more than 100,000 drone strikers, have been deployed to a valley position on the front called the Sotk Pass."

"I don't trust Davidian, Lindy. You've got to watch your back."

"You have to leave right now," she replied. "Otherwise, you'll never get through."

"But we have issues to settle," Jake insisted. "Personal issues."

Lindy looked into Jake's eyes and saw truthfulness. "Later, Jake," she said gently. "We'll have to take it up later."

"This… Conor and Tali's wedding should take no more than a week," he replied. "Then I will return, and we can settle the matter."

"Talk, Jake," Lindy said, a little more firmly now. "We can talk."

Jake was pleased. He had a plan and a promise. Outside, a convoy of military trucks was waiting.

Two hours later, the convoy arrived at the Sotk Pass crossing. Lindy and Jake got out of the Mercedes-Benz G-Class SUV. She would go no further. Mike would take Moynihan across the border to Ganja, where he would board the night-time BTK-57 to Baku.

Once again, Jake took Lindy in his arms and embraced her tenderly. But he did not kiss her as he had earlier; it would be an embarrassment before the troops. "One week," he said. "I see you again in one week." She nodded and quietly waved.

Then he walked over to join Mike in an unmarked car. But before he entered, he turned back for one last look. She stood as a phantom, boldly framed against the bright lights of the military entourage.

39

Toykhana

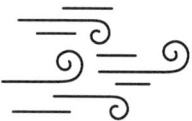

"How long have you been working for the Kedars?" Iza asked.

The limo driver was an old friend, Ali Tabak. "I stayed on after Tali was safely reunited with the family. You remember, after our big adventure at Lake Goygol."

Iza shook her head with a booming hoot, "Big adventure, indeed."

Elene, the other passenger in the car, was perplexed, "What big adventure, Iza?"

"You remember when I visited Chira last year," Elene concurred by blinking and nodding, "well, there was a side trip. Ali and I were asked to find and rescue Tali, who had been kidnapped by the Kos clan."

Ali cackled, "That one rescued herself."

"True enough. We were just facilitators."

Ali continued his story: "With Rufet and Rayna dead, the Kedars needed personal assistants for Conor and Mira, so I got the job of helping Conor while he was still in recovery. Been here ever since."

The Mercedes-Maybach began slowing as the Zümrə Estates came into view. Elene pointed at the marquee that had been erected in the open space just outside the compound. She didn't understand the Azeri signage. "It's called the toykhana, Elene," Iza said, "It's the traditional Azeri way of announcing a wedding."

Elene was unsure of her mother's explanation. "I thought you said Conor and Tali were progressives and didn't care for the old ways."

Iza pursed her lips, turned toward the friendly limo driver and said, "Help me out here, Ali."

Tabak glanced into the rearview mirror and waggled his head a tad. "The groom and the bride are very much an enlightened couple, Miss Elene," he replied. "but they are also celebrities of the Shirvan, and this wedding ceremony is a national event for all the people, not just a private affair. There had to be some compromises about old ways and the new." That's the way Ali understood it. It wasn't every day that the foreign secretary and the first female officer of the Azeri Security Service got married, after all.

As they turned onto the access road of the compound, Elene noticed the two television vans. They had been stationed there ever since the marquee announcing a wedding had been erected. When the black limo with official plates pulled up to the entry, several camera crews rushed forward. President Guliyev and other dignitaries of the recently installed government were scheduled to arrive anytime. Elene was amused.

Then, just beyond the Zümrə gate, she saw the two armored cars and the four soldiers, who were inspecting every vehicle that entered the compound. "Is something wrong, mother?"

Mother, Iza thought, *that's different.* "What do you mean, Elene?"

"The soldiers," she asked, "Why such security just for a wedding?"

Iza replied, "President Guliyev is coming," but she knew full well that her daughter would not be satisfied with such a flimsy explanation. She had her parents' journalistic instincts. "The country is on alert. Armenia has upped its war games, and everyone is… on alert."

Ali drove past the professional building and parked the charcoal gray limo in front of Conor's apartment. Once Iza and Elene stepped out, they headed for Conor's azalea garden, where two large tents had been erected – as tradition held, one was for the women and the other for the men. The day's ceremony would center on two old-fashioned events: first, the menfolk would visit the tent of the womenfolk to inspect the dowry, and afterward, if every protocol had been followed suitably, the marriage proposal would be accepted by the mother.

As the Mansour women reached the garden entrance, without warning everything stopped. The President's car was approaching, followed by a horde of media people. Georghe Markirov, the elchi or matchmaker, was positioned outside the near tent to welcome Azerbaijan's First Executive. Next to him was Jake and one of the male elders of the Kedar clan. In ancient days, such a momentous wedding lasted seven days and seven nights, but Conor and Tali insisted on something much more manageable – three days and two nights. They thought it enough time for a nation to celebrate. The Markirov Bey had announced the marriage at the end of the nightly news on the first day. That was October 18th, and by coincidence, it was the same day that the new government of Azerbaijan had been sworn in.

The bride's acceptance was, of course, a foregone conclusion, so the Mehendi ceremony began in the early afternoon. A sisterhood of Azeri women spent an hour decorating Tali's hands and legs with beautiful Mehendi art, and shortly after that, some fun-filled competitions between the two families began. That evening the air was filled song and dance as the wedding guests partied away the night.

Conor and Tali, however, retired to their apartment at 9:30. Because Jake was leaving for the States shortly, they invite him to join them for a private dinner at ten. All the foods for the wedding itself were homemade; to do otherwise would have been an insult to a nation's pride. But Conor and Tali had decided to have this evening's meal catered. They chose Scalini, an Italian restaurant in downtown Baku, and a Mediterranean menu: ravioli with ricotta and spinach, a mixed salad with sautéed calamari and sundried tomatoes, tiramisu, and, of course, a bottle of Barbera d'Asti from the Piedmont region.

Tali offered the evening's first toast, "To Jake Moynihan, who traveled a nerve-wracking 6,000 miles to see his brother married to a quiet, country girl."

Jake laughed. "No one, Tali, would call you quiet or country."

"Especially anyone from the House of Kos," Conor added. All three smiled at that notion, then ticked glasses to a job well done. At that instant, the waiter began serving the ravioli, then topped off their wine.

Tali continued her cordial chit-chat, "We are grateful you came. We know you have that election next month. It must be exciting."

"Will you win?" Conor asked.

Jake replied, "I think so. At least, my campaign people tell me I will."

Conor made the second toast, "Then we will have to visit you in Washington, DC and celebrate my brother's brilliant victory. Imagine, both of us politicians!"

They drank again, and then Tali changed the subject, "Soooo... how is Lindy, and what is she doing these days?" It was a natural question, one likely to be asked during any casual conversation.

"We broke up some time ago... more than a year," said Jake.

"Do you ever see her?"

It was the second question that threw Jake. He sat erect, took a deep breath, and felt a bit uneasy. Did Tali somehow know of his recent visit to Nagorno-Karabakh, or know about the VDW recon incursions along the border? Of course, she knew. After all, she was now an officer of the Azeri Security Service. But he wondered, *Have I been followed all along?*

"Her Uncle Mike is married to my Aunt Sonia, actually, so I'm often informed of the many Bedrosian comings and goings. It can be a little tedious." It was a clever dodge, but Tali noticed Jake's shifting posture. Next, Jake sent the conversation in a new direction. "I'm curious, Tali, about your new job. What does it entail?"

It was Tali's turn to squirm. "Nothing really different. For some time, I've been reporting directly to President Guliyev about international affairs. Now it will be domestic affairs."

"Domestic military affairs?"

This time, Conor noticed the odd turn to the military question. "Enough shop talk, Jake," he chided lightly. "Mira tells me that you will be traveling with her back to Gobustan."

"That's right. I want to see our father's gravesite one more time before I go. I don't know that I'll ever be back, you know."

"Don't say that, Jake," argued the older brother. "You and I have many things to do, and fate will bring us together again."

"If God wills it," Tali added.

Lastly, Conor asked, "Are we good, Jake?"

Appreciating his brother at last, Jake didn't hesitate, "We're good, Conor Moynihan."

The rest of the evening was spent in casual conversation. Nevertheless, the anxiety Jake felt returned more than once. But each time, Jake hesitated to tell them about the drone army. He was deeply troubled about it. The revelation would betray Lindy and his old comrades, but not disclosing it was equally troubling – the drone army was lethal, and the Armenians would not hesitate to employ it.

Around eleven the next morning, the mullah arrived to officiate at the nikah al Mutah, the legal agreement that is completed on the last day of the marriage.

Contrary to the ways of Sunnis, Shiites believe in a temporary marriage arrangement. The bride and the groom enter into nuptials that are valid for a fixed time period. The couple is expected to abide by this and stay together after the contract expires only if they elect, of their own free will, to do so. Conor and Tali asked the Mansours to be the witnesses to the marriage contract, but Mira and Seyfulla were also present, and so was Jake. It didn't take long. By noon the three-day marriage ceremony had been completed, and the camera crews were gone.

Chira had agreed to fly back to Tbilisi, so Ali drove the Mansours to the airport for an afternoon flight to Georgia. Jake was the only out-of-towner left of the wedding party, and he felt pressured to get back to Chicago and the campaign as soon as possible. The visit to Tom's gravesite, however, was an immediate priority. Mira's chauffeur, David, brought her car to the apartment at 2:30 pm for his final sendoff.

Jake had always been uncomfortable with goodbyes, but this one was especially difficult. He felt guilty. Lindy, the VDW, and the drone army were ever-present on his mind, and now his brother and his new bride were there as well. But again, he said nothing as he departed Baku.

The ride to Gobustan took about an hour, and both he and Mira were quiet throughout the journey – three days of wedding fun is always exhausting. When they arrived at the village, they went directly to the cottage. David unlocked the gate and then parked the car near the azalea garden. As they walked toward the gravesite, they heard a songbird nearby. Jake perked up. "Is that…?"

"I think so," said Mira.

Jake recalled, "You and I were walking in this very garden the last time we heard a nightingale."

Mira asked, "You remember which one sings, don't you?"

"I do."

Then she offered sagely, "It is your father welcoming you home."

A surge of sadness filled his heart as they sat down on the iron bench next to the giant Oriental plane tree. Unrelenting guilt filled his consciousness. "Mira, I have something important to tell you."

"What's that, Jacob?" It was a name not often used for Moynihan. He thought of Jacob of the Bible and that one's betrayal long ago.

"Conor and…," he hesitated, "Conor and all of you in this country are in great peril."

"How so?"

"Armenia is…"

"We know this, Jake," Mira said. "They have been threatening us for generations."

"I did not come to the wedding directly," he explained. "I went to the Black Garden to visit my old girlfriend and what I saw there was frightening. They have a new weapon."

Mira perked up. "New weapon?"

"A drone army that cannot be stopped."

She pursed her lips and said, "I'm sure that Tali knows about it." Mira gave off an air of confidence, but deep down, she was unsure. "Why didn't you tell Conor or Tali, or somebody?"

"I don't have a good reason. I guess I thought this trouble would just go away."

"No need to fuss about it now," said Mira. "Let's get back to the cottage. We can decide tomorrow before you leave."

It was a long night, fraught with anxiety.

The next morning, Jake woke up early. The train for Tbilisi would arrive in 90 minutes, and Jake was ready. He wandered into the kitchen and found a continental breakfast waiting. There was a note on the table. It read: "Had to go back to Baku for business last night. Shahin will drive you to the train station. Have a safe trip, Mira."

At two o'clock that afternoon, Jake arrived at the Ganja train depot. The high wispy sky of the Gobustan morning had turned into low-lying gray clouds in Ganja. The air was muggy, and it felt like a storm was on its way. Jake was at the meeting place he and Mike Bedrosian had agreed upon, but the man was nowhere to be found. Jake's feeling of isolation was paramount because the BTK-57 had departed, and all the people who had come to pick up their relatives had disappeared. Moynihan was alone. There was little for him to do but ignore the weather and wait.

An hour passed, but killing time was not what Jake did well. *Something has happened to Mike*, he reasoned. More seriously, Jake was troubled by the thought that somehow VDW spies had uncovered the fact that he had had dinner with an Azeri Security Services officer. He now worried, *Does Lindy think I have betrayed her and the VDW?*

He stood up and searched his surroundings, anxious to find a solution. That's when he spotted a lone taxi in the parking lot. So Jake walked to the end of the station and asked the driver, "Do you know the Sotk Pass?"

The man flipped his cigarette into the air, thinking he had a fare. "Taxi, Müserif? Ganja?"

Jake shook his head, "No." Obviously, the man didn't speak English, and Jake's Azerbaijani was rudimentary, at best. "Do you know the road to the Sotk Pass?"

The driver waved an instructive finger at Jake. "Sotk, Armenia… no, no, no!" He jumped into his taxi and drove off.

Jake was unnerved by his aloneness, *a stranger in a strange land*. Not knowing what to do next, Jake returned to the depot. There was a clerk at the ticket counter, so he went inside.

"Is there another train tonight?" he asked. "The man I was supposed to meet never showed up."

"Old 49 be here in 90 minutes," the man replied in broken English. "It's the overnight –lots of stops – no dining, no sleeping."

"Can you sell me a ticket to Tbilisi?"

"Just get on," the clerk said, clearly eager to lock up and get home. "Buy from man with hat." Jake understood that to mean conductor. He nodded and then meandered outside and found a seat on the platform.

Just before dusk, Jake saw an SUV coming down from the hillside. *Delivered*, he thought with a knob in his throat. *Lindy!* But would she be pleased to see him? He wondered how he would explain the dinner meeting with Tali and Conor. As the vehicle came to the curb and parked, Jake's heart fell when he saw only one person inside, a thousand questions raced through his mind.

It was Mike. As he got out of the car, Jake shouted out, "Where's Lindy?"

With a bottle of Jameson and two paper cups in hand, Mike said, "Let's go inside, Jake." They sat at a bench and watched the clerk leave. "I have a message from Lindy." He opened the Jameson and poured two cups full.

"What's going on, Mike?"

"Lindy decided not to come," he said. "She's made up her mind and wanted me to tell you it's over – your relationship. She has moved on. She was embarrassed to tell you she has work here, that the moment has become desperate, and that you should go home."

That didn't square with Jake's notion of the woman he'd been with for years. She never had a problem being direct and honest with Jake. "Doesn't sound like Lindy to me."

Mike hesitated, then, "She's gone ahead… to the jumping off point."

"Jumping off point," Jake replied. "What the hell does that mean?"

Mike didn't respond right away, then, "I've gotta go, Jake. Barely had time for this meeting."

"What is going on Mike?" Jake insisted. "I'm not leaving until I get an explanation."

"Okay," replied the VDW captain. "The whole of the Armenian army is on the move. A VDW recon team last night spotted the Azerbaijani forces head for the Sotk Pass crossing. We had to move to higher ground."

"It's begun, then?"

"War is eminent. All hell will break loose within hours. You've gotta get out now!"

"I gotta talk to Lindy," said Jake. "I have…."

"Can't do it, Jake. You have to get on that train." Mike got up, handed his old Freedom Army buddy the Jameson, and headed for the door.

Five minutes later, Jake was alone once more. The dusty trail Mike had made into the mountains had all but disappeared. He leaned against the platform steps, trying to puzzle out what had just happened. Then he knew it was over.

Jake had made up his mind, *Armenia, Azerbaijan, both for the birds – my future is in Chicago, the US of A!*

Just after six pm, he heard the train whistle: three shorts toots, then a long, and another short – the Old 49 was approaching the station. It was time for Jake to leave Azerbaijan. Once on board, Jake took a window seat so he could look out at the mountains of Azerbaijan one last time. It was still gloomy and now almost dark.

In the distance, somewhere beyond Lake Goygol and the Sotk Pass, the setting sun peeked through the clouds fleetingly. *A ray of hope*, the thought crossed Jake's mind. Then it disappeared, and a flash of lightning, or something like it, arced across the night sky. That's when the Old 49 started its descent into the Tbilisi valley, and everything Jake knew about the land of Fire and Wind fell away as darkness.

He thought about Lindy and Tali and the two civilizations on the brink of catastrophe. Could anyone reverse the enmities of the generations? That's when he remembered his brother and all the things that had transpired in recent days.

Could Conor be the one, he wondered? Jake couldn't be sure.

THE END